Ali Mc...
thing —...
when s...
stories...
Ronan...
as a fu...
realised...
doing, but something others enjoy...
Cambridgeshire with her family and beloved Labrador dogs.

To find out more about Ali visit her website at:
www.alimcnamara.co.uk

Follow her on Twitter and Instagram: @AliMcNamara
Or like her Facebook page: Ali McNamara

Also by this author

From Notting Hill with Love ... Actually

Breakfast at Darcy's

From Notting Hill to New York ... Actually

Step Back in Time

From Notting Hill with Four Weddings ... Actually

The Little Flower Shop by the Sea

Letters from Lighthouse Cottage

The Summer of Serendipity

Daisy's Vintage Cornish Camper Van

Secrets and Seashells at Rainbow Bay

Ali McNamara

sphere

SPHERE

First published in Great Britain in 2019 by Sphere

1 3 5 7 9 10 8 6 4 2

ISBN 978-0-7515-7432-6

Typeset in Caslon by M Rules
Printed and bound in Great Britain by
Clays Ltd, Elcograf S.p.A.

Papers used by Sphere are from well-managed forests
and other responsible sources.

Sphere
An imprint of
Little, Brown Book Group
Carmelite House
50 Victoria Embankment
London EC4Y 0DZ

An Hachette UK Company
www.hachette.co.uk

www.littlebrown.co.uk

'When it rains look for rainbows,
when it's dark look for stars'

Oscar Wilde

One

'Yes, Mrs Greening, I quite understand; really I do. I'll certainly speak to Charlie about this. Thank you for bringing it to my attention.'

I stand up and excuse myself from the room, feeling as though I've gone back in time twenty years, and I'm once more the pupil, summoned to the headmistress's office for misbehaviour that was not *always* my fault.

'Come on, you,' I say to my nervous-looking son as he waits outside the office on a long wooden bench. 'Let's go home.'

'Exactly how much trouble am I in, Mum?' Charlie asks as we walk through the school gates and out on to the street.

'At the moment, not too much.' I see him grin with relief, so I hurriedly continue, '*But*, if you hang around with the sort of boys you are at the moment, then I've a feeling it could get much more serious in the future.'

Charlie looks down at his scuffed trainers.

'You're ten years old; you're too young for me to be worrying about this sort of thing. I'd have expected you to at least be at secondary school before I got called to the headmistress's

1

office because she's concerned that the sort of people you're making friends with could be affecting your behaviour *and* your schoolwork.'

Charlie pauses by the bus stop and looks up at me hopefully.

'Sorry,' I apologise, 'no money for the bus today. We'll have to walk. Anyway,' I carry on as he sighs, 'it's a lovely afternoon; it will do us good and we can have a nice chat on the way home.'

Charlie rolls his eyes, but I pretend not to notice.

'So, what's going on?' I ask as we set off along the road together. 'Who are these boys that Mrs Greening is so worried about you being friends with at school?'

Charlie shrugs.

'Charlie?' I prompt.

'They're not at my school,' Charlie says eventually in a low voice.

'So who are they, then?' I ask, starting to worry even more. You hear such horrific things these days about gangs and ... I shake my head; I don't even want to think about my little boy involved in anything worse. 'Why aren't you spending time with your friends from school?'

Charlie shrugs, and kicks at a tin can rolling along the pavement.

'Come on, love, you can talk to me, you know you can; we've always been a team, haven't we, you and me?' I nudge him playfully, trying to lighten the mood, and he smiles ruefully up at me. 'That's better. Now pop that can in the bin instead of kicking it around. There's one just over there.'

Begrudgingly Charlie picks up the tin and tosses it into the bin. 'The reason I hang around with those boys is because they live on our estate,' he says quietly as he returns to my side.

2

I desperately want to take hold of his hand like I used to when he was little, to protect him and cosset him away from any trouble he might be in. But I know those days are sadly now long gone, and I have to deal with this in a mature way. Charlie is growing up – faster than I'd like, and I just have to get used to that.

I put my hand firmly in my pocket.

'Go on,' I encourage him.

'All my old school friends live in the posh area of Hamilton, don't they?' Charlie continues. 'Where we *used* to live. And you won't let me go all the way back there on my own after school, *will* you?' He looks at me accusingly.

So that's it. I breathe a huge sigh of relief. No drugs or gangs – for the moment, anyway. Just the simple case of a ten-year-old boy whose mother won't let him travel back to the place they used to live.

'You could always ask some of your friends to come to ours after school?' I suggest helpfully. 'Maybe their parents could drop them off in one of their *many* cars.'

'Tried that. Their mums won't let them come. They say where we live now is dangerous.'

We turn a corner and walk past the row of shops that we often pass on our way home, and I'm saddened to see yet another has closed its doors and boarded up its windows. Already some colourful graffiti has appeared to decorate the newly erected boards.

'That's ridiculous. The Spencer estate isn't dangerous – it's just not a cosy little close or an exclusive avenue, that's all.' My mood is swiftly changing from anxious to irritated. *Bloody stuck-up parents with their four-by-four cars and their triple-glazed five-bedroom houses.* There's nothing wrong with where we live.

3

Fair enough, it might not be the prettiest area, or the most sought-after, but the community spirit is high, especially in the block of flats we live in.

Charlie shrugs. 'That's what they said. Maybe I should have changed schools when we moved instead of staying at my old one. That way the kids I went to school with would be the same ones I saw after it.'

I'd wondered whether keeping Charlie at his old school was going to work when we'd had to move to our new home, but I'd wanted to keep the upheaval in his life to a minimum.

'Perhaps,' I say diplomatically. *Or perhaps we shouldn't have had to move here in the first place.* 'Anyway, this is the situation we find ourselves in now your dad's gone, so we have to make the best of what we've got. And,' I remind him, 'we must remember that just because other people think and do things differently to us, it doesn't mean *we* have to, does it? Does it?' I ask again, ruffling Charlie's sandy hair. 'You're your own person, Charlie, with your own thoughts and opinions; don't let anyone tell you differently.'

Charlie nods.

'And remember, everyone is equal in this world. Just because some people are lucky enough to have comfortable lives and plenty of money, doesn't make them any better than those that don't.'

'Yeah, I know.'

'Good boy. Now, as long as these new friends don't get you into any trouble,' I warn him, 'or affect your school work, then I'm happy for you to continue hanging out with them – okay?'

Charlie smiles.

'Just don't tell Mrs Greening, all right?' I wink at him.

He winks back. 'You're the best, Mum!'

'I know.' I grin. 'Now, what would you like for tea? I got some pizza in earlier, how about that?'

Charlie's smile broadens. Pizza is his favourite.

We walk the rest of the way back to the Spencer estate, the place we've called home for the last six months. It's not ideal, and probably not where I'd have chosen to bring up my son, but currently it is all we can afford.

We both look hopefully at the lift as we enter the building where our fourth-floor flat is, but it still has an out-of-order sign hanging from its doors.

'Looks like it's the stairs again,' I say brightly. 'At least it keeps us fit!'

We race each other up the staircase – a game we've played far too often since we moved in here, with Charlie as always getting there first. Then I unlock our door, and let us into our flat. While I carefully lock and bolt the three locks on the back of the door behind us, Charlie heads off to wash his hands, knowing he won't be allowed any snacks until he's done just that.

There's a pile of letters on the floor by the door. *Bills, no doubt*, I think, barely glancing at them. Instead, I toss them on the little wooden table by the door, planning to look at them later when Charlie isn't around. At least two of them will have bright red writing somewhere on the envelope, and I don't want Charlie to worry. He's a smart kid for ten, but he already knows far too much about the adult world for my liking.

There's another pile of envelopes on the table that I didn't deal with yesterday, so my new bundle simply slides off the top of them and on to the floor.

Damn, I think, bending down to pick them up. I begin to

stack them into a neat pile, but one envelope stands out from the others – instead of having a clear window with my name and address typed neatly into it, this one is handwritten in black ink, and the envelope is made out of a thick, cream paper.

I turn it over in case there's a return address, but it's blank.

'Mum, can I have a biscuit?' Charlie calls from the kitchen. 'I've washed my hands.'

'Sure,' I call back absent-mindedly, still looking at the envelope. 'Only one, mind; we'll probably have dinner early.'

I tear open the envelope, still having no idea who it might be from. Inside is a piece of equally thick paper, and the text covering it is also handwritten.

Dear Ms Chesterford,

Wait, that's what's unusual about the envelope – I knew there was something other than the writing. It's addressed to my maiden name of Chesterford.

I haven't been known as Amelia Chesterford for eleven years. How strange? I continue to read:

I write to you today with what I hope will be good news.

My name is Alexander Benjamin, and I am a genealogist. I was recently hired by the law firm Davies & Davies to find the beneficiary of an estate that came into their possession some months ago.

I am delighted to inform you that after much research, I now believe that the beneficiaries of this estate may be yourself and your son, Charles.

So I write today to ask if you would initially

confirm that you are indeed Amelia Jane
Chesterford, your date of birth is 1 November
1980, and you were born in St Mildred's Hospital,
Southampton. We may then proceed further with the
application for you and your son to inherit the estate
known currently as Article C.

You may contact me in any of the ways listed
at the top of this letter. But I ask that you do so,
please, at your earliest convenience.

Yours sincerely,
Alexander Benjamin

I read the letter through twice and then I laugh: these spammers are getting far too silly for their own good these days. As if I'm going to ring someone and divulge all my personal information – do they think I'm stupid?

I throw the letter on the pile with the others, and I'm about to head into the kitchen to find Charlie when I stop.

But they already know all of my personal information, don't they? And more importantly, they know about Charlie. If they're spammers, that's particularly worrying.

I pick up the letter and head into the tiny kitchen/diner/living room. Charlie is already sitting down in front of the television.

'Can I borrow your laptop?' I ask him, putting the letter on the table.

'Why?' he asks, not taking his eyes from the screen.

'Because I want to use the internet and I've run out of data on my phone,' I lie. The truth is I haven't got the money to top it up right now, and I need to go easy on the little credit I have left in case Charlie needs to call me in an emergency.

'Why don't you connect your phone to the Wi-Fi then?' Charlie asks smartly.

'You know my phone isn't great with Wi-Fi,' It was far too old and basic. 'It's too slow, and I need to search for something. Can I use it or not?'

'Sure, okay then,' Charlie shrugs amiably, his eyes still glued to the TV.

I pull Charlie's laptop from his bag and open it up. Then, relieved we haven't had our own internet cut off just yet, I pull up Google.

First I type in 'Davies & Davies Solicitors', and find there is indeed a law firm in Berwick-Upon-Tweed with that name. *Could be a coincidence*, I think, still suspicious. Then I type in 'Alexander Benjamin – genealogist' and I find to my surprise a professional-looking website telling me all about this Alexander, with very authentic-sounding testimonials from satisfied clients who have found long-lost relatives, and law firms just like Davies & Davies who Alexander has worked for with amazing results.

I close up the laptop and think.

It's becoming harder and harder for me to believe this is a scam. But why would someone leave me anything in a will? An estate, the letter said. That was usually more than a few pounds or an antique vase. And for this law firm to have hired this Alexander fellow, it must be pretty important.

I stand up and head into our little kitchenette. I fill the kettle and put it on to boil. Then I open up the fridge to get out some milk.

The emptiness of the fridge suddenly scares me. There's the pizza I'd promised Charlie for his tea, a nearly empty bottle of milk, some cheap margarine and half a tin of beans left over from last night's tea of beans on toast. But that's it. I know there isn't a lot more in the cupboards, either, and it's still three days until I'll get paid again.

What if this will thing *was* a small sum of money? It would come in very handy, that's for sure. My job at the local supermarket is never going to pay me much; maybe this 'estate' might be enough for me to start that little business I've been thinking about for a while. After all, what's the point in spending three years at university to end up working part time in a supermarket? And even if it isn't that much money, it might still pay a few of those 'red' bills that are waiting for me on the hall table.

Stop right there, I tell myself. *You're getting carried away as usual. Good things like that don't happen to you, Amelia. Not any more. This estate will probably be a scruffy dog you've inherited or something else worthless, something that's going to cost* you *money.*

But as I sip on my weak tea – made for the second time with the same teabag – I can't help but wonder . . .

'Just going to make a quick phone call,' I tell Charlie. 'Won't be a mo.'

'Thought you didn't have much credit?' Charlie asks distractedly, changing the channel on the TV.

'And I thought you had a school project to finish tonight?' I retort as I head towards my bedroom.

'Yeah, I do. But you said you'd help me with it, didn't you?'

'Did I?' I ask, hovering in the doorway. 'Which one is it?'

'The one about castles – remember? We've been studying all about them this term and Miss said we had to make our own model of one. That's what I've been saving all the boxes for.'

'Oh, yes, that's right, I remember,' I fib. 'And when has that got to be in?' I ask. *Please don't say tomorrow . . .*

'Er . . . next week, I think.'

Phew. 'Sure, I'll help you. Let me just make this call first and I'll be right out.'

I close my bedroom door and then I perch on the bed and look at my phone. Should I really be wasting my credit on this possible wild-goose chase? But what if the wild goose turns out to be a golden one? It could be the answer to so many of my problems right now. I have to at least take the chance.

I dial the number at the top of the letter and wait, expecting to be greeted by an answer phone or a receptionist, but instead I suddenly hear a smooth and very polished voice say: 'Good afternoon. Alexander Benjamin speaking, how may I help you?'

'Oh, hullo ...' I reply, thrown for a moment by the voice. 'Er ... my name is Amelia. Amelia Harris. I ... I mean Chesterford. Harris is ... *was* my married name. Chesterford is my maiden name.'

'Ah, the elusive Ms Chesterford at last! How wonderful to finally speak with you. As I just said, I'm Alexander Benjamin. You got my letter, I presume?'

'I did.'

'Now, if you'll just give me a moment I'll locate your file.'

The line goes quiet for a few seconds.

'Right, I have it to hand now,' the voice says, coming back on the line. 'Now, would you mind confirming a few details for me?'

I'm immediately suspicious, but Alexander simply asks me for confirmation of the same details he had in the letter. He doesn't ask me to divulge anything new, like my bank details or credit card number, as I'd originally suspected he might.

'That's super, Ms Chesterford, or would you prefer me to call you Harris? That *is* your name now?'

'I'd prefer Amelia, actually.'

10

'Of course, Amelia it is then. Now—'

'How did you find me?' I suddenly blurt out.

'I'm sorry?'

'How did you find me – to send me the letter?'

'Ah, I have many resources that I use to trace people. You were a particularly difficult case, I have to admit.'

'Why?'

'Because you seem to have had several addresses in the past few years, and you are yet to show on the electoral register for your current one. When clients are not on the register it makes them much harder to find.'

'Oh, I see.'

'You've moved quite a lot, have you?'

He's right: I have, but I don't see how that's any of his business.

'Yes.'

'I see. Anyhow, that is of no consequence when it comes to the estate in question.'

'You kept mentioning an estate in your letter. What exactly have I inherited?'

'I have to say it is most thrilling,' he says, sounding excited. 'When John Davies came to me with this particular case, I was incredibly eager to take it on.'

'Yes, I'm sure,' I say, trying to remain patient. 'But what is it?'

'Subject to certain checks and verification of the appropriate documents, you, Amelia, have inherited— *Beeeep*.'

'Hello … Hello … Mr Benjamin, can you still hear me?' I shake the phone in my hand and stare at it, but the line has gone dead.

Immediately I attempt to call him back, but my worst fears are confirmed when a text message pops up on my phone to tell me … I've run out of credit.

11

Two

The next morning, after I've taken Charlie to school, I walk slowly back to the flat. My shift at the supermarket doesn't start until this afternoon, so I have the rest of the morning to tidy up and take our dirty clothes to the local launderette – a job I detest. So I'm in no hurry to get home.

I hate myself for thinking it, but how I miss our old three-bedroomed house with its built-in washing machine and tumble dryer. When we lived there I'd totally taken it all for granted – the fancy appliances, the central heating, our little garden at the back where Charlie had taken his first steps across the grass on a warm spring day not unlike this one.

But that had all been taken away from us when Charlie's dad abandoned us. He'd simply left for work one day and never come back. I'd been beside myself with worry, and about to call the police, when I found his note. It had fallen down from our kitchen table on to the floor, and in my panic I hadn't seen it until the following day.

I know the words on that note will be etched in my head for ever.

Amelia,

I'm so sorry but I just can't live this lie any more.
I need to get away for a while to get my head
together.
Tell Charlie I love him.
G x

I shake my head to rid my mind of the words that have poisoned my thoughts for too long. *I just can't live this lie any more* . . . No, I refuse to let you come back to haunt me. Charlie and I have moved on from you now.

We've moved on several times, actually. From our original family home when I defaulted on the mortgage, to several different flats when the council kept moving us around between temporary accommodation, before they could house us more permanently. Finally, we settled at the small flat we're in now, which compared to some of the places we've found ourselves living in is a virtual palace. Is it ideal? No. Perfect? Far from it. But it is warm – most of the time – our neighbours are friendly, and most importantly, until yesterday I'd had no doubt that Charlie is getting on okay at school.

A little more money would come in handy, of course; I still struggle to pay all our bills on the part-time wage I bring home and the benefits I receive, so yesterday I'd desperately hoped that this Alexander chap was going to tell me that's what I'd inherited when we'd got cut off. Just a small amount of extra cash would be incredibly helpful right now, and could tide me over until I got a full-time job again.

But on the bright side, my benefit money should come through in a couple of days, so until then, when I'll be able to top up my phone with the minimum credit and phone him back, I'll simply have to wait and hope.

I walk up the stairs so deep in thought about what the contents of this inheritance could be that I barely notice a man standing on my landing leaning out over the top of the railings.

'Ms Chesterford?' a deep, curiously familiar voice asks.

I jump. 'Who wants to know?' I ask automatically, even though I know within two seconds the voice belongs to the same person I'd been talking to on the phone last night.

The man looks surprised. 'Alexander Benjamin. I spoke with you yesterday evening?'

I look at the man no longer leaning on the railings, but standing upright in front of me. He's tall and impeccably dressed in a pair of smart grey trousers, a blue open-necked shirt and shiny tan brogues. He carries a matching suit jacket over one arm, and a tan briefcase to complement his shoes in the other.

'Oh yes, hello again. But what are you doing here on my landing?'

'We got cut off – at a most untimely moment, if I may say – and I hoped we might continue our conversation in person?'

'Er . . . ' I think about the inside of the flat. Charlie and I were late getting up this morning because I overslept, after lying awake into the early hours thinking about the letter. The flat really isn't looking its best on the other side of the door right now. 'Yes, of course; perhaps we could go and get a coffee somewhere?' The minute I say this I regret it. The cost of a cappuccino at the nearest coffee shop will take the contents of my purse down to approximately £4.64, and that's if I only have to pay for my own.

Alexander glances at my door and then at my anxious face and quickly says, 'Why not? The coffee is on me, of course.'

Although I hate myself for doing so, I don't contradict him. I

14

just smile and say thank you. Then I lead him back down the stairs – apologising for the faulty lift, and then we're back out into the sunshine, where everything immediately seems better.

'There's quite a nice coffee shop over on the high street, if that's all right with you?' I ask.

'Perfect.'

Alexander has long legs to match his height and I have to hurry along to keep up with him as we walk together towards the coffee shop.

'After you,' he says, holding the door open for me as we arrive.

'Thank you,' I say, touched by his polite gesture. Manners are always important to me.

We order two cups of coffee, which Alexander pays for, and then we sit at a quiet table by the window.

'Now,' Alexander says, 'firstly you told me last night you would prefer it if I called you Amelia, is that still correct?'

'Yes,' I say, taking another sip of my coffee. It's such a treat to taste good coffee again. My daily cup has come from a jar for so long now I've almost forgotten what freshly brewed coffee tastes like.

'Then I would like it if you called me Benji, as that's what I prefer.'

I stare at him for a second. How had Benji come from Alexander?

Ah, Alexander Benjamin. Of course. 'Sure,' I agree. It's a bit odd, but kind of suits him, I suppose. Even though Benji dresses like a solicitor, I suspect from the look of his slightly unkempt hair and the Harry Potter socks I'd glimpsed when we sat down, he might have a less formal, wilder side to him.

'Good,' Benji says, sounding pleased. 'Now we've got that out of the way, you must still be wondering what I've got to tell you.'

'I am a bit, yes.'

'You have every right to feel enormous anticipation, Amelia.'

I smile at him. He obviously takes great pleasure in using as many long words as he can when he speaks.

Benji reaches for his briefcase and pulls out a slim cardboard file. He lays it unopened on the table.

'In this file,' he begins, 'are details of the estate you have inherited.' He taps the file for effect, and I hope that the apparent emptiness of the file is a good indication that inside is a rather large cheque bearing my name. 'Would you like to see?'

'Yes please.'

Benji opens up the file and pulls from it several large photos, which he keeps turned away from me.

It's going to be photos of a dog, isn't it? I know it.

'Here,' he says triumphantly, turning around the first photo with a flourish, 'is your inheritance.' He lays the photo on the table in front of me.

'It's a castle,' I say blankly, as I stare at a picture of a large medieval-looking building standing on top of a hill.

'This,' Benji continues, laying another photo next to the first, 'is Chesterford Castle, to be precise. Your ancestral home.'

I laugh – a big out-loud laugh that makes the few other people in the coffee shop look over at us.

'Sorry,' I apologise, 'but I thought you said my *ancestral home*. We've just come from my home – a two-bedroom, fourth-floor flat on a slightly dodgy estate in Hamilton.'

'Not for much longer, Amelia,' Benji says, laying down a third photo with another view of the same castle on it. 'If you accept your inheritance, then this *twelve*-bedroom castle in Northumberland will be your new home.'

Three

'You're bonkers!' I say, looking incredulously at Benji. 'How can a castle be my home? There must be some mistake.'

Benji shakes his head and some of his grey coiffured hair flops over one of his eyes. He hurriedly pushes it back with his hand. 'No, no mistake. Chesterford Castle has been without an heir since the last Chesterford passed away – almost a year ago now, I believe.'

I simply stare at Benji – suddenly wondering if this is some sort of joke. I look surreptitiously around for concealed TV cameras, and then I scan Benji for a hidden microphone or a tiny earpiece. When I don't speak, he continues: 'John Crawford Chesterford, the seventeenth Earl, died without an heir to either his estate or his title. Without going into too many details right now – that information is in the documents both his family solicitor and I have access to – we have been trying to trace a suitable heir since his death.'

I still stare incredulously at Benji, and then back down at the photos on the table, then back up at him again as he talks.

But I realise he's stopped talking now, and is waiting for me to say something back to him.

'A . . . suitable heir?' I repeat. 'How do you find one of those – on eBay?'

Benji stares at me, his eyes narrowing as if he's trying to work out if I'm being serious, flippant or just plain stupid.

Usually it would be flippant – my sense of humour has got me into trouble on more than one occasion – but this time Benji would be correct in veering more towards the stupid. I just can't comprehend what he is telling me.

But he obviously chooses the flippant option – and laughs.

'Aha, funny!' he says, waggling his finger at me. 'If only it was that easy – actually no, strike that. If it *were* that easy I'd be out of a job. Like I said, this particular case has been extremely tricky, and I've had to go across several branches of the Chesterford family tree to find you.'

There is a Chesterford family tree? All the Chesterfords I know barely have two twigs to rub together, let alone a tree.

'You're serious, then?' I ask, looking at the castle in the photo again. 'You're telling me that this inheritance you keep talking about, it's this castle?' I tap the photo on the table. 'This one right here?'

This is mad. I'm going to wake up in a minute and find that Charlie and I are even later for school because I'd nodded off to sleep again and started dreaming.

'Yes,' Benji continues in a calm voice, 'as I said before, subject to the appropriate checks, you, Amelia, are the next Chesterford in the family lineage. The last Earl died without any children or any siblings. I've had to go back up through his father's brothers and then back down through their children to find you – the closet direct descendant still alive. It's been a

18

very complex process – one of the most extensive searches I've ever completed, in fact.'

'So you're telling me that it would have been my father, if he was still alive, who would have been the closest direct descendant?'

'That is correct – your father was related very distantly to the Northumberland Chesterfords by marriage on his great-grandmother's side. But surprisingly, through all the Chesterfords I researched, and all the branches of the family tree I studied, you are actually the most direct descendant from one of the original Earls, and therefore you now inherit the family seat – Chesterford Castle.'

I sit back in my chair and shake my head. I reach forward for my coffee but I find my hands are shaking – through shock or the fact I'm not used to this much caffeine any more, I'm not sure. But I hurriedly put my cup back down when it wobbles in my hand.

'I can only imagine what a huge shock this is for you, Amelia,' Benji says kindly. 'It's one of the biggest bequests I've ever dealt with, too. To find you're now not only the owner of this magnificent medieval castle, but also a direct descend-ant of one of the oldest noble families in England must be inconceivable.'

I nod slowly, wishing there was something a bit stronger in my cup than coffee right now. 'And you're sure?' I ask steadily. 'There's no chance you've made a mistake?'

'No, as I said, provided you have all the appropriate paperwork to verify your identity then Chesterford Castle is all yours.'

I think again for a moment. It's no good; I simply have to voice the question on the tip of my tongue. 'How much is it worth?' I blurt out, almost ashamed to ask. It seems so rude to talk about money when Benji is so thrilled and excited by my family history.

'I'm sorry?'

'How much is the castle worth? When it goes on the market, how much am I likely to get for it?' *This might be better than a cheque. A castle – how much was that worth these days? It could be millions.* I swallow hard while I await his answer.

Benji stares at me for a moment. 'I think you may have misunderstood me, Amelia. I apologise if I've misled you in any way, but the castle is not for sale.'

'Yet.'

'No, not at all. The terms of the ancient bequest state that any Chesterford who may inherit in the future must work towards the upkeep and maintenance of the castle. They should live in the castle and—'

'Wait, did you just say *live* in the castle?'

'I did.'

'But I can't live in a castle! Let alone one in Northumberland. I have responsibilities. I have a ten-year-old son who is at school just down the road from here – we can't just turn our lives upside down to go and live in a castle!'

'Yes, I know about Charlie. I was just about to come on to him.'

'What do you mean? What has Charlie got to do with this nonsense?'

For the first time since I've met him, Benji looks uncomfortable. He fiddles with one of his cufflinks. 'How much of a feminist are you, Amelia?' he asks, looking a little apprehensive.

'Why? What has that got to do with anything?'

'Because the strength of your views will likely affect how you receive my next piece of information.'

'What do you mean?'

'You see, the tenth Earl was quite a forward-thinking man for his time. He realised that there wouldn't always be a male heir in the Chesterford family to inherit the castle and the title Earl of Chesterford. So it might not always be possible for his family home to be passed down directly through his family. It has always been common practice in the aristocracy for male heirs to inherit titles and land. Females were simply passed over. So sometimes property and titles ended up going to a deceased's brother or a distant cousin, instead of to his children.'

'Yes, I did know that – talk about sexist! But all that's changed now, hasn't it? Before Prince George was born they changed it so girls could inherit titles too, didn't they?'

'Royalty did yes, but not the peerage.'

'What do you mean?'

'I mean that it is still law today that a hereditary title of the peerage must be passed down through the male line of descendants. It's a type of primogeniture.'

'You're kidding me?'

Benji shakes his head. 'Nope; madness, isn't it, in this day and age. There have been some pretty high-profile cases over the last few years where daughters that should have inherited their family's estate and title have been passed over in favour of a distant male relative.'

'I can't believe that,' I say incredulously. 'This is the twenty-first century we're living in, not the fifteenth. We're fighting for women's rights all over the world, but this is still going on in our own country. How can that be?'

Benji sympathetically nods his agreement.

'But why are you telling *me* this, Benji?' I ask. 'And what did you mean about this Earl being forward thinking?'

'Yes, as I said, the tenth Earl of Chesterford realised that something like this might happen somewhere down the line, and although he couldn't change the law that said a male must inherit a title, he *could* dictate where his money and his estate would go in the future. So he decreed that if a suitable male heir could not be found that was a direct descendant of the family, then the next appropriate female would be allowed to inherit both the castle and any monies that went with it, but not the title.'

'Okay . . .'

'So that is where you come in, Amelia. You are indeed the next appropriate female and you will inherit both the castle and the estate of John Crawford Chesterford, the seventeenth Earl, to run as you see fit. But your son, Charlie, as the next direct male descendant, will in fact inherit the last Earl's title and now becomes the eighteenth Earl of Chesterford.'

Four

'Whoa!' I say, holding up my hand. 'Stop right there. That is never going to happen. I will not be inflicting that noose around my son's neck. Nah-ah, not now, not ever.'

'Whether you choose to accept the estate or Charlie chooses to accept the title,' Benji says calmly, 'he is still the eighteenth Earl by birth.'

'Look, Benny, Benji, whatever your name is,' I say, trying, but not succeeding very well, to control my fury, 'I thought when I rang you that you were going to tell me I'd inherited something. At best I hoped it might be money. At worst I thought it might be a dog.'

Benji grins, then changes his expression to one of severity when he realises that this time I'm not joking.

'But now you're telling me,' I continue, 'not only have I inherited a draughty old castle somewhere, but my son has inherited some rich man's privileged shroud too?'

'I hardly think it's a shroud,' Benji begins.

'Well, I do. Charlie is being brought up to believe that everyone is equal. No one is better than anyone else. Titles only exist to emphasise the opposite. Calling someone Duke or Countess, or whatever it is, immediately makes them different. It makes them think they're above normal folk, those that aren't born into privilege, and I won't stand for it. I might not be able to change this country's heritage, a heritage that dictates we all must have a class, but I can make damn sure my son doesn't buy into all that pompous nonsense.'

I sit back in my chair again, breathing heavily. I've let rip on one of my soapbox topics, and Benji has borne the brunt of my wrath.

'Have you finished now?' Benji asks calmly, looking at me across the table with a steady expression.

I nod.

'Good. As a matter of fact, I happen to agree with you. I might be a historian by trade, but the British class system is archaic, out-dated and obsolete. I detest it as much as you do.'

I look at Benji in astonishment. I hadn't expected him to say that.

'However,' he continues, 'as much as I detest the class system, I think our country's history must be preserved as much as humanly possible – and that includes houses and buildings of historic interest. You may only see Chesterford Castle as a money-making opportunity, but you must remember, Amelia, that it is not only your family history inside that house, but our country's history too.'

I'm impressed by his impassioned speech.

'Now,' Benji continues in a friendlier tone, his own rant over, 'you may think I'm speaking out of place here, and by all means tell me to mind my own business if you like, but the situation you currently find yourself in is hardly ideal, is it?'

'How do you mean?' I ask cautiously.

'I mean you're a single mother with a young son to raise. You live in a tiny council flat in a tower block that should have been demolished years ago. You have little money and no prospects of getting much more any time soon.'

I look down at the table uncomfortably. Benji knows far too much about me for my liking.

'Your parents have both sadly passed away, you have no siblings and no inheritance of your own. You are over-qualified for the job you do currently, but you can't get a better one because of childcare issues, even though I believe you ran your own small business for a while a number of years ago?' He looks at me questioningly. 'Feel free to correct me if I'm wrong on any of these counts.'

'How do you know about my qualifications?' I ask suspiciously. 'And my recruitment business.'

'Amelia, it's my job to know these things. You graduated from university with an honours degree in business and economics, yes?'

I nod.

'Yet you are currently working as a part-time check-out assistant in a supermarket?'

'There's nothing wrong in that!' I reply defensively. 'It's good honest work. Don't turn your nose up at it.'

'I'm not. My mother worked in a shop all her life, as a matter of fact, and I was born over the top of one.'

I look at Benji with interest. But he doesn't continue with the potted history of his own life; instead he resumes his assault on mine.

'You are destined for so much more than the life you're living at the moment, Amelia. Life has dealt you some rough blows, I know that. Don't ask me how,' he insists, holding his hand up. 'But when life tries to make it up to you by giving you another

25

chance, don't let your pride knock it back. Take that chance, and go and make a better life for yourself and for your son.'

'But—' I begin.

'But what? I've heard your excuses, and they can all be overcome. Charlie can go to a new school; you can both move into the modern apartments at the castle – yes, there are some, I'm not asking you to move into a ruin! And most importantly you can make a difference. You can choose the type of landlord you want to be; yes, you could be the owner who lords it up over the locals, as in times gone by. Or you could be the sort of owner who makes the castle work for the locals and the community that surround it.'

I gaze over the table at Benji. I hadn't thought about it that way.

'I do like the sound of the latter option ... I still have one big but, though,' I say apologetically.

Benji's lips twitch slightly with amusement, and I realise what I've just said. But instead of making a comment he clears his throat and says, 'Go on.'

'*But* I don't know how to run a castle, do I?'

Benji smiles kindly. 'That skill I'm sure can be learned. There are already staff there who will show you the ropes. As I said before, Chesterford Castle isn't a ruin; it's a fully habitable castle already open to the public. I visited it once when I was holidaying up in Northumberland.'

'Did you? What was it like?'

'Old.' Benji winks. 'It's quite a magnificent place, actually. It stands, as you can see from the photo, on a hill that looks out over Rainbow Bay.'

'Rainbow Bay?' I enquire, smiling. 'That makes it sound like a fairy-tale castle.'

'I can assure you that the history of Chesterford has been no fairy tale. There is all sorts of bloody history associated with that place.'

I grimace. 'Sounds lovely. You're really selling it to me.'

'I believe it's called Rainbow Bay because of an ancient myth about a rainbow shining over the castle. Either that or it's to do with the rocks the castle stands upon: if I remember, there are many colours in them – like a rainbow, I suppose?'

I look at the photo again.

'But what I do remember is the place was definitely in need of some new blood, and now it has some.' Benji grins at me.

'I haven't agreed to any of this yet.'

'But you're thinking about it – yes?'

'Maybe . . . just a bit.'

Benji claps his hands together. 'Wonderful! When shall I arrange a visit?'

'Whoa, steady on, I only said I was thinking about it. I have another question.'

'Yes?'

'What happens if I don't agree to take the castle on? You said I couldn't sell it.'

'That is correct. *If* you were silly enough to reject this offer,' Benji eyes me meaningfully, 'then the castle would be passed immediately to National Heritage to do with as they see fit. You would get nothing.'

'I see.'

'So, Amelia,' Benji asks, 'what's it to be? Are you going to embrace this wonderful offer of a brand-new life for you and Charlie? Or are you going to reject this amazing opportunity, and continue living the dull, monotonous life you are now?'

27

Five

'So, Charlie, what do you think of our new home?'

Charlie stares through the windscreen of the old Morris Minor we've driven up to Northumberland in. The car had been my grandfather's prized possession many years ago, and was the one thing he left me in his will. I have many happy childhood memories of trips with him in the open-top car, zooming about the countryside, but there have been far too many more recent times when I've come close to selling the vintage vehicle. Luckily something has always come along just at the last minute to bail me out and save me from having to do so. I like to think it was Granddad looking out for me and 'Bella', as he used to call the car. It would break my heart if I had to part with her; she's one of the few links I have left to my family.

So we'd piled as many of our things as we could into the back of the car; the rest of our possessions are due to follow in a removal van, which Benji had helped me organise.

The car had been in storage for so long, I'd wondered a number of times if she was going to make the long journey up to Northumberland. But make it she had, and I felt that by bringing Bella with me, I was bringing a part of my old family to my new home.

'Is that it?' Charlie asks excitedly, looking across the rolling Northumbrian hills to the majestic castle on the horizon. 'Our very own castle?'

'It's not just ours,' I say, looking with equal awe at the magnificent building in the distance. Today the castle is cloaked in a sunny golden hue as it soars up into the bright blue sky behind it, as if it's floating on its own set of clouds. 'We do have to share it with a few other people.'

'Our servants?'

'No!' I say sharply. 'I explained all this to you, remember? Even though we own the castle now, there are other people who are going to help us run it. They are not servants; they are members of the castle staff.'

'But we're in charge, right?'

'Technically, yes,' I'm forced to agree. 'But we're going to need all of their help if we're going to make a go of living here.'

'I can't believe we're actually going to live in our own castle,' Charlie says, fidgeting impatiently in his seat. 'We spent all last term learning about them at school and now I'm going to be king of one.'

I sigh. I'd spent a lot of time since I agreed to accept this challenge talking to Charlie about what was going to happen, and what it might be like for us living in our new home. But Charlie had spent most of last term learning about lords, ladies, knights and medieval battles. His idea of living in a castle is more akin to King Arthur than the modern reality of running a historical visitors' attraction. Not that my knowledge is a lot broader. All I know of Chesterford Castle is what I learned on the quick day trip I'd taken here before I finally agreed to accept the Chesterford inheritance and move us up here to Northumberland.

Benji had been right, of course: this was too great an opportunity for me to turn down. Charlie would definitely have a better life living here in the fresh air of the Northumbrian coast than on the outskirts of a big, dirty, polluted city.

When I first told him about it he'd taken to the idea without any hesitation. There was no question to him that living in a huge rambling castle was far more appealing than living in a rundown high-rise.

I wished I could share his sense of excitement, but I still had too many worries and concerns that we were doing the right thing.

'Come on, Mum!' Charlie says, banging his hand impatiently on the dashboard. 'Let's get going. It's all right for you, you've been here before. I want to see our castle! Benji has told me all about it, but now I want to see it for myself!'

Benji has been wonderful to us throughout this huge transition in our lives. I'm sure he's done much more than was required of him. He's not only kept us informed about what's going on, he's also helped me a great deal with the paperwork side of things, and with the practical stuff too, like changing Charlie's schools and working out how we could move all our stuff up here. There was only one thing we disagreed on. Against the advice of Benji, when I was still in two minds about what to do, I'd decided to pay my first visit to the castle alone. Benji had offered to come with me and introduce me to the staff, but I wanted to see what the place was really like, on my own as a visitor, without people bowing and scraping to me because I was possibly going to be the new owner.

So Benji had very generously paid for a return train ticket for me up to Northumberland (I'd insisted I'd pay him back just as soon as I could afford to). He'd offered to book a hotel, too, but I'd decided that wasn't necessary: I'd simply travel on a very early train, and return on a late one.

Chesterford Castle hadn't been busy at all the day I'd visited. *It is a Wednesday in late March*, I'd told myself as I paid to go in and politely turned down the offer of a guidebook from the young man in the small ticket booth by the entrance.

'Been here before, have ye?' he'd asked as I'd picked up my ticket and put my purse away.

'No; first time, actually.'

'Ah, I thought as much. Not many come back for a second visit.'

I'd just smiled and carried on through the huge gateway that led from the outer grounds, along a path, across a stone bridge, and under a scary-looking portcullis. The Northumberland coastal skies were dark and heavy above me, and it hadn't seemed the best time to be wandering around outside, so I'd started with the interior of the castle.

There weren't any guides waiting for me as I'd ventured inside through a huge solid wooden door, or any signs denoting a particular route I was supposed to follow. So I'd stood for a moment, gazing in awe at the vast marble staircase that swept elegantly from the entrance hall up to the second floor. I'd always wanted to live in a house that had an ornate staircase – the sort people placed a beautifully decorated tree under at Christmas. But when no one came to speak to me, or asked to see my ticket, I'd simply spent the next hour or so wandering

31

aimlessly from room to room, admiring the architecture and interiors I passed.

I'd quickly decided the interior was more like being in a large stately home than a castle. The rooms I visited were full of old paintings and furniture, most of which could have done with a good clean in my opinion, but none of which seemed all that interesting without having a guidebook to look them up in.

But what did impress me as I toured the endless rooms and walked along the long corridors were the huge crystal chandeliers that hung from nearly every ceiling.

'You look like you could do with a dust too,' I'd whispered as I'd stood beneath one looking up at it. 'I bet you'd sparkle even more, then.'

Other than the young man at the ticket booth, I didn't see many staff on my visit. In my limited experience of visiting these types of buildings, usually there would at least be a bored-looking person sitting in the corner of each room you visited or an over-enthusiastic guide who wanted to share with you everything they knew. So either they were very trusting of the visitors they had at Chesterford or there was a great CCTV system secreted away somewhere; or perhaps the antiques in the castle weren't actually worth all that much. I quickly decided it was probably the latter.

After I'd finished my tour of inside, the skies outside were surprisingly clear. So I'd had a brief wander around the gravel-filled courtyard at the centre of the castle, and up along one of the battlements with its giant black cannons pointed ominously out to sea. Then I'd climbed to the top of one of the four towers that framed the building's thick strong walls, up what seemed like a never-ending spiral staircase. And for my efforts, at the top, I'd been rewarded with a magnificent view. One side of the tower looked out over Rainbow Bay – an endless sandy beach, edged by the infamous North Sea extending as far as I could see into the distance – and the other side of the tower looked out over a different if not equally pretty view: the small chocolate-box village of Chesterford.

'It's a bit better than the view from our flat,' I'd joked to no one in particular as I'd stood on my own surveying what might soon be the view from my home. 'Perhaps we could make a go of living here after all? I mean, who wouldn't want to wake up to this every morning?'

But even though I'd run a small business before, I had to admit the thought of taking on the running of this ancient castle was incredibly daunting. Where would I even begin? Benji had said there were staff here that would help me, but I hadn't seen many of them yet.

If they were all like the young guy on the gate, I'd be fighting an uphill battle steeper than the gradient the castle stood on. Was this actually such a good idea after all?

My doubtful thoughts had been broken by something spooking me. I'd shuddered and turned swiftly around, certain that someone was standing behind me listening to what I was saying. But of course there was no one there, just the sound of a strong sea breeze circling around my head, and a cool wind chilling my already cold body.

'Well, if we do come here we'll definitely need some warmer clothes,' I'd murmured, shivering. 'How chilly is it up here – even in the springtime!'

But although the castle was vast, the walls were thick, and the rooms that I'd seen were a bit tired looking, there was definitely something about this place. Something that made me feel not only positive about the future, but a little excited, too, about the thought of coming to live here. I wasn't sure why, but for some reason I already felt very content at Chesterford.

'Come again!' a cheery-looking woman had called across the courtyard as I headed for the exit. She'd smiled warmly at me. 'We could do with a few more visitors.'

'You know something? I think I just might,' I'd called back as I'd waved goodbye. 'And sooner than you think,' I'd whispered to myself.

And now, as I smile at Charlie and put the car back into gear, I'm about to make my return visit to Chesterford Castle; not as a paying guest this time, but as its new owner.

Six

Charlie and I drive through a pair of huge wrought-iron gates at the centre of the high stone wall that encircles the grounds of the castle, and continue up a long driveway. We pull up in the visitors' car park, just outside the entrance where I'd paid to go in last time, and we climb out.

'Wow, it's even bigger than I thought it would be!' Charlie exclaims, his neck tilted right back as he gazes up in awe at the impenetrable castle walls. 'Can we live in one of the towers, Mum, purrlease?'

'We'll be living in the apartments we're allocated,' I tell him, 'like Benji told us.'

Benji really has been too good to us. In addition to assisting me with the practicalities of moving to a castle, he's been really helpful about finding out everything we needed to know before moving – like exactly where we would be living when we got here. He'd joked to Charlie that it would be in the dungeons, but instead of being horrified, Charlie was even more thrilled to hear this.

We've spent so much time with Benji over the last few

weeks that I was quite sad when I realised that when we finally did move we wouldn't be seeing him any more. He's become more than just an advisor to us; I like to think he's become our friend, too.

But as friendly as our transition has been so far, I had no choice but to be very formal when I requested that both Benji and the staff at Davies & Davies were on no account to tell Charlie about his title. I haven't fully decided what I'm going to do about that yet, and I don't want the issue confused by Charlie knowing about it. So they've agreed that for now the title Earl of Chesterford will be a silent one. I think they were so grateful to have found someone to take on the castle at last that names were the least of their worries. Plus, I've been having enough trouble making Charlie understand we aren't going to be lording it up in grand halls with servants dancing to our every whim without informing him he is actually an Earl!

'Well, I hope our apartments *are* in one of those towers,' Charlie says, still gazing at the castle. 'That would be so cool. But how are we going to get all our stuff inside, Mum, if we have to park out here?'

'I'm hoping someone will open up the big gate over there, so that we can park inside the courtyard.'

I point to a second set of black gates that bar the entrance to unwanted (or these days – non-paying) guests. These gates are the last barrier between the exterior castle walls we've just driven through and the inner part of the castle. I'd entered through a much smaller side gate when I'd come on my day trip, but even that seems to be closed at the moment.

'Let's see if there's anyone about,' I say, walking with Charlie towards the gates. 'Maybe the castle is closed to visitors today?'

The little wooden ticket kiosk is indeed closed as we arrive at the entrance.

'Damn,' I say, looking around. 'I'm sure Benji said they'd be expecting us.'

'Is Benji coming to live here too?' Charlie asks keenly. 'I'd really like him to.'

Benji and Charlie, to my surprise, had hit it off incredibly well in the few times that Benji had popped around to the flat. Benji seemed to have a natural easy way about him that Charlie liked, and Charlie, continually wary of men since his father left, had always been sad to see him leave.

'No, I'm afraid not. Benji has his own life back in London, hasn't he? We talked about that.'

Charlie's face drops.

'But he has promised to come and visit us when we're settled in.'

'Goody!' Charlie grins now. 'I like Benji, he's fun.'

'I know you do.' I put my arm around Charlie's narrow shoulders protectively as we both look up at the ominous gates in front of us. Having Benji with us today would have made things that little bit easier, no doubt. But I have to be brave and stand on my own two feet now. 'Benji gave me a number to call if we have any problems,' I tell him. 'I think it's for the caretaker. I'll see if he can help us.'

I call the number stored in my phone, but it just rings out and there's no answer.

'Damn,' I say, looking down at the phone in my hand. 'What now?'

'We could press this bell,' Charlie says, pointing to a brass button on the wall. 'Maybe someone might come then?'

'Worth a try. Go on, you press it then.'

Charlie pushes hard on the brass bell. We don't hear anything our end, but we can only hope someone does inside the castle.

Then we stand back and wait.

After a couple of minutes of nothing happening, I press the bell this time, and again we wait.

'I could get over those gates easy enough,' Charlie suggests, looking up at the gates, which must be over nine feet high. 'I've got over some that size before. These look like they'd be easy enough to climb, then I could go and see if I can find anyone inside.'

'Ha, I don't think so,' I reply, not wanting to know under what circumstances Charlie has been climbing over gates like these. 'There's a reason those gates are that high and have those nasty points on top: to *prevent* intruders from getting in.'

'But I wouldn't be an intruder, would I? It's our castle now.'

'True. But if you fell from up there then you'd be dead, or severely injured at the very least, so there would be no living in a castle for you then, would there?'

'If I was dead I could be a ghost and haunt the place instead,' Charlie says, quick as a flash. 'Ooh ... ' His eyes light up. 'Do you think there *are* any ghosts here?'

'Don't be silly – there's no such thing as ghosts.'

'But this building is really old – I bet loads of people have lived and died here, some of them probably really gruesomely too.'

I shake my head. What is it with boys and the macabre?

'A lot of them from ringing this bell when it clearly says on the kiosk we're *closed*,' a gruff voice says behind us.

I jump at the new voice, and turn to see an older, thick-set man standing on the other side of the gate with his hands in his pockets. He's wearing a tweed suit with a shirt and tie and green wellingtons, and he looks annoyed.

'Oh, hello there; sorry to disturb you. I do know you're not open today but—'

'Exactly, we're *closed* to visitors.'

'But we're not visitors.'

'Then we don't want any,' the man says brusquely.

'You don't want any what?'

'Whatever it is you're selling,' he snaps, turning his back on us and beginning to walk away.

'But I'm not selling anything!' I call through the gates after him. 'I'm Amelia. Amelia Harris ... I mean Chesterford. I'm the new owner of the castle.'

The man stops walking and turns slowly around.

'You? You're the new owner?'

I nod hurriedly.

'But the new owner isn't due to arrive until tomorrow.'

'No, I'm sure I have it right. I was told I could move in on the fifteenth of April, and today's the fifteenth.'

'We were told the new owner would be here on the sixteenth,' he says suspiciously.

'Er, no, it's definitely the fifteenth. Look, I have it right here on my phone.' I begin to look for the email I had from Davies & Davies.

'No matter, miss,' the man says, walking back towards the gates. 'You're here now. Let me just unlock this gate and we'll get you inside. No doubt that silly girl got it wrong again.'

The man pulls a large bundle of keys from his pocket and begins to unlock the side gate.

'I think we might need the big gates open, I'm afraid,' I say apologetically. 'We have a car outside loaded with our things.'

39

'The big ones?' the man says, looking anxiously up at the gates. 'Are you sure?'

'Yes, I'm afraid so,' I smile apologetically, 'and there's a rather large van not that far behind us, too, with the rest of our stuff.'

'Hmm.' The man eyes us up and down. 'If we need to open the big gates I'll need Joey to come down and help me.' He pulls a large old-fashioned walkie-talkie from his pocket. 'Joey, are you there?' he asks, speaking into it.

There's a sort of hissing crackling sound and then a voice at the other end says, 'This is Lancelot here. What's your beef, King Arthur?'

The man rolls his eyes. 'Stop with all your gibberish, Joey. I need you by the front gate. The new owner is here and wants to be let in.'

'The new owner? But I thought she wasn't arriving until tomorrow, Arthur?'

'So did I,' Arthur murmurs. 'But she's here now, and they need the big gates opening, so I need you down here pronto, Joey.'

'Got it!' Joey calls. 'Be there before you can say Camelot!'

Arthur shakes his head and puts the walkie-talkie back in his pocket.

'He's a good worker,' he says almost apologetically, 'but he'd be even better if he zipped it shut sometimes.'

I smile at Arthur through the gate. 'Have you got many staff here?'

'There's four of us in all.'

'Four of you to manage all this!' I ask in amazement. 'Isn't that a lot of work?'

'Aye, but we manage. We're the ones that live in, anyway. We sometimes get in casual help from the village if we need it.'

'Who are the four?' I ask to make conversation until Joey gets here. 'You, obviously. What do you do, Arthur? Is it all right to call you Arthur?'

'It is, miss. That'd be my name. I was once the butler here many a year ago, but now I'm part caretaker, part manager, part everything really. The old Earl called me his right-hand man.'

'I see.'

'And then there's Joey who you just heard from. He helps me out with whatever needs doing, really. Like I said, he's a good lad. Not the sharpest tool sometimes, but a good worker, none the less.'

'That's two of you. Who else?'

'There's my wife, Dorothy; she was once the housekeeper, but now she cooks, cleans, and again does a bit of everything. We all pitch in here.' He looks meaningfully at me.

'Of course. So who's the fourth?'

'That would be the young girl; Tiffany she calls herself. Mainly works in the office – doing accounts and suchlike. I think the last Earl only hired her because he felt sorry for her. Her head's always far too up in the clouds for my liking. I prefer to be on solid ground meself.'

'Joey to the rescue!' a voice calls, and I recognise the young man who sold me my entrance ticket the last time I was here zig-zagging back and forth across the path like he's a superhero with his hands in the air.

Charlie, who's been pacing up and down impatiently behind me while I've been talking to Arthur, immediately looks up with interest.

'Enough of your shenanigans, Joey,' Arthur says. 'Did you bring the key?'

'I did!' Joey says, brandishing a large silver key.

'Good.' Arthur takes the key from him and begins to undo the large padlocks on the gates. 'You'd best go and get that car of yours, miss,' he instructs. 'It'll only take Joey here a moment to lift the gates across.'

'Superman, me!' Joey says, flexing his biceps. He winks at Charlie, and Charlie smiles shyly at him.

'Where should I park once I'm through the gates?' I ask Arthur.

'Just carry on through over the bridge and under the portcullis.' He looks down the path past us. 'This van that's on the way will fit under there, I assume?'

I look up at the ominous portcullis that I'd walked under the first time I came here. 'Yes, I think so. At least, I hope it will.'

Arthur looks at me like I should have thought of that before hiring it. He probably has a point, but I guessed the van-hire company didn't have much call for large vans that were guaranteed to fit underneath a castle portcullis. I was pretty sure it wasn't on the Frequently Asked Questions page of their website, anyway.

Charlie and I climb back into Bella and drive ourselves and the mountain of luggage we have piled up in the back safely over the bridge, just as our removals van arrives behind us. Luckily it manages to squeeze underneath the archway with inches to spare, and we all arrive in the castle courtyard together.

My vintage car doesn't look too conspicuous as we climb out, but the large white van looks completely out of place surrounded by all this history. I'm sure not many past owners of the castle have arrived at their new home in this fashion: a horse and carriage would have been much more appropriate.

Arthur has obviously radioed ahead to warn the others of our imminent arrival because two very different-looking women come rushing out of a door to greet us.

'Your Ladyship,' the elder and plumper of the two women says, curtseying before me. 'What a pleasure it is to welcome you to Chesterford.'

'Er, yes. Hello,' I reply, somewhat taken aback by her formalities. 'You must be Dorothy?'

'I am, Lady Chesterford. I'm the housekeeper here.'

'Yes, we've met before – briefly. I came to visit the castle a few weeks ago now.'

Dorothy looks horrified that she hasn't remembered this event.

'Please don't worry,' I hurriedly assure her, 'I was incognito that day; I wanted to see the castle like a visitor sees it to begin with.'

'Oh, of course, Your Ladyship.'

'And please, I'd much prefer it if you called me Amelia.'

Dorothy looks even more horrified by this request.

'And you must be Tiffany,' I say, turning to the younger girl. I hold out my hand purposefully to her so she doesn't curtsey this time. But Tiffany is even more confused by my request, and instead takes hold of my outstretched hand, bobs a curtsey, and then, to my horror, proceeds to kiss the back of my hand.

'Please, all of this formality is not necessary. I would like you *all* to call me Amelia,' I say to everyone as the men join the line-up now. 'And this is my son, Charlie.' Charlie turns a deep shade of crimson as everyone stares at him. 'I want us to be friends as well as colleagues. You all know so much more about running a castle than I do, and I want us

43

to work together to make Chesterford Castle the success it deserves to be.'

Dorothy breaks out into spontaneous applause, which Tiffany quickly joins in with. Joey whoops, and Arthur simply stands there, his hands thrust into his pockets, wearing the same gruff look on his face that he's had since we arrived.

Seven

'I love it here, Mum!' Charlie says, racing up the spiral staircase for the umpteenth time. 'Have you seen the view from the top windows? It's amazing!'

'Be careful on those stairs,' I say, gazing around the room at the boxes and suitcases filled with all our things. 'They're steep and you're not used to them yet.'

Much to Charlie's delight, our apartment *is* in one of the towers. Apparently, as Joey explained as he helped us move all our stuff from the van up the many stairs of the North East tower, one of the previous Earls had been very forward thinking and had had this particular tower completely renovated in the 1950s, so he and his wife could live privately in this part of the castle, whilst allowing the rest of building to be open to the public.

Our new accommodation is set over four levels. On the ground floor is the entrance, with a pretty black-and-white tiled hallway and a tiny scullery that is home to a washing machine and tumble dryer. Then on the second floor there is a cosy kitchen/diner with solid oak units, a white butler's sink and a modern cooker. Up on the third floor there are two comfortable-looking bedrooms with amazing views of the castle and the beach from their pretty arched windows, then finally at the top of the tower, this time with a superb 360-degree view of the surrounding coast and countryside, is a large, bright, circular sitting room. Each one of the four floors is joined by the same spiral (and likely original) stone staircase that Charlie is enjoying so much right now.

I'd been pleasantly surprised by how modern everything was. I'd imagined the last Earl to be a miserly old man who'd died in a dusty cobwebbed room all on his own. But according to Dorothy he was quite the opposite and liked his home comforts.

'Daft as a brush, mind,' she'd said as she'd showed me around my new home with great delight. 'That's why it took so long to find the new heir. He should have done something about it sooner himself, but I think the silly old bugger thought he'd live for ever. Ooh, pardon me French, ma'am,' she'd apologised immediately, bowing her head a little, to my irritation.

'*Please*, it's Amelia,' I'd insisted.

'Yes, ma'am, I mean, Miss Amelia. Ooh, is that Arthur back with help?' she'd said, glancing out of the window, and we'd seen Arthur followed by two burly-looking men traipsing across the castle courtyard on their way to help us move my belongings – most of which were currently scattered all over the castle courtyard – up into the tower. Apparently, in my haste I'd paid for a van and a driver only, and our driver had informed us that on no account was he climbing up several flights of spiral stairs carrying all my stuff like some sort of lackey, even after Arthur had offered him a hefty tip if he did. So our possessions had been unceremoniously unloaded on to the gravel, while Arthur went in search of help and the driver set off back down south.

But even after Arthur had found help, the process still wasn't without trial; carrying boxes and bags up the narrow stairs was fine, but moving the few items of modern furniture I owned up the spiral staircase and into the appropriate rooms proved extremely tricky and at times almost impossible.

To my intense relief, eventually we'd succeeded, and all our helpers had followed Dorothy to the castle kitchen for tea and biscuits as a reward for all their efforts. Now it's just Charlie and me again – the way I like it best.

I unpack a few necessary things, insisting that Charlie helps me, even though it is all I can do to stop him abseiling down the tower wall to escape this torture. Then when I can stand his miserable face no longer, I agree we can go and take Charlie's first proper look around his new home.

While the Northumbrian skies show no signs of rain, we decide to explore the exterior first. Chesterford has more extensive grounds than I'd first realised. In the areas directly outside the inner castle walls there are wide expanses of green grass, dotted occasionally with large beds of luscious shrubs and pretty spring bulbs. We walk on a little further and find a few outbuildings – most of which seem empty, and some pretty derelict – and then on the very edge of the walled border are a series of tiny cottages, only one of which seems to be inhabited.

'Big, isn't it?' Charlie says as we walk along the seaward side of the castle.

'A bit bigger than our old flat, that's for sure!'

'And the house we used to live in with Dad. We had a garden there, didn't we?'

I nod silently. My stomach still twists sharply when Charlie mentions his father.

'But it was nothing like this!' Charlie carries on excitedly. 'Ooh, where does this lead, do you think?' he asks as we stumble upon a little gateway in the wall.

I shrug and shake my head, but as always Charlie's enthusiasm is not only contagious, it lifts me immediately from my melancholy.

'Let's see, shall we?' I suggest in a lighter voice, delighted to see some colour already appearing in Charlie's pale cheeks. There's a large rusty key already in the lock, so I turn it and we swing open the door.

The gateway leads down a small walled pathway towards the sea, and at the end we find ourselves stepping directly on to the beach.

'How cool is that?' Charlie says, running on to the sand. 'Our own private entrance to a beach!'

As he scampers off in front of me, I take a moment to breathe in the fresh sea air.

Glorious.

We spend about twenty minutes on the sand together, walking along the water's edge, jumping when the waves nearly wash over our inappropriately shod feet, and picking up pretty shells and interestingly shaped pebbles with which Charlie insists on filling his trouser pockets.

'Why don't you just choose one special shell or pebble?' I suggest. 'You're going to be coming down here quite a lot. If you only pick one each time then you'll still leave some for the sand to look after.'

Charlie thinks about this. Then he empties his pockets, and after much careful consideration chooses one conical shell.

'This will be my first-day-here shell,' he announces proudly. 'When I look at this shell I will remember our first day in our new home together.'

'Excellent idea,' I tell him proudly, pulling him towards me for a hug. 'Oh, I do hope we'll be happy here, Charlie.' I sigh wistfully and gaze up at the castle behind us.

'Of course we will, Mum,' Charlie tells me pragmatically. 'We're always happy as long as we're together, aren't we?'

I'm so touched by his words, I can't reply. So I just pull him into me again until I've blinked away my tell-tale tears.

Reluctantly we eventually have to leave the beach. So we head back up the path, through the gate, which I'm careful to lock behind us, and then I take Charlie on a tour around the parts of the castle I saw on my first visit. Charlie is mostly bored by this, not appreciating at all the antique furniture and *objets d'art* we find in all the public rooms, that is until we walk into the large ground-floor room known as the Great Hall and he spies a suit of armour standing guard in the corner. While he hurries over to examine it, I take a closer look at this vast room with its intricate wooden panelling and high vaulted ceilings, and in particular the many paintings that hang in between tapestries on the impressive dark oak walls.

Many of the paintings are portraits of past Earls of Chesterford – my ancestors, I suppose. *This is a very masculine room*, I decide as I move along the rows of portraits, a motley crew of men lined up within their ornate gold frames. *I wonder what went on here throughout the castle's history?*

'That's the last Earl you're looking at there,' Arthur's voice says behind me as I gaze up at one of the more modern portraits. 'A fine man he was too. Perhaps a tad unstable towards the end, but he was a wonderful master to serve.'

I flinch at the word master, and think it best not to mention what Dorothy had said earlier about her old boss.

'The paintings in here are all of past Earls, then?'

'They are indeed. Many banquets, meetings and important decisions have taken place in this very room over the years, right back to the Norman Conquest.'

'Obviously decisions made by men,' I add, looking at all the paintings. 'Has there never been a female in charge at Chesterford? What about all the countesses; where are the portraits of them?'

Arthur eyes me warily. 'One of them feminist types, are you?' he asks.

'That depends on what *type* you mean? Am I in favour of equality for women? Then yes. But do I take offence if a man holds a door open for me? Well, no, definitely not.'

'Nothing wrong with a bit of chivalry,' Arthur says approvingly.

'Indeed not. Be careful with that, Charlie, you mustn't touch it,' I call to Charlie who is still inspecting the suit of armour.

'But can't I try it on, Mum? We do own it now.'

I feel my cheeks flush. 'No, and *we* don't own it – the castle does.'

I glance apologetically at Arthur, but he simply nods his approval at my choice of words.

'I'm sure I can find an old shield or something similar for you to play with, young sir, if you'd like?' he offers.

'Ooh, yes please,' Charlie says, stepping away from the armour and coming over to Arthur and me. 'That would be awesome. Do you think you might find me a sword too?'

'No, no swords!' I insist. 'And please call my son Charlie.'

Arthur nods at me and winks at Charlie. 'Maybe just a blunt

one. Now your mum wants to see paintings of some ladies, so if you'd both follow me.'

Arthur leads us across the hall to some wood panelling with roses carved on it. He reaches up and presses on one of the flowers and suddenly one of the panels slides magically across, revealing another room beyond.

'A secret room!' Charlie exclaims. 'Cool.'

'This room was known as the Ladies' Chamber,' Arthur says, gesturing for us to go inside. 'When feasts where held in the Great Hall, afterwards the men would retire to the Billiards Room down the hall, and the ladies would retire here.'

The Ladies' Chamber is furnished entirely in shades of turquoise and gold. Embossed turquoise wallpaper adorns the walls, and turquoise and gold upholstered furniture sits amongst walnut tables and bookcases. The walls are covered in more portraits – this time, I'm pleased to see, they are of females.

I go over to look while Charlie is captivated by a tiny piano in the corner of the room.

'That is Clara, fifteenth Countess of Chesterford,' Arthur tells me as I gaze at a portrait of a pretty, but proud-looking woman wearing what looks to me like an Edwardian outfit. 'She was supposed to be quite the socialite – apparently, she hosted many luxurious house parties here; the future King Edward VII was her guest on more than one occasion, I believe.'

'Really?' I look hard at the woman in the painting. She reminds me a little of my grandmother. 'What happened to her?'

'She almost brought the castle to bankruptcy. Racked up huge gambling debts and couldn't pay them back. Her husband, the fifteenth Earl, died young, so she had to sell off some precious family heirlooms to repay her creditors. The rest of the family were none too happy with her; she was somewhat regarded as the black sheep of the family, I believe.'

I look again at the serene face gazing down at me, and I sympathise with my ancestor. Debt is never much fun, whatever form it takes.

Arthur then proceeds to tell me as much as he can about all the other paintings in the room. It seems there were some pretty formidable females in the Chesterford family. And suddenly I find myself feeling proud that I'm becoming one of them.

'Would you like me to show you around some more of the castle?' Arthur asks.

'I've actually seen most of what the visitors see before,' I tell him, 'when I came to visit myself. What I'd really like to see is the behind-the-scenes stuff; you know, the well-oiled cogs that make everything run smoothly.'

Arthur pulls a face. 'I'd hardly call it well oiled, but we get by. Come this way, then, and I'll show you the castle offices.'

Arthur leads us out into the Great Hall, and then we follow him down a long corridor, up some stone stairs that are roped off to the public, and finally through a heavy wood door marked 'PRIVATE. NO ENTRY'.

On the other side is another narrow corridor, and at the end of that Arthur opens yet another door. This time we find ourselves in a small modern office with several filing cabinets and two wooden desks. Tiffany sits at one of them in front of a computer screen.

'Hello again, Tiffany,' I say, smiling at her.

'Ooh, ma'am, er miss, er . . . ' she says, scrambling to her feet.

'Amelia,' I remind her.

'Miss Amelia.'

Why is everyone incapable of speaking to me without using a title?

'Really, it's just Amelia. Please carry on with what you're doing, Tiffany; Arthur is just giving us a bit of a tour around the castle.'

'Er ... yes ... er ...'

'What *are* you doing, anyway?' I ask, hoping to show interest.

'I'm ...' She stares at Arthur and flushes. 'I'm ... well, you see, it's a bit quiet today, and Dorothy said if ever I got all my work done it was okay to use the computer for ... well ... personal stuff.'

'What sort of personal stuff?' Arthur barks, glaring at her. 'And Dorothy has no business interfering in what goes on in here; the office is not her jurisdiction.'

Tiffany glances at the screen in the very second it changes to the screen saver, but not before I've had time to see the words, '... your ideal match is ...'

'I see no harm if Tiffany has got all her work done,' I say, hoping to dilute Arthur's anger a tad. 'As long as she's always *safe* about what she's doing ...' I wink at Tiffany.

'Hmm, well, I'm sure I could find you some work to be getting on with,' Arthur says gruffly. 'There's always something that wants polishing.'

'Dorothy says there's a lot of things that need polishing,' Tiffany pipes up. 'I'm happy to help,' she says to me now, 'but Dorothy says I'm dangerous with a duster. Too many things get broken when I'm around.'

I smile at Tiffany.

'Let me get settled in and we'll have to find someone to help Dorothy dust and polish. This castle is too big for one person to clean on their own.'

'More staff?' Arthur asks. 'We'll need more money before we can hire more staff. I wasn't going to mention this to you today, but we will need to go through the books together sometime. I'm afraid they don't make for pleasant reading.'

'Of course, that's not a problem. We'll need to do a good deal more than go through the books, though, Arthur. My intention is to make this castle a profitable and successful business in the future. I have a background in economics,' I add, hoping this might add a little gravitas to my statement. 'And I have run my own small business before.'

'Yes . . . ' Arthur says, sounding less than convinced. 'I'm sure that will come in very handy.'

'Right, perhaps we should leave Tiffany to her . . . well, her *endeavours*, and see the rest of the castle now.' I look around the office for Charlie. 'Where's Charlie?' I ask, spinning around. This office is far too small for him to be hiding somewhere.

The other two look around them. 'I don't think he's here,' Tiffany says vacantly.

'Ya think?' I snap, beginning to panic now. 'Charlie!' I call. 'Charlie, where are you? Where has my son gone?' I ask, fear spreading rapidly through me. 'Charlie!' I call desperately again.

But there's no answer.

Eight

'Don't fret, miss,' Arthur says confidently when we've checked the corridor and nearby rooms. 'He can't come to much harm here. We'll soon find him.'

'He can't come to much harm?' I reply, my eyes wide. 'He's a ten-year-old boy in a huge great castle! There must be hundreds of ways he could come to harm!'

'Ah yes, you could be right,' Arthur says, considering this. 'Don't you worry, though; we'll get right on it.' Arthur pulls out his walkie-talkie.

'Is there another way out of this office?' I ask Tiffany, looking wildly around me.

'Yes, there's a door behind that plant over there,' Tiffany says, leading me over to a tall pot plant in a colourful ceramic bowl. 'We don't use it any more, though; that's why it's behind the plant.'

'Where does it go?' I ask, pulling on the door handle. There's just enough of a gap behind the plant to pull the door ajar. And just enough for Charlie to slide through without being noticed.

'It leads to the old servants' quarters,' Tiffany says, pulling

55

the plant aside so we can open the door wider. She follows me out into a dark corridor. 'I think there might be a staircase there that leads down to the big kitchen somewhere too.'

'Have you got a torch on your phone?' I ask her. 'Er ... mine's broken at the moment.'

The truth is my basic phone isn't fancy enough to have a torch.

'It's okay, there's electricity through most of the castle. It was put in in the 1920s.' I hear a satisfying click as Tiffany pulls on an old Bakelite switch, and some rudimentary bulbs hanging from the ceiling light our way.

We dash along the bare corridor, opening doors along the way and calling Charlie's name, but all we find are rooms filled with junk, boxes and bits of old furniture. Finally, we reach a set of stone stairs that seem to go on for ever until finally we reach a flagstoned floor and yet another corridor, this one even more dingy than the last.

'Which way now?' I ask Tiffany.

'I don't know. We're never allowed down here. Arthur always says it's out of bounds.'

'This way, then,' I say, taking the lead, and we make our way slowly along the dim corridor using Tiffany's phone for light this time. At regular intervals along the walls there are wrought-iron sconces that must once have held candles to light the way; obviously the electricity never reached this far down.

'I don't like it down here,' Tiffany says apprehensively. 'It's spooky.'

'Neither do I particularly, but if Charlie came down here then we have to find him.'

'You don't think this leads to the *dungeons*, do you?' Tiffany says, her voice trembling a little. 'Cos I *really* don't want to go down there.'

The dungeons! Of course, that's exactly where Charlie would try to explore given the chance.

Suddenly we reach the end of the corridor, and in front of us is a huge wooden door with black iron bars nailed horizontally across it. There's an equally sturdy-looking bolt to pull it open, but also an extremely large padlock.

'He can't have gone through there,' Tiffany says, stating the obvious. 'He wouldn't have the key.'

'Really?' I reply scathingly. Usually I'm not prone to sarcasm, but I'm starting to get really worried now. These areas aren't open to the public; in fact, I doubt anyone visits them these days; they could be dangerous and unsafe – especially for a ten-year-old boy. 'What *is* through there, then – why is it locked up?'

'I dunno; like I said, we're not allowed down here. I think Arthur is the only one who ever comes down here, and that's not very often.'

Hmm . . . ' I look around. 'What about this way, then? What's through here?'

Tiffany holds up her phone and through a small archway we see another stone staircase, this time winding its way tightly upward. 'Come on,' I say to an even more worried-looking Tiffany. 'He must have gone up here.'

'What if he never came down this far in the first place?' Tiffany says as she passes me her phone so I can lead the way up the narrow staircase. 'He might have been hiding in one of them rooms with all the junk? That's what my little brother would do – he's a right little shi— I . . . I mean scoundrel.'

'No, Charlie is obsessed by gory stuff like dungeons; I'm sure that's where he would have tried to go.'

'But we're going up now, ain't we? Dungeons aren't up.'

She's right, but what choice do I have? Charlie might not have the key to that door back there, but neither do we.

We climb a little higher until suddenly I spy light up ahead – daylight, I realise, as we climb a few more of the stone steps – and then there in front of us is another stone archway leading out into the castle courtyard.

'Phew,' Tiffany says, gulping deep dramatic breaths. 'It's good to be able to breathe fresh air again.'

'We were only down there a few minutes,' I tell her. 'You've hardly been incarcerated underground for years.'

Joey comes rushing over to see us, closely followed by Dorothy.

'Did you find him?' he asks anxiously.

I shake my head.

'Damn, we're doing our best, but this castle is a big place. He could be anywhere, and there are only a few of us here today to look. If we don't find him soon I'll call in some back-up from the village.'

Joey's radio crackles on his belt and he swiftly pulls it loose. 'Arthur, how's it going?'

'No sign here in the north wing; you haven't found him yet, then?'

'Negative to that. The others the same.'

Suddenly before Arthur has a chance to reply we hear a distant voice.

'Mum! Up here!'

We all swivel around on the gravel of the courtyard and look up.

'There!' Tiffany says, pointing. 'Up on the tower.'

We look to where she's pointing and see Charlie waving at

us. He's standing on the topmost part of the tower, in a similar place to where I'd stood surveying the surrounding countryside on my first visit.

'Charlie,' I cry, 'don't move!'

'But Mum, the view from here is amazing; you should come up and see it.'

'I will. Just stay where you are. No, don't lean over that far, Charlie. It's dangerous.'

But Charlie can't quite hear what I'm saying and leans even further over the turret.

'Charlie, no!' I shout, about to dash across the gravel. But then another figure appears next to Charlie – a man. He says something to him and to my huge relief Charlie moves back a little.

'Don't worry!' the man calls. 'I've got him. I'll bring him back down.'

And then they both disappear from view.

'Oh my God,' I say to the others, 'I thought my heart was going to stop beating then when he leaned out like that. Now it's only going nine to the dozen. Who's that man?'

The others look blankly back at me.

'I have no idea,' Dorothy says, crossing herself. 'But thank the lord he was there.'

'We have him, Arthur,' Joey says into his radio. 'Up on the South East Tower he was. Yup, will do.'

After what seems like an age, but is probably only a few minutes, Charlie comes dashing out of the door at the bottom of the tower. He runs over to me and I envelop him in a huge bear hug.

'You shouldn't have run off like that!' I admonish him in an affectionate voice that doesn't match my stern words. 'And you must never go up to the top of one of the towers on your own, it's very dangerous.'

'But I wasn't on my own,' Charlie begins as another figure emerges from the door.

'Yes, I can see that,' I say, as I watch a young, well-built man walk calmly towards us. He's wearing jeans and a casual pale blue shirt that fits snugly across his broad chest.

Arthur has emerged from the castle and immediately intercepts the stranger before he reaches us.

'I must thank you,' he says gratefully, holding his hand out to the man, 'for looking out for the boy like that.' They shake hands. 'But I must also enquire,' Arthur says, his voice changing, 'what you're doing trespassing in the grounds of Chesterford Castle? We're not open to the public today.'

'Hi,' the man says, clearly not too bothered by Arthur's stern tone. He holds his hand up to the rest of us in greeting. 'Don't fear, I'm friend not foe.' He grins at his joke, but everyone just stares at him. 'I was just passing the castle looking for work, actually.'

'But we're closed today,' Arthur insists. 'How did you get in?'

'Through the front gate back there,' the man gestures behind him. 'It was unlocked, and no one came when I rang the bell.'

Arthur turns and glares at Joey, who is suddenly busy examining the gravel below him. 'Joey! Did you leave the gate unlocked?' he demands.

Joey shrugs. 'I might have. It was just so hectic earlier with the mistress arriving with all her furniture and the guys that came in to help – I sort of lost track.'

Arthur's face is now bright red.

'Arthur, calm down,' Dorothy says, stepping in. 'Remember

your blood pressure, and no harm has been done. In fact, something good came of it: this young man saved the master here.'

I grimace internally at their words.

'For all we know he could have lured him up there,' Arthur says, looking suspiciously at the man.

'I can assure you I did nothing of the sort. I simply wandered in here *unchallenged*,' he looks meaningfully at Arthur, 'and saw him up there looking lost. When I shouted up if there was anyone with him he said no, so I found my way up there in case I could help.'

'Tom is my friend,' Charlie says now, walking over to him. 'He rescued me from the tower like a knight in shining armour.'

Tom smiles down at him. 'Hardly, fella, but thanks for the vote of confidence.'

'Well, *I'd* like to thank you,' I say, stepping in now. 'If you hadn't gone up to the tower goodness knows what might have happened.' I go over to shake his hand, like Arthur had done.

'You must be Amelia,' Tom says, smiling as he takes hold of my outstretched hand in a firm grip. I notice now I'm close to him he's not quite as young as I'd first thought. There are distinct laughter lines around his blue eyes, which only deepen as he smiles, and a few odd grey strands at his temples that pepper his otherwise jet-black hair.

'I am,' I reply, a little surprised he knows my name. 'How do you know that?'

'Benji sent me.'

'He did?'

'He said you might be in need of my services. So here I am!'

'And what services are they, exactly?' I ask, a little suspiciously now. Why hadn't Benji said he was sending someone over?

'Here.' Tom reaches into his top pocket and pulls out a business card. 'This is me.'

I look at Tom and then I look down at the card:

Tom Barber
Antique furniture restoration service.
All types of work undertaken.
15 years' experience.
Member of the British Antique Furniture
Restorers' Association.

'Benji seemed to think I might be of some help here,' he says, looking at me. 'What do you think, Amelia; might I be of some service to you?'

Nine

'Amazing view,' Tom comments as he glances out of one of the tower windows. 'You've fallen on your feet here.'

'Some might say,' I reply, pacing back and forth across the circular room as I wait for Benji to answer his phone.

'Well, I'd definitely be one of them.'

I watch Tom as he sits down on one of the armchairs and waits for me to finish my phone call. I'd thought of him as well built when I'd first seen him follow Charlie out of the tower, but now I'm closer I can see that he's extremely fit, with toned, well-developed muscles that sit neatly under his well-fitting clothes. He looks up at me watching him, and smiles before taking a sip from the mug of tea I've just made him.

Hesitantly I smile back. *Come on, Benji, where are you?*

Eventually Benji's voicemail cuts in.

'Hi, Benji; it's Amelia,' I say into the phone. 'Er ...' I glance at Tom again. 'Could you call me when you get this, please?'

'Busy man,' Tom says as I hang up the phone.

'Yes, he is, isn't he?' I pick up my own mug and cross the

room to sit down opposite him. 'Is your tea all right? Only I haven't had a chance to get out and stock up yet on food – so my teabags are courtesy of Dorothy, who you met before in the courtyard.'

'Perfect, thank you,' Tom says, raising his mug at me.

'So, tell me about yourself,' I ask awkwardly. 'And just why you've come here to Chesterford?'

'Is this a job interview?' Tom asks, grinning. 'I'd better sit up a bit straighter if it is.'

'No. Well, possibly. What I mean is, there is a possibility we might need someone to restore some furniture here. To be honest, I haven't had a chance to look into things like that just yet.'

'I see. Benji probably thought I wouldn't come so soon, but I didn't really have much on so I thought I might as well come straight away.' He smiles again.

'So how long have you been restoring furniture?'

'I don't just do furniture, I do paintings, silverware, ceramics – you name it I can turn my hand to it – a master of all trades, you might say.'

'That's good. So what are your qualifications?' I sigh internally. I know I'm making this sound exactly like a job interview, but Tom has caught me unawares; I haven't even thought about things like restoration yet. There are definitely quite a lot of things that will need restoring here – my initial tour of the castle had shown me that – but whether we needed someone permanently on site I'm not so sure.

'Qualifications? Now that's a tricky one. I don't exactly have any of those. But what I lack in certificates I make up for with bags of experience and, more importantly, enthusiasm.'

He certainly has plenty of the latter.

'Did you train with someone?'

'I did.'

'Who?'

Tom looks at me as if he's assessing whether it's imperative he answer this.

'My father.'

'Oh, it's a family business, then?'

'It was. We fell out.'

'I'm sorry to hear that.'

'Yeah, well . . . ' For the first time since I met him in the castle courtyard, Tom seems decidedly edgy. 'It happens.' He gets up and walks over to the window. 'Did I say what an amazing view this is?'

'You did.' I wonder what has happened between Tom and his father to make him this uncomfortable talking about it.

'Is that why you're free to come and work here?' I enquire as politely as I can.

Tom turns around. 'Oh no, that happened years ago. I've just finished working at a stately home down in Bedfordshire, but it was only a temporary contract for National Heritage – some pipes burst and they had terrible flood damage. But now everything has been repaired and restored they don't need anyone full time any more.'

'Ah, I see.' I think about this. National Heritage were reputable; if they'd employed Tom he must know his stuff.

'So National Heritage would be able to give you a reference?'

'Of course. So you do have some work?' Tom asks hopefully.

'The thing is, Tom . . . ' I begin.

Tom grimaces. 'I don't like the sound of this . . . '

'I would love to give you a job here, and if Benji has sent you, that's good enough for me. But—'

'Please don't say but!' Tom says, holding up his hand. 'I have other talents. If you don't think you need a full-time restorer I can turn my hand to other things.'

Golly, he's keen. I have to give him that. 'Like?'

'Anything,' he says with assurance. 'You name it; I can do it.'

I can't help but smile. I admire his confidence. I would have said something similar many years ago if I'd wanted a job badly enough. But my own self-confidence has been knocked a bit too far from its perch in the last few years.

'Okay then,' I say, thinking quickly. 'If you can do *anything* – impress Arthur.'

'What?' Tom asks, puzzled, two tiny crinkles appearing between his dark eyebrows.

'Impress Arthur and Dorothy. They've been here for years. Stay here at the castle for a week, work with them both and see if you can impress them. Dorothy won't be too hard to win over, I'm sure; but Arthur, now if you can get him onside, then you can indeed do anything.'

Tom's eyes twinkle as he surveys me for a moment. 'Interesting ... I like your style, Amelia. All right, you're on,' he says, bounding over to shake my hand. 'Give me a week and I'll impress not only Dorothy and Arthur, but hopefully you as well, boss.'

He holds on to my hand as his eyes gaze directly into mine. 'And I get the feeling that you, Amelia, might be my hardest challenge of all.'

'So Tom is staying, then?' Charlie asks that night when I'm tucking him into his old bed in his new room. Charlie has happily spent the rest of the day with Dorothy in the castle kitchen learning how to bake cakes, while I'd spent it finding a room for Tom to stay in, along with the somewhat harder task of persuading Arthur to give him a chance.

Eventually a spare room had been found alongside Joey, who like Tiffany has his own small room tucked away in the north wing of the castle – an area that had been used in the past for the staff of any visiting guests. I discover too that Arthur and Dorothy are the inhabitants of the little cottage in the grounds we'd seen earlier, and that they've lived there since they first got married.

'Yes, Tom is staying, for now anyway.'

'Goody, I like him.'

'I know you do. But then you did have a bit of an adventure with him today in the tower.'

'Yeah . . . ' Charlie frowns. 'Sort of.'

'What do you mean, sort of?'

'Well, the end of the adventure was with Tom when he rescued me from the tower, but the beginning was with some-one else.'

'Who?' I ask, sitting down next to Charlie on the edge of the bed.

'Ruby.'

'Who's Ruby?' I ask, puzzled.

'My new friend.'

I look at Charlie lying snug as a bug under his dinosaur duvet. Surely I'd been introduced to everyone at the castle today. Who was Ruby?

'Your new friend, eh?'

'Yeah, she's cool; she can just appear and disappear like that.' He lifts his hand from under the duvet and clicks his fingers.

'Can she now? Does Ruby live in the village?' I ask, thinking perhaps one of the local schoolchildren knew their way around the castle.

'No, she lives here at the castle. She told me.'

'She does, does she?' Did one of the staff have a child they'd not told me about? But whose child could it be? Arthur and Dorothy were far too old to have a young child. Joey wasn't a dad, was he? Perhaps it was Tiffany's child? But she was a bit young too.

'This *is* a child you're talking about, isn't it?' I suddenly ask, in case Charlie has made friends with a dog or a cat or something. He'd said she'd spoken to him, but Charlie, being an only child, had a very, very vivid imagination, and talking to animals certainly wouldn't be beyond the realms of his creativity.

'Yeah,' Charlie says indignantly. 'Of course, she's a kid like me.'

'Sorry, of course she is, and she's called Ruby?'

'Yup, and she's lived here at the castle for over a hundred years. She told me that, too.'

I blink a couple of times in disbelief. 'Surely you misheard her, Charlie? She can't possibly have lived here all that time now, can she?'

'She can if she's a ghost,' Charlie says matter-of-factly. 'Night, night, Mum.' He yawns, pulling the duvet up around his ears. 'I'm really tired now.' And he closes his eyes. 'See you in the morning.'

Ten

'He said what?' Tom asks as he puts down his axe for a moment and ceases chopping up the fallen tree that Arthur has tasked him with this morning.

'He said his new friend Ruby was a ghost. I tried talking to him this morning at breakfast to see if he was making it up, but he's adamant that's what she is.'

Tom had eaten breakfast in the main kitchen with the rest of the staff. Apparently he'd settled in well last night and seemed to be a popular addition to the household with everyone but Arthur (as I suspected might be the case). Even Joey had taken this newcomer in his stride, and said that at least he wouldn't be left to do *all* of the manual labour on the castle estate now.

Although I already love our tower apartment, I do feel a little isolated up there with everyone else living in the main castle. But I guess isolation was the fate of many of the castle's previous owners, and I'll get used to it in time.

This morning, after Charlie had gone off with Arthur to look for a shield, I'd decided to see how Tom was getting on on his first morning with us. I hadn't heard back from Benji, and although Tom seemed pleasant enough, I still didn't really know that much about him.

I tried to make it seem like I wasn't checking up on him by engaging him in casual conversation about Charlie, but I think Tom guessed my motives for coming to find him.

'Kids have great imaginations at that age,' Tom says, wiping some beads of sweat from his brow. 'Even I had an imaginary friend when I was young.'

'Did you?'

'Yeah, of course. Didn't you?'

I shake my head. 'No, I don't think so.'

Tom surveys me for a moment, his steely blue eyes seeming to take in every part of me in one quick gaze. 'Practical, are you?' he suddenly asks.

'What do you mean?'

'I mean, you excel in the logical aspects of life, not the creative ones. Your best subjects at school would probably have been maths, sciences, that sort of thing. You didn't really understand *artistic* types, as you'd call them – you probably still don't. Am I getting close?'

'Perhaps,' I reply, wondering how he could possibly know this about me.

'Did you go to university?' Tom enquires. 'Wait, of course you did – you'd be far too organised not to have missed that opportunity. What did you study? Maths, chemistry?'

'Business and economics, actually.'

Tom holds up his hands in a there-you-go gesture.

'What did you study, then?' I ask defiantly. 'No, let *me* guess this one – it has to be history of art?'

Tom shakes his head. 'Nope, you're wrong. I didn't need to go to uni. Got all the training I needed on the job.'

'Of course you did,' I say, wryly shaking my head. 'Anyway, what does it matter what subjects I liked at school or what I studied at uni?'

'It matters not a jot to me. I'm just saying that even if your son *was* talking to ghosts, you would be the last person he'd want to talk to about it because there's no way you'd believe in them.'

He's right, of course: I don't believe in anything like that – I never have. But I don't like the suggestion that Charlie can't talk to me about anything if he wants to.

'Do *you* believe in the supernatural, then?' I ask.

'Not really. But I've worked in enough old buildings to know that there're things that go on in them that can't always be explained.'

'Exactly. There's always a rational explanation to everything, even if you don't always know what it is,' I reply, nodding to make my point. 'And let me assure you that if my son needs to talk he knows he can come to me about anything.'

'Sorry,' Tom apologises. 'The last thing I wanted to do was offend my new boss. Not making a great impression on my first day, am I?'

Actually, Tom is making a very different impression on me right now. With his foot perched up on the log he's in the process of chopping, his arm resting on his axe, and sweat glistening off him from his forehead down into his open-necked shirt so I can just see it dampening down the beginnings of his chest hair, I feel anything *but* offended by him.

I swallow hard. This is not how I want to feel about *any* of my staff – especially not on my first day.

'It's fine,' I tell him, quickly averting my eyes. 'No harm done. Oh, here comes Joey,' I say, relieved to see Joey travelling

71

across one of the great lawns that surround the castle on a quad bike.

'What oh, boss!' he says as he pulls up next to us. 'I didn't expect to find you out here this morning.'

'I came to see how Tom was doing on his first day,' I reply hurriedly, my face flushing, much to my annoyance.

'Course you did.' Joey winks at me. 'Tom mate, what ya doing chopping wood with that rusty old thing?' He points at the axe in Tom's hand.

'It's what Arthur gave me,' Tom says, looking at the axe. 'It could do with a good sharpen, I reckon.'

'It could do with the chop – get it: *chop*!' Joey says, grinning with glee at his own joke. 'Ah, never mind,' he says when we don't laugh. 'This is what we usually chop the fallen trees up with.' He lifts a chainsaw from the back of the quad bike's trailer. 'Arthur should have given you this.'

Tom smiles ruefully at the petrol-powered chainsaw in Joey's arms. 'Yeah, I bet he should.'

'Sorry,' I tell him. 'I did say you'd have to work hard to impress Arthur, didn't I? I guess this was just his idea of a little joke.'

'If you believe that, Amelia,' Tom says, turning to me now, 'then you really won't have any trouble believing in a few ghosts.'

'And just who is this?' I ask as Charlie bounds across the castle courtyard later with a small hairy dog at his side.

'This is Chester; he's the castle's dog,' Charlie explains, bending down to fuss the hound.

'He belonged to the last Earl,' Arthur explains. 'Dorothy and I have been looking after him at our cottage since the Earl died. He's been a forlorn little fella for the last few months, which is to be expected, I suppose, but he cheered up no end this morning when he met your Charlie.'

Arthur really has taken Charlie under his wing today. After I'd checked on Tom, I'd spent the rest of the morning in the office with Tiffany learning how the castle runs on a day-to-day basis. There's a lot more to it than I'd imagined, but surprisingly, Tiffany proved to be a very thorough and knowledgeable teacher. I'd learned about the staff and how over the years they'd been reduced bit by bit, until all that was left was the skeleton crew that lived at the castle today. When required there was a small team of temporary helpers that they called upon from the village – mainly retired residents who had worked at the castle in the past.

I'd learned about how costly it is to run the place. Even though a lot of the rooms aren't in use any more, the electricity costs alone are staggering, and the maintenance that has to be undertaken simply to keep the castle walls from crumbling around us is so complex that in the last year alone seven different tradesmen had been brought in just to prevent the castle from becoming a ruin of the future.

If I'd been daunted before about simply coming to live here, all this new information is only adding to my already burdened shoulders.

But I try to shake some of that burden away as I bend down to fuss over Charlie's new friend. 'I always knew there would be a dog involved in all this,' I murmur, stroking him under the chin. Chester eagerly licks my hand in return.

'Oh, who's that?' I ask as I stand up again and notice a strange couple wandering across the courtyard.

'Just visitors,' Arthur says. 'We're open to the public again today, aren't we?'

'Of course we are; I completely forgot.'

I watch the couple for a moment as they wander aimlessly around.

'You'll get used to it,' Arthur says. 'We don't get too many visitors at this time of the year – at any time of the year, really.'

'I'll be right back,' I say to Arthur and Charlie, and I sprint across the gravel towards the couple.

'Hello!' I call cheerily as I approach them. 'How are you today?'

The woman looks at me suspiciously from under the hood of her raincoat, and the man nods politely.

'I'm Amelia Ha ... Chesterford,' I correct myself. 'Welcome to Chesterford Castle, how are you finding your trip today?'

'Fine, thank you,' the man says at the same time as the woman replies: 'It's okay, I suppose.'

'Is there anything we could improve on?'

'You could make it a bit cheaper, for one thing,' the woman says grimly. 'There's not much to see when you get through them gates is there, Brian?'

Brian shakes his head.

'Oh, I'm sorry to hear that,' I apologise. 'What would you like to see more of?'

'It's not the amount of things as such,' Brian says, almost apologetically, 'more the quality of things on show. Many are in quite a shabby condition, if you don't mind me saying. And we've noticed quite a lot of dust, haven't we, Marjory?'

'Yes, dust,' Marjory repeats. 'Antiques ageing I can excuse, but a quick flick with a feather duster once in a while would get rid of a little bit of dust; there's no excuse for shoddy housekeeping, even in somewhere as big as this.'

'Of course.' I nod, glad Dorothy can't hear this. 'I'm actually quite new here, so I haven't had time to address these small, but *necessary* things,' I add when Marjory glares at me. 'But believe me, I will. In the meantime, may I offer you free return passes to the castle in six months by means of an apology, by which time I intend to have everything running ship shape, or is that castle shape!' I smile, hoping to lighten their mood.

But Marjory looks unimpressed. 'We won't be on holiday in six months, will we? What good are free passes then?'

'It's very kind of you,' Brian says, attempting to guide Marjory away. 'Perhaps we *will* come back and see you again, then? Good luck with your endeavours. From what I've seen this morning, you're going to need it.'

'I knew I should have believed those TripAdvisor reviews,' I hear Marjory grumble as they head towards the stone steps that lead to the top of the ruined tower. 'But you said it would be all right. There's not even a tea shop, and that gift shop is an absolute joke . . .'

I walk desolately back to Arthur, Charlie and Chester.

'What did you go and do that for?' Arthur asks, glancing after the departing couple 'Never ask them what they think. Best to leave them well alone, I find.'

'But why? If we don't know what our visitors think, how can we know what to improve on?'

'We don't have the money for improving,' Arthur states. 'Haven't you looked at the books yet?'

'Tiffany showed me *some* figures this morning, but there must be something we can do. I do have a little fund I can dip into if needed . . .'

'What little fund?' Arthur asks suspiciously.

'Along with the castle,' I explain, 'I was left some money in a private bank account. Not a never-ending amount of money,' I hastily add. 'But apparently the last Earl was quite frugal with his cash, which is probably why the castle itself is in a bit of a state.'

'Dorothy said he was a tight-fisted so-and-so,' Charlie pipes up from where he's playing fetch with Chester. 'What does that mean exactly?'

'It means he was careful when it came to spending money,' I tell him quickly, blushing. 'But it also means that as a result I do have some funds I can use to improve things here,' I tell Arthur, 'and the first thing we're going to do with that money is hire extra staff to allow us to run things more efficiently on a day-to-day basis.'

'You've already gone and hired that antiques dealer fella,' Arthur says gruffly. 'Isn't that enough?'

'Tom is a furniture restorer, not an antiques dealer; plus I haven't hired him, he's on trial. A fair trial, too.' I look knowingly at Arthur. 'Stop making things harder for him than they need be – I saw the axe this morning, Arthur; that was hardly fair, now, was it?'

'It's how we used to chop wood,' Arthur says, smiling smugly. 'If it was good enough for my father then it's good enough for him.'

I shake my head. 'I think Tom could be a great help to us if we give him a chance. He's certainly enthusiastic, and I think that's just what this castle needs to push it into the twenty-first century: a bit of enthusiasm, passion and above all hope.'

Eleven

'So that's what I propose to do,' I announce as I stand awkwardly at the head of the scrubbed wooden kitchen table, addressing the others. 'I do hope you all agree with me. Now, has anyone got anything they wish to say, or even suggest? If this is going to work then I think we all need to pull together as a team to make Chesterford Castle the success it deserves to be.'

There's silence around the table, as everyone glances at anything rather than at me.

We've been at Chesterford for a few days now, and in that time I've learned even more about the castle and how it presently runs. Actually, *survives* might be a better word to describe the state the castle is currently in – it really is hanging by an ancient thread like the ones that bind its huge tapestries together. So during the evenings when Charlie has gone to bed, I've sat up in my tower thinking, writing notes and eventually coming up with my own rescue plan, which this morning I'm tentatively sharing with the staff.

'Shall I put the kettle on?' Dorothy suggests, breaking the silence. She looks longingly at her Aga cooker.

Murmurs of 'yes please' and 'I'd love a cuppa' flow around the room.

'Righty-ho, then.' She gets up and scurries past the scrubbed wooden cupboards to claim a huge black kettle into which she proceeds to pour fresh water.

'Someone must have something to say?' I look round the table at the others. I'd expected many things to happen once I'd shared my plans, but silence wasn't one of them.

'I think it's a great idea,' Tom says from where he casually sits cross-legged on one of the wooden chairs.

'You would, you just want to get on her good side,' Arthur grumbles.

'What's the problem, Arthur?' I ask. 'You must know we need more staff.'

'We've done all right just us for the last year or two, haven't we?' he asks, looking around at the others. 'Why do we need to bring strangers in now?'

'They won't be strangers, Arthur. I intend to recruit from the village if we can. You already have some people that help you out occasionally, don't you?'

'The boss is right, Arthur,' Joey says. 'I've been saying for ages we need someone to help us out in the grounds. Just having Tom here has cut my workload by half in the last few days.'

'Anything to shirk a bit of hard work,' Arthur says grudgingly.

'If I had some extra help with the cleaning we could have the whole castle looking neat and shiny as a new pin in days,' Dorothy says, turning from the counter where she's been arranging some cups and saucers ready for the tea. 'I try my best,' she says to me, 'but there're a lot of rooms here.'

'I know, Dorothy; I think you've done amazingly well to keep it in such good shape on your own.'

Dorothy flushes a little and turns proudly back to her teacups.

'I'm more than happy to continue working in the office,' Tiffany says, 'but I'd quite like to get involved in the practical side of running the castle too, if there was a chance.'

'We'll need someone to run the new gift shop,' I say, latching on to this tiny bit of enthusiasm immediately. 'I'd like it to offer something for everyone, so it would be quite the challenge to set up. Would that be something you might be interested in, Tiffany?'

'Ooh, I'd love to!' Tiffany says, grinning. 'I've wanted to run my own shop since I was little, and I'd have time to do it – as you saw the other day, I don't always have a full day's work in that office.'

She glances nervously at Arthur.

'Tiffany has brought up a good point,' I say to the others. 'Like I just said to Dorothy, you've all done amazingly well covering all these various jobs on your own up to this point. But now I think we need to specialise a little bit more, so that the jobs we do we can all do *really* well, and that will only reflect positively on the castle. So if there's something you fancy specialising in, now is the time to shout.' There's silence again. 'Joey?' I ask, turning to him. 'What would *you* like to do?'

It's Joey's turn to glance hesitantly at Arthur.

Arthur gives him a knowing look.

'I'm quite happy working with King Arthur over there,' he says, to Arthur's immense pleasure.

'But what is your *actual* job description?'

'General dogsbody, I reckon.' Joey grins.

'Okay . . . ' I say, trying to remain patient. 'But is there any particular part of what you do here you like best?'

'I quite like doing the gardening. Anything outdoor is always preferable to being inside for me.'

'Right, head groundsman it is, then,' I tell him instantly.

'What? Just like that?' Joey looks astonished.

'Just like that. I'll leave it with you to hire some staff to help you out. I'm guessing you'll need more seasonal staff during the summer months, but can maybe make do with slightly less help during the winter?'

Joey nods slowly. 'Yeah, that's right. But what about Arthur?' He nods in Arthur's direction. 'Won't I be stepping on his toes?'

'Nope, not at all. Arthur will still be in overall charge. I'd like to promote you to general manager, if that's all right, Arthur? Your job will be to oversee *all* aspects of the castle on a daily basis.'

'Ooh, Arthur,' Dorothy says proudly, 'it'll be like the old days when you were butler and all the staff looked up to you.'

Arthur shrugs. 'Don't be silly, woman. It could *never* be like that any more; things have changed *too* much.'

I know he's partly referring to me, but I choose to pretend I don't.

'Arthur's right, things have changed,' I insist, seizing the chance. 'Chesterford Castle must move with the times to have a chance of surviving in the future. But if we can move forward alongside it together as a team, in a spirit of hard work, understanding and above all enjoyment at this new challenge we have ahead, we can not only help the castle to survive, but I know we can make Chesterford Castle *the* number one tourist destination in Northumberland!'

*

'That was quite a speech you made back there,' Tom says as everyone exits the kitchen chattering excitedly about their new roles, even Dorothy, aka our new tea room manager. When asked if she knew anyone in the village who might like to run the new tea room, Dorothy had replied adamantly that no food was going to be served in this castle unless she was the person in charge of serving it. So the job was hers, and I'd tasked her with finding some staff to help her out with her new role.

'Thanks. I don't know where most of it came from, actually. I've never really addressed a room full of people like that before.'

'You wouldn't know it. You seemed to say all the right things to keep everyone happy.'

'Everyone except Arthur.'

'He'll come round. If he doesn't want to be general manager, you can always take him on as a full-time nanny!'

I smile; Charlie had yet again gone off happily with Arthur and Chester – this time to investigate some stonework that's become loose on one of the castle's exterior walls.

I felt a bit guilty letting Arthur look after Charlie again, but both of them seemed to enjoy spending time with each other. When I'd confessed to Dorothy that I thought I might be burdening Arthur with this role, she'd told me not to worry. Apparently, they'd never been blessed with any children, so Arthur was revelling in his new role of teacher and guardian to the young Earl.

I'd tried not to wince too visibly when she'd called Charlie that. I was beginning to understand they couldn't help it. Dorothy and Arthur had lived in this castle all their lives; they were programmed to be subservient to their bosses. They simply didn't know a different way.

'It's a relief, I must say,' I tell Tom as we walk together towards Tom's latest job. He was to clean all the castle's silverware, beginning in the Great Hall with the suits of armour and all the weaponry.

I'm pretty sure this wasn't exactly what Dorothy had meant when she'd asked Tom to clean the silver, but Arthur had insisted that this needed doing first.

'After that first day in the tower, I'd wondered how I was going to keep an eye on him all the time. It won't be too bad once he starts at his new school next week, but until then, I need eyes like a hawk!'

'Boys will be boys,' Tom says, pulling open one of the two heavy wooden doors that lead into the Great Hall. 'Madam,' he says, pretending to bow as he stands back to let me pass.

'Thank you, kind sir,' I say, playing along. Tom is one of the few people here who treats me like a regular person. I never need to reprimand him for being over-formal with me, and that makes me like him all the more.

The Great Hall is eerily quiet as the door closes behind us and we stand looking up at our stately surroundings. 'At least you haven't got to fight your way through the crowds to get to everything,' I say. 'We've only had about eight visitors in total today.'

'It can't be that bad, can it?'

'I think it can. But hopefully things will get better as the season moves on. We've only just had Easter; it's early days.'

'It is indeed, and with all your new ideas, those awful reviews will soon become things of the past!'

'What awful reviews?' I ask, staring at him.

'Oh ... er ... I assumed you'd seen them.'

'No, where? Oh, let me guess, on TripAdvisor, right?'

Tom nods apologetically.

'I guess I'd better take a look. Oh, I don't have my phone on me,' I lie, feeling towards my pocket. The truth is I'd only just got around to ordering myself a better phone; I'd quickly found my basic model just isn't suitable for running this place. People need to get hold of me all the time, and I need to keep up to date on emails and messages. Arthur offered me a walkie-talkie to keep in touch, but I turned it down, saying that as soon as my phone arrived, we could just all text each other when we needed someone, or perhaps we could have a castle WhatsApp group?

Arthur hadn't even dignified this suggestion with a reply.

'Here, use mine,' Tom says, passing me his iPhone. 'There's pretty good 4G here, the castle doesn't have Wi-Fi in the public rooms yet, does it?'

'Thank you,' I say, taking it from him. 'No, only in the offices and some of the private rooms. But it's definitely something we should think about for the future. It's what people want these days.'

I open the internet via the 4G on Tom's phone and find TripAdvisor, then I search for Chesterford Castle. The results are not pretty.

'Tired, dated (and I don't just mean the castle!) and very, very dull.' 3 stars.

'My kids were bored stiff, and there were not enough toilets.' 2 stars.

'No tour guide to speak of – unless you count the grumpy old man we met while wandering around, who told us to keep off the grass! And nowhere to get refreshments.' 1 star.

'No free Wi-Fi & no interactive experiences.' 1 star.

And so it goes on. Review after bad review. There are a few

good ones scattered in amongst the poor ones, but even they're bad in their own way.

'Loved how basic everything was. A true historical experience.' 5 stars.

'No fuss. No frills. Just history.' 5 stars.

'Cheer up!' Tom says from the window where he's been attempting to dismantle one of the suits of armour. 'Things can only get better – as the song says.'

'I do hope you're right,' I say, still staring at the phone. 'Oh, you have a call.' I hurriedly pass Tom back his phone, as I see the letter J flash on the display.

'Do you mind if I take this?' Tom says, glancing at the screen.

'No, of course not, go ahead.'

Tom hesitates.

'I'll just go in here,' I say and I press the rose on the panel behind me so the secret door magically slides open.

'Nice!' Tom says as he runs his thumb across the screen of his phone. 'Jo, hi, how's things?'

I hurry through the opening into the privacy of the Ladies' Chamber, expecting I'll still be able to hear Tom talking, but the room is surprisingly soundproof, even with the door still open.

I gaze at the portraits again, and once more my eyes rest on the largest canvas in the room – the one of the fifteenth Countess, Clara Chesterford.

She looks extremely elegant as she stands with her long white fingers resting on the top of an ornate dresser behind her. She's wearing a pale green satin dress, her tiny waist pulled in no doubt by an uncomfortable corset beneath it. Her dark hair is piled up neatly on top of her head with a diamond tiara adorning it, and at her neck is a beautiful jewelled necklace encrusted with what again might be diamonds, with the addition this time of jade gemstones. Her other hand rests at her side, but in it she holds a leather book.

What a strange painting, I think as I gaze up at the canvas. *You're dressed like you're about to go to the fanciest of parties, and yet you have a book in your hand as though you've just been reading?*

'Hi again,' Tom says, appearing at the door. 'Sorry about that. Bad manners and all, but there are some calls you just have to take, aren't there?'

I nod as though I totally understand, but the truth is that not that many people ring me any more. Most of my friends were friends of my ex-husband too, and once he left, they all seemed to fade away with him. Perhaps they were never really my friends at all.

'This is quite the clandestine little room hidden away in here,' Tom continues. 'You'd never know it was here, would you?'

'No, I only know about it because Arthur showed me a few days ago.'

Was that only a few days ago? So much has happened since we arrived, it feels as though we've been here weeks already, not a matter of days.

'It's a ladies' room,' I explain, 'for after dinner when the men retire to smoke cigars and play billiards.'

'Just like mealtimes today, then?' Tom grins. 'Except now when people have eaten, it's separate screens they all inhabit instead of separate rooms.'

'Very sad,' I agree. 'But I'm afraid very true.'

'She looks quite the formidable woman,' he says, looking up at Clara.

'Apparently she was a bit of a tearaway: she nearly bankrupted the place when she lived here.'

'*Really?* She doesn't look the type, does she?'

'How can you tell? They all looked pretty proper back in Edwardian England, didn't they?'

'Ah, it was all going on beneath those tight corsets, I bet.' He winks. 'In my experience of history, the tighter the corset the more secrets are hidden beneath it.'

I grin.

'It's true,' he insists. 'Think about it, as women's clothing became looser and more comfortable, so did they. They got stronger and more vociferous in their thoughts and actions – for the good, I may add,' he says. 'Don't worry; I'm not against women's emancipation. I'm all for women having equal rights with men.'

'I'm glad to hear it, you having a female boss and all.'

Tom salutes me. 'Talking of which, I'd better get back to work or King Arthur will have my guts for garters!'

'You can't call him that.' I smile. 'Only Joey seems to get away with it.'

'To his face.' Tom winks again. 'Right, gotta go a-polishing!'

I watch Tom head back out of the door, then I take one last look at Clara before following him.

'I bet you'd have some tales to tell if you could talk, Clara, wouldn't you? Tales I'd be *very* interested in sitting down and listening to.'

Twelve

'Gah, he's still not answering,' I say to Charlie as we stand in the kitchen preparing our evening meal.

We've been living on bits and pieces that I've managed to scrounge from Dorothy's kitchen and the village shop for the last few days. Even though Dorothy has offered on numerous occasions to cook for us, I want to hold on to some independence, and not be 'waited on by staff'.

But I managed to spend half an hour early this morning doing an internet grocery order on Charlie's laptop from the nearest large supermarket, and it arrived, to my delight but Arthur's horror, about an hour ago.

'That can't come in here,' Arthur said when I asked Joey to open the gate for the delivery vehicle. 'It's not right.'

'I think it's a bit unfair to ask the driver to carry the baskets from the car park, Arthur. It's bad enough he's got to carry them up my spiral stairs when he does get in here.'

To give the driver his credit, he carried everything upstairs – and without grumbling, too. So I gave him a small tip before he left, which he was very grateful for.

'We don't see many of them these days,' he said, popping the note in his top pocket. 'I can tell you're gentry, ma'am.'

I was about to explain that I wasn't anything of the sort when I decided it was just easier to let it go this time. So I bade him farewell and notched up yet another first for the castle – this time in the form of online grocery shopping.

'Maybe Benji is on holiday?' Charlie says, putting our cutlery on a tray ready to carry upstairs.

'Without his phone?'

'Why not?'

'I guess it might be possible.' But Benji didn't strike me as the sort of person who would go anywhere without his phone. So I decide not to leave yet another message – I'd left three already asking him to call me back.

Besides, Tom was getting on quite well right now; it had only been a few days, but I thought so far he had coped admirably with everything that had been thrown at him.

Perhaps I might be able to persuade Arthur to let him have a go at some proper restoration soon. He'd made an incredible job of the Great Hall. The armour and weaponry now gleamed like it was about to go into battle for the very first time. Even Arthur had been impressed, if saying it wasn't 'a bad job' was praise. Tom and I both chose to see it that way, and when Arthur left the hall, we had a congratulatory high-five between us and a rather nice hug, which I thought had gone on for a little bit longer than was strictly necessary.

'So have you had a nice day today?' I ask Charlie as we sit down to eat our food by the window. I'd chosen to place the table there when we'd been rearranging some of our inherited furniture yesterday, so now we could enjoy a gorgeous view from all the windows – whether we were eating, just lounging on one of the sofas or sitting at the old antique desk we'd dis-covered hidden under a felt cloth when we'd been unpacking.

'It's been mega,' Charlie says, ladling beans on toast into his mouth.

I felt a bit guilty giving him this when I knew Dorothy was serving up homemade chicken pie, roast potatoes and green veg down in the kitchen tonight.

But Charlie (and me, too, for that matter!) really enjoys beans on toast, so the guilt didn't linger too long.

'And you were happy enough being with Arthur?'

Charlie thinks about this for a moment.

'Arthur is great – he knows so much about the castle and its history, and he says we can look for that sword tomorrow to go with the shield he found for me. Joey is going to help us, too. We think it's packed away in one of the unused rooms upstairs in the main building.'

'That's nice.' I make a mental note to speak with Arthur about this.

'But when I'm with Arthur, Ruby doesn't appear.'

Oh no, here we go again. I thought he'd forgotten about Ruby.

'Maybe that's a good thing?'

Charlie looks crossly at me. 'How can it be a good thing? Ruby's my friend. I think she's scared of Arthur; everyone else is.'

'They're not really scared, they're just ...' I search for the right word. 'In awe of him. He's quite formidable.'

'What does fomimible mean?'

'Formidable,' I correct him. 'It means someone who isn't to be messed with; they might come across as a little bit scary but their bark is worse than their bite – a bit like Chester.'

'I love Chester; he's great too.'

'Yes, he is a cute little dog,' I agree, pleased I've led his

89

thoughts away from Ruby. 'Perhaps we can take him for a nice long walk one day on the beach.'

'That would be great. But Chester is not the same as being with Ruby,' Charlie says, staring out of the window. 'She's lots of fun.'

I sigh.

'Tom was telling me the other day that when he was little he had an imaginary friend . . . ' I venture. 'Maybe Ruby is *your* imaginary friend. Moving to somewhere new can sometimes be a bit tricky; I wouldn't blame you for inventing a new friend.'

'Ruby isn't imaginary,' Charlie says, looking at me with a steely gaze that immediately reminds me of his father. 'I've told you she's a ghost, and she's not the only one here.'

'Really? There's more than one ghost at Chesterford?'

'Uh-huh.' Charlie nods adamantly.

'Have you met any of these other ghosts?'

'Not yet; Ruby said I might be able to meet them, but only if they wanted me to.'

'I see. They're picky about who they show themselves to, are they?' Even though I'm trying hard not to, I can feel the corners of my mouth turning up.

'It's not a joke, Mum. It's true. If the ghosts don't want you to see them they won't show themselves to you.'

'Okay, okay. So how would I go about seeing one, then?' I ask, deciding to humour him. 'This is my castle, after all. I'd like to meet everyone who's living in my home.'

'You can believe in them to start with,' Charlie says perceptively. 'Because at the moment I don't think you do, do you, Mum?' He stares knowingly at me.

'It's difficult to believe in something when you haven't seen it with your own eyes.'

'What about gravity?'

'What?'

'Gravity. You can't see that but you believe in it.'

'That's different. It's—'

'And radio waves,' Charlie continues. 'You can't see them but you know they're there. Otherwise we wouldn't have had these baked beans tonight.'

'How do you work that out?'

'If you hadn't had the internet you wouldn't have been able to order them. The internet works by radio waves. We learned that at school.'

I shake my head. I know when I'm beaten.

'Then there's oxygen and—'

'Enough, enough! Okay, you win, I'll believe in your friend Ruby. But you and she will have to forgive me if I don't mention her and any of her *friends* to anyone else just yet.'

'Not until you've seen them.'

'That's right, not until I've seen them.'

Charlie holds out his hand. 'Let's shake on it.'

I take Charlie's hand, but instead of simply shaking it, I get up and pull him off his chair towards me. Then I envelop him in a huge hug.

'You are far too clever to have only been on this earth for ten years,' I tell him. 'But I love you all the more for it!'

'Perhaps I've been incarcerated?' Charlie suggests from the protection of my arms.

I think about this for a moment.

'Do you mean reincarnated?'

'Yeah, that too. I could tell you all about that if you like?'

'I think I've learned plenty for one night, thank you, mister. Perhaps we can continue this another time when my mind is just that little bit more open.'

91

Thirteen

A week later I'm walking through the castle grounds on my way to speak to a builder who's here to give us a quote on our proposed new café and gift shop.

I'm keen for both Dorothy and Tiffany to be involved in these new projects from the start, so I've asked them to meet me on the proposed site so we can put forward all our ideas together.

At the second group meeting we'd had to discuss the castle's renovations, Arthur had poo-pooed every one of our initial ideas, so I had purposely left him out of today's discussions. When it comes to dragging this castle into the twenty-first century, I only want people involved who are enthusiastic and positive about the future of the castle, and Arthur, lovely though he is, seems determined to bring everything down.

Joey, at the same meeting, had made the huge mistake of wondering out loud whether three women should be left alone with a builder to make 'technical' decisions. The sentence had barely left his lips when he'd immediately been hit by a barrage of protests and derision from the females around the table, which I noticed Tom had found most amusing.

'I can't believe you said that, mate,' I heard him commenting to Joey afterwards. 'You should have known they'd lynch you.'

'Didn't think, did I?' Joey had grimaced. 'Opened me mouth before me brain had a chance to stop me.'

Since that moment, Dorothy, Tiffany and I had formed a tight little alliance, and we were more determined than ever to make this new project a success.

I'm the first to arrive in the outbuildings we've chosen for our renovations. Originally this area in the outer bailey had been used to defend the inner part of the castle – the inner bailey. Although he might not have approved, Arthur had been keen to inform me what this area had been used for in the past. Apparently, this part of the castle would have held domestic buildings – workshops, livestock stalls and possibly even some servants' quarters. Arthur said there had even been talk of the castle having its own brewery here, but the area we are hoping to transform – two large buildings – had originally been used as stables.

While I wait for the builder to arrive, I look around at the inside of the old structure.

It doesn't look much like a stable any more, the walls – still pretty solid – are just plain stone bricks and the uneven floors are made up of colourful flagstones in varying shades of grey through to terracotta. The room I'm in now – the proposed tea room – is surprisingly bright and airy; it currently has quite a few glassless windows that will hopefully allow sunlight to stream through if our plans come to fruition. I'm convinced it will make a lovely area for visitors to enjoy a cup of tea and a scone. And if they wander through to the next room – the proposed gift shop – to buy a few souvenirs of a day they will hopefully want to remember, they'll find a room with no windows, but one that will make an ideal place to display our new gift stock over its many solid walls. And it's from that room that I now hear distant footsteps, so I assume that either Tiffany or Dorothy must have arrived before me.

'I'm in here!' I call, expecting to hear one of their voices reply. But instead there's silence.

I listen again and once more hear footsteps. *Actually no*, I think, listening hard with my head tipped to one side, *that's more like the sound of hooves trotting over the cobbles.* I hurry through to the next room, but find to my surprise that it's empty.

Okay, that was a bit odd. How could there be the sound of horses' hooves if there aren't actually any horses in here?

Suddenly, from the corner of my eye, I see something move. I turn swiftly, but not rapidly enough to see what it is – and there's the same noise again: the sound of clip-clopping on the stone floor, as though someone is just preparing to take a horse out for a ride.

'Who's there?' I ask timidly into the dimly lit room. 'Come on, who's playing a joke on me? Is it you, Arthur? I know you don't like this idea, but this is going a bit far, isn't it?'

But there's no reply.

I nearly jump out of my skin when at last I do hear a voice. But then I realise this is a very real voice belonging to a very real body. 'Hello,' it says again. 'Am I in the right place? Are you Lady Chesterford?'

'Ah,' I say with relief, turning to the voice. 'You must be Bill?' I walk quickly across the flagstones to greet a friendly-looking, middle-aged man wearing jeans and a checked shirt. I reach out my hand to shake Bill's, and notice it's trembling a little. 'Sorry about that. Yes, I'm Amelia Chesterford – we spoke on the phone. If you don't mind, though, I prefer to dispense with formalities,' I tell him in a voice that I hope sounds convincing. 'So please call me Amelia.'

Bill looks a little hesitant at my request, but nods anyway.

'You didn't happen to see someone riding a horse on your way in, did you?' I ask, still feeling a little unnerved.

'Er, no,' Bill says, looking at me oddly. 'I don't think so. Only a guy on a ride-on-lawnmower cutting the grass – hardly the same thing, though.'

I smile. 'No, indeed.'

'Helloo!' I hear Dorothy's voice just outside. 'Anyone there?'

'We're in here, Dorothy,' I call back. 'We'll come to you.'

Bill and I walk back through to the other room and find Tiffany and Dorothy waiting for us.

'Bill, this is Dorothy, who's going to be running the tea room, and Tiffany, who will be in charge of the gift shop. Dorothy, Tiffany, this is Bill our builder.'

'You should have been Bob not Bill,' Tiffany says, grinning.

Bill looks puzzled.

'Bob the Builder?' she continues. 'That was one of my favourites when I was a kid. Scoop, Muck and Dizzy?' she suggests. 'No? Roly and Wendy?'

'Er, yes,' Bill says, stopping her before she goes any further. 'I am familiar with *Bob the Builder*. And you're not the first to make that joke.'

'I bet she's not,' I say quickly. 'Now then, *Bill,* to business. As you've probably guessed, these stables are where we'd like to put our new tea room and gift shop. So the first question is, do you think it's possible?'

We spend the next three-quarters of an hour talking Bill through our ideas. He makes lots of builderish sounds – sharp intakes of breath and tutting interspersed with ooh and ahs – then occasionally he gets out his tape measure and takes a few random measurements, followed by more noises of consternation.

'So what's your verdict, Bill? Can we do it?' I ask eventually when this has gone on for some time.

'Yes, and no,' he says, cautiously pocketing his tape measure.

'Yes *and* no?' I ask.

'Yes, it's doable, but you'll have to do some major reconstruction work in here.'

'Like for instance?'

'Like you're going to need secondary walls constructing, so we can insulate between the two, otherwise you'll never be able to heat the place, or keep draughts out.'

'Sure.'

'And we'll need to put in several RSJs to reinforce that old ceiling and the new one that will have to be erected under it, and that's only the big stuff.'

'Right . . . I see. But when you've done all that, we can have our new tea room and gift shop? You can do it?'

Bill nods slowly. 'Yes, I can do it.'

'You mean you can fix it!' Tiffany says with delight. 'Can we fix it? Yes, we can!'

Bill scowls at her.

'Enough now, Tiffany,' I say kindly. 'I think we've all got the joke.'

Tiffany nods huffily.

'I realise you'll have to get me a proper quote together and everything,' I say, turning back to Bill. 'But can you give me a *rough* timescale of how long this all might take?'

'Ooh . . .' Bill says, pulling another pained expression. 'Six . . . maybe seven months – depending on—'

'We have three,' I say, cutting him off. 'I want this up and running by peak tourist season, and peak season begins in July.'

'No chance,' Bill says matter-of-factly.

'Not an option,' I reply resolutely, seeing where this is going. I'd dealt with builders before in our old house – you gave them an inch and they'd take a mile where timescales were concerned. 'I'm sure there are other builders I can get quotes from if you feel this is a bit beyond your capabilities ...'

I may as well have punched Bill in the face, he looks so wounded by this suggestion.

'I'll have you know I'm the most well-respected, in-demand builder this side of Hadrian's Wall. You won't get better.'

'I know; Arthur said as much when he recommended you,' I tell him, even if it was grudgingly, I think. 'And that is exactly why I've offered *you* the opportunity of taking on this job first. I'm sure working at Chesterford Castle will look very impressive on your builder's CV, won't it?'

'We don't exactly have CVs ...' Bill begins.

'I bet in centuries gone by working at the castle brought with it great clout and respect from other tradesmen, didn't it?' I continue.

Bill nods. 'I'm sure it did, but things are a bit different now.'

'Bill Bailey,' Dorothy cuts in now, 'I've known your wife Hetty since she was in nappies and I used to push her pram up the hill to this castle when I was babysitting her. Even if *you* don't think working here is anything special, I know Hetty would heartily disagree.'

Bill's cheeks flush.

'Is Hetty involved in any local groups?' I ask, inspiration striking.

'Hetty is the President of the Chesterford WI,' Dorothy

97

says. 'She's in the local craft society too, and she's Brown Owl at Chesterford First Brownies.'

'She'd be most welcome to bring *any* of her societies here,' I tell Bill. 'I'm sure we could give them a private tour of the castle when everything is up and running properly.'

'Hetty would like that,' Bill says, thinking. 'That'd get me in her good books, too, which is something that happens very rarely these days, I can tell you.'

'Excellent!' I say, attempting to seal the deal.

'But it still won't get the job done any faster,' Bill says firmly.

'Will money?' I ask. 'Money to employ more staff to work with you?'

'It will take a *lot* of extra labour – skilled labour,' he adds.

'I know.'

'And they may have to work overtime . . .'

'That's fine. But we will have a completion date, Bill,' I say firmly, in case he thinks he can pull a fast one on me. 'And there will be penalties attached to our contract if you run over that completion date.'

Bill looks surprised, but then impressed by my meticulousness. He narrows his eyes and studies me for a moment.

'Arthur said you were a canny lass,' he says, and then he smiles. 'That's a good thing in these parts, in case you didn't know.'

I feel myself blush that Arthur should say anything so nice about me.

'Shall we shake on it for now, then?' I ask, smiling at Bill and holding out my hand to him. 'Just until we've agreed fully on the terms and conditions?'

'We will that, m'lady,' Bill says, taking my hand and shaking it firmly.

'*Amelia*,' I implore. 'Please, my name is *Amelia*.'

Fourteen

Bill and I eventually come to a verbal and then a written agreement about the cost and duration of the stable renovations, and finally the building work gets under way with Bill and his friendly team arriving early in the mornings and heading home by teatime every day.

Our search for new staff is well under way too, and we've already filled several key positions with people from the village, which pleases me greatly. Just as Benji had suggested in the coffee shop on the very first day we met, I want to be the sort of landlord who would make the castle work for the village, not against it. We still have a few more vacancies to fill over the next few weeks, but everything so far is going to plan.

As a matter of fact, I'm beginning to get a little worried about Benji. We've been here just over three weeks and I still haven't heard back from him – it seems so out of character for him not to return my calls.

I've even thought about ringing Davies & Davies to see if they know where he is, but I stopped myself. After all, I'm just a client, there's no need for him to keep in touch with me once the job is finished. I just felt we'd become more than that in the time we'd spent together. I'd hoped we'd become friends, too.

Perhaps I was mistaken?

But then why had he sent Tom to see me if he wasn't interested in helping us any more? Tom is getting on absolutely fine, I have no worries there. To our complete astonishment, Arthur was most affable when Tom's 'trial' period had come to an end. Both he and Dorothy had no issues with welcoming him into our little castle family, and Tom seemed extremely pleased to become a part of it. In fact, he'd been promoted and had now begun to do a little bit of restoration work as well as all his odd jobs.

So I don't need Tom to be verified by Benji any more; my concern is simply for Benji's well-being.

I've walked down to the village quite a number of times since we arrived at the castle and on each of those occasions I've been struck by two things – firstly, how much the castle looms over the tiny village of Chesterford, and secondly, the esteem in which the villagers seem to hold it.

Everyone I come into contact with greets me in a friendly manner. News hadn't taken long to spread that there was someone new at the castle, and the villagers were obviously keen to find out just who I am, and what plans I have for Chesterford.

I've made a promise to them all that I will do my best to live up to my ancestors' name, and that I will provide lots of new jobs and visitors to the area once we are up and running properly.

I think some of them believe me. But I can tell a few are a bit doubtful.

In addition to my concerns about the castle and Benji, I've

also been extremely anxious about Charlie starting his new school. I've put him through so much upheaval in the last few months and I'm worried that asking him to fit into yet another new environment might be one move too far.

And to be honest, I wasn't just worried about Charlie on his first day at Chesterford Primary School. I was nervous about how the other parents would be with me, too.

It's difficult enough trying to fit in with the 'playground parents' when you are a regular mum bringing your child to a new school, but now I was what most of the villagers saw as 'the lady of the manor' I feared it might be nigh on impossible. I certainly didn't want Charlie's relationships with his classmates to suffer as a result of how people perceived me.

So as I walked Charlie down the hill towards his school that first day I'd felt extremely self-conscious (I'd secretly changed my outfit three times before we'd left the castle).

'You all right, Mum?' Charlie had asked as I gripped his hand far too tightly. 'You seem worried.'

'Me? No! I'm just a bit nervous for you, that's all – it's your first day in a new school, it's another big challenge for you, isn't it?'

'I'll be fine,' Charlie had replied matter-of-factly. 'Been there, done that before.'

'Aren't you even a little nervous?' I'd asked, hoping this wasn't simply bravado on his part.

'Nah, not really. I think you might be, though.' He'd looked perceptively up at me. 'You'll be fine,' he'd said, reversing our roles. 'Just be yourself, Mum, and people will forget where we live and who we are.'

My heart had melted as I'd squeezed his hand. 'I hope you're right, Charlie. I *really* do hope you're right.'

And to my amazement he had been. Just as easily as Charlie had slipped into his new classroom and been welcomed by his classmates, the other mothers and a couple of the fathers had gone out of their way to welcome me too.

So now when I walked Charlie the short distance to and from school, I always tried to go that little bit early so I had time to have a quick chat with anyone that wanted to speak to me. Charlie, to my immense relief, appears to be just as happy at his new school as he is in his new home.

All of the castle staff have taken Charlie under their wing in their own way – Arthur has taught him about the history of the castle, which Charlie loves. Joey shows him how to do practical stuff like gardening and DIY. Dorothy lets him help with her baking, and Tiffany just seems to make him giggle. It's like having permanently on-call babysitters; I don't have to worry about what Charlie is up to when he's here in the castle, because I always know he's being well looked after.

It's only Tom that Charlie is a little awkward with. He still seems to see him as some sort of hero after he 'rescued' him from the tower. Tom tries super hard with Charlie, but Charlie seems adamant that Tom must be revered, while he's happy to accept everyone else as his friends – including Chester the dog, from whom Charlie is inseparable when he's at the castle.

One of the best things about Charlie being so preoccupied, whether at school or at home, is that he hasn't mentioned Ruby in a long time.

I haven't heard any further odd sounds either. Bill seems happy enough working away in the stables; he certainly hasn't mentioned anything untoward about being there. So I'm beginning to wonder if I might have imagined ever hearing anything at all.

*

This morning I'm on my way to the office. I dropped Charlie off at school a little while ago, and now I'm off to catch up on any castle correspondence and, more likely, on any bills.

My now-familiar route takes me along a lengthy corridor that holds some of the rooms that are open to the public. Occasionally I might actually witness people wandering around them too. Our visitor numbers are starting to grow; I suspect a lot of the increase is due to people from the village coming to have a nose at what's going on in their castle, or to check out the new 'Lady Chesterford', as I still kept being called. But after the last disastrous time, I've learned not to approach visitors unless they approach me first, in which case I'm always polite and as helpful as I can be. But I do often try to eavesdrop in case I can hear anything that might be helpful to us in the future.

Today as I pass by the Blue Bedroom – a lovely ornate room with an original four-poster bed and some pretty Georgian furniture – I'm sure I can hear someone moving around in there.

I look at my watch. *That's early for a visitor*, I think, *it's barely 9 a.m. Actually, wait, it's a Monday – we're closed to visitors on Mondays. So who is in there?*

I hesitate at the entrance, and then stick my head around the door. But I see no one.

That's strange, I'm sure I heard something.

Happy there's no one there I turn away, but then I hear it again, and this time there's laughter.

I turn back towards the room again.

'Hello, who's there?' I ask, wondering if someone is in the little dressing room that leads off the main bedroom. I walk hesitantly across the room towards the dressing-room door, but it's gone quiet again now. I turn the door knob and open the door purposefully to confront any intruder, but the room is completely empty.

How very odd.

I walk back across the main bedroom about to leave when suddenly there's a creaking sound – it's coming from this room again. I turn around and to my astonishment I'm sure I can see the bed moving.

The blue silk eiderdown is definitely moving up and down on top of the bed – it's like someone it sitting down on it so it creases at the edges and there's a large dent in the usually immaculate cover.

Is there a bird or a mouse caught between the covers? I wonder.

I walk slowly across to the bed and cautiously pull back the covers in case something scuttles or flies out, but when there's nothing there I feel over the top of the bed in case I can touch the shape of an animal or bird trapped in between the layers. But again, nothing.

I straighten up the bed, and shake my head. I must have been imagining it. I didn't get much sleep last night; a seagull had decided it would be a great idea to build a nest just outside my bedroom window. So from about 4 a.m. all I'd heard was it toing and froing as it created its masterpiece maternity home. Maybe my lack of sleep was making my mind play tricks on me?

I walk towards the door and turn back to take one last look at the room. Everything seems fine now, no noises, no movement on the ... I stare in disbelief at the bed. The blue eiderdown which I straightened less than a minute ago is dented again – exactly like someone has sat on it.

'Too weird,' I say out loud, shaking my head. 'Really, way too freaky.'

And then I hear it again: the very definite sound of a man laughing.

'Morning, miss,' Tiffany says as I enter the office. 'Ooh, what's up with you? You look like you've seen a ghost!'

I stare at her.

'You're all white,' she says, looking at me with concern. 'Do you want a cuppa? I've got something a bit stronger hidden in the bottom drawer of my desk if you'd like that? Don't tell Arthur, though.'

'No, tea will be fine,' I tell her. I pull out the chair at my newly created desk and I sit down while Tiffany puts the kettle on.

'So what's occurring?' she asks, perching herself on the edge of my desk now. 'You're very pale, you know.'

'Tiffany . . . ' I say slowly. 'This may seem like an odd question, but do you know if this castle is haunted?'

'Yeah, that's what they say.'

'Who says?'

'Er, people who've worked here in the past. I just assumed it was stories – you know like they pass down through the generations for entertainment?'

I nod.

'Why, do you think differently, then?' she asks. 'Have you seen something?'

'Not *seen*, exactly, more heard.'

'Ooh, really? What sort of things have you heard? Like chains rattling and stuff?'

'*No*, we're not talking about a ghost in a Charles Dickens

novel! What I heard was ... ' – I feel silly even saying it now – '... laughter.'

'Ooh, a friendly ghost, then – like Casper?'

I stare at Tiffany – she probably wasn't the best person to talk to about this.

'Perhaps. And perhaps I was just imagining it.' I shake my head. 'Never mind. Now, what have you got for me this morning? More bills?' I look at the paperwork already piled up in front of me.

'Morning, Arthur,' I say as Arthur pops his head around the office door later. I've just finished dealing with all my paperwork and emails, and after two cups of Tiffany's overly sweet tea I've decided that it was definitely my mind playing tricks on me this morning and nothing else.

'Morning,' Arthur says. 'I was just wondering if you'd rung Doug Longstaff yet? He wants to talk to you about supplying the bread and stuff for the café. Doug is the local baker?' he reminds me unnecessarily.

'Yes, I do remember, Arthur. It's next on my list.'

Arthur just nods. 'Are you all right? You look a little pale this morning.'

Still?

'Miss Amelia saw a ghost!' Tiffany pipes up.

Tiffany still insists on calling me 'Miss Amelia'. It's better than 'madam', I suppose, or 'your grace' as she had on one occasion.

'No, I didn't,' I hurriedly insist. 'I heard something odd, that's all – in the Blue Bedroom.'

'What sort of odd?' Arthur asks.

Reluctantly I tell Arthur what had happened on my way to

106

the office, feeling quite silly and sure he will simply dismiss it as nothing but nonsense. In fact, instead of pale, my face feels quite flushed when I'm finished.

'Sounds like Percy,' he says matter-of-factly.

'Who?'

'Percy, he was the fourth Earl. He died in that room.'

I stare at Arthur. 'Arthur, are you telling me what I think you are? Are you saying this Percy is a ghost?'

'Ghost, spirit, whatever you want to call them.' He shrugs. 'Percy is said to have haunted that room for centuries.'

My eyes are wide now. 'And *you* believe that?' I ask, astonished at Arthur's calm composed responses.

Arthur shrugs. 'No reason not to.'

'Have you seen this Percy, Arthur?' Tiffany asks, her eyes wide.

'Nope. I may have heard a few things over the years I've worked here, though, and I've known a few that claim to have seen him.'

'And what did they say?' I ask, still not quite believing we're having this conversation.

'Varies. Apparently, the more Percy likes you, the more he's likely to show himself to you. That's why not many visitors see him. Percy likes to get to know you before he shows himself.'

'A picky ghost – nice.' I have to smile now. This is crazy, and I can't quite believe Arthur is a part of it. 'You said this Percy died in the Blue Bedroom? Was it natural causes?'

Arthur looks a little embarrassed and extremely uncomfortable. He fiddles with the green tie he always wears with his tweed suit when he's 'on duty', although, as far as I can see, Arthur never seems to be 'off duty', even when he's at his little cottage with Dorothy.

'Oh, Arthur has gone all red!' Tiffany grins. 'What's up, Arthur, cat got your tongue?'

'No.' Arthur clears his throat. 'The rumour surrounding this particular Earl's death is a little ... how can I put this delicately? A little ... risqué.'

Tiffany and I exchange looks of amusement.

'Go on, Arthur,' I encourage. 'Please tell us.'

'It's claimed – and believe me, I have no proof of this – that he died while ...' Arthur clears his throat again. 'While in the act of consummating a relationship with a lady.'

My eyes widen and I can feel myself grinning – partly at the cause of the Earl's death, but mostly at Arthur's carefully chosen description of it.

'He died having sex?' Tiffany states to Arthur's obvious discomfort. 'What a way to go!'

'I believe so ...' Arthur says. He looks awkwardly around the office.

'Is there more to it, Arthur?' I ask, sensing this isn't the full story.

Arthur looks at me in dismay, as though he really doesn't want to go on with this torment any longer.

'I bet there is!' Tiffany says keenly. 'Let me guess, was it a man in bed with him?'

Arthur pulls a horrified expression.

'No?' Tiffany says, continuing unabated. 'Ooh, what about a lady of the night then? Or his mistress? They all had mistresses back then, didn't they, these old codgers?'

'How do you know he was old when he died?' I ask her.

'That's true – was he, Arthur?'

Arthur sighs, obviously deciding it'll be easier to answer our questions than fight against them. 'He was a good age for that time, I believe, and yes he was with his mistress. Now is that enough for the two of you?'

'So that's why the bed moves?' Tiffany says, thinking out loud. 'He's still there having it away with his mistress!'

Arthur and I both pull looks of revulsion this time.

'Eww! Tiffany!' I say. 'I don't want to know that, thank you.'

'I believe Percy simply haunts the room,' Arthur says, his eyebrows raised sternly in Tiffany's direction. 'The reports of people seeing him are usually him simply sitting on the edge of the bed or moving between the bedroom and the dressing room.'

Tiffany looks a tad disappointed.

'Well, that's a relief,' I say, then I hear myself. *Wait, we are talking about a ghost here. I don't believe in ghosts, spirits, an afterlife or anything remotely connected to any of them.*

'Anyway, I must be going,' Arthur says, looking desperate to get away. 'I only popped up to ask you about Doug. Oh, and to tell you to expect a visitor later.'

'A visitor – who?'

'I think he said his name was Benjamin?' Arthur says. 'He telephoned earlier to check you were here, and asked for his visit to be a surprise. I don't know about you but I hate surprises, I much prefer to be prepared. So I thought I'd better mention it.'

'That's fine, Arthur. Thank you for informing me,' I say calmly, although internally my mind is whizzing.

Benji is coming here – to the castle. But why?

Fifteen

'Benji!' I call happily, as he makes his way across the draw-bridge and under the portcullis later that day. 'What are you doing here?'

'Surprise!' Benji calls back. 'Although by the look of your calm face perhaps I'm not quite the surprise I'd hoped to be.'

'Arthur may have let slip you'd be calling in,' I apologise, as Benji puts his arms around me and we hug. 'Sorry about that. How come you *are* here, though?'

'I've been up in Scotland visiting my parents – Stirling, to be precise – and I thought I'd call in on my way back down south.'

'Well, it's wonderful to see you.'

'So this is Chez Amelia,' Benji says, looking around him. 'Very impressive.'

'It is pretty special.'

'You're getting on all right, then? No teething problems just yet?'

'Ah, I wouldn't go that far. But I think it's going okay just now. Come on, let me show you around, or would you prefer something to drink first?'

'Tea first, then a tour?' Benji suggests. 'I'm parched.'

I take Benji up to the top of my tower, and while he admires the view I make us a pot of tea, then I carry it up the winding stone staircase on a tray, an act I quickly learned requires a lot of balance, and a fair amount of dexterity.

'You look like you've done that a few times before,' Benji says, taking the tray from me and placing it on the coffee table between the two sofas.

'I'm getting better at it. The first few times there wasn't a lot of tea left in the pot by the time I got up here, I can tell you!'

Benji pours the tea and we settle down opposite each other on the sofas.

'So where have you been?' I ask him. 'I tried calling you several times, but you didn't reply. I was starting to get a bit worried.' I try to ask this in the lightest, breeziest way I can. But the truth is I'd been more than a little concerned, and I had to admit a little hurt by his lack of contact.

'Holiday,' Benji says. 'I always switch my phone off and leave it at home when I'm away, otherwise I never get a break. The joys of being self-employed.'

'But what if you need to contact someone? Or someone needs to contact you? Like family, I mean,' I add, in case he thinks I mean me.

'I have this!' Benji says, pulling a phone from his pocket. 'It's a spare. I only give the number to close friends and family.'

'Oh . . . I see. Good idea.'

'I'll give *you* the number if you like?' Benji says, sensing my disappointment.

'Oh no . . . I didn't mean you to think—'

'Amelia, it's fine. We're friends, aren't we?'

I nod.

111

'And I do feel partly responsible for forcing you to come and live here.'

'You didn't force me.'

'Persuaded then.'

'Helped me come to an informed decision.'

Benji grins. 'Fair play. So why were you trying to call me? Something wrong?'

'No, not at all. Well, not now there's not. It was when Tom turned up here unannounced. I just wanted you to verify who he was.'

Benji looks confused. 'Tom?'

'Tom Barber – he restores antiques?'

'Oh Tom! Is he here, then? I didn't know if he'd come.'

'Yes, he's here; he turned up the same day I arrived, actually. Bit of a shock having to decide whether to hire a new member of staff on the spot.'

'But you did?'

'I gave him a trial – which he passed with flying colours, I'm pleased to say. I can't imagine the place without him now.'

Benji smiles knowingly. 'I thought he might impress you.'

'So how do you two know each other? I don't think Tom has actually ever told me?'

'I know Tom through one of his siblings – Jo. We used to date.'

'Ah, I see.'

'That was a good few years ago now, though,' Benji says, looking thoughtful. 'I hadn't seen Tom for ages when we bumped into each other in a bar. He said he was looking for work so I immediately thought of you. He's very good, you know.'

'Yes, I've seen him in action already. He's very thorough.'

Benji grins. 'Oh, have you?'

'Not like that!' I insist, feeling heat spread all the way from my neck to my face. I'm surprised by his comment; the Benji I'd known before had been a little more prim than this. Perhaps I'm seeing the real Benji now that he is 'off duty'; he seems much more relaxed, and he has an air of mischief about him.

'Shame,' Benji says, winking. 'No, you've nothing to worry about there. Tom is as sound as these castle walls.'

'That's not a great recommendation; they're crumbling pretty badly in places, you know.'

'Ah, well, Tom is still solid. Very reliable chap. Much more reliable than Jo was ...' Benji looks down into his tea for a moment. 'Anyway,' he says brightly, 'other than strange men turning up on your doorstep, what else has been happening since you got here?'

I tell Benji everything that's happened so far, with the exception of those peculiar events I can't quite explain. I'm still not sure about those myself yet, and I don't think now is the time to begin discussing the possibility of ghostly goings-on at Chesterford with him.

After we've finished our tea I take Benji on a walk through the castle, introducing him to a few of the staff we meet along the way, then we wander out into the grounds.

'I wonder where Tom is,' I say, looking out across the wide expanse of grass that leads down to the front gates of the castle. 'I'm sure he'd like to see you while you're here. I think he was helping Joey plant some new trees this afternoon.'

'You're keeping him busy, then? He's not just on restoration.'

'At the moment he's covering anywhere he's needed. But I hope to have him as a full-time conservator when all our new members of staff start work.'

'Wonderful, he'll like that.'

'So how much of your holidays do you have left?' I ask as

113

we stroll down the hill along the drive towards the main gate. It's already time to collect Charlie, and we thought it would be a nice surprise for him if Benji came to the school to meet him too. 'You must have been away a good few weeks already.'

'That is a very good question,' Benji says mysteriously.

'Does it deserve a good answer?'

'I could be on holiday indefinitely,' Benji says, not looking at me.

'How come?'

'Well, when I said I'd been to visit my parents that wasn't the whole truth. I *was* visiting them, but I was also having a good think while I was there too.'

'About?'

'About whether to diversify.'

'Diversify into what?'

'Writing; I've been asked to pen a book.'

'Really? That's amazing. A book about what?'

'It's a bit of a mish-mash, really. The publishers want a book about how to trace your family tree, but to give it a twist they want me to add my own anecdotes from my years of tracing other people's.'

'That sounds great, Benji. Are you going to do it?' I unlock the small side gate next to the main one, and we step through.

'That's what I've been thinking about.'

'Not that I've ever been asked to write a book,' I say, locking the gate behind us, and leading Benji down the path towards the village, 'but isn't it a huge honour that they want you?'

Benji nods. 'Yes, it was a bit of a bolt out of the blue and I'm very keen to do it, it's just . . .'

'What?'

'They want me to write it in a few months – they have a

114

publication slot available early next year that will coincide with a new TV programme the BBC are showing about tracing your family tree.'

'And . . . ?' I couldn't really see what Benji's problem was.

'I can't do my normal job *and* write a book, Amelia, it's impossible. When I'm working on a case it's pretty full on – people want results as fast as possible.'

'But can't you take some time out? You've just had a little holiday; surely you could just extend it?'

'But how would I pay my bills and my rent? I'm self-employed, I don't get paid holiday.' Benji sighs. 'I know I'm sounding incredibly ungrateful; some people would give their right arm to be offered a book deal—'

'Yes, but they wouldn't be able to type the book then, would they?' I wink at Benji, and he smiles.

'I'm being a churlish fool, aren't I?' he says, shaking his head.

'Nope, but there must be a way around this – let me think about it. I'm good at solving problems.'

'Economics background kicking in again, eh?'

'Nope, too many hours with a *Puzzler* magazine!'

Benji laughs now.

'That's better,' I say, smiling. 'Ooh, there's the school bell, we'll just be on time if we hurry.'

We collect a very hyper Charlie from school, and he becomes even more excited when he sees Benji, and delights in telling him all about his day on our walk back to the castle.

I half listen to them as we walk, but most of my brain is tied up thinking about Benji's dilemma. There must be a way around this and I'm determined to find it. Benji has helped me, now it's my turn to help Benji.

*

'How long are you staying, Benji?' Charlie asks, as they play with Chester in the late-afternoon sunshine that streams across the castle courtyard.

'Just a flying visit, my young friend,' Benji says, throwing Chester's favourite red ball across the gravel for him to fetch.

In an instant, Charlie's expression changes from exuberant to miserable. 'But why can't you stay with us for a while? We have *lots* of rooms here, don't we, Mum? And *lots* of beds. Some of them are a bit high and a bit stinky, though.' Charlie wrinkles up his nose.

Benji laughs. 'That's very kind of you to offer me a stinky bed, Charlie, but I have to get back to London.'

Charlie throws Chester's ball furiously across the court-yard so hard it hits the far wall and springs back again so that Chester has to do a sharp U-turn to chase it.

'Charlie!' I admonish him. 'Be careful.'

'Nearly had my eye out there, mate,' Tom says amiably as he appears through the doorway next to where the errant ball has just been. 'Benj!' he says when he spots his friend sitting beside me on the bench. 'What are you doing here?'

Benji and Tom greet each other with a handshake and a brief hug.

'Thought I'd better call in on Amelia and see how she's faring,' Benji says. 'I didn't realise until today you'd listened to my advice and come up here. How's it going?'

'Well, the boss is a bit of a slave driver,' Tom says, winking at me, 'but other than that I'm having a grand time.'

'I hope you're referring to Arthur,' I tell him sternly, then I smile.

Benji watches the two of us with interest.

'Amelia says she's seen you in action, Tom,' Benji says, his

116

eyes glinting. 'And she commented to me how thorough you are . . . '

My face reddens again. 'At *restoring* things,' I insist.

But Tom just grins. 'You always were a troublemaker, Benj,' he says good-humouredly. 'Take no notice of him, boss. How long are you here for, anyway?'

'Benji's not staying with us,' Charlie pipes up dismally. 'Are you, Benji?'

'It's not that I wouldn't like to, Charlie,' Benji says sadly. 'I'd love nothing more than to stay here in a castle – especially with you and your mum. I bet there's loads of interesting and exciting stories to uncover here, and you know how much I like a story.'

Benji had entertained Charlie for many an hour while I'd been sorting out our move, telling him stories of the families he'd reunited and the history he'd uncovered while doing so.

'That's it!' I suddenly say. 'The answer to both our problems.'

'What is?' Benji looks confused.

'You can stay here with us at Chesterford while you write your book.' I wave my hand at him before he can protest. 'No, let me finish. You'll have to earn your keep, mind – no freebies here.'

'But how? I'm not like Tom, am I – built like an Olympic athlete with the power to lift heavy objects and the ability to wield a shovel in a muscular manner?'

Tom helpfully flexes his biceps for us in a comical way.

'No, you're not, but luckily your muscles aren't what I want you for – it's your brain.'

'That's a relief, then!' Benji grins. 'But I still don't understand.'

'You can stay here with us at Chesterford and write your book, but in exchange for board and lodgings, I would like you to discover all of Chesterford's secrets – you know, the juicy stuff that visitors would be interested in hearing from our new tour guides. Not the bog-standard historical facts, we have tomes of those already, but all the gossip about the past residents, the real stories that made this place what it is today. What do you say, Benji? Would you be up for it?'

We all look eagerly at Benji.

'Please, Benji,' Charlie begs. 'Please come and stay with us at Chesterford. It would be ace.'

Sixteen

'When is he getting here?' Charlie asks me for the umpteenth time this morning.

'Later,' I tell him. 'He didn't specify an exact time – it depends on traffic and all sorts of things.'

'Is he bringing a big van like we did?'

'No, just a big car, I think, with a big boot. Benji doesn't have as much cr— er, stuff, as we did when we moved.'

Benji, to my delight, has finally agreed to move here. It had taken us the rest of the day, and a wonderful and plentiful dinner provided by Dorothy, to finally persuade him.

But eventually we established that he would come and stay here for free in exchange for research into the castle's past, so that I could provide my new tour guides with tales of heroes and heroines, mystery and intrigue, with which to delight the many visitors I hoped would pour into the castle grounds over the summer.

'Hopefully the traffic will behave for him,' I tell Charlie. 'It's Sunday, so it shouldn't be too bad on the A1.'

'I'm so excited!' Charlie says, hopping from one foot to the other.

'I know you are,' I tell him from my place by the window of our living room, where I'm currently sitting at my desk going through some paperwork that Arthur said wouldn't wait until Monday. 'Why do you like Benji so much anyway?' I ask Charlie, turning away from the paperwork for now. 'Obviously I like him. But I'm interested to know why you do too?'

Charlie stops hopping around for a moment and thinks. 'He's funny,' he begins, 'and he makes me laugh. He's good at telling stories – he makes them sound really interesting – even when they're not.'

I smile – that is indeed a talent.

'And Chester likes him too.'

Chester is Charlie's go-to about most things now. When he's allowed to, the little dog follows him everywhere. I know it won't be long before Charlie wants him to come and live here with us in the tower, and I've already thought of my excuse – too many floors to go down then up again when Chester wants to go pee-pee in the middle of the night.

'Chester likes Tom as well, but you're not so keen on him, are you?'

Charlie thinks about this in the deep way he always does with his brow furrowed.

'No, that's not right. I like Tom.'

'You do?'

'Yeah, but he's different to Benji.'

'Well, yes, I suppose he is,' I reply, not really sure where Charlie is going with this.

'Benji is like my friend, and Tom is like . . . ' Charlie struggles to find the right word. 'He's sort of like what I want to be like when I grow up.'

120

I'm stunned for a moment. This is *not* what I was expecting him to say.

'Really?'

Charlie nods in a matter-of-fact way.

'You want to be like Tom. Why?'

'He's cool,' Charlie says, and he gazes out of the window at a seagull that's landed on the window ledge. 'And sort of handsome – like a hero in a book or a film.'

'Yes, I suppose he is.' I think about this. 'Well, I'm glad you like him. I thought for a bit you didn't.'

'No.' Charlie shrugs. 'He's just not Benji, that's all.'

'We'll see a few new faces around the castle this week, you know. We have more new staff starting tomorrow.'

'What are they going to do?' Charlie turns his head away from the window for a moment to look at me. 'The café and shop aren't finished yet.'

'Well, they're going to do all sorts to begin with – a bit like Tom did when he first arrived. They're going to help out where needed.'

'I expect Dorothy will have lots of dusting for them to do,' Charlie says knowingly. 'There's *a lot* of dust here.'

'There is indeed,' I say, smiling at him.

'Benji!' he suddenly shrieks out of the window. I stand up too, so I can see Benji arriving in the courtyard in a large four-by-four vehicle.

'Charlie, go steady on those stairs!' I call in vain as he leaps from his seat and heads for the spiral staircase.

'Stop fussing, Mum!' he calls, his footsteps growing fainter as he descends safely to the bottom.

I watch Benji climb out of his vehicle. He must be able to sense me because he looks up and waves. I wave back, but

Benji is already wrestling with Charlie who has enveloped him in a huge hug.

It's good to see Charlie so happy again. He's smiled so much more since we've been here at Chesterford, and now Benji's here too I know he'll smile even more.

'How's it going?' I ask Dorothy the next day as I watch her overseeing her new team of cleaners polishing and dusting in the long drawing room.

'Very well,' Dorothy says, looking on proudly. 'I can't remember the last time the old place looked so clean.'

'Super. It is looking good – even I can see that.' I wander over to one of the ladies, who is currently wiping a painting that's been lifted down from its place on the wall. 'How are you getting on?' I ask her.

'Wonderful, m'lady, thank you,' she says, blushing a little.

'Please call me Amelia. Well, this is only the first of many jobs around the castle, Mrs . . . Lewis?' I say, desperately trying to remember her name from her interview. To my relief she nods. 'I'm hoping to keep everyone's roles as varied as possible.'

'I'm more than happy working here with Mrs Davidson. I'm having a lovely time.'

I wonder for a moment who she's talking about, and then I realise she means Dorothy. I only knew her and Arthur by their Christian names.

'That's good to hear.'

'What's going on in here?' a voice suddenly calls, bursting into the drawing room. 'Why are you polishing that? Oh my God, what are you polishing it with?'

'Tom!' I say, surprised to hear him talking in this way. 'What on earth is wrong?'

'That painting is a sixteenth-century oil – it can't simply be wiped down with a cloth. Please tell me you didn't use that on it,' he says, looking with horror at a can of Mr Sheen.

'But it's bringing it up lovely, it is,' Mrs Lewis says proudly, looking up at Tom. 'See?' She shows him her dirty cloth.

'No!' Tom says, barricading himself in front of the painting. 'No, don't touch it with that ever again, do you hear me?'

Mrs Lewis's face now changes to anger. She ignores Tom and simply marches over to Dorothy. 'I'm sorry, Mrs Davidson, I don't want to cause a fuss, but I will not be spoken to in that way.' She puts down her cloth with purpose, then she folds her arms across her chest.

I glare at Tom, but he looks equally unwavering as he stands in front of the painting.

Dorothy, now looking equally as annoyed as Mrs Lewis at Tom's outburst, turns to me with a look that suggests 'you're the boss – it's up to you to sort this out'.

I swallow. The other staff in the room are all gawping at this unfolding drama, so I beckon those involved over to me and we step outside into the hall.

'Mrs Lewis, I do apologise,' I say quickly, trying to think how to resolve this without upsetting either party. 'You're new here; of course you weren't to know the best way to clean the painting. Perhaps Tom here needs to give Dorothy – I mean Mrs Davidson – a list of all the more valuable items in each room?' I look at Tom. He nods. 'And then those items can be left for Tom to look after. Would that make things easier?'

'Good idea,' Tom says gruffly.

'I think that might be best,' Dorothy says, looking at Tom reprovingly. 'I didn't know that Mrs Lewis had the can of Mr

Sheen anywhere near the painting. But as you pointed out, madam, she's new to this so she wasn't to know.'

'That still doesn't give him the right to speak to me like that,' Mrs Lewis retorts huffily.

I look at Tom with my eyes wide.

He sighs.

'I can only apologise, Mrs Lewis,' Tom says with as much grace as he can muster. 'I should not have spoken to you in the way I did.'

Mrs Lewis nods.

'It's just I'm very protective of the contents of this castle – as we all are,' he says, looking at me and Dorothy. 'And I would be gutted if anything should happen to ruin any of its mighty history.'

'Yes ... well,' Mrs Lewis says, visibly softening, 'I think we all feel like that. That's one of the reasons I wanted to come and work here – to help preserve the past. My family have lived in Chesterford since the eighteenth century. This castle is part of my family history too.'

'I think we're agreed that the castle is at the forefront of all our minds,' I say calmly, glad the explosive situation seems to have been defused. 'So how about we all calm down and go back to what we do best – looking after it? Tom, perhaps you could make that list for Dorothy asap, just for this room to begin with, so she knows what she's doing in here.'

'Sure,' Tom says, looking a little ashamed now. 'And then I'll go around doing the same in the rest of the state rooms.'

'That would be good, thank you. Dorothy, are you happy with that?'

Dorothy nods.

'Great! Then we're all friends again. Tom, when you're finished your list could you come and find me – I'd like a word.'

'Of course,' Tom says, glancing warily at me.

I leave everyone getting on with their jobs, and as soon as I get a safe distance away I lean my head back against the wall and sigh.

'I think you dealt with that pretty well, Ms Chesterford,' I whisper to myself. 'Even if you do say so yourself.'

'Very well,' I suddenly hear whispered back to me. I turn quickly in the direction of the voice, but there's no one in the corridor but me.

'Who's there?' I say in the most commanding voice I can muster. 'Who said that?'

But just like the bedroom and the stables before it – when challenged, there's silence.

Seventeen

'Ah, found you at last,' Tom says, bounding across the grass towards me. 'I've been looking everywhere.'

'I've been inspecting the renovations on the stables,' I tell him. 'And now I'm on my way to look at a tree that Joey's found, it's got some disease that might mean it has to be chopped down. It's really old, apparently, and Joey won't do it without my say-so.'

'Never a dull moment here, is there?' Tom says, falling into step next to me.

'No, there's not, especially when certain members of staff that I've come to rely on make a scene in front of our newer employees ...'

'Ah,' Tom says, looking ashamed. 'That.'

'Yes that. What on earth got into you, Tom? You can't just burst in and start having a go at people. We're lucky Mrs Lewis didn't walk out.'

'I know and I'm sorry – I said that, didn't I? It's just I feel very protective of everything here. I want the chance to restore it all to its former glory – or as close as I can get to that.'

I smile at Tom. It's amazing how quickly this place gets under your skin. We've only been here a few weeks, yet I can't imagine life anywhere else. Living here is a huge challenge on a daily basis, but it's an enjoyable one, and most importantly this old castle with its dusty rooms and crumbling walls already feels more like home than anywhere I've lived in a very long time.

'I completely understand, Tom – really I do. But can you at least try to curb your natural enthusiasm – just a tad? Otherwise it will get you into trouble – especially with Dorothy if you behave like that with one of her staff again.'

Tom nods. 'Don't worry, I'll make it up to Dorothy. Are *we* okay, though?' He sounds quite concerned. 'I haven't upset you, have I?'

'No, of course not. You threw me in at the deep end, though – making me deal with my first staff crisis like that.'

'I think you dealt with it admirably.'

'Hardly, but thanks.'

'You don't give yourself enough credit, Amelia. I think you're doing a wonderful job here, and so does everyone else.'

'Do they?' I ask in disbelief. 'What about Arthur?'

'Arthur is Arthur. You know as well as I do that under that hard shell of his is a heart softer than anyone's.'

'You're probably right.'

'You know I am.' He pauses for a second. 'I'll always be grateful to you for giving *me* a chance, Amelia. You didn't have to, and yet you did. What made you take that chance? I was a stranger to you, I could have been anyone.'

I consider this. 'Gut instinct, I suppose, and you seemed quite trustworthy.'

'Trustworthy,' Tom repeats. 'I guess I'll take that. Anything else?'

'Are you fishing for compliments?' I ask, smiling at him.

'Maybe ... ' Tom casts out an imaginary fishing line.

I roll my eyes. 'Er ... Charlie seemed to like you, and he's always a good judge of character. So that went in your favour, too.'

Tom nods. 'He's a good kid, your boy.'

'Yes, he is. I bet you didn't know he wants to be like you when he grows up, did you?'

Tom stops walking so abruptly I have to stop and turn around to see him.

'What's up?' I ask.

'He wants to be like *me*?' he asks, looking quite stunned. 'But why?'

'He thinks you're a hero – for saving him in the tower, and also how you look, I guess – sort of ... ' I search for the right word. 'Well, macho,' I say, berating myself for not coming up with anything better. 'All boys want to be heroes when they're young, don't they? All brave and bold and ... '

'Macho?' Tom finishes for me, grinning.

'All right,' I say, still annoyed with myself. Of all the ways I could have described Tom – intelligent, smart, funny, handsome – I had to say that! 'I couldn't think of a better word to describe you, could I?'

Tom pulls a serious expression. 'So then I have a very important question for you.'

'Go on.'

'Is *macho* a good thing?' His eyes glint mischievously.

'Charlie seems to think it is,' I reply, dodging his question.

'But what about you, Amelia?' he asks, his penetrating gaze holding me involuntarily captive now. 'Is it a good thing in your book, too?'

128

I feel myself blush. 'Who knows?' I say, turning quickly away. 'Oh look, there's Joey,' I say with relief. 'And that must be the tree he's talking about. It *does* look old, doesn't it?'

'There's not much to go on, is there?' Benji says when I find him later that day in the castle's library – a stunningly beautiful room filled with hundreds of books that line the walls from top to bottom. There's a small narrow gallery that runs around the outside of the room, and this can be accessed from some wooden steps on wheels that glide from shelf to shelf allowing the books on the higher shelves to be reached with more ease.

'Are you telling me in all these books you can't find "much to go on"?' I ask, grinning down at him as he sits at a large dark wooden desk with a green leather trim. 'What are they filled with then, fairy tales?'

'Funny!' Benji pulls a wry face. 'There *is* quite a large section on the local area and the history of the castle, actually, and I found out more about the Rainbow Bay myth we talked about before. Apparently in times of trouble at the castle, a rainbow will always shine over the bay when things are right again. According to the records it's happened numerous times throughout history – after sieges and battles, and in times of illness and plague. Whenever there's trouble, seeing a rainbow means everything is A-okay again.'

'Mmm, interesting … So it's not just to do with a spectrum in the sky caused by the reflection, refraction and dispersion of light in water droplets?'

'Aha!' Benji grins. 'You know your science! Not in this case if the books up there are to be believed. But rainbows aside, I've spent a number of hours this morning up and down that ladder looking through all the books in that particular section of the library over there.' He waves his hand in the direction of the bookshelves. 'Sadly it's just your usual stuff – facts and figures, and details about the previous Earls. All important stuff,' he adds, 'and I'm sure I can use some of it for your tour guides, but there's nothing juicy to get my teeth into – no intrigue.'

'I see.' I look up at the book-filled walls. 'Perhaps there hasn't been any?'

Benji laughs. 'I hardly think that's likely in a place as old as this. Believe me, there's always some intrigue, even in the most modern of families.' He snaps the book he's been reading shut. 'Don't you worry, though – I'll dig some out. It's in my blood! Now, how's everything with you?' He hops up on to the desk and perches himself on the edge looking enquiringly at me.

'Everything's fine.' I shrug. 'As far as I'm concerned all our plans for the castle are progressing very well right now.'

Benji nods. 'Good, good. Now answer my actual question – how is everything with *you*, Amelia?'

'That's fine too ... Why wouldn't it be? Like I said, everything is going really well. Charlie is happier than I've seen him in a long time. I've got a steady wage coming in at last – well, I will do for the first time at the end of this month – and I have a permanent home to live in. Life couldn't be better.'

Benji narrows his eyes. 'You're still avoiding the question.'

'No, I'm not.'

'*Yes*, you are. How's your love life?'

'I beg your pardon?' I say, stunned by his question.

'Don't play the innocent – you heard me.'

'I don't mean to be rude, Benji,' I say, moving away from the desk towards one of the long windows that look down towards the sea, 'but I'm not quite sure how that's any of your business?'

'True, it's not. But I just thought I'd ask in case there was anything going on?'

'Well, there's not,' I say stoutly, still a little surprised by the frankness of his question.

'Could there be, though?' Benji says, pressing on. 'Do I sense a frisson of excitement when you and Tom are together?'

'No!' I say a little too vehemently. 'You most certainly do not.'

'Not a tremor of desire passing invisibly between the two of you?'

'No,' I repeat, folding my arms protectively across my chest.

'Oh, I must have got it wrong, then,' Benji says innocently, picking up his book and heading towards the ladder. 'Perhaps your heart beats that little bit faster when Joey is around then?'

'I don't think so! Joey is way too young for me.'

'Like an older man, do you?' Benji says with his back to me so I can't see his expression.

'No, not at all. I don't have a preference, actually, and again how is this any of your business?'

Benji climbs back down from the ladder and turns to face me. 'Let's just say I'm an interested party, that's all.' He winks at me. 'Now I've done my time here for today. I need to get on with my other job or my book will never get written. See you later, alligator!' And with that he glides elegantly through the library door and is gone.

What was all that about? I think as I'm left standing in the middle of the library. Why is Benji so interested in my love life, or more accurately, the lack of it?

Eighteen

'How's it going, Dorothy?' I ask as I put my head around the kitchen door.

Dorothy jumps. 'Ooh, m'lady, don't you be making me jump like that, not when I'm getting ready to prepare one of me soufflés.'

'Sorry, is that for dinner?' I ask, my mouth watering. I hadn't had time to prepare anything for Charlie and me yet, and the smells in Dorothy's kitchen right now are amazing.

'It is, yes. I'm going to try a new cheese soufflé recipe as a starter tonight. It's a bit fancy for Arthur, but I'm sure the others will like it.'

'I'm sure they will.'

'You'd be more than welcome to join us, you know,' Dorothy says coyly, not looking up at me, but concentrating instead on her ingredients. 'I know it isn't the done thing, the family dining with the staff, but I don't like to think of you and young Charlie eating up in that tower all on your own.'

I cringe at her words. I wasn't avoiding eating with the others because I thought I was of a higher standing than them, far from it. I'd avoided it because I didn't want Dorothy to make a fuss. But eating in the kitchen with all the others wasn't exactly being waited on hand and foot, now, was it? Arthur wasn't going to don his old butler gear and put on white gloves. What harm could one night do?

'I'd love to if you've enough to go around,' I reply eagerly. 'I know Charlie will jump at the chance, he's always going on about your cooking, Dorothy. I don't think mine quite lives up to your high standard.'

'Nonsense!' Dorothy says, shaking her head dismissively. 'I'm sure it does. We'd be delighted to have you both dine with us though,' she adds, flushing with pride. 'Ooh, perhaps we could get Arthur to set up the dining room if there's to be enough of us. *We* wouldn't eat in there of course, but—'

'No, no dining room,' I insist. 'We'll eat right here in the kitchen with everyone else. It's cosier,' I add when Dorothy looks surprised at my outburst.

'Of course, m'lady.'

'*Dorothy* . . . please call me Amelia,' I beg.

But Dorothy's mind is already elsewhere. 'I wonder whether the silver is clean?' she mutters, popping her head in a cupboard.

'Dorothy, no fuss, please,' I sigh. 'Just carry on as you usually do. Charlie and I will fit in with everyone else.'

'Of course, m— I mean, Miss Amelia.'

It's better than 'm'lady', I suppose.

'Great, we'll both see you later then. Ooh, Dorothy, you've been here at the castle a long time, haven't you?'

'Born in the very cottage me and Arthur live in now, miss.'

'Gosh, really? I had no idea you'd been here that long . . . Anyway, I was wondering if you knew any stories about the castle's past residents – you know, gossipy stories?'

'Gossipy stories?' Dorothy repeats as though she's never passed on a bit of gossip in her life.

I smile. 'Yes, Benji is looking for some to pass on to the new tour guides when they start, but we're having trouble finding any.'

Dorothy's face immediately fills with joy at the mention of Benji's name. 'Lovely young man that Benji is,' she says knowingly. 'Polite, knows his manners. Very clean looking too – if you know what I mean?'

I didn't, but I nod anyway.

'I know a few stories ...' Dorothy says, thinking. 'But the place you want to go is up in the west wing.'

'The west wing?'

'Yes, in them corridors at the back of the office. There's rooms filled with stuff up there. I've wanted to get up there for years and sort through it all – but there's never been the time. It's on my list of things to do one day.'

'But isn't that all junk?' I ask. 'I saw some of those rooms when we were looking for Charlie that day he went missing.'

'A lot of it probably is,' Dorothy agrees, 'but I think I saw some diaries and books the last time I was up there. The last Earl had a fancy dress party to go to and we were looking for his old robes for him to wear. Ah, he looked mighty fine that night—'

'Thanks, Dorothy,' I say, aware that she's likely to launch into a long story about the past at any moment. 'I'll be sure to take a look. Sorry, I have to dash right now. I've got to collect Charlie from school.'

'Of course. You go. I'll look forward to seeing you and the young master for dinner later.'

Eager to get away, this time I don't even try to correct her.

*

134

'Why do you want to go rooting about in there?' Arthur asks the next morning when I tell him what I'm thinking about doing. 'I thought we talked about this yesterday?'

Last night we'd all sat down together and eaten a delicious dinner around the huge kitchen table. There had been the odd comment about 'the fancy china' and the 'good cutlery' from Joey, to which Dorothy had thrown him a fierce look that might have singed the top of the soufflé if we hadn't already been tucking in to it. But other than that everyone had been in good spirits and appeared to be behaving completely normally in the presence of their extra guests.

'No, you said there was nothing to find in there, Arthur,' I tell him now. 'But Dorothy appears to think otherwise.'

Arthur purses his lips shut, obviously thinking Dorothy should have done the same. 'Why do you want to rake up the past anyway?' he asks. 'Why do you need tales and gossip about folk? Can't we just remember them by what the history books tell us?'

'We could, but that isn't much fun, is it? People like a bit of intrigue; I want to make their visit here exciting, not just full of facts and dates.'

'On your own head be it then,' Arthur says, sighing. 'You'll be days if not weeks sorting through all the rubbish in them rooms.'

'It's fine; I've got a bit of time. There's not too much I can do now until the stable renovations are closer to completion, and everything out here seems to be running smoothly thanks to you and Tiffany.'

Arthur makes a sort of harrumphing noise, and mutters something about there being 'always something to do'.

'I'll see you later, Arthur,' I say purposefully, heading towards the door at the back of the office. 'Wish me luck!'

'You're going up there now?' Arthur asks, looking horrified. 'I thought you were just thinking of doing it sometime?'

'No time like the present,' I say, already turning the door knob. 'See you later.'

Arthur simply shakes his head and returns to the paperwork on his desk.

About an hour later I'm beginning to wish I'd listened to Arthur's advice. I'm currently waist high in boxes, most of which contain a lot of junk. Old tennis rackets and antique fishing gear sit alongside shabby curtains covering boxes of paperwork and books. But the books I've found so far are just old trashy novels, and any paperwork appears to be ancient electricity bills and poll tax statements, of all things, followed by their council tax equivalent. It seems you still can't escape the mundane, even living in a castle! There's some furniture – nothing that Tom might be able to restore, just seventies and eighties stools, chairs and some melamine bedroom furniture. I've even found an ancient Amstrad computer tucked away in a corner with some even older-looking computer games.

I'm currently trying to sort the junk into piles – rubbish to go, things that might have some saleable value and things we need to keep.

Sadly, the *keep* pile is by far the smallest. My recent ancestors had obviously all been hoarders.

Jeez, if I was back on the Spencer estate I'd be rubbing my hands in glee at some of this stuff, I think as I look at the possibly saleable pile. I'd have eBay-ed a lot of this, and maybe even had a car boot sale with some of it to make a bit of cash.

Wait, that's it! I think as I stare at the ever-growing piles. We'll have a giant car boot sale and try to sell a lot of it. The

136

proceeds can go to the renovation work on the stables. I might not be interested in keeping some old vinyl records and a pile of vintage detective novels, but I bet there would be a few people who would like them.

With new-found vigour I begin sorting again and by the end of the morning I've managed to clear one room. It's not a bad start, but considering there are at least six rooms up here just like this, I've only just dipped my toe in the ocean of junk.

'How's it going?' Benji asks me at lunch-time when I find him sitting outside on one of the benches that line the inner courtyard eating a sandwich.

'Slowly,' I reply, grimacing. 'How about you? Did you get many words done this morning?'

'Not enough,' Benji says equally grimly. 'I got caught up doing some research, and time just flew away . . . ' He illustrates this by waving his hand in the air like a bird flapping its wings.

'Research for your book, I hope?'

'Research on the castle, actually.'

'Benji, you know we agreed you'd split your time evenly.'

'Yes I know, but I found out some really interesting facts about one of your ancestors and once I started searching I couldn't stop – occupational hazard, I guess.'

I tut and shake my head disapprovingly, but I can't help asking, 'Which of my ancestors would that be?'

'Clara Chesterford? She was the wife of one of the Earls here in the early 1900s – apparently, she was quite the rebel.'

'Yes, I've heard of her. There's a huge portrait of her in the Ladies' Chamber – it's a secret little room off the Great Hall.'

'Oh really?' Benji says, his eyebrows raised. 'I had no idea we had secret rooms here.'

'It's hardly a secret – everyone here seems to know about

it. Arthur told me all about Clara when he showed me around. She was quite the party girl.'

'I know; I've been reading all about her this morning – would you like me to forward the pages to you in case it's stuff you don't already know?'

'Sure, why not? I quite like her, from what I've heard so far. She sounds like she had spirit.'

Benji nods. 'A bit like you.'

'Me?'

'Uh-huh, and that's not the only thing you have in common – she inherited the house through birth too.'

'How do you mean? I thought it only went to males?'

'Not in this case. Clara was actually the previous Earl's daughter – the Earl she was married to became an Earl because he married Clara, not because he inherited it through his family.'

'But I thought that couldn't happen?'

'It's rare, but it did happen. Apparently, both of Clara's younger brothers died without leaving any children, and there was a clause in her father's will that stated on no terms should the family estate be passed down through his cousin's line – he didn't have any brothers either, so as long as Clara was married then she could inherit the estate – well, her husband could and so she would be allowed to live there.'

'Her husband inherited her family estate, even though it was Clara's by birth? That's shocking.'

'Yes, but not in the way you think. The clause in her father's will was very forward thinking for the time: even if it did mean Clara's husband was the benefactor, it meant she didn't have to give up her family home. Otherwise it would indeed have gone to a distant cousin, and let me tell you, if it had, you wouldn't be here now.'

'I wouldn't?'

Benji shakes his head. 'Your side of the family descends from Clara's lineage – even if it is a bit distant now. If it had gone to her father's cousin you wouldn't have got a look-in, I'm afraid. I'd have been tracing a very different line of Chesterfords.'

Good old Clara – well, Clara's father. Seems like we have something else in common – not just our debt problems.

'Funny how life turns out,' I say, thinking out loud. 'Just think, we might never have met – then where would you have written your book?' I take a bite of my own sandwich, which is just starting to crisp a little as it's been sitting untouched on my plate in the sun for so long.

'Not in the grand surroundings of a castle – that's for sure. Thank you, Amelia, I'm really enjoying being here.'

'And we're enjoying having you stay. It's quite the little family we've got going on here now. I like it.'

'So do I. It was good to see you eating dinner with the others last night. It made you seem more like part of that family.'

'Didn't I before then?' I ask, a little shocked to hear this.

Benji shrugs. 'Eating on your own with Charlie does make you seem a little remote.'

I put down my sandwich. 'The last thing I want is to create a divide. I've been trying my hardest since I got here to do anything but that.'

'I know. That's why I thought I should say.'

'Perhaps we should eat dinner with you all every night, then?'

'Maybe not every night. I think it's important for you and Charlie to have some time together too.'

I nod in agreement.

'What if you arranged with Dorothy which nights you'll eat

139

with us and which you'll spend with Charlie, then she won't be offended if you suddenly don't appear at dinner.'

'Good idea.' I smile at Benji and place my hand on his arm. 'What would I do without you?' As I realise how this sounds, my face reddens.

'It's okay,' Benji says, sensing my embarrassment. He pats my hand still resting on his arm companionably 'The feeling is completely mutual, I can assure you.'

'Can I join you in the sun?' a voice calls across the courtyard, and we see Tom walking towards us carrying his own plate. 'The rest of the courtyard is in shade at the moment.'

'Sure, come on over,' I call, and Benji and I shuffle along the bench a little so there's room for three.

'I feel like I'm interrupting,' Tom says as we all sit in a line on the bench. 'The two of you looked deep in conversation when I came outside.'

'Don't be silly,' I say. 'You're not interrupting at all. We were just chatting, weren't we, Benji?'

'Absolutely.'

'How's the spring cleaning going upstairs?' Tom asks. 'Joey told me you'd decided to have a go at clearing those unused rooms against Arthur's advice.'

'Gossip travels fast around here! Yes, I am, and it's going very well right now, thank you.'

'Glad to hear it.' Tom takes a large bite of his sandwich.

'Talking of gossip, I don't suppose you've found any up there?' Benji asks. 'It would save me a job if you did.'

'Nope, nothing as yet, but I have decided to hold a car boot sale.'

Benji snorts with laughter, as Tom hurriedly swallows his mouthful of sandwich, before asking, 'Where? Here?'

140

'Yes, here; what's wrong with that? There's loads of old junk up there. It's stuff that we really don't need to keep, but someone else might like. I thought it would be a good way of raising some extra cash for the renovations.'

The money that the last Earl left me was diminishing fast, and I was starting to worry that I would run out before we got everything up and running.

'Your idea is admirable,' Benji says, 'but a car boot sale? There's not many cars around here – a horse and carriage sale maybe?'

'Okay, a *yard* sale then. No, make that a *courtyard* sale. We can set up some tables right here, and invite people to come and sell their stuff alongside our old tat. It might be fun. Our first proper event.'

'There're some trestle tables in one of the sheds – I saw them the other day when I was looking for some tools,' Tom suggests helpfully. 'They'd be perfect.'

'Great.'

'It's not a bad idea, actually,' Benji admits. 'Now you've omitted the car boot part.'

'Glad to hear you approve. I'll talk to Arthur later about some possible dates.'

'Be careful what you select to throw out, though, won't you?' Benji warns. 'Remember one man's trash is another man's treasure.'

'And one woman's rubbish is another tile on the floor of our tea room!' I remind him. 'Don't worry, I'll be careful. If there's anything worth discovering up in those rooms, then I'm going to find it!'

Nineteen

After lunch I return to my sorting. The afternoon is much like the morning – three piles, and this time I remember the bin bags, so one of the piles quickly becomes a mound of black shiny plastic.

I'm just thinking it might be time to call it a day, so I've time to smarten myself up a little before collecting Charlie from school, when I discover an old tea chest. It had been hidden in the corner of the room behind what I'd thought was an old roll of carpet, but in fact turned out to be a very large Persian-style rug.

I'm about to leave it until I come back tomorrow, when I notice that the box seems to be filled with books. Nothing new there, I've already found enough old books to start a second library downstairs, but these books seem different: from the outside they look like leather-bound notebooks. I lift one from the box, expecting it to be filled with more tiny print – my ancestors' eyesight must have been a lot better than mine is, to be able to read all the fine print I've seen today. Perhaps they'd all worn glasses?

But as I open the cover of this book, immediately I see it's different.

The writing inside is still tiny, but instead of coming from a printing press the words have been written with a fountain pen.

'It's a diary!' I say as I notice the first entry has a date. 'Oooh, I wonder who wrote it—'

Suddenly there's a crash from the next room. I look up, wondering if one of the piles I'd made this morning has toppled over.

I put the diary down and hurry back next door, but it appears nothing has moved. *That's very odd*, I think, looking around. *What made the noise?*

I go back to the room I've just come from and pick up the diary, but just as I open the cover to begin to read I hear the noise again – it's like someone is banging something together.

I rush back next door – but again nothing. I look around the corridor outside, pausing for a moment in case I hear the noise again. But all is silent.

Not this again, I think. *First it was the stables, then the bedroom. Now here.*

'Hello,' I call a little hesitantly. 'If anyone is there you might as well show yourself.'

I brace myself. I'm not quite sure what for – it's hardly likely that a bunch of ghosts will suddenly appear through the walls and waft their way over my head now, is it?

As I suspected (and secretly hoped) nothing happens.

'Right, well, if you're not going to show yourself then I'm going to collect my son from school,' I say to the empty corridor, suddenly sounding a lot braver than I had a few moments ago.

I walk confidently back into the room I've just been clearing to collect the diary for me to read later. But it's not where I left it, balanced on the edge of the packing case.

'What the ...?' I say, looking around me. I was sure I'd dumped it here before I'd hurried out of the room. Where had it gone?

I search the box again in case it has fallen back inside. But it's not there. All the other books, which also appear to be handwritten journals, still remain, but where had that particular diary disappeared to?

'This is madness!' I mutter. 'A book can't just move on its own.'

But that's exactly what seems to have happened.

I glance at my watch. 'Right, you win,' I say to the room. 'I have to go. But I'll be back,' I warn it. 'And I *will* find that diary. This is my castle, and *I* say what goes on here, do you understand?' I waggle my finger in a menacing way, and then I look at my hand in embarrassment. What am I doing threatening an empty room? All this sorting of old junk is driving me insane. I need to find some real people to talk to and fast!

'Charlie?' I ask as we walk back from the school. 'Have you seen much of Ruby lately?'

Charlie looks at me suspiciously, as though I'm asking him a trick question. 'I thought you didn't believe in Ruby?'

I shrug. I feel silly even asking my son this. Even more silly than I'd felt after leaving the rooms upstairs and realising I'd been talking to an empty room. 'It's just I've heard some odd noises around the castle lately.'

'That might be Bill,' Charlie says matter-of-factly. 'He's using some new power tools in the stables right now.'

'No, it's not Bill. These noises are ... well, they're not explainable.'

Charlie looks up at me. 'It might be the other ghosts.'

I swallow. This is so difficult for me. 'You mentioned some *other* ghosts before. Do you know how many there are?'

'No, Ruby never said. All I know is they're pretty protective of the castle. They don't really like change.'

'Oh dear; well, they won't like me, then. There's been a lot of change since we arrived.' Charlie and I walk through the main gates – unlocked today because we're open to the public – and then along the bridge towards the castle.

'Yeah ... Ruby did mention something about that.'

'She's talked about me?' I ask, partly horrified a ghost might be talking about me, but probably more so that I'm actually having this conversation with my son. 'What did she say?'

Charlie pulls a face. 'I'm not sure I should tell you.'

'Charlie Harris, I am your mother – if someone is speaking badly of me I very much think you *should* tell me.'

'It's not that they're saying bad things about you ... ' Charlie's obviously still torn. 'It's more like you're unsettling them.'

'How so? Everything I'm doing here is to improve this castle and make it more profitable in the long run. I would have thought they'd have been happy I'm trying to save their home.'

Charlie shrugs. 'Like I said, they don't like change, that's all. I guess they've lived here a long time – a lot longer than we have.'

I open my mouth to speak, and then I close it again. Something Charlie said has struck a chord. I'd been so busy thinking about the future of the castle, I hadn't ever stopped to think about its past all that much. No wonder Arthur was resistant to all my changes; this had been his home for a long time too.

'I understand,' I say quietly. 'I guess I should be more considerate of the castle's past. But . . . ' I hesitate as we walk under the portcullis and into the courtyard. 'If your . . . *friend* could pass on a message for me . . . to the others?'

Charlie nods.

'Tell them . . . tell them I only mean good in anything I do. I only want what's best for Chesterford Castle; it's my home now as well as theirs and I want it to survive and prosper well into the future.' I look at Charlie. 'Will you do that for me? Will you tell this Ruby what I just said?'

'I don't need to,' Charlie says. 'You just did.'

'What do you mean?'

Charlie looks towards one of the doors that leads off the courtyard into the part of the castle that houses the Great Hall.

'Look,' he says, pointing.

'Look at what?' I say, turning in that direction.

'Can't you see her?'

'Who?'

'Ruby. She was here with us when we came into the castle grounds. She heard everything you just said.' He holds up his hand and waves. 'She's waving at you, and smiling,' he says, smiling back. 'I think you've made her happy.'

I feel my hand reach up and give a tiny wave. 'But I can't see anything,' I whisper to Charlie.

'You will do,' Charlie says, 'once your belief becomes stronger, Mum. You will do.'

Twenty

The next day I go back up upstairs to finish sorting the rooms.

I'm still not one hundred per cent convinced that everything Charlie was saying is true – I don't think he was lying, but I'm still leaning towards Tom's explanation that it might just be his imagination creating all this.

But a ten-year-old's overactive mind doesn't explain the things I've seen and heard myself since I've been at the castle. Perhaps my imagination has been working overtime too? I mean, why wouldn't it? We've gone from living in a modern high-rise flat that had been built in the early eighties to an ancient castle that had been built hundreds of years ago. It's understandable our brains might need a little time to adjust to the more unusual aspects of living here. But since my conversation yesterday with Charlie, I have to admit I do feel much more confident about the situation, and strangely not so afraid of things I don't understand.

But as I enter the room to recommence my clearing, I'm amazed at what I find waiting for me on the corner of the packing case where I'd sworn I'd left it yesterday: the diary.

'How did you get here again?' I ask, lifting it up and looking around as if I expected to see some magical fairies flitting away after doing their good deed.

I tuck the diary safely into the top pocket of the dungarees I've chosen to wear today. 'You're not going anywhere this time,' I say, tapping the pocket. 'I'll look at you later.'

But after I've sorted a few carrier bags and moved a few boxes around, the pull of the diary is too much. So I sit on the edge of an old toilet (goodness knows how that got up here), remove the book from my pocket, and open the cover.

It only takes me a few pages (and a bit of skipping forward) to work out whose diary this is: it belonged to Clara, the Countess from the painting downstairs.

I know this because each entry is dated in the year 1910. Most of the entries talk about the daily running of the castle, interspersed with anecdotes about dress fittings and parties. Then in the later entries the light tone becomes much darker, when Clara begins to talk about her money worries after the death of her husband, and finally her debt.

'Gosh, this must have all happened so fast for you,' I say to the diary. 'One minute you're living this comfortable carefree life of parties and social climbing, and the next you seem to have all the cares of the world on your shoulders.'

A bit like you did, I think, suddenly reflecting on my own struggles. *You were happy and settled, and then – boom – one day it all changed.*

But my husband didn't die – he left me. And you didn't have a child to look after, Clara – you had a castle instead.

But still, the similarities in our two situations are easy to see.

'You okay?'

I jump at the voice, but it's just Benji.

148

'You looked deep in thought there.' Benji comes through the door. 'What are you reading?'

'It's Clara's diary – well, one of them. I assume there must be more. This one only covers about six months of 1910.'

'Clara? You mean the Countess we were talking about yesterday lunch-time?'

I nod.

'I bet her diaries make interesting reading.' Benji winks, but I remain serious.

'This one talks about how she found herself in so much debt, actually. Death duties, apparently, after her husband died; not gambling debts, after all. Perhaps that was just gossip that got embellished over the years?'

'Oh.' Benji looks a little ashamed that he's been one of the people passing on that titbit of information. He looks down into the box where all the other books still reside. 'Are these books *all* Clara's diaries?'

'I'm not sure; I haven't looked through the rest yet.'

Benji reaches into the box and pulls out another book. 'This one is,' he says, opening the cover. 'And this,' he adds, flicking through another. 'Look, same handwriting.'

Bit by bit we examine all of the books, and find they're a mix of Clara's diaries and some other journals kept by another of the former Countesses.

'Are there any more boxes like this?' Benji asks, looking around the room. 'You might have stumbled upon something worthwhile here.'

'Let's look, shall we?' I put Clara's diaries safely to one side, determined to read through them all later, and then I help Benji search through any boxes that look like they might contain diaries or journals.

Excitingly we do find more diaries belonging to Clara. Some are in old suitcases and trunks, one is in a battered leather satchel, and we even find a couple stashed inside a large chipped garden urn that I imagine might have stood proudly in the castle grounds at one time.

'Well,' Benji says, brushing the dust from his trousers when we've exhausted all the hiding places we can think of, 'there's a good bit of reading here. Do you want to take them to read first? She is your family.'

'If that's all right with you?'

'Of course. There's obviously a connection between the two of you. It's understandable you'd want to explore it further. Go for it. Just let me know how you get on.'

'Hey, how's the sorting going?' Tom asks me later when he finds me curled up under a tree on one of the new blue and white striped deckchairs that we've decided to put out for the visitors to rest on this summer. 'Taking a well-earned break?'

'Something like that. I'm doing a bit of research, actually.'

'Oh yes?' Tom asks, pulling another deckchair up next to me. 'Into what?'

'Into *who*, really – I'm reading Clara's diaries.'

Tom looks puzzled for a second. 'Oh, *Clara* – the woman in the painting you showed me?'

'Yes, that's the one. Benji and I found a load of her diaries up in one of the rooms and I'm reading through them one by one.'

'*Interesting* reading?' Tom asks, raising his eyebrows suggestively.

'If by interesting you mean saucy, then at times they are a bit racy, yes.'

'I thought as much,' Tom says, glancing with interest at the page I'm currently reading.

150

I shut the cover. 'But once you get past that, you realise that Clara was actually quite a lonely woman, especially when her husband was alive.'

Tom looks surprised. 'Ah, that's quite sad, then. Why especially when her husband was alive?'

I look at the book in my hand again, wondering if by telling Tom I was betraying Clara's trust by giving away her secrets.

'Going by what I've read so far, I think Clara might have been gay.'

'Really?' Tom looks surprised. 'What makes you think that? No, wait, I don't need to know details.'

'It's okay, there's not that many of them. I just get the feeling that she might have been. Perhaps when I've read a few more of her diaries I'll know for sure.'

Tom nods. 'But you said she was married? Was that just a ruse, then, so people didn't guess?'

'I think it might have been partly that, but it was mainly to do with the fact she wouldn't have been able to continue living here if she didn't have a husband. She needed to be married to allow her to inherit when her father died, so I think she only married because of that. It's to do with her father's legacy and an ancient law. It's complicated,' I say when Tom looks a little lost.

'Isn't it always when families are concerned,' he says knowingly.

'Yes, I guess so.' I wonder if Tom is talking from experience. 'Anyway, *I'm* reading Clara's diaries, and Benji is reading through a lot of the other journals we found up there, to see what he can discover.'

'Good-oh, and have you found any more bits for your car—your *courtyard* sale?'

'Lots; we'll have quite a bit of stuff on our stall. I just hope we can entice some other people to come and sell here.'

'Are you kidding? They'll love it – a chance to sell your old junk in the grounds of a castle? They'll be queuing up to book a stall once you advertise it.'

'You think?'

'I know it. You might not know this, but I spend a bit of time in the local pub, and there's always someone talking about you or what's going on at the castle.'

'Really?'

'Yup. You're quite the local celebrity.'

'I hardly think so.'

Tom shrugs. 'I only speak what I hear. Do you want some help advertising the event? You know, posters, that kind of thing? I can see you're really, really busy right now with your reading . . . ' He winks.

I give him a wry smile. 'That would be lovely, Tom, thank you. I hereby put you in charge of advertising and organising the car boot— I mean, the *courtyard* sale.'

'Wait, I didn't say I wanted to organise it,' Tom says, looking dismayed.

'I could ask someone else, but with all your *connections* down at the pub, I think you'd be the ideal person, don't you? And you do sort of owe me a favour after the Mr Sheen incident . . . ' I wink at him.

Tom sighs. 'You're a hard taskmaster, do you know that?' he says, shaking his head. 'Your ancestors would be proud of you.'

'All in the blood, my good friend,' I say, tapping the diary. 'It's all in the blood.'

Twenty-one

As it turns out Tom does a great job of organising the sale. Posters quickly appear all over the village advertising Chesterford Castle's very first courtyard sale, and very shortly after that spaces at the twenty or so tables we've decided we can fit in the courtyard rapidly begin to sell out. So when the day of the sale finally arrives, just over two weeks after we'd sat on the deckchairs discussing it, the castle courtyard is filled with people chattering happily away in the sunshine I'd prayed for, getting ready to sell their wares to the customers that are just starting to filter through the castle gates.

I'm really proud of how we've all pulled together as a team today. Joey is on the gate, taking a reduced entry fee from people on the understanding that they can wander around the outside of the castle as well as visit the courtyard sale, but the inside rooms of the castle will not be open to the public today. Dorothy is serving teas, coffees and cakes on a makeshift stall ably abetted by her new favourite – Benji, who is wearing a very fetching straw panama hat to shelter him from the sun – and her always favourite – Charlie, who is more excited than anyone about the sale. He'd offered up some of his old toys and books for us to sell, on the understanding I was to allow him to buy anything he wanted with his pocket money from the other stalls. This had seemed like a good deal, until I saw a man unpacking several large models of various spaceships and figurines from one of Charlie's favourite film franchises. At this rate we'd be bringing more stuff back to the tower tonight than I was selling.

But I don't have time to worry about that; Tiffany and Tom are helping me out on the castle's stall and we are already surrounded by potential buyers perusing our stock. Over the top of their heads I can just see Arthur wafting about the crowds generally overseeing everything and everyone as usual.

'You have a wonderful stall, Lady Chesterford,' a well-dressed woman says as she looks over the several trestle tables we've managed to fill. 'With some . . . *unique* items.' She pauses at three vintage toilet flushes.

'Thank you,' I reply cheerfully, deciding it would be impolite on this occasion to correct her way of addressing me. 'We've had a good clear-out. I hope there's something for everyone here.'

'I'm sure there will be. Bill's been keeping me up to date about this and everything that's been going on at the castle since you arrived.'

'Oh, you must be Hetty,' I say, pleased I'd remembered the name of Bill's wife. 'How lovely to meet you.' I hold out my hand. 'I'm Amelia Chesterford.'

'Yes, I know,' Hetty says, shaking my hand. 'Bill's told me all about you.'

It was difficult to know by Hetty's tone whether this was good or bad.

'And Bill's mentioned you too,' I say, keeping up my smile. 'I understand you're the president of our local WI.'

'I am, amongst many other things.'

'Well, I hope Bill has also told you that we'd love it if you'd bring some of your groups to visit the castle. Once the new tea room and gift shop are open I hope to welcome lots of local societies to the castle for visits and tours.'

'He did, and I'm sure we'd be delighted to accept your offer. Of course, as the new Countess, you would be most welcome to join us any time at one of our WI group meetings.'

'Er . . . yes, of course . . . that would be lovely. But I think I should point out I'm not actually a countess.'

Hetty raises an eyebrow and gives me a peculiar look.

I'm aware that lots of new customers are approaching the stall. Tiffany and Tom are dealing with most of them, but I'm soon going to be needed.

Hetty looks as though she's about to launch into some very detailed questioning about why I'm not a countess, so smiling at her I say, 'It's been lovely to meet you, Hetty, but as you can see we are starting to get a little busy now. I do hope you enjoy the sale.'

'I'm sure I shall,' Hetty says, obviously deciding now is not the appropriate time for her questions. She picks up one of the romance novels and I see her eyes widen as she glances at the text on a random page.

I leave Hetty and begin to take money from people eager to make purchases from us. Ours is by far the most popular stall at the moment – with everyone making a bee-line towards it when they come through the gates. Partly to buy things, I note, and partly just to have a nose at what we're getting rid of.

But soon all the stalls seem to be equally busy and I feel a tad less guilty at hogging all the customers.

In a rare lull, I notice Tom talking to an attractive woman with highlighted hair tied up into a bouncy ponytail on top of her head. The woman doesn't seem to be that interested in buying anything that's on our stall. Her interest appears to be solely in the stall-holder behind it.

'Amelia,' Tom calls, beckoning me across. 'Come and meet Rachel; she works at the Chesterford Arms – the pub I was telling you about.'

'Hi,' Rachel says, nodding her blonde head towards me in greeting. 'You must be the new lady of the manor I've heard so much about.'

'Hardly,' I say, smiling at her. 'Someone just left me in charge, that's all.'

'U-ha,' Rachel says, weakly acknowledging my joke.

'I was just saying to Rachel that we should get you down to the pub and introduce you to a few more people,' Tom says eagerly. 'They're a good crowd down there. I'm sure they'd love to see you one night.'

Rachel's expression suggests this was not likely to have been her idea. I get the feeling she'd probably prefer to have Tom to herself.

'That could be fun,' I say, smiling deliberately at Rachel. 'What sort of things do you get up to down there – apart from drink beer, obviously?'

'We've got a pool table, and a dartboard,' Rachel says flatly, as though this should be more than enough entertainment for anyone.

'Cool.' I nod.

'So what do you reckon, Amelia?' Tom asks. 'You up for coming down there one night?'

'Sure.' I smile. 'Why not? Oh, do excuse me, won't you? We have customers again. Nice to meet you, Rachel.'

'Likewise,' Rachel says, barely able to hide the disdain in her voice, and I wonder if the local pub might not be quite as friendly towards me as the school playground has been so far.

'How can I help you, sir?' I ask, bounding over to a stout little man waving his hand impatiently at me.

'How much is this?' He's holding up an ancient stuffed dog with a crazy wild-eyed expression, one of my least favourite items on the stall.

'Er, twenty pounds?'

He pulls a face. 'I was thinking more like ten.'

'Shall we meet in the middle, then?' I suggest cheerfully. 'How about fifteen pounds?'

He thinks about this. 'Twelve,' he says flatly. 'It's probably flea ridden.'

'Twelve pounds it is, then,' I agree through gritted teeth.

I hold out my hand and he dumps two five-pound notes along with two one-pound coins unceremoniously into it, then he simply walks away.

'Charming,' I mutter under my breath.

'Don't sweat about it,' Tom says, moving next to me now Rachel has gone. 'These people aren't all locals to Chesterford, you know; some of them have come quite a way for this.'

'Really. Why?'

'Probably think they'll get a bargain this being a castle 'n' all. Something that might prove to be worth a lot of money.'

'But I checked really carefully to make sure I wasn't getting rid of anything valuable.'

'Ah, but they don't know that, do they?' He winks.

'That's true.'

'So you're up for a trip down the pub one night?' Tom asks as though he's clarifying that I genuinely meant what I'd said.

'Of course. I'm not sure I'm going to receive quite the welcome you think I am, though.'

'What makes you say that?'

'Your barmaid friend was hardly welcoming, was she?'

'Rachel?' Tom asks, apparently oblivious to Rachel's offhand manner. 'Nah, she's okay. Always friendly and attentive when she's behind the bar.'

'Well, of course she is to you!' I laugh.

Tom looks blankly at me.

'Don't you see it?' I ask him. 'She quite obviously fancies you.'

'Don't be daft,' Tom says, his cheeks reddening. 'She's just being friendly – that's her job.'

'Didn't you see her face when you said you wanted to bring me down to the pub – it was stonier than some of our gargoyles.'

Tom thinks about this. 'No, you're just being paranoid.'

'I am not. I know a jealous woman when I see one.'

'What has she to be jealous of?' Tom asks. 'It's not like we're a couple or anything. It's hardly a date we're going on ... is it?' And I wonder if I detect a hopeful note to his last question.

'No,' I insist hurriedly. 'It's not a date. Just a way for me to meet a few more of the locals.'

'Yeah ...' Tom says, nodding quickly. 'It's just that. Nothing else.'

The people continue to flood in to the sale, and we continue to sell, so by the time two hours have passed our three trestle tables have been reduced to one.

'It's going well, isn't it?' Tiffany says. 'We're not the only ones who have almost sold out.'

I glance at some of the other stall-holders and see their tables are beginning to look a little bare too, and everywhere around us there are people sitting on benches in the sun happily drinking cups of tea and coffee, eating cakes and sandwiches, with their new purchases sitting firmly by their feet.

A great sense of achievement washes over me. Our first event appears to have been a success!

'I'd like a refund,' a voice says next to me, bursting my bubble. I look towards the voice and see the rude man who had bought the stuffed dog earlier clutching it under his arm.

'I'm sorry?' I ask, wondering if I've heard him correctly.

'I'd like a refund; my wife doesn't like it, she said it's haunted.'

'*Haunted* – what's haunted?'

The man looks uncomfortable. 'She thinks the dog is haunted. She's funny about these sorts of things.' He shrugs. 'She said there was no way she could possibly have it in our house. So I'd like a refund.'

'But this is a car boot— I mean a courtyard sale. We're not a high-street shop.'

'Makes no difference. I know my rights and I want a refund.' He places his empty hand defiantly on his hip.

I feel myself start to redden. It wasn't the man's request so much – strange though that was – it was his attitude. I detest rudeness and bad manners in all their forms.

'Course you can have a refund, mate,' I hear Tom say next to me. 'Here's a tenner.'

'I paid twelve,' the man says petulantly.

'Got a receipt, have you?' Tom asks in the same light but firm tone.

'No ... but—'

'Then you ain't got no rights, mate. I suggest you take this and be grateful for it.' Tom thrusts a ten-pound note in the man's face.

The man glares at Tom, then at me, then he dumps the dog unceremoniously on the table, snatches the note from Tom's hand, and storms off.

I grin at Tom. 'That was amazing. Well done.'

Tom shrugs. 'Ars— I mean, idiot.'

'Nah, I think you were right the first time.' I wink at Tom and he grins back at me. 'I think we make quite a team,' I say, holding out my hand for him to shake, but instead Tom takes hold of my hand and kisses the back of it.

'I am only here to serve you, m'lady,' he says, bowing.

'Oh Lord, don't *you* start with all that nonsense,' I tell him.

'Aw, I think it's sweet,' Tiffany says, grinning at the two of us. 'Tom is quite the hero after saving Charlie on that roof. He could be Prince Charming to your Cinderella.'

'Tiffany,' I say, blushing furiously, 'I'm hardly Cinderella, am I? This isn't some rags-to-riches fairy tale.'

'I dunno.' Tom winks. 'It *is* a bit of pantomime at times living in this castle. Talk of the devil, here comes the villain of the piece.'

I look over to see Arthur walking towards our stall.

'Aw, that's not fair,' I whisper to Tom. 'Arthur is a lovely man and you know it.'

'Yeah, I know,' he says, digging me gently in the ribs with his elbow. 'I'm only kidding.'

'How's it going, Arthur?' I ask as he arrives at our stall. 'Have we made a profit?'

'Oh, we've done very well out of this. Very well indeed,'

160

Arthur says, smiling for once. 'I won't have the final figures until later, but I must admit although I wasn't keen on this idea when you first suggested it, I now stand corrected. It seems there are a lot of people who are very keen on buying other people's junk. I had no idea.'

'I'm pleased you're pleased,' I tell him. 'I think it's been a great day. Everyone seems very happy.'

'Everybody's certainly smiling on this stall!' Benji says, joining us now. 'What *have* you all been up to?' he asks, lifting his hat so he can see us better. 'You look like you've all been on the happy juice!'

I turn to Tom and find he's looking at me with a similarly affectionate expression as I am him.

'It's behind you,' Tom calls suddenly.

As everyone turns around to see what he means, I feel Tom's hand gently caress the small of my back, but he's so fast that by the time everyone has turned back again his hand is casually running itself through his dark hair.

'Pantomime joke,' he explains to the others. 'Isn't that right, Amelia? Or should I call you ... Cinders?'

Twenty-two

'Benji, can I ask you something?' I say one evening as Benji and I sit at the top of my tower watching the sun go down over the sea. Benji had brought along a bottle of Pino Grigio to celebrate the fact that at last the renovations on the stables are nearing completion and we've just set a date for the grand opening in two weeks' time.

'Anything, sweetie; you know that,' Benji says laconically, as he stretches out on the deckchairs we've borrowed from the castle grounds, so we can sit up here together and wait for the stars to appear in the clear night sky above us.

I've just put Charlie to bed, so it's time to relax at last.

'Do you believe in ghosts?'

Benji's eyes open wide. 'That I was not expecting. I thought you were going to ask me something about Tom!'

'Tom? Why would I ask you something about him?' I try to keep my voice as steady as possible, but Benji isn't fooled for a moment.

'Really?' he says, looking over the top of his glass. 'We're playing that game, are we?'

'I really don't know what you're referring to,' I say in my most refined voice, then I grin.

'I've seen you whenever he's around – you go all coy.'

'I do not!'

'Yes, you do; your cheeks go pink, just here,' Benji reaches across and gently touches the centre of my cheek, 'and you go all Princess Diana.'

'What on earth does that mean?'

Benji tips his head forward and looks up at me with a doe-eyed expression, then he bats his eyelids.

'I *do not* do that!' I say, laughing at him.

'Well, maybe not quite that bad, but it's similar. You like him, don't you?' Benji asks, studying the contents of his wine glass thoughtfully.

'Maybe . . . ' I admit reluctantly. 'Just a bit.'

'I thought so.' Benji gets up and begins to examine the collection of shells that Charlie keeps on one of the window sills from his many visits to the beach. 'I'm overjoyed for you both. Tom is a top guy.'

'There's nothing going on yet,' I insist.

'*Yet* being the operative word!' Benji says triumphantly. 'Sorry, I'm teasing you. It's nice you've found someone. Like I said, I'm pleased for you. You deserve to be happy.' He turns to examine Charlie's shells again.

'Benji, is something wrong?' I ask quietly, sensing it might be. Benji has behaved oddly before when we've talked about Tom. It was almost as if . . . No, it couldn't be . . . I was stupid to even think it. But it did seem like he might be a tiny bit jealous.

'No, of course not,' Benji says, turning to look at me again. 'Why would it be?'

'No reason.' I shake my head, feeling relieved. Benji and I

163

are just friends. There's nothing more to our relationship than that. There had been a time once, before we moved to the castle, when Benji had been spending a lot of time with us that I'd wondered briefly if it might develop into something else, but I'd quickly realised that my feelings for him were not of a romantic nature at all. I thought he was great: funny, smart, kind and articulate. But I simply didn't find him attractive – not in *that* way, anyway – and I was pretty sure Benji felt the same way about me.

'Charlie sure has a lot of shells now, eh?' Benji says. 'He's quite the conchologist. Shell collector,' Benji explains when I look puzzled. 'That's what they're called.'

'Ah, I see. Well, there's a word I didn't know.'

'I'm here to educate,' Benji says, grinning. He sits back down on his deckchair and picks up his glass. 'I'm glad you and Tom are getting on well,' he says. 'It was one of the reasons I suggested he come here.'

'It was?' I'm shocked to hear this.

'Yeah, I've known Tom a good few years now. I had a feeling the two of you might hit it off.'

'We're hardly hitting it off – we're just going down the pub together on Friday.' I slap my hand over my mouth. I haven't told anyone about this yet.

'Oh, you are, are you?' Benji says, raising his eyebrows in exaggerated fashion. 'The *pub* ... And they say romance is dead.'

'It's not a date or anything,' I say hurriedly. 'Tom thinks it would be a good idea if I got to know some of the locals a bit better – and apparently the pub on a Friday night is the best place to do that. We talked about it at the sale, and then he asked me properly yesterday.'

'I've heard the pub is pretty busy on a Friday night. I guess you'll get to know a few more of the locals that way than only the school mums, and Hetty and her WI members.'

'That's the idea. You're welcome to come along too if you'd like to?' I offer.

'No, no,' Benji says, dismissively waving his hand at me. 'I don't want to cut into your one-on-one time with Prince Charming . . .'

'Don't you start calling him that too. Tiffany seems to think we're all living in some sort of fairy tale here, with me as Cinderella and Tom as my Prince Charming.'

'What does that make me, then, your fairy godmother?' Benji pretends to wave a magic wand. 'You shall go to the ball, Cinders! Or is that the Chesterford Arms in this version?'

'I think you'd make an admirable fairy godmother,' I tell him. 'You've helped me out enough over the last few months. I don't know what I'd have done without you.'

I reach over and pat Benji on the arm, and unlike the last time I'd done this, this time I don't feel that my actions and words might be misconstrued. Something has very definitely changed between us. But I feel it's only for the good.

Benji looks at my hand and then at me, and I get the feeling he wants to tell me something.

'What's wrong, Benji?' I ask gently. 'Is there something you want to say?'

Benji hesitates, and then he smiles. 'Yes, what was it you were going to ask me earlier? Something about ghosts?' After expertly changing the subject, he takes a large gulp from his wine glass.

'Oh yes, I quite forgot.' With all the talk about Tom we'd gone completely off course. 'I asked you if you believed in them.'

'That's right, so you did.' Benji puzzles for a few moments. 'Hmm . . . well, I've never actually seen one. But then I don't *dis*believe in things just because I haven't seen them – why do you ask?'

I tell Benji everything that's happened so far at the castle – from the unexplained noises in the stables to the ghostly goings-on in the Blue Bedroom. 'And then that man brought back a stuffed dog to the courtyard sale because he said his wife thought it was haunted.'

'How very odd – how can a stuffed dog be haunted?'

'I have no idea. But never mind that, what about all the other things – the noises and stuff? And what about Charlie? He seems to think that it's all very real. He even speaks to them . . .'

'Does he?'

'Yes. And you know Charlie pretty well by now; he doesn't lie, does he?'

Benji thinks about this. 'No. He's an honest kid. But then he has had a lot of upheaval in his life just lately, hasn't he?'

'Are you saying you think he's making all this up?'

'No, but the mind is a very clever thing. It can sometimes trick you into thinking something is real even when it's not.'

'I suppose.'

'And I imagine you've both been told a lot of unexplained things happen in a castle such as this from the moment you first came here.'

I shrug. 'Possibly. But I'm not imagining these things, am I? Even Arthur seemed to verify the Blue Bedroom ghost.'

'Seemed to, or did?'

I think about this. 'I guess he didn't actually say he'd seen anything with his own eyes.'

166

'There you go, then.'

'But that doesn't mean it isn't real, does it?'

Benji shakes his head. 'Nope. On the other hand, it doesn't prove anything either.'

'Ooh, you're a tricky one, Fairy Godmother, aren't you?' I say, lifting the half-empty bottle, first to top up Benji's glass and then my own.

'Cinders, you never said a truer word,' Benji says, lifting his glass and toasting me. 'You never said a truer word.'

Twenty-three

'What can I get you?' Tom asks me on Friday night as we enter the pub and weave our way through the throngs of people up to the bar.

'I'll have an orange juice, please,' I say, looking up at him.

Tom pulls a face. 'Really? I can't tempt you into anything stronger?'

I'm not usually a big drinker. In fact, the few glasses of wine I had with Benji the other night was more alcohol than I'd drunk in a very long time.

'All right then, er . . . ' I scan the bottles behind the bar. 'I'll have a gin and tonic, please.'

'Gin and tonic coming right up – any particular type of gin, or for that matter tonic?'

I shake my head. 'Nope, anything is fine.'

Tom pushes himself a little further forward, but doesn't appear to have any difficulty in catching Rachel's eye amongst all the other people waiting to be served at the bar.

While he gets our drinks I take a quick look around. The outside of the Chesterford Arms looks much like any other country pub might – a small whitewashed building with a thatched roof and a pub sign hanging outside with a painting of a castle – my castle – on it.

Inside the décor is modern and clean with occasional prints of picturesque Northumbrian vistas hanging on the ivory-coloured walls. There are exposed timbers above me with a few named silver tankards hanging from them – presumably for the regulars – and hanging from the wall timbers are various brass objects to add to the traditional feel.

The pub is so crammed right now that there's not a seat to be had anywhere – from the cosy little booths around the outside walls to the bar stools that surround the large U-shaped bar.

'Excuse me, love,' a man says, pushing past me. 'Oh, Lady Chesterford – I do beg your pardon; I didn't recognise you.'

'Hello, Bill, how are you?' I ask as Bill stares in astonishment at me. 'And it's Amelia, remember?'

'Yes ... yes, of course. I'm very well, Lady ... I mean, Miss Amelia. What are you doing down here?'

'I'm having a drink with Tom,' I say, gesturing back to where Tom is still waiting patiently at the bar.

'*Oh, I see ...* ' Bill winks at me and taps his nose secretively. 'Say no more.'

'No, Bill, it's not like that,' I protest. But suddenly I'm not the only one to be recognised.

'Bill, mate!' a burly man says, slapping Bill on the back. 'How goes it? You finished that moneysucker up at the castle yet? Has her ladyship flushed any more money down the drain this week?'

'Er ... ' Bill, looking horrified, glances wildly from the man to me and then back again.

'What's up, mate?' the man asks him. 'Dodgy curry? Hello,

love,' he says jovially to me. 'Haven't seen you around here before.'

'Les, let me introduce you,' Bill says, grinning manically. '*This* is Amelia – the new Lady Chesterford.'

'Hi, Amel— What? Bloody hell-fire, I mean … oh boll— Greetings, your majesty,' Les says finally, and in his panic he gives a small bow.

'Amelia is just fine,' I say, grinning at him. 'Pleased to meet you, Les; and what do you do around here?'

'I … I'm a farmer.'

'Oh, what sort? I mean, what do you specialise in?'

'Livestock,' Les says, finally finding his feet on a topic he feels comfortable with. 'Cows and pigs mainly. We have a few chickens, too.'

'Organic?' I ask, an idea unexpectedly forming.

'Oh, yes. It's the only way forward these days.'

'I totally agree. I'd like to offer as much organic produce as I can when we open up the new tea room. I've been thinking about offering some organic produce as part of our gift shop, too – you know, like a small farm shop?'

'I do indeed,' Les says, his eyes lighting up. 'I'd be more than happy to provide some samples for you, if you were thinking of sourcing the food locally.'

'I wouldn't consider doing anything less,' I tell him, smiling. I pull one of the new business cards I've had printed from my bag. 'Here,' I say, passing it to Les, 'give me a call over the weekend and we can talk business. In fact, if you know of anyone who grows organic fruit and vegetables, too, then perhaps you can ask them to call me as well.' I give him a second card.

Les looks at the cards and nods his head. 'I'll certainly do that. Sorry about before,' he says apologetically.

'Already forgotten,' I say, smiling.

'I didn't bring you down here to pass out business cards,' Tom says, pushing his way back through the crowd with our drinks. 'This is supposed to be relaxation on a Friday night.'

'Ah, you hush, young Tom,' Les says. 'If the lady wants to do a bit of business in her local, then I'm not going to complain. I'll speak with you soon then, miss,' he says, lifting his half-empty pint of beer at me. 'And I'll leave you to your *relaxation*!'

'Me too,' Bill says. He puts his empty glass down on a nearby table. 'Nature calls!'

'See you Monday, Bill,' I call as he makes his way in the direction of the toilets.

Tom grins and passes me my drink while both Les and Bill disappear into the throng of people. 'I see you've already made some new friends, then?'

'Hardly. I already know Bill, and Les is hopefully going to supply us with organic meat for the castle.'

'But what about the suppliers we already have?'

'How do you mean?'

'The ones Dorothy uses to supply the food she cooks our dinners with.'

'That's different. This is for larger consumption and retail purposes. That would be counted as domestic use.'

'You have an answer for everything, don't you?' Tom says, grinning at me.

'No. I just know what I want, that's all.'

Tom raises his eyebrows at me. 'Oh, really . . . '

I take a sip of my drink. 'Gosh, that's strong!'

'Double,' Tom says matter-of-factly. 'Saves going up to the bar again so soon. It's manic in here tonight.'

171

'I hope you're not trying to get me drunk?' I say, eyeing up my glass.

'Now why would I want to do that?' Tom asks innocently. 'You are my boss, after all.'

'Hmm ... Pay rise?' I ask, playing him at his own game.

'That could be one reason, I suppose.'

'Hello, Tom,' a soft voice interrupts us. 'How are you?'

'Molly! Hi,' Tom says to a pretty brunette. 'I'm very well, thank you – and yourself?'

'Always better for seeing you, you know that.'

Goodness, Tom's like a bright lantern beaming out into the darkness of Chesterford. But as opposed to attracting moths and other insects, the females of the village all seem to be drawn to him, fluttering their eyelashes instead of their wings.

'This is Amelia,' Tom says, turning back to me as I smile to myself at my analogy. 'She runs the castle now.'

'Ah, the infamous Lady Chesterford,' Molly says, half smiling at me. 'I had no idea you were so ... young.'

'Amelia is just fine, thanks. Lovely to meet you, Molly. Are you local to Chesterford?'

'Lived here all my life ... sadly,' Molly says, rolling her eyes. 'Never quite escaped ... yet.' She looks at Tom as though he might be the one who could enable this escape. Likely on his white charger, while wearing chainmail and carrying a sword.

I smile. Why did everyone, including my own son, see Tom as some sort of hero?

'And what do you do here?' I ask, ignoring Molly's dig at Chesterford.

'I'm a mobile beauty therapist and hairdresser.'

'Ah ... lovely.'

'Perhaps you'd like me to pop up to the castle sometime?'

she says in a voice that suggests this isn't a genuine offer. 'I'm sure I could fit you in for a few appointments ... I do nails, as well as hair and beauty, and I do a reduced rate for block bookings.'

Cheeky mare! I think, but I politely reply: 'Thank you so much for the offer, but it's not really my thing. I prefer a more natural look.'

'Clearly,' Molly says, looking me up and down.

I'm about to open my mouth, but Tom, suddenly realising what's going on, hurriedly interrupts us. 'Well, it's good to see you, Molly,' he says in a voice that suggests this is the end of their conversation.

'Yes, likewise,' Molly says, smiling back in a sultry fashion at him. 'Perhaps we can catch up next week when you're not so ... bogged down with work?' She glances disdainfully at me.

Even though it takes all my resolve, I keep a dignified silence.

'Yeah, maybe,' Tom says hastily.

'I'll be by the pool table if you can shake off the shackles,' Molly grins, sashaying away so Tom is in no doubt as to her motives. 'You owe me a game.'

'Like I said, maybe another time.'

'Oh, that's right, you have a pool table ... ' I say, looking in the direction of the little room I'd seen when we came in. 'That sounds like fun.'

'Play, do you?' Molly enquires airily, barely glancing at me, her eyes still firmly on Tom.

'Depends – is it the one with lots of red balls, and they keep taking the balls back out of the pockets when you get them in?'

Molly's eyes light up with a mixture of glee and danger. 'Yeah ... something like that. Wanna game?'

'No, Molls,' Tom protests, waving his hand across his throat, 'Amelia doesn't want to play pool – you just heard what she—'

'Sure!' I say firmly over Tom's excuses. 'I'll try anything once. Lead the way, Molly.'

Twenty-four

Molly leads the way over to the room with the pool table in it, then she scribbles our names on the chalk board hanging on the wall to denote we'd like the next game.

The two young men already playing look at us with interest. 'Who's your friend, Molly?' one of them asks.

'Lady Penelope, ain't she?'

'Amelia,' I tell them, ignoring Molly.

'Cool,' one of them says as he watches the other one take his shot. 'You new around here, Amelia?'

'Fairly new,' I tell him, while watching what's going on on the table.

'You live local?'

'At the castle.'

'Ooh, fancy, at the castle. What do you make to the new bird up there? Tom here seems to think she's all right – don't ya, Tom? Always singing her praises.'

'Probably trying to get into her knickers, more like.' The man at the table misses his shot and he stands up. 'Am I right, Tom?'

My face goes bright red, and I daren't even look at Tom.

'You pair of numpties – this *is* the new bird, ain't it?' Molly says, pointing a pool cue at me. '*This* is Lady bloody Chesterford!'

Both the men stand upright – as if to attention. I half think they might salute, so I'm very relieved when they don't.

'Oh, I'm so sorry, m'lady, I didn't recognise you,' one of them says, looking mortified.

'Yeah, me either,' the other one says. 'I didn't expect you to look like that ... I mean, you ... you're fit, ain't ya?'

His friend nudges him hard in the ribs.

'Oi! Well, she is, Paul,' he insists as if I can't hear them.

I have to smile. 'Look, please don't stand on ceremony like this. I'm not royalty!' I say jokily, trying to defuse this awkward situation. 'I'm not a lady or even a countess – I'm just Amelia.'

'Me dad worked up at the castle for many years,' the one called Paul says, 'and me granddad before him. They wouldn't dream of calling one of the Earls or Countesses by their first name, would they, Kev?'

'Yeah,' Kev agrees. 'My aunt and me mum used to be maids up there until a few years ago. Me and my cousins was always taught to be polite to His Lordship.'

'I see nothing wrong in being polite,' I tell them. 'But would you have found the last Earl or his wife down the local pub about to have a game of pool?' I ask, grabbing a pool cue from the rack.

They shrug. 'Doubt it,' Paul says.

'Right, well in that case, just for tonight I am simply Amelia, not Lady Chesterford, or any other titled name, for that matter.'

I bend down over the pool table, and line up my shot. Then

I hit the white ball hard with my cue; the white ball knocks cleanly into the black ball, which shoots off up the table at an angle and rolls neatly into the corner pocket without touching the sides. 'Now,' I say, standing up and looking around at the others, 'who's up for a game?'

'I thought you said she couldn't play?' Molly moans at Tom as they watch me win my tenth game on the trot.

'I never said that,' Tom says, watching me with interest. 'I said she didn't *want* to play.'

'Who's next?' I ask, as the black ball rolls once more into the pocket with a satisfying click.

Over the last ninety minutes or so, the small pool room has become more and more crammed with people all intrigued by the exploits of the lady of the manor.

I've been challenged by those that thought they could beat me, bought drinks by those that had lost to me, and applauded by those that were pleasantly surprised by what they were seeing.

'Perhaps you'd better take a break?' Tom whispers into my ear as I chalk my cue up for the next game.

'Why? I'm on a roll!' I cry happily, as someone again high-fives me as they squeeze past in the small room.

'All the more reason to go out on top, then,' Tom says. 'Plus you've had quite a bit to drink now.'

It was true, I had had quite a few alcoholic beverages. Apparently, the house rules are that the loser of the game has to offer to buy the winner a drink, and even though I'd politely begun refusing drinks after my second win, my opponents seem to take offence if I don't allow them to buy me a drink, and even more so if I appear to not be drinking it. Therefore,

I'd had to down a fair few more glasses of alcohol than I'm used to, in a relatively short space of time.

'You know something,' I say, my speech slurring a little, 'it is getting harder to see the balls. I thought it was the light.' I gesticulate with my cue to the long low light that hangs over the pool table.

'Careful,' Tom says, grabbing my hand, 'or you *will* have a problem with the light if you break it.'

He gently prises the cue from my hand.

'I think the champ has had enough for one night,' he tells the assembled room. 'She retires unbeaten.'

I take a long slow bow as the room applauds. But I seem to have difficulty getting back up again as the floor starts to swim in front of my eyes.

'Need a hand?' Tom asks, taking hold of my shoulders and helping me back up again.

'No, I is fine,' I say, waving him away as I wobble on the spot.

'Glad to hear it,' Tom says, taking hold of my shoulders again, but this time he guides me out of the room, past more handshakes and high-fives along the way.

'Night, Rachel!' Tom calls, to a tired-looking Rachel behind the bar. 'Some evening, eh?'

'Looks like you've got your hands full there, Tom,' Rachel says, smiling sympathetically at him.

'He said he didn't want to get me drunk!' I tell Rachel, pulling away from Tom and heaving myself up to the bar where I hold on for dear life. 'But . . . shush,' I say putting my finger to my lips and whispering now. 'Guess what?'

'What?' Rachel asks, now grinning at me.

'He did!'

'Come on, you; we've got a long walk home,' Tom says,

taking me by the shoulders again and guiding me towards the door.

'Why, it's not far to the castle?'

'With you like this, that is gonna be one long hill we've got to climb – believe me!'

The walk back up to the castle does indeed seem to take longer than usual, and I'm glad of Tom to steady me as we make our way home.

'Did you ever think you'd be living in a castle?' I ask him as we make our way slowly towards the main gates. 'I didn't,' I continue, not waiting for his answer. 'It really is like something from a fairy tale, isn't it?'

'A bit, I guess,' Tom says, steadying me once again as I veer towards some flower beds. I feel him tighten his hold on me where our arms are linked together. 'Only with less goblins and fairy godmothers.'

'Indeed!' I say, waggling my finger at him. 'That is very true regarding the goblins, but we do have a fairy godmother in our midst, you know?'

'Do we?'

'Yes, we do! Can you guess who it is? It's your friend and mine,' I continue without a break, 'Benji!'

'Why is Benji a fairy godmother?' Tom asks with interest as he guides me up the hill.

'Because . . . ' I say slowly, trying to form my words correctly. 'One of the reasons he sent you here to Chesterford was so *we*,' I wave my hand madly between the two of us, 'could meet!'

Tom looks surprised to hear this.

'But *shush* . . . ' I say, holding my finger up in front of my mouth. 'It's a secret.'

'Right . . . ' Tom nods. 'Did Benji tell you this?'

'He did. I think he wanted to tell me something else as well . . . ' My brow furrows. 'But he didn't in the end.'

'What sort of something?' Tom asks calmly as I struggle to walk and talk at the same time.

'Dunno!' I hold up both my hands, and regret it as I nearly fall over.

Tom grabs me, we straighten up and begin to walk again.

'Are you glad Benji asked me to come here to Chesterford?' Tom asks so quietly I can barely hear him in my intoxicated state.

'Of course I am!' I reply in a loud voice. 'You're my mate now, aren't you?' I pat Tom's arm that's linked with mine.

'I am indeed,' Tom says. 'A good mate.'

'A *very* good mate,' I agree, nodding. 'The best.'

'Do you think there might ever be more to it than that?' Tom asks softly.

'More to life?' I ask, mishearing him. 'You know I was going to ask you the same thing. I think we might have ghosts at the castle, what do you reckon to that?'

Tom sighs and his grip on me weakens slightly. 'Ghosts – really? Have you seen some?'

'Nooo! But I've heard things.'

'What sort of things?' Tom asks, his voice returning to its normal pitch.

I tell Tom as much as I can currently remember about my peculiar experiences.

'Old buildings make a lot of strange noises,' he says as I sway a little on the path once more and he quickly straightens me up again. 'Are you sure it isn't just that?'

I shake my head vehemently. And quickly regret it, when for

the next few seconds I can't actually see properly as the world of Chesterford spins before me.

'Definitely not. Charlie speaks to them, you know.'

'Yes, you told me. But I thought we agreed it could just be an imaginary friend he's speaking to.'

'I thought that, but now *I've* started hearing things too . . . strange things.'

'I know,' Tom reminds me patiently. 'You just told me about those.'

'Ah, yes, so I did.' I nod slowly, comprehending this fact. 'Anyway, Charlie says if I believe in them properly, then they'll show themselves to me.'

'The ghosts will?'

'Uh-huh.'

'And you want that, do you?'

I think about this. 'Not sure.'

'Hmm, well I know I wouldn't want a load of ghosts suddenly turning up at the foot of my bed one night,' Tom says, propping me against one of the castle gate posts while he proceeds to open up the side gate for us.

'They wouldn't do that – would they?' I ask him apprehensively. 'Well, maybe Percy might, I suppose.'

'Who's Percy?'

I tell him what Arthur had told Tiffany and me about the ghost that supposedly haunts the Blue Bedroom, while Tom manoeuvres us both through the gate and then locks it up again behind us.

When I get to the bit about Arthur describing the way Percy died, Tom laughs.

'You have a nice laugh,' I tell him, my usual inhibitions completely dulled by the amount of alcohol I've ingested tonight.

'Thank you,' Tom says, turning to look at me as he links arms with me again. 'So do you.'

'You're only saying that because I just did!'

Tom shakes his head. 'On the contrary, I saw you laugh an awful lot tonight, and smile – you should smile more, you know.'

I grin inanely at Tom.

'Perhaps not quite like that.'

'I guess I got out of the habit,' I tell him after we've walked on in silence for a bit, under the great portcullis, and into the main courtyard – lit prettily tonight with the new up-lighters that Joey had fitted a few days ago, so that now all the castle walls, both outside and in, are lit with a soft yellowy glow as soon as dusk falls.

'Out of the habit of what?'

'Smiling. Until I came here life wasn't that great. I didn't have much to smile about.'

'I know.'

'How do you know? I've never told you.'

'Benji.'

'Ah, Benji again ... I should have known. But Benji only met me a little while before I moved here. He doesn't know everything.'

'I never said he did.'

'Do you want me to tell you about it?'

'Do you want to tell me?' Tom asks in that same soft voice he had before, as we stand in front of the door that leads up to the top of my tower.

'Sometime ... ' I say, looking up to the window behind which my bedroom, and more importantly right now my comfortable bed, is waiting. 'Right now I think bed is calling. For me!' I add hurriedly when Tom doesn't speak. 'I didn't mean—'

'It's okay,' Tom says, smiling at me. 'I know what you meant. However, I think getting you up those spiral stairs isn't going to be easy.'

'Why?'

'Stand on one leg,' Tom suggests.

'What?'

'Stand on one leg. Let's see what your balance is like. Even if I can get you up the stairs, there is no way I'm leaving you. If you need to come down in the night – you'll fall to your death.'

'Pah! Fall to my death. I'm perfectly fine,' I say, lifting my right leg off the ground and immediately toppling to the side. Luckily Tom is prepared, and deftly catches me.

'See,' he says. 'Dangerous. Who's babysitting Charlie?'

'Dorothy.'

'Right, let's see if we can at least get you up the stairs, then I'll relieve Dorothy and bed down on your sofa for the night.'

'Really, Tom, stop fussing; I'll be fine.'

'Let's try the stairs first, then we can re-evaluate the situation if need be, okay?'

With much grumbling – from me – Tom and I attempt to navigate the narrow stone staircase. I go first, and Tom follows up the rear – literally one at a time, when he has to put his hand on my bum to stop me falling back down on top of him.

'Sorry,' we both say at once. Then we go on in an embarrassed silence for a few steps – until finally we reach the floor that holds Charlie's and my bedroom.

I move towards the next flight of stairs, but Tom stops me.

'Whoa, lady, where do you think you're going?' he whispers so as not to wake Charlie.

'To see Dorothy, and check everything is all right,' I reply in an equally hushed tone.

'Your journey stops right here.' Tom barricades himself across the entrance to the next set of steps. 'If you go up there, you've got to come back down again to go to bed. Going up with you has been bad enough; I don't want to think what will happen if we try to attempt going down.'

'But . . . ' I say quietly, looking up again.

'Is everything all right down there?' I hear a low voice ask. 'I thought I heard you coming back in.'

'Benji, what are you doing here?' I ask, recognising his voice at once. 'Where's Dorothy?'

'Don't worry, everything is fine.' I hear Benji's footsteps on the stairs and Tom stands aside to let him through. 'Dorothy had a headache so she called me and asked if I'd take over. I've been writing all night. I haven't heard a peep from Charlie. Are you all right?' he asks, looking at me. 'You don't look too good.'

'I'm just fine,' I say, trying to stand up proudly, but failing miserably when I begin swaying immediately.

'Amelia has had a *very good* night,' Tom says, winking at Benji. 'But she needs to get to bed and sleep it off.'

Benji nods with immediate understanding. 'That sounds like a good plan. Shall we help you to your bed?'

'I am quite capable, thank you,' I reply stoutly, but again, to my annoyance, my legs fail me. 'Perhaps one of you *could* escort me?'

'Probably best if you take her, Benj,' Tom says, winking at Benji.

'Why do you two keep winking at each other?' I ask as Benji comes over and takes my arm. 'It's most disconcerting.'

'Goodnight, Amelia,' Tom whispers, ignoring my question. 'I'll see you tomorrow. Sleep well.'

*

I have an erratic night's sleep.

The first time I awake, I can't have been asleep that long because I can hear Benji and Tom talking upstairs as I make my way across the tiny hexagonal hallway towards the bathroom.

As I sit on the toilet rocking to and fro deciding whether I'm going to throw up or something else, I can hear them discussing who will stay with me tonight.

'Look, I know you like to be the hero,' Benji says to Tom, 'but I'm perfectly capable of looking after her.'

'Yeah, I know,' Tom says, 'but I feel partially responsible for letting her get in the state she's in. I think I should stay.'

'Tom,' Benji says now, 'I can assure you that when Amelia wakes up the last person in the world she's going to want to see is you – she'll feel and look as rough as a badger's arse; she really won't want to be worrying how her hair is or whether she's got any make-up on – you must know she's keen on you?'

There's silence, which I can only assume is Tom nodding, because Benji then says, 'Good, now let me do the babysitting for both of them. You know Amelia will be safe with me – you've no worries on that score. You can come and check on her when she's all lady of the manor again, okay?'

'Sure, thanks, Benj – I owe you.'

'Nonsense, we both know that is not true.'

The next time I awake, the tower is in silence. Tom must have left, and Benji presumably has bedded down on my sofa.

I have some random thoughts about whether he's found spare blankets and a pillow, before I feel myself drifting off to sleep again.

The third time I awake, I wonder for a few moments

whether it's time to get up yet – but then I realise the little bit of light that's filtering through my curtains is only dawn breaking, so I turn over in my bed. Oh Lord, my head is already starting to pound.

I reach for the water that I vaguely remember Benji leaving on my bedside table last night. Then I try to take a sip without sitting up fully, but that doesn't work, so I have no choice but to sit up.

But as I take my first thirst-quenching sip, I very nearly drop the glass – because suddenly I'm aware of someone standing at the end of my bed.

I blink a couple of times, wondering if I'm still asleep – but the figure doesn't move. She just stares at me.

'Who are you?' I ask, my brain not really computing the absurdity that someone should be in my room in the early hours of the morning.

But the young girl is silent.

'Are you lost?' I ask calmly, noting as I stare back at her that the girl is wearing a long white smock over her shabby-looking dress, and heavy leather lace-up boots.

The girl shakes her head.

'Are you Ruby?' I suddenly ask, not really knowing where that question has come from. My brain still feels drenched with alcohol, and my head is pounding with dehydration.

To my surprise, she nods. Then she smiles at me and waves her hand before disappearing in front of my eyes.

'Amelia,' I say to myself as I place my glass of water back down on the table, and my head back down on to my cool pillow, 'you must never drink this much alcohol again – do you hear? Never.'

Twenty-five

The next time I open my eyes, the sunlight is much stronger through my curtains, and I know this time it's time to wake up.

I try to sit up, but my head is still pounding, and so I reach for the water again. I gulp down what's left in the glass, and then I pull myself into a proper sitting position – and try to recall the night's events.

There had been the pub ... yes, I remember most of that. I smile as I recall my victories at the pool table, and how no one had expected it of the lady of the manor. And then there was the walk home with Tom ... It's a little hazy, but I remember bits and bobs of our journey together. Then we'd climbed the spiral staircase – ooh, that cheeky monkey had had his hand on my bum – I feel my cheeks redden at the memory.

Then Benji had been here when we'd got back ... I wonder if he's still here. I glance at my watch – golly, it's 11 a.m. already, I have slept in. I'd better check on Charlie.

I take another sip from the glass. Damn, it's empty; I've gulped that down quickly, and it's as I stare at the empty glass that I remember ... Ruby.

That must have been a dream – surely? Yes, I had an awful lot to drink last night – my mind must have been playing tricks on me. Perhaps I was still dreaming and never even awoke to have that drink of water . . .

But then why had my glass been half empty just now when I'd gone to take a drink from it? If I had been dreaming, then my glass would have been full.

I shake my head. *Gah, why won't my brain work properly? It feels all fuzzy.*

I decide to get up and see what's going on upstairs. I look down at what I'm wearing – pyjamas, great; at least I'm decent if anyone is still in the tower.

Wait, how had I got into my PJs last night? I don't remember putting them on. But then I don't remember quite a few things about the last part of yesterday.

I check on Charlie's room, which as I expect at this time of the morning is empty. He's probably taking advantage of the fact I'm late up and is upstairs watching TV. So I quickly freshen myself up in the bathroom and then head slowly downstairs to the kitchen to put the kettle on. Then I climb just as carefully back up two flights of steps to the sitting room.

It's funny – the awkwardness of this multi-storey living hasn't bothered me at all before. Now that I'm feeling under par, all this up and down stairs seems such hard work.

'Morning,' Benji says from my sofa as I enter the top floor of the tower. 'I thought I heard you up. Making tea, are we?'

'Yeah – well, trying to. Where's Charlie?'

'I sent him off with Joey for the morning, so you could sleep in.'

'Thanks, what's Joey doing today?'

'They've taken Chester for a walk along the beach, I believe. You might see them if you look out of the window.'

I walk over to the window, but I can't see Charlie or Joey in amongst the several groups of people walking their dogs along the beach this morning.

'How are you feeling?' Benji asks.

'Rough.'

'I thought you would be. Tom said you had a fair few yesterday.'

'Yeah ... how ... how did I get to bed last night?' I ask tentatively. 'Everything from the pub onwards is a bit hazy.'

'Tom brought you back and managed to get you up the stairs, and then I helped you into your bed.'

I look down at my pyjamas.

'Yes, I helped you into those as well – you did most of it, mind,' Benji insists when he sees the look of dismay on my face. 'I was very discreet.'

'Oh good,' I say, still feeling embarrassed. 'I'm sorry I caused so much trouble, Benji, and that you had to stay over.'

Benji shrugs. 'Not a problem. Besides, you have much better views here than I do from my room. I enjoyed seeing the stars last night and the sunrise this morning – nature at its very best!'

'Unlike me,' I reply dismally. 'I am not at my very best right now.'

'Aw, don't fret it,' Benji says, putting his book down and coming over to me. 'We all have our off days.' He puts his arm around me, and the simple act feels only comforting as he pulls me closer. 'How about I pop downstairs and make you that cup of tea – lots of sugar this morning?'

'Two will be plenty, thanks.'

189

'Two it is. Too early for a fry-up?'

I pull a face. 'Yeah, I'm not quite up to that just yet.'

'I thought so. Back in a jiffy.'

I go back over to the open window and breathe in the fresh sea air that's filtering steadily through it, and my queasiness is eased temporarily.

I hate being a burden to people, but that's just what I feel like I'd been last night. I should have limited myself to a couple of drinks, but then I would have offended people, and I hate doing that too.

Who would have thought that my biggest dilemma so far since taking on this castle would be accepting drinks from the locals down the village pub!

'One cup of builders' tea,' Benji says, appearing at the top of the stairs with two mugs. 'Here, get that down you; you might start to feel a bit more normal again then.'

I sip slowly on the mug of tea.

'Talking of builders, do you know some of Bill's gang are in this morning?' Benji says amiably.

'On a Saturday?'

'Yup, apparently they're running a bit behind.'

'I knew it!'

'Don't get your knickers in a twist – the red ones,' Benji winks, and I grimace, that's exactly the colour I'd been wearing last night. 'They're only a day or two behind. That's why they're working over the weekend to get back on schedule. I've never seen such well-behaved builders. You certainly have them under control.'

I shrug. 'I made it very clear to Bill that the work must not over-run, and that we will be opening on the thirtieth of June come what may. Otherwise there will be penalties.'

Benji salutes. 'Yes, sir! Whatever you say, *sir*!'

'Funny,' I reply drolly. 'It's important we get this new venture up and running as soon as possible.'

'Yeah, I know. I think you've done a marvellous job since you got here, actually – you've really stepped up.'

'Thanks.'

'Change isn't easy to implement, especially in somewhere as old as this. I think everyone has taken it really well.'

'Perhaps,' I begin when suddenly we hear a commotion coming from the outside. 'What's that?' I ask, looking at Benji.

'No idea.' Benji stands up and heads over to the window that looks over the courtyard.

I follow him.

'It looks like Arthur is talking to one of the builders,' Benji says, still looking out of the window. 'I've no idea why their voices are raised, though. Actually, strike that, it's the builder that's doing all the shouting.'

I watch for a moment and Benji is right, one of Bill's men, who I think is called Ed, appears to be remonstrating with Arthur.

'I'd better go and see what's going on,' I say, putting down my tea.

'But you're not dressed,' Benji says.

I look down. 'Ah, it'll have to do – I'll grab a dressing gown on my way downstairs.'

'Good luck,' Benji calls as I leave the top floor. 'It looks like you're going to need it.'

I hurry down the spiral staircase as fast as I can in my delicate state. Pleased as I exit from the dimly lit tower into the bright sunshine, that I've grabbed a pair of sunglasses on the way down as well as my dressing gown.

'What's going on?' I call as I hurry across the gravel.

'Ah, about time – the organ grinder and not just the aged monkey,' Ed says, glaring at Arthur.

I notice Ed's hands are covered in white plaster, as though he's simply dropped whatever he was doing to come to talk to Arthur.

'Yes, thank you, Ed,' I tell him. 'Arthur?' I ask, looking at him now. 'Would you like to explain?'

'Ask him,' Arthur says grumpily. 'He's the one spouting all the nonsense.'

'Well?' I turn back to Ed.

Ed suddenly looks a tad embarrassed. 'There's been an ... incident,' he says eventually, 'that has meant we've had to down tools.'

'What sort of an incident?' I ask, terrified he's going to say a severed limb, a nasty fall or worse.

'We all heard it,' Ed says, looking shiftily down at the ground.

'Heard what?'

'The horse. The horse neighing, and the sound of its hooves across the floor.' He looks up. 'Except there was no horse – only the sound of it.'

I'm listening intently now. This is exactly what I'd heard in the stables, the day Bill first came to see us.

'Don't talk nonsense, man,' Arthur says. 'Are you still hungover? I heard a load of you were down the pub last night.' He glances at me knowingly, and now it's my turn to look shamefully at the ground.

'Not me,' Ed says, shaking his head. 'I knew I was working this morning, so I was at home watching Netflix. I was, and still am, stone-cold sober. That's why I know what I saw.'

I notice for the first time that Ed's face is almost as white as his hands.

'Saw?' I ask. 'You said you *heard* the sound of a horse.'

'I said *several* of us heard the horse. But only I saw it.'

'Saw what exactly?'

Ed takes a deep breath, and I see along with his pale complexion, he's actually trembling. 'After the weird sounds, we all went back to work. None of us could explain what had happened so we all thought we'd better try and forget about it. But then I saw a man riding a horse.' He looks at me. 'Nothing odd in that, except when the man rides the horse right through the wall you're plastering, then you start to think something isn't quite right.'

'You saw a man ride a horse through a wall?'

'Yeah, one of the new partition walls we've only just put up.'

'What did this man look like?'

'Miss Amelia, I really don't think—' Arthur begins.

'Arthur, *I* really do think,' I warn him. 'Carry on, Ed. Can you describe him?'

Ed nods. 'He was wearing a uniform – like the sort you often see on kids' toy soldiers. You know, like a red jacket and one of them mayor type hats.' He tries to describe what he means by drawing an invisible triangle over his head.

'Do you mean a tricorne?' Arthur asks scornfully.

'Yes, that's exactly what they're called,' I say, nodding. 'What else?' I ask Ed eagerly.

'He was wearing white, maybe cream-coloured breeches and black boots, and he had long hair – braided long hair,' Ed is now the one to sound scornful.

'When would that be the uniform for?' I ask Arthur.

Arthur shrugs.

'Come on, Arthur, I know you know,' I say encouragingly.

'Possibly around the seventeen hundreds,' Arthur says begrudgingly. 'Perhaps a little later.'

'Thank you.' I turn back to Ed. 'And you say he rode his horse right through a wall?'

Ed nods. 'Like I said, the one I was just plastering.'

'You must have seen the ghost of an eighteenth-century soldier,' I tell him. 'What other explanation is there for it?'

'I know,' he says, shaking his head. 'If it had happened to anyone else I wouldn't have believed you – I don't believe in that sort of stuff, never have done. But I know what I saw.'

'Think you saw,' Arthur says.

'*Know* I saw,' Ed repeats.

'I believe you,' I tell Ed. 'I've heard things too since I've been here, and I think I might have seen something as well. I can't be one hundred per cent sure I wasn't dreaming with that one, to be fair,' I say, looking up at the tower. 'But I've definitely witnessed some odd things.'

'Thank you, miss. But the problem is the lads saw me after I'd seen the ... the thing, white as a ghost I was, funnily enough.' He rolls his eyes. 'But the problem is now they won't go back in the building because they think it's haunted.'

'And as I was telling you just a few minutes ago,' Arthur says, 'you can't just down tools because you think you've seen a ghost.'

'Try telling them that,' Ed says. 'They're all scared shi— I mean, they're really spooked by this.'

'But you have a contract,' Arthur says. 'The work must be finished for the opening in two weeks.'

Ed shrugs. 'You'd better get the local priest in, then – perform

194

an exorcism or something. Because we are not setting foot in those stables until you can guarantee no more ghosts.'

Arthur turns to me with a despairing look.

'I don't know about getting the local priest in,' I say, watching as two figures and a dog walk through the castle entrance. 'There might just be another way . . .'

Twenty-six

'Mum!' Charlie calls, running across the gravel to hug me. 'You're all right! Benji said you weren't feeling very well this morning.'

'Yes, I'm fine now,' I tell him. 'Have you had a good walk with Joey?'

'Great, thanks. We saw some Arctic terns, a kittiwake, some guillemots, and I got a new shell for my collection.' He pulls a sand-covered shell proudly from his pocket.

'Excellent!' I examine the shell in his hand.

'So what's going on here, then?' Joey says, looking suspiciously between Arthur, Ed and me. 'Ed, you're as white as a ghost, mate.'

Ed pulls a face.

'Ed has seen what we think is a ghost in the stables this morning,' I tell Joey, expecting him to look as shocked as Ed.

'Ah,' Joey nods, 'that'll be Jasper.'

'Jasper? Who's that?'

'Didn't you tell them this, Arthur?' Joey asks, looking with surprise at Arthur. 'Jasper is the ghost that haunts the stables,'

196

Joey continues when Arthur just shrugs. 'He's this dude from the Battle of Culloden that rides his horse through the castle on occasions. I've heard him a few times, but only seen him once. He usually appears when he's not happy about something. Remember when we moved all that gardening equipment out of the stables and into the new sheds His Lordship bought, Arthur? His Lordship decided he might try keeping horses again,' he says to us when Arthur doesn't respond. 'Not that he ever did. He was like that – always dreaming up new schemes he never followed through. Anyway, when we went to empty the stuff, Jasper went a bit ballistic – it was like the Grand National in there for a while.'

'Why didn't you tell us you knew about this ghost?' I ask Arthur.

'There are ghosts, spirits – whatever you want to call them – everywhere in this castle,' Arthur says stoutly, breaking his silence. 'Bound to be in a building as old as this – stands to reason. Doesn't mean I want to share those details with everyone, does it?'

I shake my head. I'd ask Arthur about this later. Now I had more important things to deal with – like my builders downing tools.

'Charlie,' I say, crouching down next to him expecting to be almost level with his face, but suddenly realising that he's grown since we've been here, and now if I do this he's actually way taller than me, 'do you think you could talk to Jasper for us?'

'Sure,' Charlie says, as though I've simply asked him to talk to Chester. 'What do you want me to say?'

'Can you ask him what the problem is? And if we can solve that problem, would he be kind enough to stay away from the stables until the work there is finished?'

Actually, would he be kind enough to stay away permanently. I don't think it will go down too well when people are tucking into their sandwiches and cups of tea if a soldier suddenly rides his horse through a wall in front of them.

But again, I'll have to deal with that possibility later.

'I can try,' Charlie says. 'He might not appear to me if he doesn't want to, though.'

'But let's at least try,' I say, looking encouragingly up at Ed. *Trying might be enough to get the men back to work ...*

We all head over to the stables, and now we are joined by Benji too, who on seeing the gathering in the middle of the courtyard had come down to find out what was going on.

At least we're not busy with visitors, I think as the motley crew troop across the courtyard towards the stables. *Goodness knows what they'd think with me still in my dressing gown and sunglasses, and Ed with his white face and plaster-covered hands.*

There is a row of builders sitting up against the outside wall of the stables – some looking anxious, some looking pleased they've been given an excuse to stop work.

'The young fella here is going to try and talk to the ghost,' Ed says, looking slightly embarrassed that he even has to utter this phrase to his colleagues.

'Should we come in with you?' I ask Charlie, as Chester darts off for some fuss from the builders.

'Yes, but only you and Chester should come,' Charlie says firmly. 'Chester is fine with ghosts, and they're usually interested in what you've got to say, Mum.'

'Really?' I ask as I put my hand out to the others to stop them following us. 'That's a first.'

Charlie calls Chester, and I follow them into the stables.

If it wasn't for the reason we were actually here, I'd actually feel quite pleased and excited as we enter the building. The stables have been transformed into two brightly lit, modern-looking rooms that, except for a lick of paint, look like they might soon be finished.

'What should I do?' I whisper to Charlie.

'Nothing, I'll ask Jasper if he'll come and speak to us, then we just need to wait and see if he wants to. Jasper?' Charlie calls quietly. 'Would you be so kind as to come and talk to us? We only want to know what's wrong. My mum is here to help you.'

Charlie and I stand in the empty room that's soon to be the gift shop, surrounded by power tools, pots of paint and a half-plastered wall.

After a minute or so of silence, Charlie asks again. 'Please, Jasper – we only want to help.'

Suddenly Chester, who's been wandering around sniffing the floor, stands to attention. His nose points forward and his usually waggy tail is stiff behind him.

I notice the hackles on the back of his neck have risen, too.

'Hello, Jasper,' I hear Charlie say as I'm still looking at Chester. 'Thanks for coming.'

I look at the place where Charlie's gaze is directed, but I can see nothing.

Charlie looks up in the air, and for a moment I think that Jasper must be about ten feet tall, and then I realise he must be still mounted on his horse.

'What's the problem?' Charlie asks. 'Why are you suddenly scaring the builders?'

It's most disconcerting seeing your ten-year-old son talking to an apparently invisible being. It's a bit like listening to someone on the phone: you can only hear one side of the conversation.

'Yep,' Charlie says now. 'Uh-huh ... Are you sure? ... Okay, then, I'll tell Mum.' Charlie turns back to me. 'Did you hear any of that?'

I shake my head.

'Jasper says he was trying to warn the builders there is danger.'

'Danger? Where?'

'In here. Jasper says they've done some work that isn't safe, and if they leave it tragedy will befall the users of this building.'

'Tragedy – what sort of tragedy?'

Charlie laughs. 'Jasper says you ask a lot of questions.'

'I should think I do. He comes here and scares the bejesus out of my workmen, then tells me he only did it to warn us of tragedy, but can't tell us what it is.'

Charlie looks up into the air again.

'Uh-huh, where? ... Okay, sure, I'll tell her that, too. He says there's something else.'

'More tragedy?'

'No – a key.'

'A key?'

'Yeah, he said, find the key – apparently, it could be important to you.'

'Right, so all Jasper has told you is there's going to be tragedy and we need to find a key.'

'What's that?' Charlie asks. 'No, I'm not telling her that.' He shakes his head. 'No way!'

'What? What is he saying now?'

Charlie swallows hard. 'He said a man wouldn't react in the same way you are. He said women are too emotional and shouldn't be left in charge.' I'm proud that Charlie looks mortified to even have to utter these words.

Chester growls next to me as I stare at the empty space that Charlie has been talking to for the last few minutes.

And then I laugh. A laugh so deep and throaty, that even I'm not certain where it's coming from.

'Now I've heard everything,' I say as Charlie stares at me, unnerved by my laughter. 'A sexist ghost. Wonderful!'

'Ruby, what are you doing here?' Charlie asks suddenly, looking to his left side. 'Yeah, he did say that.'

'What's going on?' I ask Charlie. This whole scene is getting stranger by the minute. Not only am I standing in the middle of a building site listening to my son talking to some invisible being, now he's talking to two. If you'd told me a few months ago that this is what I'd be doing in my short-term future – or at any stage in my future, actually – I'd have thought you were high on some illegal substance or other.

'Ruby is saying that Jasper shouldn't be so rude to you, and that she likes that word sexist – she hasn't heard it used before. She wants to know if it means to be rude to women.'

'It means to be derogatory about women,' I tell the empty space next to Charlie. 'To say or think that men are better than women. Because they're not.' I turn and talk to the place where Jasper is supposed to be. 'Woman can do everything men can, and sometimes they do it even better.'

'Jasper is over here now, Mum,' Charlie says, pointing to the right of him. 'He's moved.

'Hello,' Charlie says now to another empty space. 'Who are you?'

'There's three of them now?' I ask, my head spinning.

Charlie appears to be listening to the latest ghost to join the party, then he laughs.

'This is Percy,' he says, holding out his hand in front of him. 'He rarely leaves the Blue Bedroom, apparently, but he wanted to come along and join the fun.'

'Yep, this is certainly fun,' I say sarcastically. 'Welcome, Percy.'

'Percy says he's delighted to meet you at last, and is impressed by your bedroom attire.'

I pull my dressing gown around me a little tighter.

'Thank you, Percy. I do know your story, you know,' I warn him.

'He says he's glad to hear it – he likes to be infamous! Is that like mega famous?' Charlie asks me.

'Sort of. Why are they all here?'

'Why are you all here together?' Charlie asks. He listens and then says, 'They want to back up Jasper's story. Percy says that even though Jasper is a stuck-up fool, and that he's known for telling lies, on this particular occasion he's telling the truth.'

Charlie looks at the place Jasper is, and then back at Percy, and then back at Jasper again. 'They're arguing now,' he tells me.

'Arguing about what?'

'About what Percy said about Jasper being a liar.' He listens again. 'Apparently Jasper insists he died on the battlefield, and Percy is saying he didn't – the truth is he died of pneumonia here at the castle on his way to the Battle of Culloden. What's pneumonia, Mum?'

'Er ... it's a problem with your lungs. It's like a really bad cold where you can't breathe properly.'

'Ah, right, and now Percy is laughing again at what you just said. He's teasing Jasper that he simply died of a common cold.'

'Okay, okay,' I say to the assembled ghosts. 'You can have your arguments in private. Actually, I do have one question for you. Have all the ghosts that haunt the castle died here too?'

Charlie looks at Ruby.

'Yes,' he says. 'To be allowed to haunt somewhere as historically important as this, you have to have died here.'

'What did you die of, Ruby, if you don't mind me asking?' I knew Ruby was a child so it would have to have been something bad for her to have died so young.

Charlie listens, and then he looks sad.

'She died of Spanish influenza,' he says.

'I've heard of that,' I tell Ruby. 'It was an epidemic that spread through Britain during the early part of the twentieth century, I think.'

'Ruby died in 1918,' Charlie says sadly. 'Her father died in battle in the First World War, and then her mother died of the same thing as Ruby, only a few weeks before Ruby passed away.'

'I'm truly sorry to hear that, Ruby.'

'Ruby says thank you.'

'Now then, the rest of you,' I say to our invisible guests, 'perhaps you'd stop bickering for a few moments and tell me what's really going on here. Is this building dangerous?'

'Percy says yes,' Charlie answers for him. 'You should speak to your head builder and have him check it out.'

'Okay, I'll do that; and what about this key?'

'He says you should probably talk to Clara about that.'

'Clara? You mean the former Countess? Is she a ghost here too?'

Charlie listens again – this time to Ruby.

'Ruby says Clara doesn't come out very often as she's very shy. But she's also very beautiful and kind-hearted. She's been very caring to Ruby since she got stuck here.'

'That's good to know, Ruby. I'm pleased someone is looking out for you. So how do I get in touch with this Clara?'

'Percy says he'll have a word.'

'Thanks, Percy.' I'm aware of some movement outside, so I quickly hurry the conversation along. 'Right, now we've had this little chat and I've agreed to get the building checked out and look for this key, can I ask that for now anyway you cease from haunting this building? I'm looking at you in particular, Jasper.'

Well, I hope I am, I think as I glare sternly at an empty space.

But Charlie is silent.

'What's he saying?' I ask.

'He's not saying anything, but the others are trying to persuade him. Okay, he's nodding now. He says yes.'

'Good, thank you, Jasper, and thank you, everyone else, for all your ... help.' I look at Charlie. 'And thank you for speaking with Charlie like you do. It's most appreciated. Perhaps one day I'll be able to see and speak with you all too.'

'Is everything all right?' We hear Benji outside the door. 'Only you've been in there a long time.'

I look at Charlie.

'They've all left now,' he says, looking around.

I nod. 'Yes, we're fine,' I call. 'We're coming out now, Benji.'

But before Charlie and I leave the stables, I stop him.

'Charlie, I must thank you, too,' I tell him. 'I may not have believed you to begin with when you started talking about Ruby, but I certainly do now.'

204

Charlie just nods matter-of-factly. 'I knew you'd come round in the end, Mum.'

We have ghosts at Chesterford Castle, I think as I emerge with Charlie back out into the daylight. It's a prospect I should find extremely worrying, but instead I find to my surprise that it's enormously comforting.

Twenty-seven

'So, I hear you had a bit of a time of it this morning?' Tom says later that day. He's popped over to the tower to see how I'm getting on.

'You could say that. It's not a situation I'd usually choose to deal with when I'm nursing a hangover, but we seemed to get it sorted out to everyone's satisfaction in the end.' I pour Tom some iced orange juice from the jug I have next to me on the table. It's still about the only thing I've been able to stomach since I returned to the tower for some necessary peace and quiet.

Tom smiles.

'What?'

'It's just you and your turns of phrase. You're very business-like when you're dealing with people.'

'What's wrong with that?'

'Nothing,' Tom says, wisely choosing not to pursue this. 'I hear it wasn't just people you were dealing with this morning, though. I gather there might have been some uninvited visitors as well.'

'They weren't uninvited. This is their castle, too – in fact, they've lived here a lot longer than either you or I have.'

'Easy,' Tom says, holding his hands up in defence. 'I was only having a joke – feeling a bit below par today, are you?'

'Sorry. Yes, I am a bit. As you witnessed, I had a lot to drink last night – which I'm really not used to.'

'Yes, I gathered that. Don't worry about it, we've all been there. So, you really saw these ghosts that Benji told me about, then?'

I should have known it would be Benji spilling the beans. I hadn't exactly asked him to be quiet about what had happened in the stables, I'd just assumed it wasn't something he'd be telling everyone about.

'I didn't see them, exactly, but Charlie did.'

'But you heard them?'

'Well, no, Charlie did most of the … translating, I guess you'd call it.'

'Ah, I see; so it was only Charlie who saw and heard them as always. I thought it was actually you this time.'

'No, but I knew they were there.'

'How?'

'By what he was saying. There was no way he could have made up all that stuff.'

'I didn't say he was making it up.'

'No, but I can tell that's what you're thinking.' I take a gulp from my glass. Why was I so agitated today?

'I just find it hard to believe, that's all,' Tom says calmly. 'I know people say ghosts exist, and they've seen them and everything, but I haven't, and until I do you'll bear with me if I appear a little doubtful of their existence.'

'You're entitled to your opinion, of course,' I reply, knowing I probably sound haughty. I don't mean to be off with Tom, but I really couldn't cope with any more confrontation today. 'But what you don't realise is that by saying those things, you're also saying my son is a liar.'

'No, I'm not,' Tom says, shaking his head in dismay. 'I think the world of Charlie, you know that.'

'But you're saying he's making all this up?'

'Not making it up; perhaps *imagining* it is a better word. Charlie is a bright kid, he knows his stuff, but he's also an only child, and only children are renowned for having great and wild imaginations.'

'I'm an only child, and I wouldn't say my imagination is all that great. Far from it, actually; that's why, as you so rightly pointed out, I was good at practical subjects at school.'

'When did I say that?'

'Not long after you arrived here. Up on the field when Arthur had got you chopping wood with an axe. You said I was practical and probably didn't get artistic people.'

'Oh yes, so I did. Perhaps I judged you a little strongly then.'

'Yes, perhaps you did.'

There's an awkward silence in the tower.

'Look, Amelia, I'm sorry if I've upset you,' Tom says eventually. 'I really didn't mean to. I just came here to check you were okay after last night.'

'You haven't upset me; I'm still feeling a little delicate, that's all.'

Tom smiles. 'You were certainly the life and soul last night, that's for sure. I never did ask you how you learned to play pool like that.'

'I worked in a pub for a while. There was a pool table – so when it was particularly quiet – usually weekday

208

lunch-times – the landlord and I would have a game or two. He was in the pub's team, so he was pretty good. He taught me how to play.'

'Did you play in the team, too?'

I shake my head. 'No, they played at night. I had Charlie to look after then. It was after my husband left.'

Tom nods. 'Ah yes, of course. You said last night you'd tell me more about what happened.'

'I did?'

'Yeah, you said there was more to your story than Benji knew.'

'Oh . . . I don't remember saying that. But then I don't really remember a lot after we left the pub.'

This was a bit of a lie; I did remember, but I didn't feel like sharing intimate details about my life with Tom right now.

'Ah, I see.' Tom looks thoughtful for a moment. 'Perhaps I *should* go?' he says, suddenly standing up. 'You'd obviously rather be on your own right now.'

'It might be for the best,' I reply stiffly. 'Thanks for coming up, though. I appreciate it.'

'Sure.' Tom heads towards the stairs. 'Any time you want to pop down to the pub again you just let me know.'

'I'll probably give it a miss for a while, if that's all right with you. I think I've downed enough alcohol to last me a few weeks.'

Tom simply nods, then he turns and lifts his hand briefly, before heading quickly down the stairs.

I put my glass down on the table and sigh. *Looks like I've scared another one off.* Why does this always happen? I meet a perfectly nice guy and then when they start to show an interest I pull on my protective armour and they're forced to leave.

It doesn't matter what they do, I always find a reason to pick

209

a fight, and this time Charlie had been the excuse I needed to push Tom away.

Tom wasn't really having a go at Charlie, I knew that deep down, but made to choose between my son and anyone else, there was no contest. Charlie will always come first in my life. That's something that will never change, whatever we're doing and wherever we're living.

Twenty-eight

The rest of the weekend is a quiet one – well, I choose to make it quiet so I can recover from my hangover.

'How are you feeling this morning?' Benji asks me on Monday, when I've spent most of Sunday in the tower, only venturing out for a walk with Charlie and Chester along the long sandy beach. The walk had certainly blown away a few cobwebs – the weather on Sunday had been gusty and filled with heavy showers, so to get out into the bracing sea air had been a welcome escape for a few minutes, before we'd had to run back home as yet another downpour had dispensed from the dark clouds above us.

'Much better, thanks,' I tell him as I pause on my way to the stables. 'Why does it take so long these days to recover from alcohol? I'm sure it never took this long in my twenties.'

'Ah, that would be one of the joys of ageing,' Benji tells me, smiling. 'That and wrinkles, piles and dodgy knees!'

I laugh. 'Enough! I'm not *that* bad yet.'

'Where are you off to this morning?' Benji asks. 'You look like you mean business wherever you're going. You were

211

marching across this courtyard with quite the look of determination on your face.'

'The stables. I'm meeting Bill there. Apparently he's found out what the problem might be.'

'You mean the problem that Jasper warned you about?'

I love the fact Benji didn't question anything that Charlie and I had told him about the ghosts – unlike Tom.

I hadn't seen Tom since we'd parted on slightly awkward terms on Saturday afternoon. Apparently he'd gone off to visit someone, Dorothy told me when questioned, and he'd be back today.

'Yes, that problem.'

'So he was right, then?'

I shrug. 'I guess I'll find out in a moment.'

'Well, good luck,' Benji says, patting me on the shoulder. 'I get the feeling you might need it.'

'Bill,' I say as I find Bill standing in the new tea room looking up at the ceiling. 'What's happening?'

'Ah, morning, Miss Amelia,' Bill says, turning around to greet me. 'And how are you today?'

I'm sure he's heard all about my exploits at the pub, but I pretend to be unaware the precursor of my recent hangover is likely what he's referring to.

'Wonderful, thank you, Bill. So what's the problem here, then?' I ask, cutting to the chase. 'I'm assuming you've found a problem?'

'First, I can only apologise, miss,' Bill says, looking ashamed, and I assume he's talking about the problem he's found. 'Ed should never have mixed you up in his nonsense on Saturday morning.'

'It's fine, Bill, really,' I begin, but Bill continues.

'No, miss; he's always been a bit of a loose cannon that one. I don't know how he did it, but he got all the others believing in his gibberish too.'

'But—' I try again, keen for Ed not to take the blame for this.

'However,' Bill continues, 'it's just as well you phoned me and asked me to come and check on the building; it turns out we do have something of a problem.'

'We do?' I ask in surprise. Even though I'd been expecting this, it still comes as quite a shock that the ghosts might be right. 'What is it?'

Bill points up at some of the original rafters that I'd insisted we keep in the renovations. 'You see these timbers?' he says. 'Riddled with woodworm.'

'Are they?' I ask, looking up at the timbers. 'I can't see anything. Aren't there usually lots of little holes with woodworm?'

'Not if they've not hatched yet. These beams here have only eggs and larvae in them; there's just a few tiny holes beginning to appear, which mean the worms are just starting to hatch. It's possible when we originally checked this there were no holes at all. It's easily missed.'

'So what would have happened if we hadn't found it?' I ask, still staring up at the ceiling.

'Not much to begin with, but eventually the beams would have weakened and then subsequently collapsed.'

'Collapsed? What, with no warning?'

'Again, it's possible – but I'm sure someone would have noticed the holes before it got to that stage.'

'But what if they hadn't? What if one of those beams had collapsed when we had people in here? What if the whole ceiling had come down?'

I stare at Bill, my eyes wide.

213

'I think it's best we're just grateful we found it before it got to that stage,' Bill says, glancing up at the beams again.

'Indeed,' I say, thinking about Jasper. 'So how long will it take to fix? I'm assuming you can remove the woodworm?'

'We'll definitely need to get some specialists in. This isn't something I can deal with on my own.'

I sigh. 'How much is it going to cost, Bill, and almost more importantly, how long is it going to take?'

Bill makes his customary deliberating noises.

'Difficult to say, I'd need to get a quote, and then we'd need to book them in. If we're lucky it might only put us back a week or so.'

'And if we're unlucky?'

'We can still work in here until the specialists come and spray their chemicals around; the beams are still safe at the moment. But then we'll likely be out for anything from a few days to a week until the building is deemed fit to work in again.'

I sigh again. 'Sure, I understand.'

'Better that we've caught this now, miss, than after you've opened the place up to the public. It doesn't bear thinking about what might have happened had this gone unnoticed.'

'Yes, you're right, Bill, of course you are. I'm just keen to get the tea room and gift shop up and running as soon as we can.'

'I know, miss. Me and the boys will do our best for you to catch up on the lost time. I feel partly to blame we didn't see this sooner.'

'Thank you, Bill; I appreciate that. You'll get on to these exterminator people as quickly as you can?'

'Of course, miss.'

*

I leave Bill still examining the timbers while he talks on the phone to his woodworm specialist, and I wander over towards the office.

'Hey, Tiffany,' I say as I enter the open door. 'How are you this morning?'

'Good, thanks, miss.' I've got used to the way most of the staff address me now. It's not perfect, and I'd still prefer Amelia, but it's better than 'ma'am' or 'm'lady'. 'How are you? Feeling better?'

'I'm very well, thank you.' I glance at her. 'You heard about my exploits down the pub then?'

'I did, yes.' Tiffany grins. 'I think you impressed a lot of the locals, you know.'

'Really? By getting drunk and beating them at pool?'

'By becoming one of them. Also drinking someone under the table is considered quite the badge of honour around here.'

I look at Tiffany to see if she's being serious.

'Honestly, it might not have impressed Arthur, or our local vicar, but as far as the regulars at the pub go – you're quite the hero.'

'Let's just hope Hetty doesn't hear about it, or she won't be that keen to bring her WI ladies in for one of our group tours when they're up and running.'

The tour guides that we hired have been doing sterling work with the visitors that are beginning to pour into the castle as the weather has improved and the spring has turned into an early warm summer. So much so that we've had an idea for doing group tours – well, Benji had.

I already had Hetty and both her WI ladies and her Brownies lined up for some of the first tours, and we hope to welcome lots more groups, including local schools, to the castle over the next few months.

'Oh, she'll have heard about it,' Tiffany says knowingly. 'Things don't stay hidden long around here.'

'Great.'

'So how did you get on with Tom?' Tiffany asks coyly.

'Fine. Why do you ask?'

'It was kind of your first date, wasn't it?'

'It wasn't a date!' I reply sharply. 'Far from it.'

'Oops, my bad,' Tiffany says, pretending to busy herself with her computer screen again. 'I thought ... well, *hoped* it might be.'

'What is your obsession with trying to pair me and Tom off? Why can't we just be friends?' To be fair, I wasn't sure we were even that any more after Saturday afternoon. We had left things a bit awkwardly.

'It's not an obsession. I just think it would be nice. You're single. He's single. He's hot and you're ... well, you're very pretty.'

'But not hot? Thanks.' I grin at her.

'No, I didn't mean that. You could be hot; you just choose not to be.'

'Oh, do I now?'

'Well, I think that's why you're the way you are ... '

'And what way is that?' I ask, half amused, half intrigued by what Tiffany has to say.

Tiffany's face screws up and her forehead wrinkles as she searches for the right words.

'You're sort of removed, aren't you? I don't mean because you're a Lady or anything – it's not that you're snobbish, it's like you're reserved. Yes, that's a better word. It's like you're always worried we're going to get too close.'

'What do you mean *too close*? You make it sound like I'm

worried about catching something!' I'm half smiling as I say this, but Tiffany is getting a bit too close to the truth.

'Not that sort of close. I mean it's like you're worried about getting too attached to anyone. Have you been hurt in the past, is that it?'

Talk about poles apart. One minute Tiffany is virtually curt-seying and calling me Your Highness, and the next she's trying to delve far too deeply into my personal life. And I never feel comfortable talking about that – with anyone.

'I think we'd better get on with some work,' I say, leaving Tiffany in no doubt I'm changing the subject. 'Now where are those wage slips?'

'How'd you get on with Bill this morning?' Benji asks me later when I bump into him in the village on my way to collect Charlie from school.

'Good and bad,' I say, and I proceed to tell him what Bill has told me.

'At least they found it,' Benji says practically. 'If the worst had happened ... '

'Don't even go there,' I tell him. 'I'm trying to remain positive about this.'

'Until the bill comes in from the exterminators.'

'Yes, that I am a tad worried about. Money is starting to run extremely short, and until our visitor numbers increase and they hopefully start spending money in the gift shop and the tea room in addition to their entrance fee, then I can't see any way of making any fast.'

'Oh,' Benji says, 'that is a worry.'

'I know. Please don't tell the others, though; I don't want them worrying too. We need to remain positive that this

217

summer we'll see more visitors through the grounds than we've ever seen before.'

'Fingers crossed.'

'It'll take more than crossed fingers. I've been working on a comprehensive marketing and publicity plan to launch Chesterford Castle back into the public's minds and make them want to come and visit us.'

Benji, a little worryingly, simply nods.

'Are you heading back to the castle immediately?' I ask him when he doesn't say anything to back my plans. 'Or do you want to tag along and collect Charlie from school?'

'Sure, why not? I was on my way back to do some more reading this afternoon, but I guess that can wait.'

'What are you reading?' I ask as we walk along together towards the school.

'I was going to ask if I could borrow something of yours, actually.'

'Really, what?'

'Clara's diaries. I started to read some of them when I was babysitting at the weekend, and I'm keen to finish them.'

'Sure, I've not got through all of them myself yet. I never seem to get time for reading any more – there's always something to do, and I'm often too tired at night, I just want to go straight to sleep when I get into bed.'

'They're actually extremely interesting,' Benji begins. 'The reason I want to finish them is there's something that doesn't quite make sense to me.'

'Oh yes?' I ask, but then I notice several mothers and children already exiting the school gates. I glance at my watch. 'Damn,' I say, suddenly hurrying along the street. 'My watch has stopped working. We must be late!'

Luckily we're only a few minutes late, and Charlie is waiting for us at the door when we get to his classroom.

'I'm so sorry,' I tell Miss Gardener, his teacher. 'I've just realised my watch has stopped.'

'Not a problem,' Miss Gardener says, glancing with interest at Benji.

'Oh, this is Benji, I mean Mr Benjamin,' I tell her. 'He's a friend who lives at the castle with us.'

'Pleased to make your acquaintance, Miss Gardener,' Benji says, shaking hands with Charlie's teacher.

'Likewise,' Miss Gardener says, smiling shyly at Benji.

'Right, well, we'd better be going,' I say, looking between the two of them. Miss Gardener is still gazing at Benji, but Benji is already taking Charlie's PE kit off him and enquiring how his day has been.

'Bye, Charlie!' Miss Gardener calls. 'Goodbye, Mr Benjamin!'

Benji casually lifts his hand as he departs.

'She likes you,' I tell him, as we all walk back towards the castle together. Well, Benji and I do. Charlie insists on dashing on ahead, then waiting for us to catch up with him when he reaches a corner or a bend in the road.

'Who does?' Benji asks innocently.

'Don't play coy with me, Benji, you know perfectly well who – Miss Gardener, of course.'

Benji still looks none the wiser.

'Charlie's teacher?' I prompt.

'Oh her.' Benji looks like I've just disturbed him from some very deep thought. 'Sorry, what did you say?'

'I said, I think Miss Gardener likes you.' I whisper now, in case we're close enough to Charlie for him to hear us.

Benji looks genuinely surprised. 'Really? What makes you say that? I barely said two words to her, let alone enough for her to form an opinion of me.'

I grin at him. 'Are you deliberately playing dumb?'

He shakes his head in a perplexed fashion.

'You didn't see it, then? The way she looked at you?'

'Amelia, I truly have no idea what you're talking about.'

'Right ... so you don't like her, then?'

'Who, Charlie's teacher?'

'Yes, Charlie's teacher. Who else?'

'Er ... not in that way no. She's not really my type.'

'Ah.' *What is Benji's type?* I wonder.

'Sorry if I'm being a bit vague, it's just while we were in the classroom I had a thought.'

'Go on.' I wave at Charlie; the signal he was allowed to 'go on' himself.

'I think I need to read the rest of Clara's diaries first,' Benji says. 'And then I might be able to tell you more.'

'Benji!' I whine. 'That's not fair.'

'Sorry, Amelia, but for now it has to be. For if what I think might have happened actually did happen, then it changes everything.'

'You're talking in riddles now. Even more than you usually do!'

'Yes, I know,' Benji says seriously. 'But this is important. Very important. The future of Chesterford Castle could depend on it.'

Twenty-nine

'Hello, you're back, then,' I say to Tom when we bump into each other outside the office the next morning.

'Got back last night,' Tom says, looking uncomfortably at the floor. 'I did clear it with Arthur before I went.'

'I know, and it's fine. We all need a . . . break sometime.'

'Yeah.'

'Did you go anywhere nice?'

'Just to see my brother. He was staying just the other side of the border with some friends for the weekend. I hadn't seen him for a while.'

'Ah, that's nice.'

Tom nods. 'So what's been going on here – seen any more ghosts?'

The minute Tom says this I can see him regretting it; this is, after all, what he thought we'd fallen out over.

'No, no more ghosts. But we do have some other unwanted visitors.'

'Oh yes?'

'Woodworm, in the stables. We're getting exterminators in to clear them, though.'

'Good. They can be nasty if left alone.'

'I know.'

An uncomfortable silence falls between us.

'Look, I'm sorry if I upset you the other day,' Tom says, suddenly breaking the quiet. 'I really didn't mean to.'

'I know,' I say hurriedly, pleased he's brought it up. He's obviously keen to clear the air. 'It's fine. We can't all have the same beliefs, can we? That would be a dull old world for sure.'

'It would, yes; but what I wanted to tell you was—'

'Amelia!' Benji says, rushing along the corridor towards us. 'Oh hey, Tom, you're back. Did you have a nice weekend away?'

Tom just nods at Benji.

'Tom went to visit his brother,' I say keenly. 'Didn't you, Tom?'

'Er, yeah . . .' Tom says, glancing at Benji.

'Oh . . . I see.' All of a sudden Benji looks uncomfortable. 'And is he well?'

'Yeah . . . he's doing really well, thanks.'

'Good. Good,' Benji says, nodding hurriedly. 'Sorry to change the subject but I must know if you've found it yet, Amelia?'

'No, sorry,' I tell him, wondering why they were being so odd together. 'I've just come from looking. Not a sign.'

'Then we'll have to keep searching,' Benji insists anxiously. 'It really is imperative we find it.'

'What are you two looking for?' Tom asks. 'Sounds important.'

'A diary,' Benji says. 'Specifically, Clara Chesterford's *missing* diary.'

Tom still looks mystified.

'When I cleared the rooms before the courtyard sale I found some diaries,' I quickly explain. 'They belonged to Clara Chesterford – you know, the lady in the painting I showed you?'

'Yes, I remember, I found you reading one on a deckchair, didn't I?'

'So you did. Well, Benji has been reading through them – the two of us have, actually, but Benji's much faster than me.'

'Occupational hazard,' Benji says, shrugging. 'I'm used to having to read through documents quickly.'

'But last night we discovered there was one missing,' I continue, 'and Benji thinks it could be important. Annoyingly he won't tell me why, though . . . '

'I don't want to say anything yet in case I'm wrong,' Benji says. 'But if I could just find this one diary then I'd be able to tell you for sure.'

'Right . . . ' Tom says, looking between us both. 'I'm not really any the wiser after that explanation, but if you want help looking?'

'Yes, please,' Benji says at the same time as I say, 'No really, it's fine.'

'Which is it to be?' Tom asks, grinning. 'I've some paintings to clean if you don't want me?'

'*All* help would be gratefully received,' Benji says. 'It has to be here somewhere and we must find it.'

'Ace!' we hear called from the other side of the office door. 'A treasure hunt. Count me in!'

I open the door and find Tiffany standing the other side of it.

'I bet no one's ever called you subtle, have they, Tiffany?' I ask her, smiling.

'Don't be daft, miss,' Tiffany says, grinning. 'That's me middle name!'

The four of us spend the rest of the day looking for the missing diary.

It's bad enough when you lose something in a normal-sized house, but in a castle, it's truly like looking for a needle in a very large haystack!

'It's impossible,' I say, when we meet up in the kitchen at lunch-time for some refreshment. 'It could be anywhere. It's definitely not in any of the rooms I cleared of junk.'

'I've searched through the office, too, and all the surrounding rooms we keep any paperwork in,' Tiffany says. 'There's nothing like that anywhere.'

'Why do you think this particular diary wasn't kept with the others you found?' Tom asks. 'Do you think it was removed on purpose?'

We all look at Benji.

'If what I think is written in there, actually is, then I'm pretty sure it would have been removed immediately if someone read it.'

'You're going to have to tell us eventually, Benji,' I implore him. 'Perhaps it might help us to find it?'

Benji sighs. 'All right, but you have to keep it to yourselves for now, okay? Just in case I'm wrong.'

We all nod keenly.

'You've read most of Clara's diaries, haven't you, Amelia?' Benji says, looking at me. 'What did you think?'

'Er . . . she was misunderstood,' I say, thinking about the content of the diaries. 'The reputation that she had wasn't really justified if the diaries are a true reflection of her life.'

'Go on,' Benji says.

'For instance, I was led to believe that she sold important items from the Chesterford family's collection to cover her gambling debts, and yet her diaries suggest she sold them to pay the castle staff, because there was no money to pay anything when her husband died. He was the one who had gambled it all away. Clara turned to gambling to try to recoup some of the losses, so the castle could continue to run as a family home.'

'Oh, that's a shame,' Tiffany says. 'I've only ever heard the first version; it was told to me when I came to work here.'

'Exactly,' Benji says. 'That story has been embellished over the years so that now Clara has the reputation of being this Edwardian party girl, when really it seems she might just have been doing what was needed to keep her family home from crumbling around her.'

I know how that feels.

'But that still doesn't explain what you think is in this missing diary,' Tom says. 'What is it, proof that her reputation was unjustified, or something else?' He glances at me, and I know what he's thinking. Does the missing diary have some proof of Clara's sexuality?

But if it does, why would Benji be so worried about it? And why would it matter so much if she was gay?

But Benji shakes his head. 'If it were only that. No, the last diary before the one we're looking for talks about a secret, and I quote ... ' Benji reaches for a small notebook from his pocket. '"A secret so big that if anyone found out it would ruin not only my reputation, but the reputation of all Chesterfords for evermore ... "'

Perhaps it was her sexuality, after all?

'Ooh,' Tiffany says, her eyes wide. 'I wonder what it is.'

'You wonder what what is?' Dorothy comes bustling into the kitchen. 'What are you lot doing here – are you all wanting lunch? I can knock up some sandwiches if you're hungry. There's some cold chicken and salad left from last night's dinner if anyone's interested?'

'What do you reckon this secret is, then?' Tom asks me as we search for the diary again that afternoon.

We'd all sat and had lunch in the kitchen with Dorothy, being careful not to say anything about what we were doing. Then we'd all split up again and Tom and I had been sent to look for the missing diary in some of the state rooms around the castle.

Currently we're going through any drawers, chests, or anything really where someone might have hidden a diary.

'Benji didn't really have a chance to continue with his story when Dorothy came into the kitchen, did he?' Tom continues, closing up yet another empty drawer in the bedroom we're currently in. 'He seems to think it might be quite serious, though.'

'Yeah, I know. I wondered if it might be some sort of proof that Clara was gay. I know that sort of thing doesn't matter these days, but back then I bet it would have been a huge scandal.'

'It sure would,' Tom says. 'But knowing Benji, I'm sure it isn't likely to be that.'

'Yes, I haven't known Benji as long as you but he doesn't seem to be one to create drama for the sake of it.' I close the doors on the wardrobe I've been looking in.

'No, definitely not. He's straight down the line is our Benji. Well, as straight as Benji is ever going to get!' Tom grins.

'What do you mean?' I ask, pulling open the small side drawers on a pretty dressing table.

Tom stops what he's doing and looks at me.

'Are you messing with me?' he asks. 'You must know Benji is gay.'

I swivel around on my stool and stare at him.

'Obviously I was wrong,' Tom says. 'You didn't know.'

My mind rushes through everything I know about Benji, and suddenly a few things click into place. But equally some other things do not.

'But Benji told me he only knew you because he dated your sister – that's how you two met.'

Tom grins. 'I don't have a sister. Only the one brother – Joe. Well, Joseph to give him his full name. That's who I went to see this weekend.'

I think about this, and then I cringe when I realise my mistake. 'Oh, I must have assumed Joe was a girl when Benji mentioned him the first time. So that's why Benji was a bit funny with you when you said you'd been to visit your brother – his ex! God, I feel so silly now.' I bury my red-hot face in my hands.

'Don't be. Obviously I've known Benji for a long time and I've always known he was gay because of Joe. But to be fair if I hadn't I probably wouldn't know either. It's not something he makes a big deal about. I'm surprised he never mentioned it, though. You two seem quite close.'

'Yes, we are. I guess there was never a need for him to say anything. Perhaps he assumed I already knew.' I think about this, and I wonder if this might have been what Benji was trying to tell me up in the tower the night we ended up talking about Tom.

227

I feel bad that I might have stopped him from sharing something so important to him.

'If I didn't know Benji was gay I'd have been quite jealous of the two of you together all the time,' Tom continues.

'Would you?' I ask innocently, pulling myself from my thoughts about Benji. 'Why?'

'Oh, Amelia,' Tom says, coming over to where I'm still sitting at the dressing table and kneeling down next to me. 'You must know how much I like you. Haven't I made it plain enough?' He takes hold of my hands and I have to fight my natural reaction to pull away from him.

'Maybe I just missed the signs,' I say shyly, willing myself not to retreat into my protective shell like I always do.

'Really? I've tried to make it pretty clear.'

I look down into Tom's blue eyes, and I see a man desperate to make me understand how he feels.

Let him in, Amelia, I hear my inner voice instructing me. *It's time.*

'Perhaps you should try a little harder then,' I say quietly and I allow my hand to reach out and gently touch his cheek.

Tom closes his eyes at my touch, and when he opens them again he finds my lips millimetres from his.

'Amelia,' he murmurs, but annoyingly I don't hear him, my ears are trying to listen to something else.

'What was that?' I ask, looking away from him for a moment.

'Nothing,' Tom murmurs, gently turning my face back towards his.

'There it is again,' I say, looking away again. 'It's like a pinging sound. You must hear it?'

Tom sighs and his hand drops away from my face. 'Yeah, I hear it. It's probably just a bird outside.'

I listen again.

'But it's not coming from outside, is it? It sounds like it's coming from downstairs. What's directly underneath here?'

'Er ...' Tom looks down at the floor. 'The Great Hall, I think.'

'Or,' I say, leaping up, 'could it be the Ladies' Chamber?'

'You mean the room with the painting of Clara in it?' Tom asks, pulling himself to his feet.

'The very same!' I call excitedly, already heading out of the bedroom into the hall. 'I reckon I know exactly what that pinging sound is, too.'

'What?' Tom asks, chasing after me. 'What is it?'

'It's the sound of a piano playing! It's Clara,' I say as I hurry down the corridor towards the stairs. 'I think she's trying to help us!'

Thirty

I burst into the Great Hall and rush over to the wooden panelling on the far wall. Then I push the panel with the roses on it. To my relief the panel slides open to reveal the beauty of the hidden Ladies' Chamber beyond.

Tom is not many seconds behind me as I hurry over to the mini piano and lift the lid. 'It must be here somewhere,' I say, looking desperately amongst the taut piano strings.

'Are you sure it was a piano playing?' Tom asks, standing back to watch me. 'It wasn't very tuneful.'

'Yes, and it wasn't a tune that was being played; it was one note. One note constantly.'

'But why would someone play one note constantly?'

'Because that's exactly what Clara said she'd done in her diary,' I say, still searching inside the piano. 'She might have been in a loveless marriage, but she fell pregnant, then sadly suffered a miscarriage. She wrote that she sat at this very piano for hours at a time hitting one note constantly. Apparently her lady's maid had to come and prise her away when she wouldn't listen to anyone else.'

'That's very sad,' Tom says, staring at the piano. 'Poor Clara; she had some life, eh?'

'She did indeed. But I think as a result of everything she had to go through, it made her the strong woman you see in that painting.'

Tom glances at the painting while I get down on my hands and knees to look underneath the piano. 'It must be here. It must,' I mutter in frustration.

Tom's head suddenly appears upside down next to me as he investigates what I'm doing.

'Any luck?'

'No,' I say, crawling back out again. 'I was certain it was going to be here after I heard that noise when we were upstairs. I was sure it was Clara trying to help us. It was her way of giving us a sign.'

Tom looks thoughtfully at me.

'You're pretty sure these ghosts exist, aren't you?'

'Let's not fall out over this again,' I plead.

'No, you mistake me. I mean, if you really think they exist, then I'm prepared to give them a go too.'

I smile. 'I'm fairly new to this, too, you know. But I'm pretty sure you don't give ghosts a go like you're choosing a fairground ride.'

Tom grins too.

'What *do* you do, then?' he asks, moving closer to me. 'Maybe you could teach me.'

'Maybe we could learn together,' I say, looking deeply into his eyes again. But to my, and most likely Tom's annoyance too, the chances of our lips actually touching this time are dashed once more, as my gaze is redirected to the painting behind him.

'That's it!' I cry.

'What is?' Tom asks, startled. He looks behind him at what I'm staring at.

'The painting. Look,' I say, dashing over to it. 'Here.' I point to Clara's hand resting on the book. 'It's the diary.'

'How do you know it's the diary?' Tom asks, obviously trying to hide his disappointment at yet another interruption. 'Her hand could be on any book.'

'No, it looks exactly the same as all the other diaries we found; they were all written in the same style of cream leather-bound book with gilt edging around the pages. This must be the missing one. There is only one other diary after the one we're looking for, and in it Clara talks about sitting for this very painting. She even talks about there being a meaning to this painting that no one else will ever understand.' My forehead wrinkles as I try to remember. 'Something about her locking her grief and guilt away somewhere, so that no one else will ever need to know or share in it.'

I look at Tom. 'What could that mean?'

Tom shakes his head. 'No idea.' He looks more closely at the painting now. 'If that's a diary under her hand there, would it have a key, perhaps? Maybe that's what she means by locking her guilt and grief away?'

'It could be, but none of the other diaries had locks on them. Hmm . . . what about this chest of drawers thing she's standing in front of? What if the diary is locked in there now?'

'That's a bureau. If it was Clara's it was probably called her writing desk.' Again Tom examines the painting closely. 'Yes, I'd say by looking at it, it was probably designed specifically for her – it's a smaller, more delicate piece than some of the earlier writing bureaus, which tended to be bigger and less intricate. This one likely dates from the late-Edwardian era.'

I smile at Tom.

'What?' he asks, noticing.

'Nothing. You're very clever.'

Tom shrugs. 'I know my furniture – that's my job.'

'Do you think this could be the thing that's locked, then?' I look at the painting again. 'Would it have had a lock on it, do you know?'

'Oh yes, more than likely. In addition to the drawers you can see here, once open it would have had a writing slope, pigeonholes, inkwells, small slots and often secret drawers—'

'Wait! *Secret* drawers?'

Tom nods.

'So if Clara's bureau is still here at Chesterford the diary might be locked away in a secret drawer.'

'I guess.'

'Have you seen it?' I ask, looking at the painting again. 'It doesn't look familiar to me, but you've probably spent longer looking at the furniture here than I have.'

Tom stares at the bureau. 'I don't think I have. I'm sure I would have remembered it if it has the same detailing on it that's shown in this painting. It's quite unique with this inlaid marquetry.' He points to some patterns on the front of the bureau.

I sigh. That would be just our luck if it had been thrown out or sold somewhere along the line. I don't know why, but suddenly this search seems so important to me. I know why it's important to Benji – searching for missing links to piece together a family's history is right up his street. But I feel like there might be something else significant going on here.

'I'll take some photos of the painting and show it to the others. Maybe one of them will recognise it.' I pull out my phone and stand back a little from the painting to take a few snapshots. 'Look,' I say as I move a little nearer to get a close-up of the desk. 'There *is* a key shown here – on the desk next to the flowers.'

'So there is,' Tom says, looking at the painting again. 'But that's not going to be for this desk, it's far too big. That's a key for something bigger, like a door or a gate. The key to this desk would be very small and easily lost over the years, I'm afraid.'

'Well, I'm still going to try to find the bureau – with or without its key,' I say determinedly, putting my phone back in my pocket.

Wait, I suddenly think. *A key! When we were in the stables with the ghosts they'd said something about a key, and that Clara would know all about it . . .*

'Have you ever seen this writing bureau here at the castle?' I ask for what feels like the umpteenth time today. I hold out my phone to Arthur this time, after already asking Tiffany, Dorothy, Benji and the two tour guides that were in with us today. Joey is away for a few days to attend his cousin's wedding in Wales.

Arthur takes my phone from me with a puzzled look.

'That's the painting of Clara, fifteenth Countess of Chesterford,' he says, peering at the photo.

'Yes, I know; but have you seen the writing desk she's standing in front of?'

Arthur shakes his head. 'No, I don't think I have – why?'

'Ah, no reason,' I say, trying to hide my disappointment. 'I just thought it was pretty, that's all, and I might like it to sit and write at if it wasn't being used in any of the public rooms.'

Arthur looks again. 'No, I'm sure I haven't. But what you must remember is there was a lot of artistic licence that often went on in these paintings. It's quite possible that when Clara sat for this portrait she wasn't sitting in front of that desk at all, but something completely different.'

'Yes, I'd already thought of that. I mean, look at the size of that key on the desk – there's no way that would fit a desk such as this, would it?'

'No, it looks like the ceremonial key to me,' Arthur says, handing me back my phone.

'The what?'

'The ceremonial key. It's a key that's passed on to each new owner of Chesterford Castle. It's a centuries-old castle tradition.'

'But I haven't been given a key?'

'No, I was waiting for an appropriate time to give it to you. Traditionally the key is presented at the first formal gathering the new owner hosts. So far you've only hosted the courtyard sale, and I didn't think that was entirely appropriate.'

'No, you're probably right.'

'But I was thinking of having a small presentation when the stables are complete and the new tea room and gift shop are officially opened. It seemed a more apt occasion.'

I'm pleased that Arthur is finally acknowledging our new venture. He's always been very reticent to talk about it before with his extreme dislike of any sort of change. 'That's a lovely idea, Arthur, thank you.'

Arthur nods.

'So what does this key open, then?' I ask. 'The main gate or something?'

235

'I'm not sure it opens anything, really – like I said, it's ceremonial. An official moment to mark the passing of one Earl and the handing of the title on to a new Chesterford.'

'But I don't have the title, do I?' I tell him. 'The title should be Charlie's. You're not thinking of involving him in this, are you? You know how I feel about that.'

Arthur shakes his head. 'No, I wasn't going to involve young Charlie. I feel in this *special* instance that the ceremony should be more about the passing of the *ownership* of the castle from one Chesterford to another, rather than the title.'

'Thank you, Arthur, I appreciate that. So where is this key, then? I haven't seen it around. Do you have it on display?'

'No, the key is kept – funnily enough – under lock and key. It's an incredibly important artefact in the castle's history. It's said to date right back to Norman times when the castle was originally built here as a simple motte-and-bailey construction.'

'So it is more than likely it really doesn't open anything?'

'I highly doubt it. Now, if there's nothing else, I must get back to the cottage. Dorothy is hosting her sewing circle this evening and I promised I'd wash down the garden furniture so they can sit outside if it stays warm and dry.'

'Sure, Arthur, you go. Thanks for your help.'

'Any time, miss. Any time.'

I watch Arthur walk along the path that leads to his and Dorothy's small cottage. I couldn't imagine living and working at the same place like they had for so many years, although if you were going to do it, then Chesterford Castle was as good a place as any. They really had given their lives to this castle, and I for one was very grateful to have them here.

I think about my conversation with Arthur as I begin to

walk back towards the office. *I wonder if this ceremonial key has anything to do with the key that the ghosts said I was to look out for?*

I shake my head. I never thought living in a castle was going to be easy, but I didn't think my main troubles would be caused by a bunch of ghosts, an old diary, a key and very some persistent woodworm!

Thirty-one

'How much!' I ask, not even attempting to keep my voice down as I stand with Bill in the stables the next afternoon.

'It's worse than I suspected,' Bill says, looking apologetic. 'The beams – especially these two here – are riddled, apparently. Vic says we can try and exterminate the woodworm and their larvae, but he very much doubts it will be enough to clear them completely.'

Vic, the woodworm expert, had been in to look at the stables this morning, and now Bill and I were discussing his findings.

'So we have no choice?'

Bill shakes his head. 'The beams are going to have to be replaced if you want to continue with this project.'

'Can't we just cut them out?' I ask, looking up at the offending beams. 'I know it won't look as effective, but surely that would be a cheaper option.'

'We could do that, but we'd have to install something else to prop up the rest of the ceiling. These oak beams aren't just for decoration; they're an integral part of the support system of the whole building. If you don't replace them like for like, then we'd have to put something more modern, and, most importantly, something structurally sound in their place instead.'

I stare up at the beams. How can something so basic-looking cause me so much expense? There's no way I want something modern up there; it would completely ruin the look we're going for. I've got no choice.

'And you're sure this is a fair price?' I ask, looking at the estimate in my hand. 'This Vic isn't trying to pull a fast one on us because he thinks we have lots of money, is he? Because I can assure you, Bill, currently we do not.'

'It's actually a very good price,' Bill says. 'I can get some other quotes, but I don't think you'll do any better. Vic is local to this area; he'll want to do a good job for you.'

I nod. 'Okay, go ahead, then. But please emphasise to Vic to keep his costs as low as possible – without scrimping on safety, of course.'

'Of course,' Bill says. 'On the bright side, everything else is going very smoothly now, and with a bit of luck and some overtime we could still open on time.'

'That's really good to know, Bill,' I say, trying to sound pleased. 'Don't let me hold you up any more then, and as always, many thanks for sorting all this out for me.'

I leave Bill and his men whistling and bantering away with each other while they work. But as I walk away from the stables, I can't shake the cloud of doom that hangs over me.

I know exactly how much money we have in the castle's main bank account right now, and how much I have left in the secret fund that the last Earl left me. And it's nowhere near enough to cover the estimate that Bill has just shown me. I don't know where I'm going to get the money from to pay this bill; all I know is that I have to find it somewhere.

'You're quiet,' Benji says to me a couple of days later, when he's popped up to the tower with a new draft of facts for the tour guides to impart to our visitors. 'In fact, you've been quiet for a few days. Is everything all right?'

I look at Benji sitting next to me on the sofa, and suddenly I feel like bursting into tears. I've kept my money concerns to myself until now. I didn't want to worry anyone else with them, not until I'd figured out a plan for how we were going to pay for everything.

'If I tell you something, Benji, you must keep it to yourself, okay?'

'Sure, of course. What's wrong? Is it you and Tom again?'

'No, why would that be worrying me? Me and Tom are fine now – not that there really is a me and Tom ... Why, has he said something to you?' I babble, completely thrown by his question.

Benji shakes his head. 'No, but I can't think what else it would be ... unless ...'

'Unless what?'

'Nothing. You carry on.'

'Right ...' I tell Benji what Bill had said, and then my concerns about how we are going to pay for everything. At the end, to my astonishment, Benji smiles.

'Why are you smiling?' I ask. 'This is serious.'

'Yes, I know,' Benji says. 'It's very serious indeed. But I have to say I'm a little relieved.'

'You are – why?'

'It's going to sound silly now after what you've just told me,

240

but Tom confided in me that he'd let slip to you about my ...
my sexuality a couple of days ago. And it's since then you've
been a little off. I thought it was that that was bothering you,
but now I know it isn't me, it's something else, it's quite a
relief.'

'Oh, Benji, you didn't really think I'd mind that you're gay,
did you?'

Benji shrugs. 'I hoped you wouldn't, and I have to say it
really didn't seem like the way you'd react. But you just never
know these days.'

'I have to admit it *was* a bit of a surprise when Tom told me.'

'Really?'

'Yeah, I hadn't guessed at all. Perhaps I should have. I mean,
the signs were definitely there ... '

'What signs?'

'Dorothy said you were very "clean looking", for one.' I
wink at him.

'Oh, did she?'

'I think she said something along the lines of you were very
polite, and knew your manners too. And that *of course* means
you must be gay.'

'Of course it does!' Benji says, grinning now too. 'No straight
men are ever like that, are they?' He rolls his eyes dramatically.
'Ah, I'm so glad you're all right about it. I've wanted to tell
you for some time, because ... well ... ' Benji looks incredibly
embarrassed to even have to utter this next sentence. 'I did
wonder for a while if you might have ... you might have feelings for me.' His face goes bright pink and he looks down at
one of the sofa cushions.

'I did,' I say quietly, putting my hand over his so he glances
up at me. 'And I still do. Deep feelings ... as a friend!' I finish

241

when Benji starts to look worried again. 'A *very* good friend indeed.'

'Ah, Amelia, the feeling is completely mutual,' Benji says, leaning across the sofa so he can put his arm around me and give me a hug. 'So now, what are we going to do about this money – or lack of it?' he asks. 'I wish I had some savings I could help you out with. I've got a little bit of money put aside from the advance on my book, but it's not on the scale you're talking about.'

'That's kind of you, Benji, but I couldn't take your money.' I sigh. 'I really don't know what I'm going to do. Try to get a bank loan, I guess. Once the gift shop and tea rooms are up and running we're bound to be making a profit; surely they'll take that into consideration?'

'And if you can't get a loan?'

'If that doesn't work, I might have to sell a few things from the castle. It's a last resort, but what choice do I have?'

'You're starting to sound like Clara, having to sell off her valuables to pay her debts.'

'I know, tell me about it. I thought I was done with debt when I moved here, but now it seems I'm going to be buried even further in it. I'm sorry I haven't done anything more about finding Clara's missing diary,' I tell him, suddenly remembering, 'but I've had all this going on in the last couple of days. Plus, Tom and I looked everywhere; even the bureau idea didn't come to anything.'

'It did, actually,' Benji says. 'When I mentioned it to Joey he knew exactly where it was.'

'He did?' I ask, sitting forward in anticipation. 'Where was it?'

'Only in his room!' Benji says, smiling. 'When I went to look at it with him, he had a mirror, a hairdryer and all his toiletries all over it. He was using it as a dressing table.'

'Joey? I never thought he took all that much care over his appearance?'

'Apparently so, but he is very definitely *not* gay.' Benji winks. 'A straight man caring what he looks like, who would have thought it! Anyway, we checked all over it to see if we could find any secret drawers or compartments or anything, but there was nothing. So Joey knows about the diary now too.'

'That's okay, we can trust Joey. But another dead end – damn, it's so frustrating.'

'I know. Perhaps we'll never find it.'

'That would be such a shame. What do you think this big secret is – something to do with Clara's sexuality?'

'You figured that, then?'

'It wasn't exactly hard if you read between the lines.'

'No, indeed. It must have been awfully difficult for her back then if she was gay, which I too think she was. It was bad enough when I came out, but back then it simply wasn't acceptable – especially for a woman.'

'I know, she couldn't even choose to stay single and become a – what did they call women who didn't marry back then – an old maid?'

Benji nods. 'No, she was forced to live even more of a lie by having to find a husband so she could stay here.' He shakes his head. 'Mad, isn't it?'

'It seems so now, but I guess that's just the way it was. We don't know how lucky we are these days with everything so open and free.'

'We really don't. But to answer your question, no, I don't think that's what the secret is. What Clara has written, and subsequently hidden in that diary, she must have considered pretty scandalous, even more so than her sexuality. I've done enough of this kind of thing over the years to know that when an important piece of paperwork is missing, there's always a reason for it, and in this case I think it could turn out to be a very important reason indeed.'

I sit in the Ladies' Chamber on a pale green chaise longue, staring up at the painting of Clara once more.

This time I'm not looking for any clues as to where her missing diary might be. I'm simply hoping that by spending time with her, some inspiration might strike on how I'm going to solve my money worries.

Reluctantly, I've had to confide my concerns in Arthur too, and on his recommendation I've made some initial enquires at a local bank that has had dealings with the castle before. But my preliminary conversation with a financial advisor there didn't give me much hope that I will get very far with them, or more importantly get any money from them either.

'Come on, Clara,' I plead as I look into the eyes of this striking woman. 'I know you suffered similar troubles in your life. Can't you think of a way out of this without me resorting to selling more of our family's valuables?'

But Clara just stares serenely back at me.

'What about this key I'm supposed to ask you about, then?' I say quietly. 'I know you mentioned something about it to the others before. Is it this ceremonial key Arthur mentioned that you're talking about?'

Again nothing.

'I can't believe I'm talking to a painting now,' I mutter to myself. 'How desperate am I?'

I stand up and turn to leave the room. *But what choice do you have, Amelia?* I think. *You're running out of ideas, and more importantly you're running out of time. Once the woodworm have been permanently removed and the new beams are up, there's going to be a rather large bill that needs paying pretty swiftly.*

'Look, Clara,' I say, turning back to the painting, 'I know the others said you were shy, and I completely understand that. It might surprise you to know I've always been a pretty shy person myself. It's only since I've had to cope with being alone in the world as a single mother that I've had to come out of my shell, otherwise Charlie and I would have starved. I've had to fight for what I'm entitled to, fight to find us somewhere to live when the council didn't want to give us anywhere, and then fight for my job so I could feed us and pay my rent. I didn't have time to be shy. And now I'm here at the castle I've had to fight to try to bring this place into the twenty-first century so it can survive for many more years to come. I'm trying my best here, so if you know of any way to make this easier for me, then *please* tell me, or at least give me a clue.'

Again nothing happens. A breeze blows through the room from the window, just enough to disturb the thick net curtain that hangs in the window. *That's odd*, I think. *Who would have opened a window in here? I certainly didn't when I came in.*

I'm about to head towards the window to close it, when it happens again. But this time a shaft of sunlight suddenly appears through the gap the billowing net has left, allowing me to see tiny dust particles in the beam of sunlight that streams through the window.

My gaze follows the beam across the room to where it falls directly on the painting of Clara, or more specifically, on a part of the painting I hadn't noticed before. In the top right-hand

245

corner of the portrait the artist has depicted another painting hanging behind Clara on the wall. It's a painting of a dog – Clara's dog. I know this because Clara talks about her love for the dog in her diaries. She wrote about how much of a friend the little dog had been to her, and how he'd been a faithful companion when times had been tough and she'd been incredibly lonely at the castle. At the time, I'd only thought of the similarities between Charlie and Chester's relationship, but now something else resonates with me as the sun still shines on the corner of the portrait.

The little dog in the picture looks very similar to another dog I'd seen recently. Not Chester this time, but the little stuffed dog I'd sold, then had to subsequently refund at the courtyard sale ...

Thirty-two

'Tom!' I call, hurrying across the grass towards the long barn that Tom has turned into a temporary workshop while he repairs and restores items from the castle. 'Tom, I need you!'

Tom, who currently seems to be taking a leather wing-backed chair carefully apart, looks up at me as I run across the lawn.

'That's quite the greeting!' he says, winking at me, as I arrive in front of him slightly out of breath. 'We may need to find somewhere a little more private, but I'm sure I can accommodate your needs.'

'What? Oh, I see, it's a joke. Look, I haven't got time to mess about—'

'That's a shame,' Tom says, still grinning.

'What did we do with all the stuff we didn't sell at the courtyard sale?' I demand.

'Er, I think we put most of it back in one of the empty rooms upstairs, didn't we?'

'Yes, that's what I thought, but I can't find the dog.'

'What dog?'

'The dog that we sold to that rude man, remember? Then he brought it back and demanded a refund.'

'Oh the stuffed dog – but why do you want that?'

'I just do. Do you know where it is?'

'No.'

'Damn.'

'What's going on, Amelia?' Tom asks, his eyes narrowing. 'You seem very het up about this dog.'

'I'm sure it has something to do with the lost diary,' I tell him hesitantly. *Don't ask me why. Don't ask me why*, I pray. *It's going to sound really odd if I have to explain why.*

'Why?' Tom asks as if on cue.

Reluctantly I tell him what happened in the Ladies' Chamber, waiting for his sceptical reaction at the end.

'Sounds like we'd better find it, then!' is all he says, to my surprise and relief. 'We'd best ask Tiffany; she helped tidy away a lot of the unsold things that day.'

Tom puts his chair away in his barn, and then we dash back across the grass together, Tom taking hold of my hand as we go as if it's the most natural thing in the world. And I let him; it feels good to be sharing this with someone.

'Tiffany, what did you do with all the left-over stuff from the courtyard sale?' I ask as we reach the office, letting go of Tom's hand just before we go in.

'Didn't you put most of it in one of the rooms just down the corridor?' Tiffany says, looking at Tom.

'I thought I had, but apparently not all of it went in there.'

Tiffany thinks. 'I was sure we'd put it all in there. Is there something in particular you're looking for?'

'Yes, a dog. A stuffed dog. Do you remember it?'

'Oh yeah, that mangy thing,' Tiffany says, wrinkling up her

nose. 'I tossed it with some other rubbish I didn't think was worth keeping. It gave me the creeps, and it probably had fleas. Who wants to stuff their dog when it's dead, anyway? It's just plain weird.

'I didn't dump anything valuable, mind,' Tiffany continues when I simply stare open mouthed at her. 'That all went back in the rooms. What?' she asks when I don't say anything. 'Have I done something wrong?'

'When you say dumped, Tiffany,' Tom asks, 'do you mean in the rubbish – the rubbish that gets collected from outside the gates every week?'

'Yeah.'

'Right.' Tom grimaces at me.

'I saved its collar, though,' Tiffany says brightly. 'The dog's, I mean. Arthur said that dog had once belonged to the Countess of Chesterford – you know, Clara, the one whose diary we were looking for? So I thought I'd better keep the collar, in case we ever wanted to display it or something.' She grins furtively. 'Arthur doesn't even know I still have it.'

'Where is it now?' I ask.

Tiffany reaches into the bottom drawer in her desk and retrieves a worn blue leather collar. 'Here, do you want it?'

Eagerly I take the collar from her. 'Look,' I say excitedly as I turn it around in my hand. 'There's a key.'

Where there would normally be a silver dog tag, instead there hangs a tiny silver key.

'I thought that was odd too,' Tiffany says. 'Cos he's not wearing that in the picture.'

'What picture?' I ask, my ears pricking up. 'There's a painting of this dog somewhere?'

'Yeah, when we had to sort the tower out for you arriving,

we had to remove a lot of the last Earl's things. Dorothy said you'd probably like a fresh start, so we took all his things and put them in storage. A painting of that dog was hanging in the toilet, of all places; I remember because I had to take it down. The dog looked a canny wee thing when it was alive, that's why I hated that stuffed monstrosity so much.'

'Where is the painting now?'

'Er, Arthur put that and all the Earl's other personal effects into some trunks. They're down in the basement somewhere, I think.'

'Where is Arthur now?'

'Out. He's gone to look at some new fencing with Joey.'

'Do you know where he keeps the keys to these trunks?'

Tiffany goes over to Arthur's desk and rootles about in one of the drawers. 'He thinks they're hidden in here because he tucks them away at the back. But . . . ' Tiffany reaches right to the back of the drawer. 'I know what he does!' she says triumphantly, pulling a large ring of various keys from the depths of the drawer.

'Shall we?' she asks, delight that she's got one over on Arthur shining from her eyes.

'Why don't you lead the way?' I ask her, holding out my hand.

Tiffany leads us out of the back of the office and down the same corridor I'd travelled with her the first day I was here, when we'd lost Charlie.

We follow her down two flights of stairs, until we come to the locked solid wood door we'd encountered on that day.

'I didn't know Arthur had a key to this door when we were here before,' Tiffany says. 'It's only recently he's been using these keys a lot. That's how I knew where he kept them.'

'But which key is it?' I ask her, looking at the huge array she has in her hand. 'Do you know?'

Tiffany shakes her head. 'Nope, I just know it's one of these. Arthur says there are keys to open anything in the castle on here.'

Tom examines the lock on the door. 'Can I see them?' he asks, holding out his hand.

I nod at Tiffany and she passes Tom the keys. He looks through each key until he finds a suitable one, then tries it in the lock. On only his third attempt he's successful.

He unlocks the door, opens it, and we peer inside. There's a staircase leading immediately down from the doorway, and luckily a corresponding light switch, that when flicked floods the staircase with light, allowing us an easy descent into the basement.

'Ladies first,' Tom says, holding out his hand.

'Thanks,' I reply, wondering what we're going to find down there.

I walk cautiously down the stairs, followed by Tiffany and then Tom. When we get to the bottom we find a spacious room filled with various large trunks: the kind you see people using when they are going on long voyages on ships. The trunks are all different sizes and colours, but the one thing they have in common is that they are all locked with sizeable and strong padlocks.

'Any idea which one the picture might be in?' I ask Tiffany.

'Sorry,' Tiffany says, shrugging. 'Like I said, Arthur is the only one who comes down here.'

'Looks like we're going to have to try them all, then,' Tom says, shaking the keys. 'Who wants to start?'

After we've narrowed down our search by eliminating all the keys that are going to be too big to fit in the padlocks, we try each key one by one.

It takes us until our fourth key to find one that fits.

'Yes!' I shout as my key turns satisfactorily in the lock. 'We're in.'

But inside the first trunk we only discover some clothes. They are antique clothes, probably belonging to a past Countess and Earl, interesting, but sadly not what we are looking for.

Our next success opens a trunk containing some silverware and china. Tom examines the contents with much excitement.

'There's some valuable stuff in here,' he reports, carefully returning it all to the case, 'but sadly nothing we're looking for.'

We try again, and this time unlock a trunk that according to Tom contains some very old artefacts – including a bronze chalice, some unusual pewter plates and a large rusty iron key.

'This must be the ceremonial key that Arthur was talking about,' I tell the others while they examine the chalice and the plates. 'Apparently it's presented to each new owner of Chesterford – Arthur is going to present it to me the day the new tea room opens.'

We put the items carefully back in the chest – wrapping them in their worn protective fabrics – and it's on our next successful key-turn that we finally find it.

'This must be the one!' Tiffany calls, as Tom lifts a few framed photos from the trunk first. 'These are the last Earl's bits and pieces. I recognise some of his things.'

Tiffany pores over the chest, moving things around until she finds it. 'Here,' she cries triumphantly, lifting up a small painting. 'This is the picture I was talking about.'

Tom and I examine the painting with Tiffany. It is indeed a very good likeness of the little dog, looking a lot healthier and robust than its stuffed version had.

But after we've studied it for a few minutes, we realise that it is just that – a painting. It gives us no further clues; we still don't know where the missing diary is, why the dog's collar has a key attached to it, or even why we are actually here.

'It was worth a try, I suppose,' I say with a sigh. 'The painting might have had something on it that could have helped us.' I look around at the trunks we have yet to unlock. 'What else is down here, do you think?' I ask. 'I'm intrigued to see what else is hidden in this cellar.'

'Do you think we *should*?' Tiffany asks anxiously. 'I mean, it's stuff Arthur locks away.'

'If it was anything personal to Arthur surely he'd hide it in his own cottage,' I say, taking the keys over to a small but battered-looking trunk. 'Everything we've come across so far has been to do with the history of the castle. And if it's to do with the castle then I'd like to see it. I've been wondering whether to put on an exhibition of sorts,' I explain to them as I try a couple of keys before finding the correct one to unlock the padlock. 'You know, the sort of stuff you see displayed in glass cabinets because it's delicate or valuable. We don't have anything like that here, and it seems a shame to keep some of these things we've found today locked away where people can't see them.'

I open up the lid of the trunk and I'm surprised to see tissue paper. Then I realise the tissue paper contains fabric. Carefully, I fold back the paper to find a beautiful powder-blue silk organza dress. 'This looks like it might have belonged to Clara, don't you think?' I say, holding up the dress for the others to see. 'It's the right era.'

We carefully lift another six tissue-wrapped packages from the chest, all containing similar beautiful dresses.

'Someone knew what they were doing when they put these away for storage,' Tom says, wrapping another dress back in its protective paper. 'I'd say this is acid-free tissue paper; that's fairly modern stuff, so these could only have been wrapped fairly recently.'

'My sister wrapped her wedding dress in something similar to this before she put it away in her loft,' Tiffany says, feeling the paper. 'It protects it from damp and stuff.'

'I wonder why it's only recently been wrapped up? You'd have thought it would have been done years ago.'

'Perhaps it was,' Tom says knowingly. 'It might have just been *re*-wrapped recently.'

'Oh, look at this one,' I say, opening up a new package. I'd expected to see another beautiful ball gown, but instead my hands are now touching a much heavier material. It's black and scratchy and not at all like the luxurious fabrics the previous colourful outfits have been made out of. 'It's a maid's dress,' I exclaim, holding it up, 'and look, there's an apron too.'

The next few packets from the large truck contain items that must have belonged to 'downstairs staff' – some dowdy but practical shoes, a very basic brush, some hairpins, and some stout-looking stockings. There's even a little white hat, which I could just imagine one of the maids at Chesterford wearing to tend to one of the previous Countesses.

'These would look great on display in the castle,' I say as I lift another smaller package up from the trunk. 'We could get some mannequins or something similar – we could even display Clara's outfits in the Ladies' Chamber with her portrait, and maybe the maid's things in one of the bedrooms.'

'That's a great idea,' Tiffany says. 'I love to see stuff like that when I visit old houses. There's something about clothes that make history come to life that little bit more. Ooh, what's that?' she asks as I open up the tissue paper and begin unfolding what I assume is another dress.

'It's a shawl,' I say, beginning to unwrap a large, silk, embroidered shawl. 'It feels like there's something hard wrapped inside it, though – like a box.'

'It is a box!' Tiffany exclaims as the fabric reveals a small colourful box hidden within it.

'It's locked again,' I say, examining the object in my lap. 'Look, there's another small padlock on it.'

'That box is old,' Tom says, looking over my shoulder. 'It looks like enamel to me. Probably eighteenth century, by the look of the design.'

I look at the box in my hand; it looks familiar. Where had I seen it before?

'This must have been Clara's too!' I say as it dawns on me where I've seen this box before. 'It's in her portrait in the Ladies' Chamber; it's on the desk next to where her hand rests on the diary. You don't think . . . '

'We don't think what?' Tom asks impatiently as I stand up and reach into my pocket.

'You don't think that this,' I say, holding up the silver key still attached to the dog's collar, 'opens up *this*.' I hold up the box in my other hand. 'It looks like a perfect fit to me.'

'Try it. Try it!' Tiffany squeals excitedly.

I reach the key across to the lock, and to my delight it fits. I'm about to turn it when we hear a deep voice bellowing down the stairs.

'No! Don't you dare try it. I insist you put that box down immediately.'

Thirty-three

'Arthur!' I cry, jumping at both the loudness and the tone of his voice. 'Whatever's wrong?'

Arthur comes thundering down the stairs, faster than I've ever seen him move before.

'Put that down,' he says, his voice calmer but just as forceful.

'Why?' I ask, still gripping tightly to the box. 'What's inside? Why don't you want us to open it?'

Arthur swallows, obviously trying to calm himself. 'This is a private area,' he says, looking around at all the open trunks. 'You have no right to come down here ... *disturbing* everything.' He glances at the box in my hand again, and something inside me makes me grip it all the tighter. 'And you,' he says, pointing at Tiffany, 'had no right bringing them down here. How many times have I told you this area is out of bounds?'

Tiffany looks like she might burst into tears.

'Arthur, that's enough. It's not Tiffany's fault we're here. If you want to blame someone then blame me; I asked her to show us where you kept a picture, that's all, and she told us it was down here with the last Earl's things. It was only because we didn't know which key opened which trunk that we ended up opening so many.'

'Well, you've obviously found that particular trunk now,' Arthur says, looking at the painting of the dog propped up in front of one of the trunks. 'So perhaps it's time—' He suddenly notices the dog's collar in my hand, and more specifically the key I'm about to open the box with.

'Where did you get that?' he asks, his voice suddenly a bit too calm.

'This?' I ask suspiciously, holding up the collar. 'Why?'

'I thought the key for that box had been lost years ago . . . and all this time it was on a dog's collar?' Arthur seems almost mesmerised by the key.

I look questioningly at him – just what is going on here? Arthur clearly knows about all the stuff down here. Tiffany said he's been back and forth a lot just lately. Why was he so against us opening this box now we have the key?

'I think you should all leave now,' Arthur orders, his voice calm, but his face reddening, as though his anger is just beginning to boil under his cool exterior again. 'Before you do any more damage. The things down here are private – private to the family.'

I'm really not sure what the feeling is building up inside me right now. It's one that I've never felt before. But all I know is it's time to pull rank.

'*If,*' I say in a steely voice that surprises even me, 'these had been your private items, Arthur, then of course I wouldn't dream of riffling through them. But we've opened nearly every trunk down here now and all we've found are items that belonged to past owners of this castle, private items that as you have correctly pointed out belonged to past members of the

257

Chesterford family – my family, Arthur. So I think that gives me some right to look at them too.'

Arthur is silent.

'There are things down here we could display for the public to see; things I think they'd find very interesting. We make no mention throughout the castle of what went on below stairs, and I think some of the bits and pieces in this trunk in particular could be used as the basis for an exhibition about the staff of Chesterford.'

I can see Arthur's mind ticking over fast. 'That *might* be a good idea ... I suppose,' he says carefully. 'I would have no objection to you opening the rest of the trunks and seeing what you find. But, miss, I really must ask that you stop at opening the box in your hand. In fact, I beg of you that you don't.'

I notice this is the first time he's used a title to address me since he came thundering down the stairs. Normally this would please me, but all it does is make me wonder all the more why Arthur is so upset about all this.

'Why?' I ask again. 'What's in here that's so important?'

Arthur sighs and shakes his head. 'I knew you meddling would come to this. Why can't things just remain the same around here? You youngsters are obsessed with change. Change isn't always good. Sometimes change is bad.'

'Why is it bad, Arthur?' I ask, still desperate to know what he was so keen to prevent me from seeing. What on earth could be in this box that's so awful?

'Fine!' Arthur says, throwing up his hands in despair. 'Go ahead and open it, then. But don't say I didn't warn you.'

With that, Arthur turns and stomps back up the stairs without another word.

'What the hell was all that about?' Tom asks, looking mystified as we watch Arthur disappear.

'I have absolutely no idea,' I reply, shaking my head. 'But what I do know is that now I really *must* open this box and find out what's inside.'

'Wait!' Tiffany holds up her hand just as I'm about to place the tiny key, still attached to the dog collar, into the padlock. 'What if the box is cursed?'

'Excuse me?'

'What if it's cursed, and when you open it, it unleashes a whole host of misery and woe on to the castle and its inhabitants?'

'You watch too many movies, Tiffany,' I say, looking at the box. 'That is not going to happen.'

'She might be right, you know,' Tom says to my surprise. 'Arthur is pretty keen for you not to open that box. Don't get me wrong, I don't think it's cursed – sorry, Tiffany – but there must be something inside he doesn't want you to see.'

I stare down at the box in my hand, then I glance at the painting of the dog again, and across at the trunk full of Clara's dresses.

'No, we've come too far. Arthur may not want me to see what's inside here, but I'm pretty sure Clara does.'

I take a deep breath and turn the key, and as smooth as anything it immediately pops the mechanism so the padlock springs open. I remove the padlock and finally, I open up the lid.

'I knew it!' I exclaim triumphantly, lifting the contents from the box. 'It's the missing diary!'

I put the box down on the ground and begin to thumb through the pages of the book.

'What's this, though?' Tom asks, lifting up the box again and looking inside. 'There's something else in here.'

I look at what he's removing from the box. It's a small velvet pouch. Tom eases it open and pours the contents into the palm of his hand.

'It's a brooch,' Tiffany says, gazing in awe at it. 'A really pretty one, too.'

'It's more than a brooch,' Tom says. 'It's a cameo brooch.' He holds it up to the light and then to my surprise he pulls from his pocket one of those tiny magnifying eye glasses you see jewellers and antiques experts wear, and slots it into his eye.

'I'd say late nineteenth century, possibly even earlier,' he says, examining the brooch. 'These little cameos had a resurgence in popularity when Queen Victoria took to wearing them. They're usually carved from shell. This one is made from a carnelian or maybe a conch shell, I'd say by the look of its colour.'

'Can I see?' I ask.

Tom passes me the brooch. It's an exquisite white carving of a woman's head against a pale orange background. It's surrounded with gold, tiny pearls and what I think are diamonds.

'Are these real diamonds?' I ask Tom, still looking at the brooch.

'Yes, I think they are,' he says. 'I'd have to do some research, but I'd say what you're holding in your hand is pretty valuable, and possibly quite rare.'

'I wonder why it's down here with the diary?' I pick up the diary again, and put the two together. 'They must be linked. This brooch must have been Clara's too.'

'Are there any more paintings of Clara at the castle?' I ask

Tiffany. 'I've only seen the one of her in evening dress. She's definitely not wearing this brooch in that one.'

'I don't think there are,' Tiffany says, thinking. 'Not that I can remember.'

'Not to worry. So, we have a diary and a brooch,' I say, looking at the two items in my hands, 'let's put them together with the other diaries and see if we can find out what this big mystery is. And the first person we need to speak to about all that when we get back upstairs, is our friend Benji.'

Thirty-four

'Leave it with me,' is all Benji says when we find him in the library and excitedly hand him the diary.

'Is that it?' I ask, feeling a little hurt that he isn't more enthusiastic about the discovery of the missing diary. 'I thought you'd be pleased.'

'I am pleased,' Benji insists. 'Really pleased. Now I might be able to finally piece together this mystery. But it's going to take more than a quick read of this diary to do it.'

'Why? What's going on here? You've never really said, and now we've got Arthur acting strangely too. What *is* in that diary that's so important?'

I'm now beginning to wish that I'd read the diary before giving it to Benji. Perhaps I'd be able to figure it out for myself then.

'The fact you say Arthur wasn't keen for you to find this tells me that my suspicions might be correct after all. But,' Benji holds his hand up to stop me asking any more questions, 'let me do my own investigation and I'll get back to you, okay?'

'Okay . . .' I agree hesitantly.

'Amelia,' he asks, 'do you trust me?'

'Yes, of course, but—'

'Then let me do my job. I'm very good at it,' he says, smiling now, 'as you very well know . . .'

I nod. 'Sure. But you'll come and find me the minute you know anything?'

'I will.'

We leave Benji in the library opening up the first page of the diary. I thank Tiffany for her help, and then tell her to take the rest of the afternoon off so she doesn't need to bump into Arthur again today.

'But how will I be able to face him in the office tomorrow?' she asks anxiously. 'He'll still be cross with me.'

'I'll speak to Arthur before you see him again,' I tell her. 'Don't worry; I'll smooth things over for you.'

Tiffany heads back towards her room, while Tom and I stand awkwardly in the hall together.

'What are you going to do with this?' he asks, holding up the small pouch containing the brooch.

'I have no idea,' I say, taking it from him. 'I guess I'll just hold on to it for now, until I find out what's what.'

'Look after it; I reckon it might be pretty valuable.'

'Yes, I know . . .' I look down at the velvet pouch.

'Fancy a walk?' Tom asks brightly. 'After being stuck down in the cellar all that time, I could do with some fresh air.'

I look at my watch. 'Sure, I have time before I pick up Charlie.'

'Beach?' Tom suggests.

'Definitely. I'd take Chester but he's with Joey today. Although if Arthur is back then I guess Joey is too.'

'How about it's just us?' Tom asks quietly.

I nod. 'Yes, you're right. That would be nice.'

Tom and I find suitable shoes, and then we head through the grounds of the castle, and along the secret path that leads down to the beach.

'Ah,' I say, breathing in the fresh sea air, 'this feels good.'

'Doesn't it?' Tom agrees, taking hold of my hand. 'Let's walk.'

We stroll along the sand, quietly at first, each of us caught up in our own thoughts about what had happened down in the cellar.

At least that's what I'm thinking about, and I assume Tom is too.

'You've been quiet lately,' Tom says after a bit. 'I wondered why?'

'I've just got stuff on my mind, that's all.'

'What sort of stuff?'

I hesitate; I don't want more people worrying about my money troubles than is absolutely necessary.

'Financial bits and pieces,' I answer carefully.

'Oh, I thought it might be something I'd done.'

I have to smile. That was what Benji had thought, too. What is it with men? Straight or gay, they always think everything is about them. 'No, it's nothing you've done,' I reassure him.

'What's funny?' Tom asks.

'Benji said almost the same thing to me.'

Tom smiles now too. 'I guess we both care about you and want you to be happy.'

'Thank you, I appreciate both your concerns, really I do, but I'll be fine.'

'You're not great at asking for help, are you?' Tom says, stopping to look at me.

'What do you mean?'

'I mean, you've got people who want to help you make a go of this castle, but you're very reluctant to let them.'

'I am not.'

'Yes, you are. I understand why you find it difficult, Amelia, you're used to going it alone. But you really don't have to.'

I shake my head. 'No, you're wrong. I do let people help me. You and Tiffany helped me find the diary today, didn't you?'

'Only because you couldn't do it on your own.'

'What about the stables, then?' I say defiantly. 'I'm not the only one doing that. When it's open both Dorothy and Tiffany are going to be involved and have been in all the planning stages.'

'Because it suited you to have them involved. You knew it made good business sense to let them have a role.'

I look at Tom. 'What is it you want me to do, then? Hold a committee meeting regarding all my decisions both personal and professional, open my life up to all and sundry?'

'No, not to all and sundry. Only to those that are close to you – like me.'

Before I can protest further, Tom pulls me to him, and without even waiting for any sort of approval from me, or any reason for it not to happen this time, he leans down and kisses me firmly on the lips.

For the first few seconds of his kiss, I can feel myself resisting, but then I relax and allow myself to enjoy it.

My arms, which had been firmly by my sides, involuntarily reach up and wrap themselves around him, and as our kiss

265

progresses, I realise my fingers are gently caressing the back of his neck.

As we pause for a moment to catch our breath, our faces pull away from each other, but our bodies remain firmly pressed together.

'God, I've been wanting to do that for ages,' Tom says breathlessly, kissing my forehead now.

'Really?' is all I can reply.

'Of course really.' Tom looks at me with surprise. 'You are a very attractive woman, Amelia; you must know that.'

'Not really.'

'What?' He holds me back in his arms. 'You're kidding, right?'

I shake my head, and then to my embarrassment I feel a tear beginning to roll down my cheek. It's quickly followed by another one, and then a third, until suddenly my cheeks are wet and my eyesight blurred.

'Oh my, what have I said?' Tom asks, letting go of me to fumble about in his pocket for a tissue. 'Jeez, I'm useless, I don't even have a hankie to offer you.'

'It's fine,' I say, unceremoniously wiping my cheeks with the sleeve of my top. 'It's not your fault – really.'

I blink a few times to try to stop the tears from flowing, and then I dab again at my eyes with my sleeves.

'Good job I haven't got any mascara on today,' I sniff, 'or you'd be trying to retract your last statement pretty hastily by now.'

'No, I wouldn't. I'd still think you were beautiful.'

'You really have to stop saying nice things!' I hold up my hand in front of his face. 'Or there *will* be a tear tsunami.'

'Come on,' Tom says, leading me across to some rocks. 'Let's sit down for a bit so you can recover from my amazing ability to make you cry. Then you can tell me why what I said caused you so many tears. I've a feeling it might be to do with that story you promised to tell me the night we walked back from the pub.'

'What story?' I ask innocently, even though I know exactly what he means.

'The secret of why you're just like one of these before it gets washed up on to the beach,' he says, lifting a large conical shell up from the sand and passing it to me. 'Soft on the inside, but covered with a hard protective shell.'

Thirty-five

There aren't many people about on the beach this afternoon, just a couple walking a dog and a runner doing some sort of sprint training up and down the hard sand near the water's edge. So as we sit on the smooth side of some rocks, we're pretty isolated and alone.

'Right,' Tom asks gently. 'What happened that made you have such a low opinion of yourself? I know the basics, but I have a feeling there's more to this.'

I take a deep breath. It was always hard going back down this particular road to the past, but I know that if I'm going to move forward with Tom, I have to talk about it.

'You know that my husband walked out on me?' I ask, trying to judge how much Benji has told him.

'I knew you split up with your husband, but not that he walked out on you.'

Right, so Benji had been fairly discreet then.

'Yes, he just upped and left one day – no warning, nothing. I thought we were getting on fine. Obviously we had our moments, like all marriages do, but I just thought that was normal.'

'He just left you and Charlie without telling you why?'

'Uh-huh. When he'd been gone over twenty-four hours I was on the brink of reporting him missing to the police. Graham *always* warned me if he was going to be late, or anything was unusual. It was completely out of character for him just not to come home.'

Tom nods. 'So what happened then?'

'I was about to sit down and ring the police, when I found a note. It was under the table; it must have blown off on to the floor after he left so I didn't see it.'

'What did it say?' Tom prompts gently.

'It said . . . ' I take a deep breath. I don't need time to remember because I'd never forgotten. It was just difficult to voice. It always had been. 'It said he was living a lie and that he couldn't do it any more. He said he still loved me and Charlie, but that he needed to get away for a while to get his head together.'

'Did your husband have a high-powered job or something?' Tom asks. 'Was he stressed out by work?'

'Hardly. Graham worked in a bank – not as manager or anything. Just as a cashier. His job had actually helped us out when we wanted to get a house – our mortgage was that little bit easier to come by. In retrospect, we probably shouldn't have tried to take on such a big house. But we were getting married, we wanted a family. This was supposed to be our forever home.'

My voice breaks a little, and Tom puts his hand on my knee.

'And we were happy. Well, I thought we were. We had our dream wedding, then I fell pregnant with Charlie within a month of us trying – it was all so perfect. From the outside it seemed like we had everything; from the inside too, actually. But apparently he didn't see it that way.'

'So what was his problem – this *Graham*?' Tom asks harshly, with obvious disdain. 'It seems to me like he had everything a man could want. A beautiful wife, a gorgeous son, and a family home to return to every night. What could possibly have gone wrong?'

'I never really found out. I was left with a young son and no money – oh, yes, he took all that too. He probably figured I had enough with the house, but what he didn't think about was how I was going to pay the mortgage. I didn't work then, I just looked after Charlie. You can imagine how quickly my perfect life fell apart, how fast the mortgage company repossessed our home when I couldn't meet the repayments. How quickly we found ourselves without anywhere to live.'

'But couldn't you have stayed with friends or family until you got back on your feet?'

'You'd be surprised how quickly so-called friends vanish when things aren't going well for you. My problem was our friends were mainly his friends, so when he disappeared they all went very quiet.'

'Did they know where he'd gone?' Tom asks, again sounding annoyed.

'I don't think most of them did, maybe one or two. But they'd been well primed not to say anything to me.'

'What about your family, then? Couldn't they help?'

'My dad died when I was eighteen, and my mum a few months before Graham left.'

'He left you just after your mum died?' Tom asks in a voice so low it's barely audible. 'Can this ... I'll call him a fool to be polite, this fool stoop any lower?'

I shrug.

'What about any brothers or sisters – couldn't you go to them?'

I shake my head. 'Only child, me, like Charlie. That's one of the reasons I didn't want him to be. Anyway, the council kicked in eventually, and we had a few different homes before we ended up on the estate that Benji found us on. By that time I had a job and we were just about surviving on the money from that and the few benefits I was entitled to. The next part of my sorry tale is Fairy Godmother Benji turning up on my doorstep one day, telling me I now owned a castle, and then magically persuading me to come here. Tiffany said my story is a bit like a fairy tale, and I'm inclined to agree with her now after hearing myself tell it.'

'It is some tale,' Tom says, smiling sympathetically at me. 'From council estate to lady of the manor.'

'I guess. So after hearing it, can you understand why I'm a little bit wary of putting my trust in people? Why I protect myself within my "shell"?'

Tom nods. 'I can. But what I still can't get over is why your husband just left like that. And you never heard anything more from him?'

'Nope, not until about a year later when one of my ex so-called friends spotted him. I think she felt bad about abandoning me the way she had, so she got in touch again to tell me she'd seen him – over Facebook, of all things. As you can imagine I hadn't really been in the mood for updating my profile, or looking at what perfect lives others were pretending to lead, so it was a shock to get an email telling me someone had sent me a message. It was Andrea, saying she'd seen Graham in Doncaster out and about with his new partner.'

'He had a new partner!' Tom asks, his eyes wide.

'Yep, and not only that, his new partner was a man.'

271

Tom's mouth drops open. 'You're kidding me. No, I'm sorry, obviously you're not. So he's gay – or does that make him bi?'

'I wondered that too, but apparently after speaking to Andrea and doing a bit of digging myself, it turns out my ex-husband now prefers men.'

Tom shakes his head; I can only assume it's in disbelief at my sorry tale. 'So that was the lie he was living – being gay in a straight marriage?'

I shrug. 'I can only suppose so. Now do you understand why I don't tell many people about this?' I say, my own head dropping down to look at the shell still held firmly in my hand. As tightly as I've been gripping on to it, it still remains intact. No one is going to break its protective layer, a bit like no one has ever broken the one I'd put around myself and Charlie when Graham left.

'Hey, don't you dare think any of this is your fault,' Tom says, tilting my head back up to face him again. 'This isn't *anyone's* fault, let alone yours.'

'I know. But I can't help wondering if I'd done something differently ...'

'No,' Tom commands, his hand dropping away. He looks out across the sand towards the sea. 'I can never condone what your ex-husband did to you and Charlie – the way he just left like that was unforgivable. But no one can, or *should*, ever change their sexuality to suit another person.'

'You sound like you know what you're talking about.'

Tom looks down at his feet. 'I guess it's my turn to come clean,' he says, kicking at the sand.

'Oh my God, please don't tell me you're gay,' I say, only half-jokingly. 'First my husband, then Benji, not you as well. It must be me!'

Tom laughs. 'No, I'm not gay. Couldn't you tell by that kiss a few moments ago?'

'Ah yes ...' I agree as I remember Tom's passionate embrace. 'Very good point. You're doing a pretty good job of masking it if you are.'

'No, it's not me that's gay. It's my brother – Joe.'

'Joe, yes, I'd forgotten about him; the one I thought was Benji's girlfriend!'

'The very same. Joe was in a similar predicament to your husband. He wasn't married or anything, but he was hiding his sexuality. Mainly from our father who disapproved of anything that wasn't "normal", as he put it. He thought we should each settle down with a suitable girl as soon as possible once we turned twenty, have 2.4 children, and a four-bedroomed house in Surrey. Preferably continuing in the family business too. But sadly for him it didn't work out that way for either of us.'

'What happened?'

'Both Joe and I were doing exactly what Dad wanted to begin with. He'd trained us in the family firm – furniture restoration, as you know. But neither of us had settled down or wanted to. Joe because he was secretly gay, and me because,' Tom looks slightly ashamed, 'well, I was too busy playing the field.'

'At least you're honest about it.'

Tom shrugs. 'I was young; I didn't know any better. Anyway, I was always keen for Joe to come out to Mum and Dad, but he was scared; he couldn't bear the thought of them disapproving of him. To cut a very long story short, when no prospective fiancées seemed to be appearing in Joe's life, my parents stepped in and tried to set him up with a few girls. Joe went along with it, but obviously nothing ever came of it. Then

273

when they tried it with the sister of a girl I'd been dating, I had to step in.'

'What did you do?'

'I told my girlfriend the truth and of course she told her sister. Her sister wasn't the most discreet of people so word soon got out about Joe, and eventually it got back to my parents. They went ballistic.'

'I can imagine.'

'My father was furious – mainly about Joe's sexuality – but my mother was just upset that neither of us had confided in her. I felt really sorry for her, actually; I always told Joe that Mum would be okay about it.'

'What happened then?'

'There were a lot of arguments at home, before the big one. My stupid, narrow-minded father gave Joe an ultimatum.' Tom stops and shakes his head in disbelief. 'Even now I can't quite believe he said this; he told him either he stopped being gay or he moved out of the house, and the family would have nothing more to do with him.'

'He didn't? That's awful.'

'I know. You can imagine what Joe said. He packed his bags and left that night. I can still hear my mother sobbing all night in her bedroom. The next day Dad turned on me. He asked me why I'd never said anything, told me I should have been loyal to the family name, and the most ludicrous – I should have helped Joe to try harder at being straight.'

'*What?* That's madness.'

'Tell me about it. So the next day I left too. I wanted to stay for my mother's sake, but I couldn't live in a house where that sort of bigotry was present. So I packed my things and left, and I've never been back.'

'Do you have any contact with your family at all?'

'Joe and I do, obviously. Mum only through birthday and Christmas cards now. But I bet Dad doesn't know she's sending or receiving them. I haven't spoken to my father since the day I walked out.'

'I'm so sorry, Tom.' This time it's my turn to comfort him. 'Aren't humans rotten sometimes?'

Tom nods. 'Not all humans, though,' he says, and he reaches out his hand to cup my face. 'Sometimes you stumble across some pretty magnificent ones in the strangest of places ...'

Our lips meet again, and don't part for some time.

'I'm so glad I bumped into Benji again,' Tom says eventually when we do part, 'or I might not have come here and met you. When Benji mentioned you and this castle I thought it was a bit odd to begin with – I mean, what were the chances you'd need someone to restore furniture here? But he seemed so adamant I should come.'

'I know. He was trying to matchmake even then. He knew I was single and you were too – perhaps he really was living up to his fairy godmother role!'

'Ha, maybe! Anyway, I'm glad he did insist I should come. I think it's turned out rather well, don't you?'

'I do that,' I agree, leaning in towards him.

Tom puts his arm around me and we spend the rest of our time on the beach sitting close together, knowing as we look out across the sand towards the sea that whatever troubles might befall us in the future, for now we'll be facing them together.

Thirty-six

'Charlie?' I ask as we sit in the tower after school that day. 'Have you ever seen Clara?'

'Who?' Charlie asks as he munches on a ham and cheese sandwich while watching something on the old iPad that Joey lent him when he found out that Charlie doesn't have one. 'I've recently upgraded mine,' Joey had told us. 'Someone might as well get some use from this one.'

I'd felt guilty then, because Charlie still doesn't have all the things that other boys of his age seem to have. But as long as things keep progressing in the way I hope at the castle, with any luck it will soon be me that will be providing him with these types of luxuries. That's if I can ever find a way of paying for the woodworm to be permanently removed from the stables ...

'Clara,' I repeat. 'You know, the ghost that the others talked to us about in the stables.'

'Oh yeah, I remember.'

'Have you ever spoken to her?' I ask again. 'Does she pop up like the others seem to?'

I'd long ago stopped doubting Charlie's contact with the ghosts of Chesterford Castle. I had so many other things to worry about that Charlie speaking to spirits seemed the least of my worries. Besides, I could do with all the help I can get.

'Not really. The others say she's shy.'

'Yes, I understand that. It's just that I could do with asking her a few questions – about the history of the castle.'

'I'll ask Ruby to talk to her,' Charlie says, finishing off his sandwich. 'I think they're pretty close.'

'Thank you, I'd appreciate that. So ... do you know when you might see Ruby again?'

Charlie looks at me and narrows his eyes. 'You must need to see Clara pretty urgently,' he says knowingly.

'Yes, I do.'

'Why don't you just speak to her yourself?'

'I ... I wouldn't know how.' That wasn't strictly true, I'd talked to her portrait a few times.

'I think she mainly haunts the Ladies' Chamber where her portrait is, and she's appeared in the Great Hall too. That's where they used to hold all the grand balls in her day. Arthur told me.'

At the mention of Arthur's name, I'm reminded that I still need to speak to him about what happened earlier in the cellar.

'Okay, I'll bear that in mind; thank you, Charlie.'

'No worries. I'll still ask Ruby for you, though, when I see her.'

'Good boy.' I reach over to ruffle his hair, but Charlie dodges out of the way. 'Mum, I've only just done that,' he says, reaching up to smooth his untouched hair.

Since when has Charlie cared about his appearance? Perhaps he's spending too much time with Joey?

'Sorry,' I apologise automatically, and then I shake my head. 'What about a hug for your old mum, then, if I can't ruffle your hair any more?'

Charlie looks at me, and for a brief moment I think he might actually refuse. But to my relief he puts down his plate, slides across the sofa and wraps his arms around my waist while I wrap mine around his shoulders.

'Is that better?' he asks in a slightly muffled voice.

'Always,' I reply, hugging him even tighter.

Charlie might be growing up fast, but he will always be my little boy however big he gets.

The next morning, I knock on the door of Arthur and Dorothy's cottage. Unusually Arthur hadn't appeared in the office this morning, and on asking around no one had seen him.

Although the cottage is part of the castle estate, it's separated from the rest of the grounds by a picket fence, and has its own little garden filled with blossoming flowers and neatly trimmed bushes. It really is picture perfect, and could well be a photo on the front of an expensive box of chocolates, or a thousand-piece puzzle.

'Oh hello, dear,' Dorothy says on answering the door. 'I mean madam, no Lady Chest . . . er, miss?' she finishes with.

'I much prefer "dear" to "madam" or "miss",' I tell her kindly. 'Dorothy, I've just popped round to check if Arthur's all right. Only, no one has seen him about the castle this morning.'

'That's kind of you to be concerned, dear,' Dorothy says, actually listening to my preferences for once. 'Arthur is fine. His blood pressure has been a little high again, that's all. We had the doctor in this morning and he says he's to rest for a few days.'

'I'll rest for one day only!' I hear Arthur bark from inside the cottage. 'And then I'm back to work.'

Dorothy steps outside and pulls the door to behind her.

'That's what he thinks,' she whispers. 'Just between us this isn't the first time this has happened. He's on medication, but getting him to take the tablets is a fight, and getting him to take it easy is a battle that even I can't win usually. But I'm determined to this time for his own good.'

'Is there anything in particular that might have brought on this latest rise in his blood pressure?' I ask, knowing the answer before I've even asked the question.

'Your guess is as good as mine,' Dorothy says, shrugging. 'But he's not been himself for a few days, rushing here, there and everywhere like his life depended on it. I told him to slow down, but you know what he's like.'

'Yes, I do,' I say, thinking. 'Right, well, give him my best, won't you? And you keep him away from the castle for as long as is necessary, Dorothy. The castle's stood strong for many centuries; it won't quite crumble without him. Contrary to what he might think!'

'You're a good girl,' Dorothy says, patting me on the arm. 'This place wouldn't be the same without you and Charlie now, and whatever Arthur might have you think, he feels exactly the same way.'

I leave the cottage with mixed emotions. Part of me is guilt-ridden that what took place in the cellar might have caused Arthur to become ill, and part of me is feeling pleased as punch at what Dorothy had just told me.

'Amelia!' I turn around to see Benji chasing me up the path. 'I've been looking everywhere for you.'

'I've just been to see Dorothy; Arthur isn't too well – it's his blood pressure, apparently.'

'I'm not surprised his blood pressure is up, if he knows what I now know,' Benji says gravely.

'Whatever do you mean?'

'I think you'd better come with me, Amelia. We need to go somewhere quiet and comfortable for you to hear this story. It could take some time to tell.'

Thirty-seven

'So, what's all this about?' I ask Benji as we sit up in the tower with a long cool drink of Dorothy's homemade lemonade each. 'I'm guessing you've read the missing diary?'

'I have ...' Benji taps absent-mindedly on the cover of the book that sits in his lap.

'And?' I ask impatiently.

Benji looks at me. 'I think the reason this diary might have been hidden away was it contains some information, information that if it had become common knowledge might have completely changed the history of the castle.'

I open my eyes wide. *'Really?* What does it say?'

'I think you should read it for yourself in case you come up with anything different from me, but it seems that there may have been another heir apparent to Chesterford Castle when Clara took the reins.'

'What? But I thought she was the only remaining child of the previous Earl. You said he put in a special clause so she'd be able to inherit the castle.'

'No, the tenth Earl had already done that. Clara's father wanted her to inherit *everything* – the castle and grounds *and* the title. I thought originally it was simply a clause specifically for Clara, but it seems there may have been other motives for his decision.'

'Ooh, like what?' I ask, intrigued.

'This diary suggests he had another child, born before Clara – a second daughter. So in theory, as the eldest, she should have inherited the castle and the title, and not Clara.'

'Clara had a sister?' I ask, not really following this. 'But why then didn't *she* inherit everything on the Earl's death?'

'Because she was born out of wedlock,' Benji explains. 'The Earl had an affair with one of the maids at the castle before Clara was born. Reading between the lines of what Clara says in here, I would surmise that Clara's mother had trouble conceiving an heir, causing a rift in her parents' marriage. The Earl, as was common then, sought comfort, shall we say, elsewhere. Except that comfort produced a child – Clara's half-sister Mary.'

'And it says all this in that diary?' I ask. 'But why would Clara talk about it in there? She says in her previous diary she was ashamed of something. How did she put it? "A secret so big that if anyone found out it would ruin not only my reputation, but the reputation of all Chesterfords for evermore"? But why was she ashamed of her sister?'

'You're thinking about this with your twenty-first-century brain,' Benji says, 'a brain that's used to women having equal rights and a say in how their lives progress. These women didn't have that. They were bound by traditions and laws that always favoured the man.'

I think for a moment. 'She was ashamed of her because

282

she was born out of wedlock and to a maid?' I ask, starting to become irritated by Clara's snobbishness.

Benji shakes his head. 'No, I think after reading on a bit further that Clara was more ashamed of her parents' behaviour than of Mary herself. I don't think she was even aware of the sister's existence until she found some documents that suggested this had all taken place some years before. By this time her parents were both dead so she couldn't ask them about it, and she wasn't even sure that her sister knew who her father was. She'd never said anything that suggested she knew anything about him.'

'What do you mean she'd never said anything? Did Clara know her half-sister already, then?'

Benji nods. 'She worked at the castle – just like her mother had, as a lady's maid. Clara's lady's maid.'

'What? Clara's maid was her sister and they didn't know?'

'It would seem so, according to Clara's diary.'

'This is wild!'

'It gets even wilder, I can assure you.'

'Come on, Benji – spill!' I encourage. 'This is better than a soap opera.'

'With just as many twists and turns,' Benji says. 'So when Clara found out that she had a sister, Mary was still living and working in the castle grounds but she was no longer Clara's maid because she had two children of her own. She lived at the castle because her husband worked there as a groomsman, so luckily they'd been given grace-and-favour accommodation that went with the job.'

'Like Arthur and Dorothy's cottage?'

'Yes, a bit like that. Back then there were quite a few cottages like Arthur and Dorothy have now dotted about the grounds, but there were also many rooms in the castle itself that were kept for staff quarters. So Mary lived there with her two children. Sadly her husband was killed at the beginning of the First World War, but Mary was allowed to stay on in exchange for taking on some chores around the castle. Contrary to what you might be thinking about her right now, I believe Clara was a kind-hearted Countess and didn't want to see any of her staff consigned to the workhouse, especially not her sister and her nieces.'

'So she found out Mary was her sister in what year?'

'About 1912, according to the dates in the diary.'

'But she still hadn't acknowledged her by the First World War?' I ask in astonishment. 'Why on earth not?'

'Again, put on your 1912 woman's head, Amelia. Women hadn't even got the vote by then; they were still regarded as second-class citizens, especially in the aristocracy. If Clara had acknowledged Mary as the rightful heir to Chesterford Castle, and Mary hadn't been quite so kind hearted as Clara, Clara could easily have been thrown out of the castle with nothing. It's not like now where the state will help you out when things get a bit tough.'

'Hardly,' I mutter grimly. 'I've been there, remember?'

'Yes, I know, and that's why I think you'll have empathy for Clara's dilemma when you read it in her own words. But for now it falls to me to be the storyteller.'

'Go on, then. What's next?'

'So Clara chose to keep quiet. I believe she did her best to look after Mary and her children, and make sure they never went short of anything. But then tragedy struck, and Mary and one of her daughters died.'

'Oh no, what happened to them?'

284

'Spanish flu happened. There was a pandemic between 1918 and 1920; it killed hundreds of millions of people throughout the world, and it didn't miss the castle either. Mary and her daughter were immediately quarantined, and her other daughter was removed from the apartment and sent to live in the village with a local family. Luckily they managed to stem the outbreak from affecting too many people here – I read that in some books in the library, not in Clara's diary, but it did affect a few people in the village. Clara says she thinks her sister picked it up from a man that came to the castle looking for work. She says Mary took pity on him and fed him some scraps from the castle kitchen. She was probably in contact with him for no more than an hour, but that was enough: she had the virus and so did one of her daughters. They got ill, and were not strong enough to recover.'

'That is so sad,' I say, thinking how awful it must have been to get ill back then when medicine was much more basic than it is now, and the mortality rate was so high. But then something strikes me.

'Benji, does it say in Clara's diary what Mary's children were called?'

'Yes, er ... ' Benji flicks through a few pages. 'They were called Violet and Ruby.'

Ruby! My thoughts are racing faster than my mind can make sense of them. Ruby was Clara's niece. No wonder she was so kind to her in the afterlife. She felt responsible for her because of Mary.

'What's up?' Benji asks. 'You look like you've seen a ghost.' He turns around sharply. 'You haven't, have you?'

I shake my head. 'No, I leave that to Charlie. But something *has* just clicked. It doesn't matter for the moment. Is that the whole story or is there more?'

285

'Oh yes, there's more. Quite a lot more, actually.'

'You sound serious, Benji,' I say, wondering why he's treating this so sombrely. It's not a pleasant story obviously, especially the part where Mary and Ruby sadly passed away, but it wasn't anything too worrying.

'Like I said before, Mary had two children – Ruby, who passed away shortly after her, and Violet, who survived. I couldn't find out much about Violet from Clara's diaries. The mentions of Mary, as you know, seem to stop after this particular diary.' Benji taps the cover again. 'However, I've managed to do a bit of my own searching using both the castle records and some online resources, and it seems that although Violet left the castle after her mother and sister died – she was taken in by a local couple who had no children of their own, so she did stay in Chesterford – it was only later as an adult that she returned to work here again.'

'Oh, she came back? That's good. Did she have a happy life, do you know?'

'We can only hope so. She married and had two sons, David and George, I believe, but the trail seems to fizzle out after that – which is most annoying, but sadly quite common when tracing families.'

'Why does the trail fizzle out sometimes?'

'It can be for a number of reasons – records get destroyed, people change their names. Sometimes they even escape being registered at all.'

'So Violet had children; that's nice. They would have been Mary's grandchildren – am I right?'

'Yes, that's right . . .' Benji agrees hesitantly.

'What's wrong, Benji? I know something's bothering you about all this.'

'Well, you know I had my suspicions when I read the previous diary to this one. That's why I was so keen for us to find the missing diary – the missing piece of the puzzle, as it were. But now I know what I do, my suspicions have been confirmed.'

'Suspicions of what?' *What is Benji going on about?*

Benji takes a deep breath. 'That you, Amelia, might not be the rightful heir to Chesterford Castle. Now we know about Mary and her offspring, both you and Charlie might not be the last Earl's next living relatives. There could be someone else.'

Thirty-eight

'What do you mean *someone else*?' I ask, my heart beating hard against my chest. 'Who? I mean, how ...? Oh, I don't know what I mean. I'm confused.' I reach for my lemonade, wishing, unusually for me, that it was something stronger.

'That's understandable; it is somewhat confusing and, if I might say, a tad ambiguous on my part. That's why I haven't said anything before, in case I was mistaken.'

'Benji, cut the waffle and just tell me.'

Benji nods. 'Okay, let's go back to why I thought originally you were the rightful heir. If you remember it was because you were descended from Clara's side of the family. Not directly, Clara didn't have any children, but indirectly through her father's side. However, that was when I thought Clara was the only child of the fourteenth Earl. Now we know there was another *elder* sister, any claim to the Chesterford dynasty should by right come from that line – from Mary's descendants.'

'So that would be Violet and her family?'

'Exactly.'

I think about this. 'You said Violet had two sons. So it's the eldest son we should be thinking about here – David?'

Benji nods. 'Initially.'

'And did he have any children?'

'No, David died young of tuberculosis.'

'Oh, what about George, then? Did he have any children?'

'I believe so – at least one.'

'So where are they now?'

'That, I'm afraid, is where this puzzle annoyingly has its missing piece – in the form of George's child.'

'But there must be a record of their birth.'

'Frustratingly, I can't find one.' Benji looks like he's taking this as a personal failure.

'Then how do you know there is a child? I say "a child" but how old would they be now? We've spoken about so many generations that I've lost track of how old they'd be.'

'Difficult to say exactly how old, because even though there is a limited window of procreation for woman, in theory men can sometimes father children until they're well into their seventies, sometimes even beyond that.'

'Benji, try to keep on track please,' I encourage him.

Benji nods. 'So if George fathered a child with his wife, Louisa, then we'd be looking at a window of about twenty years.'

'Twenty years!'

'Yes, remember there was a lack of contraception back then, so women were having children commonly into their forties – especially if they had a big family. They didn't always survive, but I'd say we'd be likely looking for a baby born in the late 1940s to early 1960s.'

'But that's a huge span of time, Benji. They could be, what, as old as seventy now or as young as fifty?'

'Yes, as long as the child we're looking for was conceived with his wife. But as I'll go on to in a moment, I think it's likely it was. However, what this child and any offspring of this child all have in common is that they as direct descendants of Mary would have more of a right to the castle and the title than you and Charlie do.'

I drain the last of my lemonade while I think.

'But you said you couldn't find any traces of them? Why not, if you can trace all these other Chesterfords?'

'Strictly they're not Chesterfords – none of them ever had the family name, for obvious reasons when you hark back to Clara's sister, Mary.'

'But why does the family tree stop at George? And how do you know he had a child if you can't find any records of them?'

'Because of this.' Benji holds up an old newspaper clipping, yellowed with age and beginning to curl around the edges. 'I found this in one of the family record books when I was researching for the tour guides. It was in with some information on staff in the castle at that time. Here,' he passes me the paper, 'read what it says.'

I take the clipping from him, looking at the photo from the article first. It's a photo of a man, a woman and a baby. They are standing on a large expanse of grass with the castle in the background. I'd say from their dress the photo was taken in the late forties, maybe the early fifties. I begin to read what the copy says underneath the photo.

George Edwards (Chief Footman) and his wife, with their newborn baby after the fire.

'Fire?' I ask, looking at Benji.

'Read on,' Benji says.

The Chesterford family and their staff are thanking
their lucky stars that a fire that began in the library
of the castle last month was quickly intercepted by
Chief Footman, George (above), and two of his fellow
staff. The fire, which is thought to have been ignited
by an incorrectly extinguished cigarette left burning
in an ashtray, is said to have wiped out over half
of the family's extensive collection of books, and a
wall that possessed records dating back some fifty
years of many of the castle's staff. The current Earl
said, 'We are incredibly grateful to George and his
team for extinguishing the fire as quickly as they
did. Without them, it might have gone on to cause
significantly more damage to the many priceless
works of art that we have here at Chesterford.'

'So this is George?' I say, looking at the faded photo again.
'And is this the missing child?'

'It could be. There's no record of a child anywhere else that I
can find, possibly because the castle records were destroyed in
the fire. But this *is* our George, and in this photo he has a newborn baby. It could be the first of many or the only one. Like I
say, for some reason official records seem to stop around now for
George and his family. There's nothing in the later census records
for any of them, and the previous one doesn't include a child.'

'But if this child is still alive,' I hold up the newspaper
clipping, 'then the chances are they are the rightful heir to
Chesterford Castle?'

Benji nods. 'Either them or possibly even their children. So now, Amelia, it falls to you to make the difficult decision.'

'It does?'

'Yes, somewhat like Clara, your ancestor before you, you have to decide whether to come clean about this new line of Chesterfords or keep quiet and retain the castle for yourself, and the title for your son.'

Thirty-nine

'There's no way I can keep quiet about this, can I?' I say to an expectant Benji, as I pace about the top floor of the tower. 'It wouldn't be right.'

'Clara did,' Benji says pragmatically. 'She knew it was in her best interests to keep quiet about Mary.'

'Well, Clara and I are very different breeds of Chesterford then. I can't possibly take away someone's right to all this.' I gesture out of the window at the castle below. 'If this isn't rightfully mine and Charlie's, then we'll have to move out.'

As I'm saying this, an awful feeling of dread begins to spread right through me.

'Are you sure?' Benji asks. 'You're doing great things here, Amelia. Perhaps you *are* the right Chesterford to take the castle on.'

I turn away from the window to look at Benji.

'Do you want to go back to the estate?' he continues. 'What about Charlie? You've told me several times how well he's doing since he came here. Is it in *his* best interests to make him leave his new home and move elsewhere again?'

I think about Charlie now. Benji is right, he's been doing incredibly well since we came to live here; he's definitely happier, and he's doing so much better at school. By making him move again I'd likely be affecting *his* future too, not only my own.

'Perhaps you should think about it,' Benji says softly. 'And you're forgetting one thing.'

'What's that?'

'We don't even know if George's baby is still alive. I hate to sound morbid, but the fire the newspaper is referring to took place in 1952. That baby would be around sixty-seven years old now – things happen.'

'That *is* morbid, Benji,' I tell him. 'You spend too much time reading about death.'

'I speak only the truth,' Benji says, shrugging.

'*Even* if they have passed away,' I concede, 'they might have had children of their own, so then one of them would be the rightful Chesterford heir.'

Benji sighs. 'All right then, even if either the baby or one of their imaginary children is still alive, the chances of me finding him or her are minimal. Remember how long it took me to find you – and that's when I actually wanted to.'

I stare hard at Benji, and he returns my gaze with one just as steely.

'I like you being here, Amelia,' he says. 'A lot of people like you being here. You've done a tremendous amount of good, not only to the castle but to yourself and your family, too. If you want my opinion, I think you should forget all about this diary, all about Mary and her offspring, and continue doing what you already are – making sure that this castle remains here for another few centuries to come. That's all any Chesterford has ever aimed to do, and I think makes you the best person to look after this castle that there could ever be.'

'Thank you, Benji,' I say, blinking back the tears that have formed in the corner of my eyes. 'That's a lovely thing for you to say, really it is, but I need to think about this. The Chesterfords seem to be a mixed bunch – some of them honourable people, some of them not so much.' I think about Clara again. 'But what I do know is that I am an honourable person, and what you're asking me to do goes against all my principles.'

'I know that,' Benji says, 'but I beg you to give this some serious thought, Amelia. What you decide won't just affect you and Charlie, it will affect everyone else in your castle family as well. You should consider them, too, when you make your decision.'

'Are you okay, Mum?' Charlie asks me later when he's getting ready for bed. 'You've been very quiet tonight.'

After Benji dropped his bombshell, I spent the rest of the afternoon pacing around the castle trying to decide what to do. I knew what the *right* thing was; but like Benji had pointed out, was that the *best* thing for everyone?

On my travels I'd watched Joey toiling happily in the gardens, Tom studiously polishing a mahogany table until you could virtually see his reflection in it, Dorothy in the kitchens making iced cup-cakes for everyone's tea because 'Master Charlie had asked so nicely for them' and Tiffany cheerfully in charge of the office while Arthur was away. I'd even stood and watched some visitors wander around the Great Hall, and I'd enjoyed for once their funny comments and often naive observations at what they found there.

Everyone had been doing what they always did. But what had struck me today for the first time was how happy everyone was doing it.

'Come and sit down,' I say to Charlie, patting the sofa next to me. 'I want to ask you something.'

'Yes?' Charlie says cautiously as he sits down. 'What have I done?'

'You haven't done anything,' I tell him. 'I'm not going to scold you. Now we've been living here at Chesterford for a while, I want to ask you how you like it.'

Charlie still looks a tad suspicious, but he puts on his 'thinking' face. 'I like it,' he says succinctly. Then he looks at me as though that should be enough.

'You like it, is that all?'

Charlie nods. 'What more do you want? It's cool living here – much better than the flat was.'

'Yes,' I smile, 'it is a *little* bit better than the flat.'

'I like the people we live with, too. Because we've moved around a lot, we've never really made many friends, have we? I mean, I've made friends at school, but you don't make many friends, Mum, and I think you have friends here at the castle, friends that make you happy.'

'Yes, I think I have friends here too.' I'm touched Charlie is thinking about me in this.

'Actually, the people we live with here feel like more than just friends; they feel like my family. Because I've never really had much of those either, have I?'

'No, I don't suppose you have.'

'I mean, I know I must have some family somewhere, but we don't ever see them, do we? And I know I have a dad, but I never see him either.'

296

To Charlie's credit, he doesn't say this last part at all accusingly. He just states it as a fact.

'No, I'm afraid you don't. I'm sorry about that.'

'It's okay.' Charlie shrugs. 'Now we live here I sort of have a surrogate family, don't I?'

I'm surprised Charlie even knows the word surrogate, let alone how to use it in the correct way.

'I have Dorothy and Arthur, who are sort of like a granddad and grandma to me, and I have Joey and Tiffany, who are like a big brother and sister. Benji is like my fun uncle and Tom ...' He hesitates for the first time. 'Well, I think if you like him as much as he likes you, he might become my new dad in the future.'

My cheeks immediately flush a shade I can only imagine is a bright crimson. 'What makes you say that?' I try to ask as casually as possible. 'Has Tom said something to you?'

'Not really, but I know he likes you – a lot. Sometimes when we're together he asks me about you and stuff.'

'Oh, does he?'

'Yeah, just things like what you like and if you ever talk about him.'

'I see.'

'But only in a good way,' Charlie insists, seeing my face. 'Don't be cross with him, Mum.'

'I'm not cross. I like Tom too; very much, actually.'

'Good, because I don't want to have to leave here and go somewhere else. I like living at Chesterford Castle, and most of all I really *love* my new family.'

I tuck Charlie up in his bed and kiss him goodnight. Then I wander through to the lounge and stare out of the window at the sun setting over the beach.

What Charlie said tonight has affected me in several ways. Not just what he said about Tom, flattering though that was, but mainly what he said about having a brand-new family.

From the day Charlie was born I've tried to give him everything, and until I became a single mother and we had to move out of our big house and into a series of council flats, I thought I'd been doing pretty well at it.

Even then I tried to not have him want for anything, as difficult as that was. But what I haven't been able to provide him with, and what I realise he's been longing for all this time, is a stable home and a family. And now it seems that Chesterford Castle has given him both of those things.

What right do I have to take that away from him?

But what right do I have to take it away from someone else?

Forty

'Did you read it?' Benji asks me the next morning. 'The diary, I mean.'

'Of course I read it. I was up until the early hours reading it.'

'And what do you think?'

'I think we should be talking about this somewhere no one else can hear us.'

I guide Benji away from the kitchen where he and the others have just had their breakfast. Charlie had also joined them this morning, but I hadn't really felt that hungry, so I'd politely declined Dorothy's kind offer of pancakes, fruit and maple syrup.

'Perhaps I was a bit harsh on Clara,' I tell him, when I think we're safely out of earshot. 'It appears she did feel some remorse for her course of action, and she did talk very kindly of both Mary and her children, and how she wouldn't see them go without.'

'See, I told you. She did the right thing for her ...' Benji looks hopefully at me.

'I know what you're hinting at, Benji, and I'm sorry to inform you that I still haven't made my final decision yet.'

'Oh.' His face falls.

'I think we should at least try to find this child of George's, and then I'll decide what to do next.'

'Based on what? Whether he or she needs to inherit, or is even worthy of inheriting, an ancient castle by the sea in Northumberland?'

'No, not that at all. I don't know what I'll base my decision on, but I think we have to find them before we do anything else.'

'All right then,' Benji concedes. 'I'm guessing you want me to be the one to do the searching?'

'Would you? But before you start I think I may have something else for us to go on.'

'What's that?'

'This.' I hold up the velvet pouch that we'd found in the cellar along with the diary.

'What's that?' Benji asks.

'It's a brooch.' I tip the cameo on to the palm of my hand. 'I think it must have belonged to Clara. It was with the diary, locked away in the chest where we found lots of her other things.' I'd thought at the time that it was odd that servants' clothes were packed away with Clara's things. Now I realise they probably belonged to her sister, Mary.

'It looks expensive,' Benji says, examining the brooch.

'Tom thinks it might be worth quite a bit, but I'm not concerned with that right now. What is important is that Clara mentions this brooch in her diary. She says she had two pieces of jewellery commissioned: one, this cameo, was carved into a likeness of her. The other was a pendant and bore a likeness of her sister. Clara kept the brooch, but she gave the pendant to Mary on a chain, claiming it was a thank-you gift for being her lady's maid. She insisted to Mary that if she was ever in need she should sell the pendant and use the money. But Mary apparently was so moved by the gesture that she promised to keep it for ever and pass it down through her family, so they would all know the kindness of Clara, Countess of Chesterford.'

Benji stares at me with a wrinkled forehead, trying to take all this in. 'Yes, I remember reading that. But because I didn't know we had the brooch, I didn't see it as important at the time. So if a matching pendant to this *was* passed down through Mary's family, and has never been sold, then the new heir would probably own it now?'

'Yep, that's what I'm hoping.'

Benji nods. 'This is good. If we do need a way to clarify that we've got the right person, we can see if they have, or someone in their family has the pendant. But I still maintain we have to find them first,' he insists. 'And that is not going to be easy.'

'If anyone can do it, you can, Benji. Please?' I gaze imploringly at him when he still looks doubtful. 'I know you don't really want to, but for me?'

'All right then,' he begrudgingly agrees. 'But I want it on record that this is against my better judgement.'

'What are you two in cahoots about?' Tom asks, suddenly popping up next to us and making us both jump. 'If I didn't know better, I'd be jealous seeing the two of you whispering away to each other.'

'We're just discussing the brooch, actually,' I say truthfully. 'Benji thinks it might be worth something too.'

'Maybe you should sell it,' Tom suggests. 'It might cover the extra work you're worried about on the stables?'

'No! I could never sell this,' I say a bit too quickly, clutching the brooch to my chest. 'It ... it's a family heirloom.'

Tom stares doubtfully at me for a moment before turning his attention to Benji. 'Benj, what do you reckon?'

'I agree with Amelia,' Benji says rapidly. 'I think this brooch could prove too important to ever consider selling.'

Tom looks between the two of us now. 'Hmm ... I know you two are up to something. Okay, if you won't sell the brooch, what are you going to do?' he asks. 'You still haven't found a way to pay this woodworm bill yet. And I'm sure I don't need to remind you, Amelia, but time is rapidly running out before you have to do just that.'

'Actually, I might be able to help you there,' Benji says quickly. 'I have a contact who works for one of the larger banks; I haven't spoken to him for a while, but the last I heard he was specialising in loans to big businesses.'

'You do?' I ask in surprise. 'I mean ... do you think we qualify as a big business?'

'You don't get much bigger than a castle, do you?' Benji says, thrusting his hands widely in the air. 'I'll contact him and see if he can give us any advice.'

'Thanks, Benji,' I say. 'I appreciate it.'

'Now, I've got *many* things to do! Let me leave you two lovebirds alone, so you can chirp sweet nothings to each other, or whatever it is you do!' He winks at us. 'Toodle pip!'

'Word sure spreads fast around here,' I say, rolling my eyes at Tom as Benji departs down the corridor. 'About us, I mean.'

'Does that surprise you?' he asks. 'And I like hearing you say *us*.'

I smile at him and take hold of his hand. 'Nothing surprises me about this place any more,' I say, leaning my face towards his. 'Absolutely nothing.'

'So what are you up to today, then?' Tom asks after we've spent a few minutes close together doing something similar to what Benji has just suggested. Except there's more kissing involved and slightly less chirping!

I don't like lying, but I can hardly tell Tom the truth, which is that I'm going to try to speak to a ghost.

'Oh, this and that – the usual.'

'Can I take you out to dinner later?' Tom asks. 'It's about time we had our first official date.'

'That sounds lovely,' I reply coyly, suddenly feeling shy when he mentions the word date. 'Where were you thinking of taking me?'

'There's a cute little bistro in the village,' Tom says. 'It's small, but the food is delicious.'

'That sounds good ... in theory.' I hesitate. 'But if it's small and local won't someone see us there, and then it won't just be the castle that's gossiping about the "countess",' I do air quotes with my fingers, 'and her latest beau. It will be the whole village too.'

'That's true, I guess. It bothers you, then, people knowing about us?' Tom looks a little hurt.

'No, of course not,' I tell him, touching his arm. 'But this is all so new, Tom, I don't want people getting the wrong idea. Okay, I don't want Charlie getting the wrong idea. He's young and impressionable, and he's been hurt in the past.'

'If it's Charlie you're worried about, then I'll let you off,' Tom says. 'I think the world of him, you know that.'

'Yes, and that's why we mustn't confuse him.' I hold Tom's gaze with a meaningful look.

303

'I understand. Right.' He taps the side of his nose. 'You leave it with me, Countess. We shall have that date, and we shall dine like kings ... or is that queens?' He winks. 'But what I can guarantee is it will be very secretive and very, *very* private.'

Reluctantly, I leave Tom and make my way upstairs to the office. There are some things I need to check on before I go down to the Ladies' Chamber to see if I can speak to Clara.

Tiffany is already working away happily when I get there.

'Everything all right, Tiffany?' I ask, secretly hoping she might have something she needs my help with.

'Yeah, everything is fine here, boss,' Tiffany says, saluting me. 'Everything is running like clockwork, even in Arthur's absence. Don't tell him that, though, will you? He likes to think this ship can't sail without him.'

So with Tiffany giving me no reason to put this visit off any longer, I head along the corridor and down the stairs to the Great Hall. I check my watch: it's just gone ten o'clock. I should be pretty safe just yet from any visitors – the human kind, anyway – they usually don't start appearing at the castle gates until just before eleven, unless they're very keen.

I walk through the Great Hall and press the rose on the carving to allow me access to the Ladies' Chamber. As always the door slides open, and I'm granted access to the light bright turquoise room.

But today, instead of leaving the door open, I use the handle that's on the other side of the door to slide it shut again. I don't want to risk anyone witnessing what I'm about to do.

To begin I sit on the chaise longue, looking incredibly awkward with my knees together and my hands in my lap. Then I stand up and move towards the window, wondering if this might feel more comfortable. When it doesn't, I walk over and stand in front of the painting of Clara and gaze up at her, wondering exactly what you say to summon a ghost. When this doesn't bring forth anything from my lips, I go and sit down at the little piano.

And at that moment it comes to me.

I begin to tap lightly on one of the piano keys, just the one, over and over, just like Clara said she'd done in her diary, and just like I believe she had done to summon me, when Tom and I were searching for her diary.

This should feel irritating, but strangely, it actually feels quite comforting to continually hear the same familiar note.

Just as I'm becoming completely mesmerised by the sound, I feel quite chilly. I look up at the window in case it's been left open again, but it's definitely tightly shut today. And it's as I'm thinking about this that I feel something brush my hand.

Initially I jump, but then I realise this is what I'm here for. I try to think about Charlie and how he'd react to this.

'Hi,' I say to the empty room. 'I felt you just then. It's good you could join me today.' *It's good you could join me today?* I repeat in my head. *What was that?*

But whatever or whoever is in the room with me isn't put off by my stilted conversation, because I feel something brush against my hand again.

I couldn't be imagining this, could I? I wonder as I stare at my hand. *This has to be real.*

'Is that you, Clara?' I venture in a tiny voice. 'Are you really there?'

The sound of a single note on the piano begins to fill the room again. But this time it's not me who's pressing the key.

305

As I stare transfixed at the piano keyboard, I hear a distant voice.

Is it Clara? Is she speaking to me at last?

'I'm so pleased you're here, Clara,' I whisper, looking around the room. 'I have so much I need to ask you.'

Suddenly the piano stops playing and I hear another sound – the sound of the secret door sliding back on its old cranky mechanism.

I whip my head around so fast that I almost give myself whiplash.

'Wowee!' I hear as two small boys are revealed on the other side of the doorway. 'That is so cool.'

'Jamie, Luther!' A woman's voice now. 'I told you not to touch anything. Oh, I'm so sorry,' she apologises as she sees me sitting at the piano looking dazed. 'We didn't mean to disturb you.'

I stand up quickly. 'No, not at all. Your boys have simply discovered the entrance to a secret room, that's all. We sometimes have this room open to the public, but I was just ... ' I search desperately for inspiration. 'I was just tuning the piano.'

'Ah,' the woman glances doubtfully at the piano, 'I see. I do apologise again. We'll leave you to it. Come along, boys.'

'Enjoy the rest of your visit to Chesterford Castle!' I call as they depart back into the Great Hall. I hear the boys banging on the suits of armour as they pass them, even though there's a clear sign that says, 'Please Do Not Touch'.

I look around the room, but the feeling I'd had a few moments ago has now disappeared, and I am in no doubt that Clara – if she'd ever really been here at all – has definitely gone.

I leave the door to the Ladies' Chamber ajar and head back upstairs.

Am I imagining all this? I ask myself again. *Have all the things that have happened really been the result of spirits roaming the halls of Chesterford? Or am I just desperate to discover the answers to several of my most pressing problems, and this is the only way I can see of solving them?*

But then I think about Charlie. He couldn't be imagining all this, could he? Although I have to admit last night he had talked about how glad he was he had a family again here at the castle. Perhaps this ghost thing is about something similar – something he lacks in his life that he needs to find answers for.

I'm just passing the Blue Bedroom when I notice the door is pulled to. That's odd, the doors to all the state rooms are always open when visitors are in the castle.

I'm just reaching my hand towards the handle when I hear a noise coming from inside the room, and then giggling.

Is it Percy up to his old tricks?

Because I'd doubted their existence, are the ghosts showing me they are really here again?

I push open the door to enter the bedroom, expecting to see nothing as I'd done that last time I'd heard sounds on the other side of these walls. But to my surprise, and subsequent shock, I do see something, and it's something I really don't want to see before I've had my morning coffee. In fact, at any time of the day.

It's the sight of two shapes writhing about under the bedclothes.

But these definitely aren't celestial bodies, they are very real ones.

'Excuse me!' I say in a voice that sounds prim, even to me. 'What on earth do you think you're doing?'

The faces on the two bodies turn towards my voice, looking even more shocked than I feel.

'Oh God!' the young man says, grabbing at the blue silk eiderdown. 'We didn't think anyone would be up here this early.'

The girl in the bed with him attempts to cover her body as best she can. 'I told you this wasn't a good idea, Stu!' she hisses. 'You and your bloody dares.'

'I think you'd both better get out of there and get dressed as quickly as you can,' I tell them in the same stern voice. 'I assume those are your clothes over there on the chair?'

Stu nods. 'We're really sorry,' he says, trying to stand up, but he takes the blue eiderdown with him, and his girlfriend squeals.

'Oh sorry, Jen.' He drops the cover back over her, but then realises that he is now the naked one. He grabs a cushion to hide his modesty. 'Will you tell the owner?' he asks in a 'please don't' sort of voice.

'I am the owner,' I tell him, trying now I'm over the initial shock to keep a straight face. 'So I've already been told.'

'It was just a dare,' Stu pleads. 'There's a rumour that this bedroom is haunted, and my mate dared me I couldn't do it in a haunted bed.' He grimaces as he hears himself.

'Please, miss,' Jen says now. 'If you're the new owner I've heard really good things about you. How you're turning this place around, modernising it and stuff, and how liked you are in the village. My mum is always talking about you and her job here.' She slaps her hand over her mouth.

'Your mother works here?' I ask. 'No,' I shake my hand at her, 'don't tell me who she is; I don't want to know or I won't be able to look her in the face.'

308

'Come on, miss, you must have been young once,' Stu tries now. 'I bet you got up to loads of stuff like this.'

I look at them both and realise how young they are. When had I got so old and sensible? It didn't seem five minutes since I was young and carefree too.

'I may well have got up to some things,' I tell Stu, 'but I can assure you I never did anything quite like this. Now, I'm going to go downstairs and make myself a cup of coffee. When I come back up here, you'd both better be gone, that bed had better be made up just like you found it, and this room had better be absolutely spotless, do you hear?'

Two heads nod hurriedly.

'Right, you have five minutes max!'

I turn and leave them in their compromising positions, and then I wait until I'm a long way down the corridor and halfway down the stairs before I burst into uncontrollable laughter.

Oh to be young, carefree and . . . wait . . . am I already in love?

Forty-one

'Tom, you didn't have to go to all this trouble,' I tell him as I enter the Great Hall, and see a long table that looks at first glance as if it's been laid out for a magnificent banquet. Three silver candelabras have been set at intervals along the table, and in between those sit small flower posies made up of buds I recognise from the castle gardens. The table is covered in a long white cotton cloth, and there are various silver serving dishes and jugs distributed along it. But the reason I know the table isn't expecting many guests to dine at it this evening is because at one end there are just two place settings. Matching white china plates sit next to each other, with sets of silver cutlery on either side of them, above those various sizes of glass wait hopefully for wine or even champagne to be poured into them.

All that's missing are the two diners to fill the empty seats.

'I wanted to make this special,' Tom says, 'even if it is secret. Besides, I did have a little bit of help from the others.'

'Which others?' I ask, as I wander along the side of the table, admiring the elegance and sophistication of it all.

'To begin with, Joey and I had to get this huge table in

here – which was no mean feat, I can tell you; it's pretty heavy and incredibly awkward to get around corners. Joey also cut the flowers for me from the castle gardens, and Tiffany helped me to arrange them. Arthur then gave me *very* detailed instructions on how to set the table correctly, Benji helped me do it, and of course Dorothy was pretty involved in the cooking. Although I did help with that, too.'

'Wow, you have been busy.' I look up from the table and smile shyly at him. 'I'm touched, really I am.'

Tom hurries around to one side of the table and holds a chair out for me.

'Madam?' he says.

'This is where the formalities stop,' I say, waggling my finger at him. 'No titles. You know how much I hate them.'

I sit down and Tom pulls out his own chair and sits down next to me. We're not seated opposite each other, but instead we sit on two sides of the end of the table at right angles to each other. It's much cosier, and I'm glad he's set it like this.

'So why do you hate titles so much?' Tom asks after enquiring which wine I'd like. He begins to pour me a glass. 'You look gorgeous, by the way; that dress really suits you.'

I'm wearing a beautiful, floaty, scarlet-red dress lent to me from the wardrobe of Tiffany. When she found out that Tom and I were going on our first official date, she insisted on dressing 'Cinders for the ball'.

'Thank you, it's Tiffany's. I didn't really have anything glamorous enough – it's been a long time since I had to dress up for anything. You look very smart too.'

'Thanks – this is actually my own, though.' Tom gestures to his smart trousers and white shirt. 'Tiffany is one thing, but I wouldn't want to have borrowed anything from Arthur!'

I smile at him.

'Now, you were about to tell me about this title thing?' Tom asks again as he returns the bottle to the ice bucket. 'What's the big issue?'

'I would have thought that was obvious, isn't it?'

'Not really. I completely understand why you'd prefer not to be called "Lady" or "madam", but you seem *so* against it. I've seen your face when someone makes a mistake and addresses you in that way. You absolutely detest it.'

'I do; it really irritates me. I've always believed that everyone is equal in life, and I've brought Charlie up to treat everyone the same whether they're a different age, gender, colour or they come from a different background to him. I dislike people having titles bestowed upon them, whether it's through family ties or an honour from the Queen. It's not right.'

'The people who get an honour from the Queen deserve it, though, surely? Many of them have done great work for charity.'

'That's true, I suppose. All right, maybe not so much when they get an OBE or an MBE after their name – that's acceptable, I guess. But why do they have to become Sir this or Dame that? It's giving them a title that suggests they're better than someone who hasn't got one.'

Tom nods. 'You could be right.'

'I am right,' I reply adamantly. 'This is something I feel very strongly about. I've been on both sides of the fence, Tom. I've been very comfortable, with my nice house and my easy life, where I'm ashamed to admit my only worry was whether my curtains matched my sofa. But I've also found myself living on very little money, worried sick that I'd have enough food to last the week or that the meter would keep running long enough to keep us warm.'

312

'But you were still the same person throughout both those times in your life, were you not?'

'I definitely was. But other people didn't treat me the same. It was like I was a second-class citizen when we lived on the council estate. People looked down their noses at us, people who we'd once called our friends.'

'They say you find out who your friends are in times of need.'

'I can certainly vouch for that!' I lift my glass and take a sip. 'Very nice,' I say approvingly.

'And now you find yourself at the other end of the spectrum again,' Tom says, looking down the Great Hall. 'Living here as lady of the manor – even if you don't wish to be known as that,' he adds hurriedly.

'I know. I had to think very hard about bringing Charlie here when I found out about not only the castle but the Chesterford title too.'

'Why?'

'I didn't want him turning into one of *those* kids: the sort that think they're better than the others.'

'But Charlie isn't like that. He's a great kid.'

'I know; that's why I don't want him to change.'

'With you as his mother I don't think he'll stray too far from what's right. Besides, this castle is your family's history, isn't it? You both deserve to live here.'

I take another, longer sip from my glass.

'Let's talk about something else,' I say quickly. 'So, when am I going to taste some of this delicious food that you helped Dorothy cook?'

When Tom told me how much the others had helped him prepare for tonight, I wondered if they might be waiting on us too this evening, which I would have felt very uncomfortable about. So I'm quite relieved when Tom gets up and disappears for a few minutes and returns with our first course – a cold salmon mousse with mini oatcakes accompaniment.

'How did you know I liked salmon?' I ask him, tucking hungrily into the dish in front of me.

'A little bird told me.' Tom winks. 'Enjoy.'

After our delicious first course, Tom gets up again, collects our plates and heads back down to the kitchen.

'Can I help you at all?' I ask before he leaves, anxious that he's doing all the work.

'No, you just sit right there and relax,' he says, heading out of the door. 'I've got it all covered.'

So I do as he says and sit back in my chair sipping my wine, enjoying for once the sense of stillness and quiet that surrounds me. I don't usually get much peace when I'm here in the castle. I spend so much time rushing here and there trying to get things done before I have to collect Charlie from school, that I don't get to appreciate how calm and tranquil the castle can be.

But as I'm sitting having my few moments of peace, something strange happens. I feel something cold brush lightly past me, like someone has left a window open and a draught is wafting in. Nothing unusual there: this castle is full of draughty rooms, but this feels different. I feel a bit like I had in the Ladies' Chamber earlier today before I'd been disturbed by the two boys ...

'Clara?' I whisper into the vast room. 'Are you here?'

Silence is my only reply.

Perhaps I'm imagining it, I think, looking down at my glass. But I haven't had a lot of alcohol at all so far. In fact, I'm pretty clear-headed.

But then I feel it again, the same coolness, and something very definitely brushes past my seat.

I leap up and look around me wildly just as Tom walks backwards through the door carrying a large wooden tray.

'Here we go,' he says, turning around with the tray in his hands. 'Oh, what's up?'

'Nothing,' I say, sitting down again quickly. 'That smells wonderful, Tom. What is it?'

'This,' Tom says, putting down the tray and lifting the hot plates up with a white cloth, 'is a chicken and mushroom pie, with new potatoes and asparagus. Sorry it's not fancier, but I think you'll like it.' He lifts up the silver lids that cover the food on each salver.

'I don't need fancy, because again this is one of my favourites,' I tell him, smiling. 'This little bird you've been talking to, is it my son, by any chance?'

'Ah, you guessed,' Tom says, sitting down. 'I didn't think it would take you long. Yes, even Charlie has had a part in all this. He provided the menu suggestions.'

'Then it gets more perfect by the minute,' I tell him. 'Let's tuck in, shall we?'

I'm starting to feel quite full by the time we get to the end of our second course. I haven't sensed anything else since Tom has been back in the room, and the temperature has now returned to normal, but I can't help wondering if something might happen when he goes back to the kitchen.

'Shall we wait a bit before I fetch dessert?' Tom asks as I put my knife and fork down on my empty plate. 'I don't know about you, but I'm pretty full already.'

So was I, but I was also keen to find out if Clara might still be here.

315

'Maybe just a few minutes,' I reply to be polite. 'I'm very keen to know what you have for me next, though. My favourite dessert is flambéd crème brûlée. How you're going to get that from the kitchen to here while it's still alight I can't wait to see.'

I watch Tom's face drop. 'Oh ...er ... ' he falters.

'I'm only kidding.' I grin. 'You should know by now my tastes are a little simpler than that.'

'Phew,' Tom rolls his eyes, 'you had me going for a moment there! I've only done an apple crumble with vanilla ice cream.'

'Then that will be just perfect,' I say, 'just like the rest of this meal has been.' I reach out and put my hand over his. 'Thank you so much for this, Tom. If you'd suggested us dining in here earlier, I would have tried to put you off, thinking it far too formal for just the two of us. But it's been lovely, really it has.'

'Good,' Tom says, putting his hand over mine. 'I'm glad you're happy.'

'I'd be even happier if I had a plate of apple crumble and ice cream in front of me, though,' I say, smiling hopefully at him.

'Really?' Tom says. 'Already?'

'Can't wait!' I fib. Truthfully, I was probably fuller than he was.

'Right then, just give me a few minutes.'

Tom clears our plates and pops them on the tray, but he knocks the salt cellar over in the process. Grains of salt spill all over the dark wood floor.

'Damn,' Tom says, looking at the salt in horror. 'I'll bring a dustpan and brush back with me when I come back up. Won't be a few minutes.'

'Don't worry,' I say, holding the door open for him as he takes the tray of dirty plates and heads back down to the kitchen. 'Take all the time you need.'

As soon as I think he's out of earshot I turn back to the empty room. 'Right then. Are you in here, Clara, or not? I suggest if you are you make yourself known before Tom returns with our dessert.'

I stand still in the silence and listen.

To begin with there's nothing, and then I hear a strange sound. It's like someone very softly swishing something around on a hard surface. *What was that?*

I look around the room but I can see nothing, only hear this strange, barely audible scratchy sort of sound. If the room hadn't been so quiet, I probably wouldn't have heard it at all.

But apparently I don't actually need to hear anything, because my wandering gaze suddenly rests on the floor next to the table.

I stare for a moment, trying to clarify in my head that what I'm seeing with my eyes *is* actually happening in front of me.

But there's no doubt, it is.

I walk over to the spilt salt, and I see the last of a series of letters being formed in the white grains – a T, an L and an E.

I stare at the floor, unable to believe what I'm seeing.

And what I'm seeing is a message, written very clearly in the salt.

THE HEIR IS AT THE CASTLE

Forty-two

As I'm staring at the words I hear Tom coming back upstairs.

'One hot apple crumble and vanilla ice cream,' he calls cheerfully as he comes through the door. 'Oh, I forgot the dustpan and brush,' he adds as he sees me staring at the floor.

'No!' I snap, as my hand shoots up into the air to stop him. 'Don't touch it!'

'Why on earth not?' Tom asks, putting his tray down on one end of the long table before coming over to me. 'What's going on?' he asks jokily, looking over my shoulder. 'Have you been writing me love messages, Amelia? Oh.' He stops short when he reads what's written on the floor. 'The heir is at the castle? What does that mean?'

'I ... I'm not sure,' I half fib. The truth is I know exactly what the message is referring to. What I don't know is to *who* it's referring.

'Didn't you write it, then?' Tom asks, still looking at the words.

'No.'

'But if you didn't, then who did? Has someone else been here while I've been gone?'

'You could say that.'

Tom gently turns me to face him.

'Amelia?' he asks. 'Is there something going on that you're not telling me about? First you're all secretive with Benji, and now this,' he gestures at the salt, 'weird message. What's going on?'

'Oh, Tom.' I sigh, suddenly feeling the need to confide in him. 'There's so much going on, I hardly know where to start.'

'Start at the beginning, then,' Tom says, guiding me back to my chair and sitting me down. 'We've got all night.'

I tell Tom everything. From what Benji and I had discovered in the missing diary to the matching cameo brooch and necklace; I tell him about my fears that Charlie and I shouldn't even be living here at the castle, and then I tell him what I'd just witnessed.

'You actually saw the message being written?' Tom asks in amazement.

I nod.

'And the words just formed in the salt on their own – you saw no one?'

'I didn't see anyone, no; but I knew someone was there.'

'How?'

'I could feel them.'

'How do you mean?'

'I could sense a presence in the room. I've felt it before in the Ladies' Chamber – sort of cold, but not cold in a bad way, if you know what I mean. It was more cool, but calm.'

It's Tom's turn to nod this time. 'And you think this might have been Clara – am I right?'

'Yes. If this message is what I think it is, then she would be the only one who could know that.'

319

'That the real heir to Chesterford is here at the castle?'

'Yes.'

'But what if that's you?' Tom says, suggesting something I hadn't thought of. 'Or Charlie? Perhaps the message was simply clarifying that the real heir is one of you two?'

'Perhaps. But I don't think it means that. Why not just write that I'm the heir or that Charlie is? Why the cryptic message?'

'You're asking me why a supposed ghost isn't writing more clearly in a pile of salt?' Tom says, grinning now. 'Now that *is* a tricky one ...'

I smile too. 'I guess it doesn't make a lot of sense, does it?'

'You said it! But listen,' Tom says, taking my hand over the table, 'I really don't think you have anything to worry about. Even if this heir is at the castle, they don't know anything about it, do they? You've got to be the best thing to happen at Chesterford in years, Amelia. That's all I hear people saying around here. Why jeopardise yours and Charlie's security, and possibly your future happiness, by trying to uncover another heir? And what if this diary is wrong? You've only got the word of Clara to go on. What if that diary was made up, or she made a mistake – have you thought of that?'

'Of course I have. I've turned all this over in my head time and time again since I found out. But there're just too many things that add up away from the diary for it to be fabrication. And why would Clara make it up? It makes no sense for her to.'

'Why do people do a lot of things?' Tom says. 'Life often makes no sense to me. If you'd told me a few months ago that I'd be living in a castle, believing in ghosts and falling head over heels in love with a smart, funny, beautiful woman, I'd never have believed you – especially the last part.'

320

I smile shyly at Tom and squeeze his hand. He winks at me in return.

'Well, you and Benji both seem to think it's a bad idea for me to try to find this other heir, but now I know they might be here at the castle, I just have to do it. I couldn't continue to live here with that on my conscience, knowing I hadn't at least tried.'

'And your honour is just one of the things I adore about you. Your honour, your principles, your beautiful smile, your sexy, curvaceous body – need I go on?'

'I think you'd better quit while you're ahead,' I tell him, smiling on the outside, but on my inside I can feel nothing but a warm glow spreading right through me. It's been a long time since anyone said anything remotely like this to me. And possibly never in quite the same ardent way that Tom is.

'So what are you going to do?' Tom asks.

'About your enthusiastic declarations of love?'

Tom grins. 'We could go down that path if you like?' He lifts his eyebrows suggestively. 'However, I think you need to get a few things straight in your mind first – am I right?'

I nod. 'Thank you for understanding,' I tell him. 'I really need to get all this other stuff sorted out before I can commit to anything else right now. But,' I add, holding on to his hand all the tighter, '*we* are something that I'd like to give quite a lot of my time to in the future, if you're happy to wait a little while?'

'I'll wait as long as I need to,' Tom says, leaning his tall frame across the table to kiss me. 'There's just one thing, though,' he says just before he does.

'What's that?' I whisper, very aware that Tom's lips are only a tantalising distance away.

'Do you like cold apple crumble?' he asks, glancing to the end of the table where the tray of dessert still waits.

'Love it,' I whisper. 'But, I love *this* even more.' And I lean across the last little gap between us, leaving Tom in no doubt which of the two I prefer.

The next morning I find myself with a smile on my face as I walk down the hill towards Dorothy and Arthur's cottage.

Considering everything that's going on right now, I probably shouldn't be smiling quite so much. But I can't help it; every time I think about Tom and what happened last night, I find myself smiling.

And that, I tell myself as I knock on the cottage door, can only ever be a good thing.

'Hello, Arthur,' I say, bracing myself as he opens the door to me. 'How are you feeling?'

'Much better, miss, thank you,' Arthur says in his slightly gruff way. 'I'm sorry I haven't been at work the last couple of days. Dorothy is insisting I rest.'

'And rightly so,' I tell him. 'Your health must come first.'

'Nowt wrong with me,' Arthur grumbles. 'I'm only doing as she says to keep the peace.'

'Of course.' I wink at him. 'Anyway, I haven't come over here to berate you for having some time off, I've actually come to have a little chat.'

Arthur looks suspiciously at me.

'Can I come in?' I ask.

'Of course.' Arthur steps back to let me in. 'I was just going to make a cup of tea; would you like one?'

'Love one.'

After Arthur has made us both a cup of tea, we sit outside in his little back garden, which is just as neat and tidy as the front.

'You have a wonderful view here,' I tell him, sitting back in my wooden seat. Arthur and Dorothy's back garden looks out over the entire village of Chesterford.

'It's not quite the sea view you have from your side of the castle,' Arthur says, 'but it's a treat on a sunny day such as this one. You can see for miles.'

We both sit and admire the view for a few moments.

'Is Dorothy out today?' I ask, taking a sip of my tea. 'I haven't seen her around this morning.'

'Yes, she's gone to Berwick with her friend Maureen from the village. They often go shopping on a Saturday morning. Not that they do much shopping,' Arthur says, raising his eyebrows knowingly. 'More like a long gossip with tea and a slice of cake thrown in! But I don't mind; gives me a bit of peace for once.'

'I know you don't mean that, Arthur. You two adore each other.'

'Ah, maybe,' Arthur says good-naturedly. 'But a little break from her dulcet tones once in a while doesn't go amiss.'

'Actually, I'm quite glad Dorothy isn't here today,' I tell him. 'I wanted to talk to you about a couple of things.'

'Oh yes?' Arthur says apprehensively.

'The first was about the other day in the cellar,' I begin.

'I'm so sorry about that, miss,' Arthur interrupts. 'I had no right speaking to you in that way.'

'No, Arthur, it's fine really. We probably shouldn't have been poking around in things without consulting you first. But your reaction did me a favour.'

'It did?' Arthur looks even more suspicious now.

'Yes, you see, now I think I know why you might have behaved like that.'

Arthur still looks puzzled.

'Were you trying to keep something a secret from me, Arthur?'

'Perhaps ...' Arthur says hesitantly, trying not to give too much away. 'You've read the diary, I suppose?'

'Benji and I have – yes.'

'I see.'

'So we know all about Clara and her secret sister.'

'I thought you might.'

'And Benji worked out that there could still be an heir that was descended from Mary who would have more right to a claim on the castle than me.'

Arthur nods.

'But now I also have good reason to believe that that heir might already be here at the castle. So the thing I'm wondering is ...'

'Yes?' Arthur prompts when I don't finish my sentence.

'The thing I'm wondering is, Arthur, are *you* the true heir to the castle? Should it be you that becomes the new Earl of Chesterford?'

Forty-three

'*Me?*' Arthur splutters, putting his tea down on the table in front of us in case he spills it. 'Why would you think I'm the missing heir?'

'Because you were so keen to hide everything from me,' I explain. 'I know you were the person who locked everything away in the cellar, and we know that some of Clara's things had only recently been rewrapped. Because you were so annoyed at finding us down there, I put two and two together.'

'And got five,' Arthur says.

I can't really tell if he's amused or cross. His face is difficult to read right now.

'Why were you so annoyed at finding us there if you didn't have anything to hide?'

'I didn't say I didn't have anything to hide,' Arthur says cryptically. 'I said I wasn't the missing heir.'

'Right . . . I think you'd better explain.'

Arthur takes a sip of his tea before continuing. 'I've known about Clara's diaries for a long time,' he says. 'Her missing diary has been locked away in the castle since Clara herself first hid it – afraid that someone might read what she'd written and tell her secret.'

'But why didn't she simply destroy it, if she didn't want anyone to know what was in there?'

'Your guess is as good as mine – perhaps secretly she wanted someone to discover it one day? So that the true Chesterford lineage could be revealed. If the secret had died with Clara, then no one would ever have known.'

'You might be right there. So how long have you known about all this?'

'As much as I hate to speak ill of the dead,' Arthur admits, 'when the last Earl was in his later years, he wasn't really the best at running the place. He was what Dorothy would call scatter-brained. So I sort of took over all the duties usually performed by the Earl, and he seemed to prefer it that way. I was his right-hand man, and that meant I got the keys to everywhere in the castle. As you've seen, over the years things had built up, there was junk everywhere, no administration and seemingly no systems for anything really. It's a wonder the place had lasted as long as it had. You might not have thought we were very organised when you arrived, but compared to what I took on it was super-efficient, I can tell you.'

'I've never said you weren't organised, Arthur; far from it. I just thought we could modernise things a bit, that's all.'

'Yes, I understand that now . . . ' Arthur drifts and appears to be thinking about something.

'Arthur, the diary?' I remind him.

'Oh, yes, sorry. So one day I was attempting to sort through some old files and I discovered, like you did, the diaries – and just like you a missing diary, too. It didn't take me all that long to work out the clues Clara had left to find the whereabouts of the missing diary. Back then it was simply kept locked in a drawer of her old bureau – you know the one in the painting?'

'Yes, I know the one; Joey has it now in his room. How did he get that, anyway?'

Arthur shakes his head. 'I have no idea. He must have asked the Earl for it. It wasn't on show or anything in any of the state rooms. It was simply upstairs with all the other junk. But after I discovered the locked box hidden in the bureau, I knew it had to contain the diary. Unlike you, I couldn't find the original key. I would never have looked on that mangy old dog, so I . . . ' Arthur looks embarrassed.

'What? What did you do, Arthur?'

'I'm afraid to say I picked the lock.'

'Arthur,' I exclaim, pretending to be shocked, 'you didn't?'

'I did. It's not something I'm proud of – picking that lock, or even knowing how to. A lad showed me how to do it down the pub one day when I was much, much younger, and I've never forgotten. I'd never used it, mind, until that day, but I had to know what was inside the box, and of course when I read the diary I knew I had to hide it away so no one else would discover it. So I took the box and hid it somewhere a lot safer than an old desk – down in the cellar with a lot of Clara's other possessions. I thought no one would ever go looking down in a dirty dark cellar for it, and if they did, they wouldn't be able to piece together all the clues without the other diaries to help them, so I hid those diaries too – up in those disused rooms, thinking no one would ever go looking up there for anything amongst all that junk.'

'Until I started nosing around, that is,' I say. 'I bet you hated me trying to sort everything out upstairs.'

'I was a bit panicky, yes; but I thought you'd probably get

bored before you found more than one of those diaries, so I didn't worry too much. Little did I know you'd find the whole flipping set!'

'I know; I think I might have had a bit of help with that, though ... Anyway, carry on with your story, Arthur.'

'So to begin with, yes, I was a bit annoyed that you were poking your nose in and trying to change things here – not just because of the diaries, but because I didn't think anything needed to change,' Arthur admits. 'I couldn't see the point to all these modifications and new ideas, but then a different Chesterford began to emerge. I could see it becoming a happier place to live, and the people inside it were becoming happier too, and that is all thanks to you and young Charlie. I might sound like a mad old fool, but you've made this castle happy again, Amelia, and I don't think it's been happy for a very long time.'

'Arthur, what a lovely thing to say.' I'm moved by his kind words.

'And I wasn't going to let anyone change that,' Arthur continues. 'This castle is everything to me. It's been my whole life. So I knew that diary definitely had to be kept from you, in case, as I feared, you decided to try to trace the missing heir. I was just working out where I was going to re-hide it when I discovered you all down in the cellar, and by then it was too late.'

'And that's why you were so cross? Because you didn't want me to find the diary in case it meant we had to leave?'

Arthur nods. 'I like having you around, Amelia; we all do. I don't know if Dorothy has ever mentioned this, but God never blessed us with our own children, so having little Charlie around is like having our own grandson to look after. We both think the world of him.'

'And he thinks the same of you,' I tell an emotional Arthur. 'I'm so grateful, Arthur, I really am, that you would want to protect me from this.' I take his surprisingly large hand in mine. 'But I'm glad we found that diary. It's always good to know the truth about everything, and this way at least I'm prepared.'

'Prepared for what?' Arthur asks, looking worried again.

'Prepared in case I ever do discover who the missing heir is. I know most of you don't want me to look for them, and I'm touched you all feel this way – honestly I am. I didn't think Charlie and I would ever have had this much of an effect on Chesterford. But the problem is I *know* the heir is here at the castle, Arthur, and if they are I have to find them.'

Arthur sighs. 'I won't try to stop you; your mind is obviously made up.'

I nod. 'I must at least try to do the right thing, Arthur. I couldn't live with myself if I hadn't at least done that.'

Arthur nods. 'Can we help you at all? Dorothy and I? We've been here at Chesterford the longest.'

'That would be wonderful if you could. The thing is I don't have all that much to go on. It's more than likely that the person who might be the heir doesn't actually know they are. If they do, why wouldn't they have said anything before?'

'Not everyone would want to do what you're doing,' Arthur says pragmatically. 'Some people like a quiet life, don't they? Perhaps they prefer living in the shadows – I know I would. And no, before you ask again, it's definitely not me – or Dorothy, for that matter.'

'Sorry, I was going to ask you about Dorothy, though. The only thing I do have, thanks to Benji, is possibly the heir's parents' or grandparents' name. You don't happen to know what Dorothy's father was called, do you?'

'Of course: his name was Frank. Fine man he was, too – harsh but fair. He didn't say too many words, but when he did you listened.'

'I see. That rules her out, then. I'm looking for someone whose father – or it might even be their grandfather if they're a bit younger – is called George.'

'I guess you'll just have to ask around the castle, then. What makes you so sure they're here?'

I hesitate. But Arthur had been so good about the ghosts before, surely he'd understand?

'I got a message,' I say hesitantly. 'I think it was from Clara.'

'Go on,' Arthur says.

I tell Arthur about what happened last night in the Great Hall, and then what had previously happened in the Ladies' Chamber, and even right back to when the original diaries had disappeared and reappeared.

'It would seem that Clara really wants you to know,' Arthur says thoughtfully when I've finished. 'In fact, all the ghosts seem to be on your side. They must approve of you.'

'How do you mean?'

'Well, as you can imagine, the ghosts have seen many a different owner of Chesterford pass through these walls. There's been a few they've taken a big dislike to, and they've not made it easy for them to live here at all.'

'What happens if they don't like you?'

'Ghostly appearances in bedrooms, paintings falling off walls just as the owner passes by, strange unexplained noises at night, one Earl even had a vase thrown across a room at him. Oh yes, if the ghosts of Chesterford Castle don't like you, you'll know.'

'Goodness, I had no idea.'

330

'That's why I think even they approve of you being here.'

'But in that case why would Clara want me to know who the missing heir is, if that might mean I'd have to leave?'

'You're asking me to explain why a spirit chooses to do something?' Arthur says, smiling. 'Just be grateful for now that they seem to approve of you.'

'You're right. So, if this new heir is not you, Arthur, and it's not Dorothy, then who on earth is it?'

Forty-four

I spend the rest of the day surreptitiously trying to discover if anyone at the castle has either a father or a grandfather called George.

'Why are you asking?' Joey says when I find him and Tiffany having a picnic in the shade under some trees in the castle grounds. At first I'm so fixated on my mission that I don't think anything of the two of them sitting here together. Even though Saturday is one of our busier days, it's mainly run by the new staff I've hired – most of whom are getting on extremely well in their new roles. So Saturday has become a sort of unofficial day off for the rest of the live-in staff.

'I'm just wondering, that's all,' I say, knowing this is such a weak excuse for a reply.

Joey looks at me suspiciously.

'Is it to do with the diary?' Tiffany asks suddenly. 'Remember I told you about us finding this old diary and brooch down in the cellar, Joey?'

'Tiffany, that was supposed to be a secret,' I say, looking shocked. 'You're not supposed to gossip about it to just anyone.'

'Joey isn't just anyone,' Tiffany says, looking across at him with an adoring expression.

Joey returns her gaze with an equally tender look, and suddenly I get it.

'Yes, it is something to do with the diary,' I tell them, feeling bad that I haven't noticed this relationship developing before. I've been so tied up in my own thoughts and troubles that I haven't noticed two of my staff – no, make that two of my friends – coming together in this way. 'So *are* either of your fathers or grandfathers called George?'

Joey shakes his head. 'Nope, not mine. Tiff?'

'Nah, my mum's dad is called Joseph – ooh like you, Joey,' she says suddenly realising. '*My* dad's called Barry, and my other Grandad is Harry. Goodness, I've just realised that rhymes!' she suddenly squeals with delight. 'All these years and I've never realised before. Barry and Harry, do you think they knew?'

'You are just too cute,' Joey says, taking Tiffany's hand and gazing at her again.

'Right . . .well . . . thanks, you two,' I say awkwardly, feeling like the biggest gooseberry in the world. 'Er . . . just carry on with your picnic; sorry to disturb.'

I hardly think they notice me depart, as I leave them gazing at each other and walk back towards the castle.

'That's another two off my list,' I mumble to myself as I walk along. 'Now who's next?'

'What are you muttering about?' Benji calls, jogging across the grass towards me.

'I've just been asking Joey and Tiffany about their grandparents,' I tell him. 'By the way, did you know that the two of them are an item?'

'Of course,' Benji says, to my annoyance. 'It's been building for a while. Why, didn't you?'

I shrug.

'Oh dear, not keeping up with the castle gossip, eh?'

'I have had a few things on my mind, Benji; you know that.'

'How's that all going? Any luck with the missing heir?'

I shake my head. 'Nope, I've asked around nearly all of the staff now. Some of them must think I'm mad asking about their parents and grandparents. I'm getting a bit desperate.' I look at Benji suspiciously.

'Er, no!' Benji replies, knowing exactly what I'm thinking. 'It's definitely not me!'

I sigh. 'I didn't really think it was; would have been nice, though. At least you wouldn't ask me to leave.'

'You don't know the missing heir would want that either. And if you're so worried about having to leave, why are you insisting on continuing this search?'

'I just have to, that's why. Plus, Arthur said some things this morning that made me think.'

'Like?'

'Like he said that Clara must really want me to know or she wouldn't be helping me in this way. He said the ghosts of Chesterford Castle can be really awkward if they don't like you. He seems to think they like me.'

'That's good, isn't it? You've now not only got us humans rooting for you, but the afterlife too!'

'Don't tease me, Benji; I'm serious about this.'

'I know you are, and that's why I'm trying to help you by taking some of the weight off in other ways. I spoke to my friend yesterday, and he said he'd like to visit Chesterford before he makes any financial decisions.'

'What do you mean "financial decisions"? I thought he was just going to offer us some advice?'

'I just said that so I didn't get your hopes up. But Toby might actually be able to offer you some investment, too.'

'Really?'

'I hope so. He's coming on Monday.'

'But we're closed on Mondays; he won't be able to see the castle in full flow, with visitors touring around the place and the guides doing their stuff.'

'I'm sure that won't matter – plus, this way you can give him his own personal guided tour.'

'I guess . . . What's he like, this Toby? How do you know him?'

Benji raises his eyebrows at me.

'*Oh*, like that?'

'We were together for a while, yes; but it was a number of years ago now. He'd just come out of a difficult relationship; in fact, I think he'd not long come out altogether. He didn't want anything serious, and neither did I at the time. It wasn't meant to be anything long term, and it wasn't, so we parted amicably when the time came.'

'What have you told him about Chesterford?'

'That it could be a worthwhile investment for his company. The new owner is doing a wonderful job bringing the castle into the twenty-first century, as it were, but you could just do with a few extra resources to allow you to bring all your plans to fruition.'

'Nice.'

'Thank you.' Benji gives a tiny bow. 'Right, where are you off to now on your mission?'

'I don't know; I'm running out of people to speak to.'

'Looks like you'll just have to stay on as lady of the manor, then,' Benji says, winking at me.

'I *will* find this heir,' I tell him. 'Now I know they're here at the castle, I will find them, Benji; you just see if I don't.'

'So what's this guy like?' Tom asks me as we wait in the courtyard to greet our important visitor on Monday morning.

Arthur, back at work now after his few days off, and Benji are already waiting at the front gate to meet Toby and escort him up to us in the main castle.

'It will create a sense of importance and grandeur about the occasion,' Benji had insisted when we'd discussed who would greet our visitor and where. 'Like he's being escorted in to meet with nobility.'

'He's going to be a tad disappointed when he finds me, then,' I'd told him, smiling.

'Not at all. You're going to make a fabulous impression on him, I'm sure of it.'

I wasn't quite so confident. But Benji seemed to think this was the best course of action so we were going with his plan.

'I don't know what he's like,' I tell Tom. 'Benji has done all the organising. All I know is that we have to impress him enough so he gives us some money – sorry *investment*. You look very smart, by the way,' I tell him, looking him up and down. 'I didn't know you owned a full suit.'

'It's hardly a suit, I've ditched the jacket; it's far too hot for that today.'

Tom is wearing a tight-fitting waistcoat with a shirt and tie combination. His waistcoat and trousers fit him so well; they must have been tailor-made.

'Well, I like it. It's very ... you.'

'Very me meaning ... very sexy?'

I grin at him. 'Perhaps.'

336

My phone beeps in my pocket. 'He's here,' I say, looking at the message from Benji. 'Brace yourself.'

We wait in the courtyard for Benji and Arthur to escort Toby up the path, in through the archway and under the portcullis.

And as I see the small party appear in the courtyard, I suddenly realise what my ancestors must have felt likc when they saw enemies about to invade their home.

'Ah, here's our wonderful leader,' Benji says, as he leads a tall but lanky man towards us wearing an ill-fitting plain grey suit. 'Amelia, I'd like you to meet Toby. Toby, this is Amelia.'

I just stare at the man in front of me, and he does the same to me.

'Hello, Amelia,' he says eventually. 'It's been a while.'

'Hello, Toby,' I reply, my voice barely audible. 'Or should I call you Graham?'

Forty-five

Tom and Benji stand silently next to us as the stare-off continues.

'Do you two already know each other?' Benji finally asks.

'You could say that,' I reply, still glaring at the man opposite.

'Wait,' Tom suddenly asks. 'You called him Graham. Is he *that* Graham?'

I nod.

'What Graham?' Benji asks, looking perplexed. 'This is Toby.'

'That's what you're calling yourself now, is it?' I say scathingly. 'I heard you'd changed your name, amongst *other* things.'

'Please, I really don't understand. What *is* going on here?' Benji asks again.

'This ... *person*,' Tom says carefully, 'is Amelia's ex-husband, I believe. The one that abandoned her and Charlie.'

Graham glances warily at Tom, sensing his anger.

'What? No, it can't be,' Benji says, sounding horrified. 'Toby?'

'It's true,' Graham says. 'I'm sorry, Benji, but when you told me all about *Chesterford* Castle, and mentioned the owner was

338

called Amelia and she had a son called Charlie, I just knew it had to be them. Amelia is right: when I left her I changed my name to Toby so I could start afresh without anyone knowing me.'

'I ought to knock your block off,' Tom says, squaring up to him. 'How could you just abandon them like that? Whatever your issues were, you were a coward running away from your problems.'

'What would you know?' Graham says, looking angrily at Tom. To my surprise he doesn't back away from him, even though Tom is taller, broader and would surely throw a far harder punch than Graham could muster. 'Look at you; you couldn't possibly understand what I went through.'

'Actually, I do understand,' Tom says. 'I understand a lot more than you think I do. But you still shouldn't have walked away, leaving your wife and son like that. Have you no honour, man?'

'Tom, I appreciate you standing up for me like this, really I do,' I say, putting my hand across his chest to pull him back a little, 'but I'm strong enough to fight my own battles.'

Tom glares at Graham again before stepping away.

Benji is standing back from us a little, looking extremely agitated.

'Benji, did you know?' I ask him.

Benji shakes his head, clearly perplexed.

'Did you know that Graham – I mean Toby – had just left his wife and child when you hooked up with him? You said he'd not long come out when you met him. In fact, you said he'd just come out of a difficult relationship.'

I glare once more at Graham, who at least has the decency to look ashamed.

'No! Of course I didn't know,' Benji says, looking horrified.

'I just wondered if that's why you were so kind to Charlie and me when you met us, because you felt guilty that you'd been part of something similar before?'

'Amelia, how can you even ask that?' Benji says, looking hurt now. 'I think the world of you and Charlie, you know that.'

I just nod. I need time to process all this.

'How *is* Charlie?' Graham suddenly asks. 'Is he around?'

'No! You're not seeing him,' I shout, finally losing my composure now Charlie has been mentioned. 'You . . . you have no right . . . no right at all to have anything to do with either of us any more.' My voice, loud as it is, begins to tremble. 'Do you hear me?' I say to Benji and Tom. 'He's having nothing to do with Charlie! Nothing!'

I turn and I run. I'm not sure where I'm running to, but as I cross the gravel I just know I have to get away. I have to find Charlie and keep him safe from this man who has invaded both our castle and our home.

It takes me only a few minutes to remember that Charlie is at school right now in the village, and is, for the moment, safe from Graham.

So I head to the only place I know I'll be able to get some peace for a while and think – the beach.

Even though it's a warmish yet cloudy day, the beach to my utter relief is almost deserted, so I pull off my shoes and walk barefoot across the sand, breathing heavily, not only from the speed at which I've run here but from the shock I've just experienced.

Why did Graham have to try to come back into our lives

now? After all this time, just when things were starting to go well for us for once, *he* had to turn up again.

I kick angrily at the sand under my feet. Soft grains fly up in the air and land again almost as smoothly as before I'd kicked at them.

So I kick again, and the same thing happens – the beach simply smooths out my anger as soon as the grains land back down with the others.

Perhaps life is a bit like that too? I think, feeling myself beginning to calm. *As much as something tries to disturb the sands of your life, they can only do so if you let them.*

So what if Graham has found us? It doesn't mean he has the right to disrupt our lives. He can only do that if *I* let him.

And that is *not* going to happen.

I sit for a while against the side of one of the sand dunes that line the edge of the beach, letting the rhythmical sound of the waves calm my angry mind and soothe my worried soul. I wonder how many of my ancestors must have done the same when faced with a troubling time or a difficult decision.

The castle isn't the only thing that has stood solidly in this area for hundreds of years; the sea and this beach in Rainbow Bay had been here for thousands of years before it.

'How many troubles and anxieties must you have absorbed over time?' I ask the grains of sand that slide easily through my fingers. 'There must be the worries of thousands buried deep beneath your surface.'

'Hello, miss,' I hear from up above me. 'You okay down there?'

I look up and see Joey clambering down over the dunes.

'Yes, fine, Joey; thanks!' I call back, still wanting to be alone with my thoughts.

But Joey continues to clamber across the sand until he reaches me. 'I heard there was a bit of a ruckus in the court-yard,' he says, sitting down next to me. 'What's going down with your ex? Me and Tom can soon see him off if you want us to – he won't come bothering you again,' he says knowingly.

'Oh, Joey,' I say gratefully, 'it's very good of you to offer, but I don't think that's going to be necessary.'

Joey shrugs. 'The offer's there if you want it.'

'Thank you. I appreciate it.'

We sit without speaking for a few moments, the only sound between us the calling of the gulls above, and the never-ending waves continuing to wash along the sand.

'Married to him, were ye?' Joey asks after he's sat thoughtfully for a while. 'This Graham?'

I nod.

'And he's Charlie's father?'

'Yes.'

'Hmm, that's makes it tricky, then.'

'It does indeed.'

Joey sits quietly again for a bit, as if he's gathering his thoughts.

'Look, miss—' he says eventually, finding his voice.

'*Amelia*, please, Joey. You know I prefer that.'

'Sorry. So, mi— I mean, *Amelia*, I don't want to talk out of turn, but the thing is *my* father walked out on me mam and me when I was a bairn too.'

'Oh, I'm sorry to hear that.'

Joey shrugs. 'As it turns out we were better off without him. I found out afterwards he hit me mam.'

'No, that's terrible, your poor mother. But not you?' I ask gently, trying not to appear as if I'm prying.

'Nah, not me, luckily. But like I said, after he left I was sad I hadn't got a dad, but I soon realised me mam was better without him. She was happier, and a lot less bruised!'

'Indeed.'

'But the thing is I always wondered about him, you know?'

'Did you ever see him again?'

'Nope. Apparently he died a couple of years ago, up north in Glasgow of all places. We didn't find out until later, so we didn't go to the funeral or anything. Well, me mam wouldn't have gone, but I might.'

'Even after what he'd done?'

'Even after that. He was still me dad, wasn't he? People don't stop being your parents just because they do something bad. You might not like them as much, but they're still your mam and dad.'

'My father died when I was young too,' I tell him. 'He was still with my mum then, so it was hard for all of us.'

'Bet you still miss him,' Joey says perceptively.

'Yes I do. I miss them both – Mum has passed now too.'

'Terrible that is – both your parents gone.' Joey thinks about this for a moment. 'You wouldn't want that for Charlie, now, would you?'

I shake my head.

'So even though you might hate this fella Graham, he's still Charlie's dad, and Charlie might want to know him.'

'I suppose . . .'

'He didn't hit *you*, though, did he?' Joey asks, suddenly on the defensive again. 'Cos if he did, I don't think I'd be able, or even *want*, to hold Tom back. He's livid enough back there in the castle. Dorothy is trying to calm him down with a cup of tea, but I think she might need an elephant-size tranquilliser dart, he's so worked up.'

343

'Oh Tom . . . ' I say, sighing as I think about him.

'He thinks the world of you and Charlie – we all do, actually – but Tom, I think, especially so, if you get my meaning?'

'Yes, Joey, I understand. I think the world of Tom too.'

'Good. So this Graham fella isn't getting any sort of look-in?'

'Oh no, definitely not. I don't think he'd ever be interested in *me* any more – if you get *my* meaning?'

'Why not? There's nothing wrong with you, miss. Nothing at all.' Joey looks me up and down approvingly.

'Thanks for the vote of confidence, Joey, but Graham isn't interested in *any* women these days . . . ' I wait for the penny to drop.

'Oh . . . ' Joey nods perceptively. 'Makes sense.'

'Does it?' I ask. 'Does any of it, really?'

'Just do what you think is right, Miss Amelia,' Joey says, tapping my shoulder. 'That's usually the best thing, in my experience.'

'But that's the trouble, Joey; every time I've tried to do the right thing since I came here, the right thing just doesn't work out for me. Something always gets in the way. I can't do right for doing wrong.'

'Then I can only say one thing to you,' Joey says in a serious voice.

'What's that?'

'You're screwed,' he says pragmatically, 'whichever way you turn.'

'Never have you said a truer word, Joey.' I agree. 'Never have you said a truer word.'

Forty-six

Joey and I walk back to the castle together, me wondering all the way what I'm going to find when I get back.

But what I find is nothing, just a very calm castle carrying on its business as usual.

'They were taking him inside somewhere when I last spoke to Arthur,' Joey says, reading my thoughts. 'Tom went down to the kitchen with Dorothy, and Benji took this Graham in the opposite direction.'

'To the dungeons?' I ask hopefully.

Joey looks at me, his eyes wide.

'I'm joking, Joey,' I assure him, only half meaning it. How fabulous would that be, to be able to dispose of your enemies simply by sending them down to your own personal dungeon to rot away?

But I know I wouldn't have been able to condemn anyone to that fate. Even Graham, who although he's definitely my worst enemy, as Joey had rightly pointed out, is also Charlie's father.

'Ah good,' Joey says, relieved. 'Although I wouldn't blame

you for feeling that way at all. Life might have been more brutal centuries ago, but it was a lot simpler too.'

'It was indeed. I guess I'd better go and find Benji.'

'No,' Joey insists, holding up his hand. 'I won't hear of it. Benji and Graham must be brought to you. This might be the twenty-first century, but there's still some things we can do like the old days.' He grins and taps the side of his nose. 'You leave this with me. Now, where would you like to hold court? Can I suggest the Great Hall? It's the most imposing of our many rooms, and that enormous table is still in there from your dinner with Tom.'

I smile as I immediately understand what he's suggesting. 'Yes, that would be most acceptable, my good man,' I reply, playing along. 'Bring them to me at,' I look at my watch, 'midday, please.'

'Certainly.' Joey bows. 'I wanted to say "m'lady" then,' he adds, looking pleased with himself, 'but I remembered not to.'

'Just between us, Joey, today, and only today, I shall enjoy playing the part of the lady of the manor. In fact, I shall be channelling all my past ancestors that have sat in that Great Hall and dealt with their enemies. I just hope I do them proud!'

It's hard to imagine as I sit at one end of the long oak table, that only a few days ago I'd enjoyed a romantic meal in here with Tom. Today the ambience inside the Great Hall is very different; the table is stripped bare, and as I sit waiting for Benji and Graham to arrive, I feel different too.

The person sitting in one of the large carved wooden chairs (that were usually positioned up against one of the far walls like thrones, but Joey had helped me to pull to the head of the table) doesn't feel like the usual me at all. I feel powerful and in control, and I have to admit I quite like it.

I rest my hand on the table in front of me, occasionally tapping my fingers on the wood – not impatiently, but with meaning, as though this small act will bring me closer to those who have sat in this position before me, so I can draw on some of their strength and resolve.

The large grandfather clock that stands at one end of the hall chimes midday, slowly and with purpose, adding to the already dramatic atmosphere.

And then, when the last chime has sounded, someone knocks at the door.

'Come,' I say steadily.

Joey walks in first. He winks encouragingly at me before leading the other two men in.

'Mr Benjamin and Mr Harris are here to see you, m'lady,' he announces, and he gives a small bow.

Benji looks at him likes he's gone mad, but I just smile serenely and say, 'Thank you, Joseph. That will be all.'

Joey backs out of the room, leaving Benji and Graham standing at the end of the table looking a bit lost.

'What's going on, Amelia?' Benji asks. 'Are you okay?'

'I am perfectly fine, thank you, Alexander,' I say, feeling a little guilty I was treating Benji this way. But it was necessary for me to create the desired effect on Graham. 'Now if you would leave me alone with your friend here, I'd be most grateful.'

Benji looks at Graham.

Graham simply shrugs at him, and holds his hands up in a 'I have no idea what's going on' gesture.

'If that's what you want?' Benji asks me, with a 'are you sure you're okay?' look.

'I am perfectly sure, thank you.'

'All right, then. I guess I'll see you both in a bit.'

Benji leaves the room. I notice he sort of backs out, without turning his back on me. It was working already.

'Shall I sit, or do you want me to stand?' Graham asks in a sarcastic tone as the door shuts behind him.

'You can sit down,' I say, gesturing to one of the few chairs we'd left around that end of the table, at completely the opposite end to where I was sitting on my 'throne'.

'Gee, thanks,' Graham says, pulling out a chair.

I watch him, and wonder what I ever saw in him. This sarcastic tone was what he always lowered himself to when he was on the back foot.

'So, what do you want?' I ask, getting immediately down to business.

'What do you mean, what do I want?' Graham replies, folding his arms across his chest. 'You asked me to come here, didn't you? I thought you needed money?'

'You know exactly what I mean. You didn't come here to offer us money. When you realised it might be me and Charlie that were living here, you came to see us.'

'That is true, I can't deny it. I was curious; I wanted to see how you were.'

Keep calm, Amelia. Keep calm, I repeat in my head, as I feel myself beginning to tighten up. 'After all this time?' I reply steadily. 'You wondered how we were? What happed to wondering how we were in the days after you walked out? What happened to wondering how we were in the weeks and months after that? When we had no money and got thrown out of our home. Where was your wondering then, hey?'

Graham looks down at the table. 'I'm sorry,' he says, not

348

looking up at me. 'I shouldn't just have walked out on you like that.'

'Damn right you shouldn't.'

'But I couldn't help myself, I was confused. Confused about who I was. Who I wanted to be.' He looks up at me with a wretched expression.

'And who *did* you want to be?' I ask, trying my hardest to feel no sympathy for him. 'Toby?'

Graham shrugs. 'I . . . I don't know. Like I said, I was confused, I didn't really know what I was doing. I just knew I had to get out. It was like a noose around my neck pulling tighter and tighter. I couldn't breathe, Amy.'

'No,' I correct him immediately, 'you have no right to call me that any more. My name is Amelia. It stopped being Amy the day you walked out.'

'I'm sorry,' Graham says again. 'I'm so, so sorry. I never wanted to hurt you and Charlie. You were my world.'

'But not your universe, eh?'

Graham and I gaze at each other across the table.

'I should have done things differently; I know that now. If I could go back again I would do.'

'But you'd still leave?' I ask quietly.

Graham nods.

'Good,' I hear myself saying, like I'm having an out-of-body experience. 'I'm glad. We might have struggled for a while without you, and if I could go back I might do a few things a little differently too. But I'd still want you to leave.'

Graham looks shocked and a little hurt to hear this.

'You see, I'm stronger now, Graham. So much stronger and tougher than when you knew me; and it's you that's made me that way.'

349

'I can see that,' Graham says, a note of sarcasm returning to his voice again. 'But what about Charlie?'

'What about him?'

'Doesn't he need a father in his life?'

'He's managed without one for this long, and he seems to be doing just fine, thank you very much.'

'You keep saying he's doing fine. But can't … can't I even see him?'

I just stare at Graham. I knew this was coming, but I still can't deal with it. I try to remember what Joey said to me on the beach, and how his words made me feel. But any empathy I might have felt for Graham's situation is being completely blotted out by the man sitting in front of me.

'He's ten now, isn't he? Almost eleven? A boy needs some male influence in his life.'

'Male influence?' I can't help but smirk. 'Are you suggesting you should be that male influence? Now that is a twist I hadn't seen coming.'

'Don't be nasty, Amy. It doesn't suit you.'

'Amelia. And Charlie has plenty of male influence, as you call it. Since we came to live here, he has people that love and care for him – both male and female. We've made a new family, and I won't have you messing with that.'

For the first time since Graham entered the room I feel myself begin to get emotional as I talk about my new Chesterford family.

'If you mean that He-Man that tried to beat me up earlier,' Graham sneers. 'That's hardly what I'd call a role model.'

'If you mean Tom, he did not try to beat you up. I can assure you that if Tom had gone anywhere near you, you wouldn't be sitting here now, that's for sure. You'd probably be in hospital.'

It was a cheap shot, but I couldn't resist it. Tom was better-looking, bigger and stronger than Graham, and there was nothing Graham could do to match that, and he obviously knew it.

'Tom is great with Charlie, actually,' I continue, just to rub salt into the wound. 'An ideal role model, and even if he wasn't around, Charlie would have Benji and Joey and Arthur – they all love him too. So I can assure you, if you think for one moment that *my* son is going without anything, you are very, very wrong.'

Graham sits silently for a moment, so I'm quiet too waiting for his next move.

'But I'm his father,' he says eventually in a low voice. 'Please don't keep me from him.'

I bite my bottom lip. He is right, of course. I know what I have to do, but it doesn't make it any easier.

'He comes out of school at three o'clock,' I say, without looking at Graham. 'I'll walk him home and explain as best I can why you're here and that you'd like to see him. And then if, and only if, he agrees, you can see him for a *short* while.'

'Thank you, Amy ... I mean, Amelia,' Graham says. 'I appreciate this, really I do.'

I look directly at him now. '*Don't* mess this up,' I tell him in my harshest voice. 'Because if you do, so help me I'll ... I'll ... I'll have you locked up in the dungeons at the bottom of this castle, and I'll throw away the key!'

Forty-seven

As I knew he would Charlie does want to see his father.

So, when we get home from school, I permit Graham to come up to the top of the tower so Charlie is on familiar ground, and I allow them to spend some time together.

After I'm satisfied that Charlie is happy with everything, I leave them together playing with Charlie's Lego, and I head downstairs for some fresh air.

'How's it going?' Tom asks as I step out into the courtyard. I know he's been waiting patiently outside since Graham's arrival.

'Fine. Just fine,' I reply, sighing.

'Come here,' Tom says, holding out his arms, and I gratefully let him envelop me in a comforting hug. 'You've done the right thing,' he says softly, nuzzling his face into my hair. 'You know that, don't you?'

'I hope so,' I tell him. 'I really hope so.'

As Tom is holding me, I notice Joey across the courtyard watching us. He holds his thumb up and nods. So I smile and do the same to him behind Tom's back.

'Why do parents cause us so many problems?' I say, not really voicing a question, more a statement.

'How do you mean?' Tom asks, holding me back in his arms.

'Well, for one, my son is up there having his first contact in years with his dad; then there's you with your own estranged father—'

Tom nods in agreement.

'Joey has had similar troubles, too,' I continue, 'and then there's Clara – her father caused her no end of trouble producing an elder sister no one knew about.'

'It seems like it's men then, really?' Tom says, smiling at me. 'We seem to cause all the grief.'

'Some of you, perhaps,' I say, looking up at him tenderly. 'I hope not all of you, though . . .'

Tom leans forward so his face is close to mine. 'I promise, for however long we're together, that I'll do my best to never cause you any grief. How about that?'

'That could be a very long time, you know,' I whisper, my lips getting even closer to his.

'I do hope so,' Tom murmurs just before our lips meet. 'I really do.'

Against my better judgement, I agree to let Graham stay on for a couple of days so he can get to know Charlie again. He's come up from London to visit Chesterford, so instead of him staying locally I agree to him staying at the castle.

'How are you getting on with your dad?' I ask Charlie one night just before he settles down to sleep. 'Do you like spending time with him?'

'Yeah,' Charlie says, thinking about it. 'It's cool to get to know him.'

'Good.'

'But . . .' Charlie hesitates.

'What is it?' I ask anxiously in case I've done the wrong thing after all.

'Is it all right if I still like being with Tom, Joey, Benji and Arthur better? Dad's okay 'n' all, but they're all much more fun.'

I smile at him. 'Of course it is,' I insist. 'You can like whoever you want to the best. It's your life, Charlie. You make the choices, not anyone else.'

'Thanks, Mum. I love you; you're the best.'

Charlie rolls over and closes his eyes, and with tears in my own eyes I gently tuck him in, kiss him goodnight, and then I pause by the door just before I turn off the light, and I whisper, 'I love you, too, Charlie. So very, *very* much.'

'So,' Graham says as we prepare to see him off after his short stay. 'This was fun.'

'I wouldn't call it that exactly,' I say, trying to remain polite for Charlie's sake. 'But Charlie has enjoyed having you here, so that's all right with me.' I swallow hard. 'You can come again if you like.'

'Thank you, Amelia; you know I'd love that. Perhaps he could come and stay with me too sometime?'

'Let's not get too carried away just yet; it's early days,' I say diplomatically.

'Of course. Of course.' Graham nods. 'You've done a good job bringing him up, you know? A very good job. I'm just sorry I haven't been there to help you.' He pauses. 'I know I've said it before, but I am sorry, for everything. Truly I am.'

'I know,' I relent. 'Are you happy now, Graham? With your new life, I mean?'

Graham sighs. 'I don't think I'm as happy as you are living here at Chesterford. This,' he waves his hand around at the castle, 'it suits you, you know that? You've blossomed from my little Amy Harris into a very grown-up Amelia Chesterford.'

'Thank you, I think.'

'No, it's a compliment. This place has been good for you and good for Charlie too. He's told me how much he enjoys living here, and I'm glad. All any parent wants for their child is for them to be happy.'

'That's true.'

'So that's why I'm going to make sure you stay here.'

'What do you mean?'

'I'm going to recommend to my company that we invest some money here. Not just for you to complete the renovations on the stables – which I may add are very impressive indeed. But Arthur has spent a long time going through everything with me; he's guided me around the place, told me all the history, and all about your plans for the future – including the costume and servants' exhibitions, which I think are an excellent idea. He's also gone through all your books, so I know you could do with quite a lot of investment elsewhere in the castle. This place is going to be great under your leadership, Amelia, and I'm certain Keystone Financial will want to be part of that.'

There's a tiny part of me that wants to tell him no – stick your money. Isn't it bad enough you have to be involved in any part of my life now? But I know I can't; I have to think of the castle and of everyone here.

'Thank you, Graham,' I say through slightly gritted teeth. 'I really appreciate that. I'm certain we can do great things with your investment.'

He nods. 'I'll be in touch when I've got some figures together. But just between you and me, Amelia, Arthur's input would have been enough, you know? You didn't need to go to all that trouble with the special effects; you already had me on board.'

'What special effects?' I ask, having no idea what he's talking about.

Graham smiles. 'Yep that's right – you keep playing along. Maybe we can use that in the marketing for this place: Chesterford, Northumberland's number-one haunted castle. I have to say they were all very realistic – especially the guy riding the horse through the wall in my bedroom. That was the *pièce de résistance*. Excellent stuff.'

I just stare at Graham. Was he saying what I thought he was? Had the ghosts paid him a little visit in the night? Were they trying to do their bit to keep Chesterford Castle alive too?

'Right,' Graham says, appearing not to notice my hesitance, 'I think it's time to go. Say goodbye to Charlie for me again, won't you? I wish he was here to see me off – but school must come first.' Graham looks at the others who have all been standing back a little so we could say goodbye privately. 'Arthur,' he says, holding out his hand to him, 'thank you for making me see what a wonderful place this is.'

Arthur nods as he shakes Graham's hand.

'Dorothy, thank you for all the delicious food.'

'My pleasure,' Dorothy says, smiling.

'Benji, sorry I caused you strife.'

'Not a problem,' Benji says, giving him a quick hug. 'Amelia and I have already made up, haven't we?'

I nod. 'I couldn't stay mad with this one for long, could I?' I say, slipping my arm through Benji's.

356

'Joey, Tiffany, thank you for making my stay here a pleasant one.'

Joey half smiles and Tiffany waves.

Graham turns finally to Tom and holds out his hand. 'I know you don't think much of me,' he says to Tom's stony face, 'but look after Amelia, won't you? She deserves someone that will stick around.'

'I intend to,' Tom says, taking a firm hold of Graham's hand. I notice Graham wince a little at Tom's grip and I smile.

We all walk down to the gate with Graham and wave him goodbye.

'Now,' I say, turning to the others when he's finally gone, 'can we just get on with running this castle normally and without drama for a bit? I believe we've got a grand opening taking place in less than a week, and we've got a lot to do!'

We all walk back up to the castle together. And for once I feel relaxed and happy that things here at Chesterford are going to be all right . . . for a while, anyway.

Forty-eight

I stand looking in the mirror at my reflection.

'You look older,' I think, narrowing my eyes and peering at myself a little more closely.

But do I actually look older? Or do I just look a more confident and self-assured person than the nervous, worried one that had arrived here at Chesterford earlier this year?

Graham was right when he'd said I'd grown up. I had, and in a good way. I felt comfortable within myself and confident about my abilities.

'You look gorgeous,' Tom says, popping his head around the door. He comes over to the mirror and puts his arms around me so we're both looking at our reflections.

He kisses the side of my neck. 'Have we time for me to rip that dress off you, and whisk you back into bed?'

'Sadly, no.' I sigh, wrapping one of my arms around the back of his head. 'And you might crease me!'

'I'd do more than that!' Tom says, grinning at me.

It hasn't taken us long to move our relationship up to the next level, and Tom has taken to spending most evenings with us up here in the tower, rather than in his room at the castle. And once Charlie's gone to bed, he usually spends the night too.

We tried to hide it from Charlie at first, with Tom creeping out in the early hours before he awoke, but Charlie being Charlie soon let us know that he was quite aware Tom was staying the night, and he was happy for him to do so.

'Nothing against you, Mum,' he'd said, 'but I like having someone else to talk to over breakfast. Tom actually knows something about football; he doesn't just pretend to like it, like you do for my sake.'

And so, with Tom staying at the tower, and all our new extended family in the rest of the castle, both Charlie and I feel at last that we totally belong here.

I've also decided, after much thought, not to continue searching for the missing heir. It feels like I'm supposed to be here now, and everyone else seems to want me to be here too; fate, the mystical spirits that haunted Chesterford and my new friends and family certainly want me to stay, and so for once I'm listening to them.

'Ah, well,' Tom concedes, 'if I can't persuade you in other ways, perhaps we had better go. May I escort you downstairs, m'lady?' Tom holds out his arm to me.

'You certainly can, m'lord,' I reply, for once not getting my knickers in a twist about titles. Since the whole Graham incident in the Great Hall, I've felt much better about the few instances when someone gets it wrong. I'll never feel happy about someone addressing me as Lady Chesterford, but I know it will happen from time to time and I can deal with that now.

We walk downstairs and out into a bright sunny courtyard;

then we head over to the stables, which are looking glorious today bedecked for their grand opening.

'I'll go and find Charlie' Tom says, looking around for him. 'He said he was going to come down early and see if he could wangle a cake out of Dorothy.'

I watch Tom go, and then I pause while I've got a moment's peace to take everything in.

Bill and his gang have transformed the stables into two rooms perfect for their new uses. First, we have our gift shop, which today looks inviting and attractive with its many products neatly lined up on the wooden and glass shelves. Our keen staff, wearing their brand-new castle uniform – a black skirt or trousers with a white shirt and a black waistcoat – wait eagerly to serve their first customers. Then there's our bright and cosy tea room, which looks amazing with its newly restored black beams contrasting magnificently against the whitewashed walls. Paintings and prints of the castle hang on the walls, some of which are also for sale in the gift shop. There are scrubbed wooden tables dotted about this room, with little menus standing neatly on top of the gingham tablecloths that cover them. Then at one end is the serving counter that separates the dining area from the kitchen. This is bedecked with glass domes filled with delicious-looking cakes, scones and pastries.

'You've done a grand job, lass,' Arthur murmurs behind me. 'You should be proud.'

'It's not just me, Arthur,' I say, turning around. 'Everyone has worked hard to get us to this point, and I'm grateful to every one of you.'

Arthur does something unusual then: he puts his hand on my shoulder. 'I'm glad you decided to let that *other* matter go,'

360

he says quietly. 'You and young Charlie deserve to be here, not anyone else. I might not have been that welcoming when you first arrived, but I'm very glad you're both here now.'

'Thank you, Arthur,' I say, and I do something a little out of character as well: I give him a kiss on the cheek. 'That means a lot.'

Arthur's cheeks turn pink.

'I can safely say the last Earl never did that!' he says, smiling. 'And I for one am very glad he didn't!'

Arthur and I walk out of the stables into the little outdoor seating area where we have installed more tables, chairs and parasols to keep the sun – which I'm pleased to see is still shining today – off our visitors. The walls outside the stables are decorated in colourful bunting, which billows gently in the breeze.

'It's perfect,' I whisper, momentarily caught off guard by my emotions at seeing everything finally coming together like this. 'Absolutely perfect.'

People are just beginning to filter in to the castle for the official opening in half an hour, and everyone seems to want to speak to me.

There's Bill and his wife, Hetty, and some of the other builders that have worked on the stables, including Ed and his girlfriend. I recognise some of the locals from the pub, including Rachel and Molly, followed by many other people from the village who have come to wish us well today. So that when the time comes for the official opening and cutting of the ribbon, which Tiffany and Joey hold up between them across the entrance, we've quite a crowd squashed into the little area in front of the stables.

'Good afternoon,' I say, standing up on a small box that Joey has put in front of a microphone. 'And thank you all for coming to Chesterford Castle on this beautiful afternoon.'

I look out into the crowd, and recognise not only the faces of all the local residents that I know, but also the faces of my new family, all looking up at me with affection in their eyes, willing me to do well.

'When I came to Chesterford I really didn't know what to expect. I mean, you can't do an evening class in how to run a castle, can you?'

There are a few polite titters.

'But nothing prepared me for what I would find when I eventually did arrive. Not only this remarkable castle, which has stood so resolutely and so magnificently on the Northumbrian coast for centuries, but a community of people that love and adore it too. Stepping into someone else's shoes is never easy, but when it's a woman stepping into a man's shoes, it's often doubly difficult.'

A few of the women in the crowd nod their agreement.

'But none of you made it that way for me,' I continue. 'You all accepted me, and helped me, and together we have hopefully not only created something in the new stables that will bring more pleasure to our many visitors, but we have begun together a new era for Chesterford, one that will bring much prosperity to the castle and to you all in the local community.'

Some spontaneous applause breaks out, so I wait.

'But before I cut this ceremonial ribbon, I must thank a few special people without whom I really couldn't have done this. First, to the two people you see holding the ribbon next to me.' I gesture towards Tiffany and Joey. 'Tiffany, my right-hand woman, you've been an absolute rock throughout all of this. I simply couldn't have got through it without you. And

Joey – you are a rock too. You're strong and brave and wise. Never forget that.'

Tiffany and Joey both look highly embarrassed but thrilled at my words.

'Arthur and Dorothy, you've been totally amazing, welcoming us and helping us to understand the ways of the castle. You've not only become good friends to me, but you've become surrogate grandparents to my son, too. Charlie and I can't thank you enough.'

Charlie, holding Chester in his arms, grins up at Arthur and Dorothy, who he's standing next to. Arthur gives me a small salute, and Dorothy fumbles for a tissue to dab at her tear-filled eyes.

'My good friend Benji, like me, is new to Chesterford,' I say, looking across at Benji. 'But without him I definitely wouldn't be standing here right now. Thank you, Benji, for helping me to see I was good enough to do this.' Benji blows me a kiss.

'And finally Tom.' I look at Tom, who is standing in the crowd looking proudly back at me. 'What can I say? Thank you for being not only Charlie's knight in shining armour, but mine too. I didn't think this princess needed rescuing, but perhaps I was wrong. Perhaps I did need a handsome prince to sweep me off my feet?'

Tom winks at me, and I gaze back at him for a moment. *Thank you*, I silently mouth.

'Now,' I say, looking into the crowd once more, 'without further ado, let's finally get this place open!' I take some shiny new scissors from Joey and I hold them over the ribbon. 'I now declare The Stables gift shop and tea room officially *open*!'

There's rapturous applause as I snip at the white ribbon, and I breathe a sigh of relief as people begin to pour into the stables to get their free refreshments and browse the goods in the gift shop.

'Here,' Benji says, thrusting a glass of bubbly into my hand. 'You look like you need it.'

'If you knew how long I've been practising that speech,' I tell him.

'It was superb!' Benji says, clinking glasses with me. 'Here's to many more like it in the future!'

I screw up my face.

'If you've finally accepted that you're the rightful lady of the manor then you'd better get used to it. That's what they do, don't they – open things and make speeches?'

'Benji, stop teasing me,' I tell him, gulping down some prosecco. 'Just be happy I'm doing what you all want at last.'

Benji grins. 'I am! We all are, you know that.'

'You were great,' Tom says, coming over to us and putting his arm around me. 'I'm very proud of you.' He kisses my cheek.

'Thank you.' I snuggle into his embrace a little. I always feel safe when Tom's arm is around me, and after making that speech I need all the reassurance I can get.

'Mum!' Charlie says, running through the crowd with Chester on a lead, tugging Dorothy behind him. 'You were fab! I loved your speech. It was a bit like the one my headmaster gave the other day in assembly, only better, and fewer people fell asleep.'

'The ultimate compliment!' I hug Charlie, and look at Dorothy. 'I hope he's not giving you too much trouble, Dorothy, dragging you around?'

'Not at all,' Dorothy says, looking adoringly at Charlie. 'He's a poppet, as is Chester.'

As if on cue, Chester barks his agreement.

364

'You're looking very swish today, Dorothy,' I tell her. 'I like your dress.'

'Thank you,' Dorothy says, smiling. 'I thought I'd make an effort since it was an important day for you and for the castle. It's new.'

'And very nice it is too. You look lovely.' I'm about to take another sip of my drink, when something about Dorothy's manner makes my eyes remain upon her. She's sort of staring at me as though she wants me to notice something.

I look at her again, and then I see it. With her lovely new dress, Dorothy is wearing what looks like quite an old necklace. But it's not the age of the chain that piques my interest, but the item that's hanging delicately from it.

Because around Dorothy's neck is a cameo pendant, and it's not just any cameo she has resting against her ample chest, but one that matches the brooch I'm wearing today.

For this momentous day at the castle I've chosen to wear Clara's precious cameo brooch pinned to my dress, and it would seem that Dorothy has chosen to wear Mary's missing necklace.

Forty-nine

Dorothy doesn't seem in the least bit surprised when I drag her away from the crowds and try to find a quiet bit of the castle in which we can talk. But there seem to be people milling around everywhere today, so finally I guide her into the Great Hall, and eventually through to the Ladies' Chamber, where I know if we close the door, we will at last have some privacy.

'Where did you get that necklace, Dorothy?' I ask, sitting next to Dorothy on the chaise longue, and staring at the cameo pendant.

'It's a family heirloom,' Dorothy says calmly. 'Do you like it?'

'Yes I do. It's like *my* brooch, isn't it?' I say, pointing to my own jewellery.

'It is. I thought you'd notice it; that's why I chose to wear it today.'

I look at Dorothy, trying to work her out.

'You know, don't you?' I say suddenly. 'You know about Mary and Clara?'

Dorothy nods. 'Of course I know. This necklace has been in my family for decades. All us Edwards know.'

'But why haven't you or your family ever said anything? Some of you could have been the Earls or the Countesses of Chesterford if you'd said something; it would have been a direct line.'

'Because we were happy as we were. The story, along with this pendant, has been passed down through each generation of Edwards. Everyone the story was told to understood exactly what it might mean if we ever shared it with anyone outside the family. We were never told *not* to share, or not to go looking for Clara's diary, it was always our choice. We've always been happy working for whoever the Earl and Countess were at the time; we didn't want the responsibility of being in charge. The Edwards family have always been happy being in service. We like being *downstairs* here at the castle. It suits us. We're content with our lot in life.'

I continue to stare at Dorothy.

'But what about when they couldn't find someone to take over here when the last Earl died? Didn't you think then you might like to step up?'

'I did think about it,' Dorothy says steadily. 'And if they *hadn't* found someone I might have said something. This castle has been mine and Arthur's whole life; I wouldn't see it go to ruin. But luckily they found you, didn't they, my dear?' She pats my hand. 'So I didn't have to.'

'But . . . ' I'm lost for words. *The missing heir had been Dorothy all this time, and not only that, but she knew she was too.*

'But Arthur said your father was called Frank,' I say, finding my voice at last. 'If you are the direct descendant of Clara's sister Mary, then your father was supposed to have been called George?'

'He was,' Dorothy explains. 'Silly old duffer changed his name to Frank because he had a friend called George and he

367

said it was confusing when they played on the local cricket team together. Frank was his nickname and it stuck. After a while not many knew his real name was George at all.'

I stare at Dorothy again, still trying to make sense of what she's telling me.

'Does Arthur know about this?' I suddenly ask. Arthur had sworn blind he knew nothing about the heir. I couldn't bear to think of him lying to me.

Dorothy shakes her head. 'No, we Edwardses have kept this in our family for years. Not even our spouses know the full story. I can only imagine what some of them might have tried to do if they sensed a bit of money or power might be in the offing.'

'That is true, I guess.'

'Arthur told me you were looking, though,' Dorothy admits. 'And we both said the same thing – that we didn't want you to find another heir. We both love having you and little Charlie around, and we couldn't bear the thought of someone else moving in and starting again, and, besides,' she adds sadly, 'what good would it have been if I had come forward as being the rightful heir? Arthur and I haven't been blessed with any children, so the line would have stopped with us. This way the Chesterford family tree continues with you, then Charlie, and possibly even Charlie's children in the future. It's for the best this way, my dear, really it is.'

'So why tell me today, Dorothy? Why not keep it a secret?'

'Because I knew you'd keep looking. Yes, I know you said you'd stopped; Arthur was pleased as punch the day you told him that. But I knew differently; I could tell you'd always wonder. Wonder if you should actually be here. Wonder if the castle was rightfully yours. Wonder if one day someone was going to pop up and take it all away from you both. But now you know the truth, you can stop wondering. You can settle down here with Charlie and with Tom.' She raises her eyebrows and pats my hand again. 'And the three of you can make Chesterford not only a great castle again, but a wonderful home.' She holds her hand up as I'm about to speak.

'And don't you try to persuade me otherwise, young lady, do you hear? Because now you know who the missing heir is, you also know that you have her permission, and most importantly her blessing, for you not only to live here now but for your future generations to live here too. It's what I and all the others want, including my great-aunt Ruby and my great-great-aunt Clara.'

Dorothy looks behind me, and as I turn to see what she's looking at I expect to see the portrait of Clara on the wall, but Dorothy is looking away from that at what appears to be an empty space on the rug.

'Are they here?' I ask, amazed, as I suddenly realise that Dorothy can see the ghosts too. 'Clara and Ruby? You can see them, Dorothy?'

'I can,' Dorothy nods, 'and they look pleased, very pleased.'

'Why can't I?' I ask in an anguished voice.

'Because it's not quite the right time for you yet. You will see them, my dearest Amelia. You will, I promise.'

Dorothy and I walk back outside to the others arm in arm.

'Where have you been?' Benji asks anxiously as he spies us walking across the courtyard towards him. 'Arthur is going bananas looking for you, something about a key ceremony?'

'Oh yes, the ceremonial key! I'd forgotten he was going to do that today. Where is he?' I ask, looking around.

'Over by the stables. You'd best go find him.'

I leave Dorothy with Benji and hurry back to the stables.

'Here you are at last!' Arthur says with relief when he sees me. 'I want to do this before people start leaving.'

'Sure, sorry, Arthur. I had some . . . business to take care of. Is that the special key?' I ask, looking at a large iron key in Arthur's hands. It looks exactly like the one we'd found hidden in the trunks in the cellar.

'It is; now we just need to get everyone's attention.'

'Tom, can you get everyone together again?' I ask him as he comes wandering over. 'Arthur has an announcement he wants to make.'

'Sure,' Tom says, leaping up on to the box in front of the microphone. 'Joey, can you switch this thing on again?' he calls. Joey waves and does as he asks.

'Ladies and gentlemen, if I could just have your attention one more time, please. Arthur, our beloved stalwart of Chesterford, would like to say a few words.'

People begin to gather around the mic again as Arthur steps up on to the box.

'Ahem . . . as some of you may know,' he begins, looking a tad self-conscious, 'when a new owner takes control of Chesterford Castle, they are traditionally presented with this ceremonial key to signify not only their possession of the castle but their allegiance to Chesterford village and the people that live here. It is an ancient ceremony that has taken place many, many times over the centuries, yet one that is still equally important and relevant today in the often troubled times in which we live. Chesterford Castle is something solid and reliable, in a world where everything has to be fast and disposable, and I for one welcome that security.' There's a small ripple of approving applause, and Arthur waits until it has died down before continuing. 'I think you will all agree that our new owner has come to Chesterford and not only brought about solid change for the good of the castle and the community, but she has done it with style and grace, and most importantly a good heart, and I am delighted that she and her son Charlie are going to be a permanent part of our Chesterford family. So without further ado, I ask you, Amelia Chesterford, to accept this key as a symbol of your allegiance and ownership of Chesterford Castle. May your time here bring you good health, much wealth, and above all lots of happiness.'

I take the key from Arthur and hold it above my head so the photographer who is still here from the local newspaper can get a good shot.

'Oh look!' someone suddenly cries. 'There's a rainbow over the bay!'

Everyone in the crowd turns to look, then they begin to rush over to the exterior wall of the castle to get a better view. Mobile phones are suddenly produced, and people begin taking photos of this magnificent phenomenon of nature as it radiates its magic in the sky above us.

I look up at the incredibly bright, vibrant rainbow and I smile. I knew exactly what that means – everything is A-okay again here at the castle. Just like Benji had said.

I look for Charlie in amongst the people, but when I see him I notice he's not looking at the rainbow, instead he's gazing up at the top of the castle behind me.

I turn to see what he's staring so intently at, and then I see for myself: up on the castle ramparts, in between two of the towers, stand four figures – an older man wearing Elizabethan-style clothing, a young girl in a white apron and a shabby brown dress, a red-coated soldier on top of a white horse, and, lastly, an elegant woman in a pale green evening gown, wearing emerald and diamond jewellery.

Percy, Ruby, Jasper and, at long last, Clara.

They all look down at me and wave, then Clara blows me a kiss. I glance back at Charlie and find he's grinning at me, and then we both look immediately back up at the castle again, but the figures have disappeared.

The ghosts of Chesterford Castle have given me their own unique seal of approval, just like the rainbow had.

It seems Charlie and I have finally found our way back home.

Acknowledgements

Wow, this is my tenth book, and that means my tenth set of acknowledgements!

Surprisingly, and rather gratifyingly, the people I have to thank now are mostly the same people I thanked ten books ago.

My amazing agent, Hannah Ferguson for believing in me and 'Scarlett and Sean' all those years ago.

All the team at Sphere and Little, Brown who published book number one and are still publishing my stories ten books later. And my editors over that time: Caroline Hogg, Rebecca Saunders and currently, marvellous Maddie West.

You, my loyal and avid readers. Some of you have been with me from the beginning (thank you!) and some of you are just finding my books now. Never underestimate how much your messages of joy, happiness, thanks and support are appreciated. They never fail to put a smile on this author's face.

And last, but *never* least, my wonderful family: my husband Jim, my daughter Rosie and my son Tom, whose never-ending love and support mean more every day.

Until the next time . . .

Ali x